THE CURE

BOOKS BY PEDRO URVI

STANDALONE NOVELS

The Cure

THE SECRET OF THE GOLDEN GODS SERIES

Origin

Rebellion

Rebirth

THE PATH OF THE RANGER SERIES

The Traitor's Son

The King's Secret

Mystery in the Tundra

Treason in the North

The Secret Refuge

Path of the Specialist

The King of the West

The Turquoise Queen

Power Conspiracy

The Great Council

Frozen Origins

Dragon Spirit

Arcane Call

Mission in the East

Rise of the Immortal

The Druid Queen

The Secret of the Dragon

The Throne of the North

Deep Threat

The King's Sacrifice

THE ILENIAN ENIGMA SERIES

Marked

Conflict

Trials

Destiny

THE PATH OF DRAGONS SERIES

Flameborn

Elemental Power

Golden Magic

Dragon Rider

Deadly Rescue

THE CURE

PEDRO URVI

Copyright © 2026 by Pedro Urvi
Published in 2026 by Blackstone Publishing
Cover design by Bookfly
Book design by Blackstone Publishing

All rights reserved. This book or any portion thereof may not be reproduced or used in any manner whatsoever without the express written permission of the publisher except for the use of brief quotations in a book review.

The characters and events in this book are fictitious. Any similarity to real persons, living or dead, is coincidental and not intended by the author.

Printed in the United States of America
Originally published in hardcover by Blackstone Publishing in 2026

First paperback edition: 2026
ISBN 979-8-228-64879-1
Fiction / Science Fiction / Apocalyptic & Post-Apocalyptic

Version 1

Blackstone Publishing
31 Mistletoe Rd.
Ashland, OR 97520

www.BlackstonePublishing.com

To my father, who always believed in me

CHAPTER 1

Ava felt a shock that went down from the nape of her neck to the tips of her toes. The impact was intense, and she began to feel very sick. She was lying there—or perhaps she wasn't. She was feeling very odd, as if she were seeing her inert body from the outside. She became aware in some unconscious way that she was not awake. She must be in the middle of a nightmare, which for some reason was hurting her body intensely. She tried to wake up, to escape from the pain. For a long moment she was unable to, and then there came another shock. She fought to wake up, and at last succeeded. She saw the ceiling of her hut of adobe and straw above her head, and the hard cot under her body.

She woke up feeling dizzy and sick, with a burning pain throughout her whole body. She tried to sit up but was unable to. Her mind knew she was awake, but her aching body still would not respond to her wishes, as if it were in a state of suspension. Or maybe it was the other way round. Perhaps the Curse had already killed her, and she was not yet aware of the fact.

As she gazed at her little room, her recognition of it made

her mind and body wake up at last. She was still alive. She got to her feet, but then nearly lost her balance. She had no idea why she was having these difficult nightmares and awakenings more and more frequently. She knew that she was not sick, or at least not in her body. She left the room, then very slowly went up the stairs that led to the flat roof. Here she sat down with her legs crossed and stared up at the starry sky, while the breeze from the delta caressed her face. She took a deep breath and began to feel a little better.

The moon was shining high in the sky, bathing the deserts and the great river that crossed the lands of the Kemet with her silver light. She enjoyed getting up before dawn so that she could watch it shining over the Pyramid and the Great Sphinx in front of her. The image filled her with peace and transmitted a joy that her frozen heart never experienced in any other way. She sighed. This might be the last time she would watch it, because today was the Day of the Chosen.

She was feeling rather melancholy. When she felt like this, she always thought of the Ancient Ones. She wondered whether they, too, had watched the eternal moon in their era, as she was doing now. She pictured a girl like herself, sixteen years old, before the Apocalypse, in that same place, lost in her own thoughts, as she herself was now. What had it been like to live in that vanished epoch? What had that girl's life been like? It must have been really fascinating to be able to enjoy a life full of progress, of knowledge, of technology and entertainment. Everything that she and her people would never come to know.

Ava could only begin to imagine it, since the Kemet knew so little of that remote time. They had not been able to glean much information from the few fragments of knowledge they had managed to find and rescue: the "relics," as they called them. It must have been a fantastic era, full of life, joy, and prosperity.

Her cat, Guardian, black as night, came up to her, rubbed himself against her leg, and began to purr. She picked him up and hugged him.

"Good boy, my guardian," she said with a smile. "Don't you worry, the Curse doesn't affect animals, only humans. It's our punishment for causing the Apocalypse. You animals are good and noble, that's why you're immune to the punishment of the God Siaais."

Guardian stared back at her with his enigmatic cat eyes, half-closing them to enjoy her petting. After a moment he leaped from her arms. Ava liked animals, cats in particular. She respected them. They were their own masters, and would never allow themselves to be subservient.

The sun began to make its appearance over the land of the Kemet, and with the arrival of dawn, Ava went downstairs to get dressed. Today was a special day, the most important one of the year. She took her healer's bag, where she carried the medicinal plants and ingredients she needed for her craft. If she had time she would go to the oasis to gather plants to make ointments against infections, because her stock was low and she needed to make more.

As she was leaving her house she saw her cousin Amelia, who greeted her with her usual broad smile. They were both dressed in black, with long plain tunics embroidered in silver and wide leather belts, as was the custom among the people of the deserts.

"Hi there, Ava!"

"Why are you smiling so early in the morning?"

"Because today's going to be a wonderful day."

Ava shook her head. "I don't see what's wonderful about it."

Amelia ignored her cousin's comment. "Don't tell me you got up before dawn again."

"I like it. I find it soothing."

"I don't understand why you do it. Do you want to gain the favor of the Archaic gods by seeing Tout off so that you can receive luminous Ra?"

"What I don't understand is your fascination with those false Archaic gods. Tout is simply the representation of the moon and Ra that of the sun. And I know that, because you've told me about them. You're a scholar."

"An apprentice scholar. I'm still learning the craft."

"You know more than half the tribe put together."

Amelia smiled and blushed. "I like studying the relics and learning."

"I don't see what we gain by studying the gods the Ancient Ones worshipped."

"Correction," Amelia said with a lively glint in her eyes. "The first gods were created and worshipped thousands of years before the Apocalypse. The Ancient Ones no longer worshipped them when it happened. Those are the gods of the Archaic Ones."

"Ancient, Archaic, whatever . . . they're all extinct. That's a good reason to forget about them."

"But they're all we have left from that lost world. The relics are our inheritance, and we have to keep them safe and study them."

"You spend too much time studying those Archaic papyruses and paintings, hieroglyphs and murals," Ava said.

"I love studying the hieroglyphs and their symbolism and the few tomes of knowledge we have left. There's so much to learn. I've asked to be part of the next expedition to the southern temples, downriver. There are still priceless pieces being kept down there. Here at the delta there's almost nothing that the passage of time, the desert, or the great river haven't destroyed."

Ava sighed. "Luckily I was destined to the House of Life, to Healing."

Amelia shrugged and smiled. "The House of Knowledge and its scholars will guide our people to a new future."

"I hope so," Ava replied without much conviction. "Come on, let's go down to the Great Pyramid."

They entered the ruins of what had once been a great city of steel and glass with incredibly tall towers and endless paved avenues, temples, and homes for thousands of people. All that remained were the half-buried remnants of a metropolis. The whole city had succumbed long ago. The relentless desert, with the help of the passage of time, had buried it almost completely. The exceptions were those areas where the tribe dug in search of relics and knowledge.

"You're too fond of those relics," Ava told her cousin. "They're just rubble and useless bits the desert has yet to swallow up completely. But sooner or later it will."

Amelia shrugged. She was gazing around in fascination. "I know. I like to walk among the ruins and imagine what it must have been like . . . it must have been a beautiful city . . ."

They walked past a structure like a long warehouse their people had turned into a school. It was built entirely of stone, and for that reason had survived the passage of time. Where steel and concrete had crumbled, stone and clay had held.

"What had their life been like?" Amelia asked, more to herself than to Ava. She was gazing at what remained of a huge collapsed building half-covered by sand.

"Better than ours, I hope. I always think that, and I believe it must have been better—before the Apocalypse, of course . . ."

"Don't be a pessimist, our lives will get better. There's hope."

"I'm a realist, not a pessimist, cousin. There's no hope. We're fooling ourselves."

Amelia made a gesture of disapproval. She took her cousin's arm and smiled, and they walked on, leaving the ruins behind and going down a long hill. The breeze caressed their long hair, and they laughed when a stronger gust suddenly ruffled it.

Ava looked at her smiling cousin out of the corner of her eye. They did not look much alike. Amelia's skin was intensely brown, her eyes dark and bright. Her straight hair, black as jet, fell to her shoulders. Like most of the women of their tribe, she was slender and not very tall. According to the saying, the scorching sun toasted and consumed the bodies of those who lived beneath its harshness. She stood out because she was very pretty. Wherever she went, the boys turned their heads to look at her and smiled at her like idiots. But for Ava what was most noticeable in her dear cousin was not her beauty, it was the fact that she was joyful and optimistic.

Ava was very different, and she knew it. Her brown skin was much lighter, her hair completely curly, and her eyes emerald green—a combination that was considered less attractive in a tribe where straight tresses and darker skin tones were the qualities most valued. Nor was she as pretty as Amelia, and she certainly did not have Amelia's sympathetic nature, much less her optimism about the future. Nonetheless, Ava knew herself and she accepted who she was without resentment.

"Didn't you sleep well?" Amelia asked her suddenly, sounding worried.

"Does nothing get past you?"

"Nope," she said, smiling, and tilted her head in amusement.

Ava stared accusingly at her cousin's right forearm. "You haven't been Feeling me, have you?"

"Of course not. I know you don't like it, though I don't know why. It's a blessing all-powerful Siaais has granted us. He urges us to use it, and I follow his wishes."

"He's also Cursed us, don't forget. This sickness will kill us both."

"Don't say that, there's always hope . . ."

"I don't believe in vain hopes. But let's not argue. How do you know I slept badly if you haven't Felt me?"

"By the circles under your eyes."

"Oh . . . I see . . ."

"Is it because today's the Day of the Chosen?"

"Maybe . . . I don't know . . ."

"I think it is. I'm very excited too, and a little nervous. We're sixteen now. We can volunteer."

"I'm not turning up at that meaningless ritual voluntarily."

"Why not?" Amelia asked, with disappointment in her voice.

"For two reasons. First: Those who volunteer and are Chosen die. Second: because it makes no sense. If Siaais wanted to give us the Cure for the Curse, he would. The Day of the Chosen is simply a savage entertainment for a capricious god, amusing himself at our expense."

"Shhhhhh, don't say that," Amelia urged her. She was looking around, as if Siaais could hear them. "The fact that nobody's ever come back doesn't mean they died . . ."

Ava folded her arms. "That's exactly what it means."

"The God Siaais gives us an opportunity to show him our courage, our determination, to earn the Cure so we can heal our people from the Curse. It's our duty."

"All I know is that every year three reckless fools are chosen from among all the volunteers, they set out in search of a cure, and nobody hears from them again. Ever. It's a death sentence."

"You say that because of your father . . ."

"My father was a fool like all the others. He died because he volunteered. As they all did."

"Shhhhhh! He's going to hear you." Amelia put her hand over Ava's mouth and looked around with eyes wide. "He sees it all, he's the eye in the sky. He's watching us."

"He's an abominable god who laughs while we suffer and fall victim to the sickness, then die a horrible death," Ava whispered. "You know that as well as I do."

Amelia looked up at the sky, then toward the river. "Please don't talk like that anymore," she said uneasily, and took Ava's arm as they carried on along the dirt path.

They greeted the workers who were on their way to the riverbank to work in the fertile irrigated land. Further down they passed several fishermen who were carrying large nets to their boats. They sailed the great river all day long to catch fresh fish to sell in the market. Everybody in the tribe knew everybody else. Although their lands were extensive, the Kemet numbered no more than five thousand in all and lived in a single large community. Nobody settled very far from the Great Pyramid. It had been so ever since the Apocalypse.

There was one other significant fact they all shared: There was no one in the whole tribe older than thirty. The Curse, that ruthless, terrible sickness, took them all before they reached that age. And many of them it took much earlier. Surviving the sickness beyond twenty-five was considered an achievement. Everyone in the tribe knew they would not live beyond that age, including Ava and Amelia.

Their way took them through the craftsmen's area. Three forges and a sawmill made up the first of the working areas, where two dozen muscular youths were already starting to light fires and sharpen tools. When they saw the two girls, they straightened up and greeted them, trying to make themselves look strong and attractive. Amelia noticed this and waved at them, so that they puffed themselves up like roosters, pleased and smiling. Tanners, weavers, potters, butchers, greengrocers, and other lesser trades formed the second of the working areas. These represented all the technological advances that were now available to them: more or less the same as the Archaic civilization that had built the Pyramid and the Sphinx thousands of years before. Ava shook her head at the thought.

In front of the Sphinx was a huge earthen square. On one side they had dug a well from which two oxen drew water by turning a system of pulleys under the orders of the water-carrier. The market was located on the other side, beside the Sphinx, and here the trade in fruit, fish, and fresh meat took place. It was the nerve center of the tribe, and there were always people there chatting, trading, or worshipping the Sphinx. Ava did not understand why people did this, since after all it had been built by the Archaic Ones, and both they and the Ancient Ones were long since dead and gone.

Amelia exchanged greetings, and several women chatted with her animatedly. Ava, who did not like empty chatter, stayed a little behind. If there was one thing they could not afford to waste in the short life they had been granted, it was time. She watched Amelia behaving so naturally, easily, and gracefully that she felt a trace of envy, but it was over in a moment. Ava was Amelia's only family, as her cousin was her own. Amelia's parents had succumbed to the Curse shortly before turning thirty. They had not left instructions for how they wished to leave this world, so Amelia, as was her right as their only child, had decided that their last days should be spent inside the Pyramid.

Ava's parents had not suffered that dark fate. Luckily, they had left earlier. Her father had volunteered as a valiant and been selected on the Day of the Chosen, shortly after she had been born. He had left and was never heard from again. Her mother had not died from the Curse or the whim of Siaais, but in a dreadful accident eight years ago that had marked Ava forever. She would never forgive herself for her failure to save her mother.

Amelia brought her out of her thoughts. "We have to go to the Pyramid now or we'll be late for the ceremony."

"Don't worry, it's not until noon, we have time," Ava replied. She was looking at the blazing sun in the sky.

"I want to go there early to see it all. It's a very important day."

Ava shook her head, but did not argue. She followed her cousin without a word.

On the way to the Pyramid, they passed the six military buildings: the barracks. Here they saw a hundred-odd valiants practicing in each of the horseshoe-shaped buildings. Boys and girls, under the orders of a dozen instructors only slightly older than Ava and Amelia, were giving their all for the good of the tribe. Amelia stopped to watch them, as she always did, especially one in particular: Amos. Ava could not blame her, because Amos was tall, well-built, and strong, as well as a very good fighter. More than that, he was quite handsome for such a muscular hunk of a boy.

When Ava had first learned the reason the children trained every day with such ardor, she was shocked. It was not to defend the Kemet from other enemy tribes. There had been a time when expeditions had been sent to search for other tribes that had survived the Apocalypse, but all had failed. After so long without outside contact, the consensus among the Kemet was that they were the only survivors in the world. Nor did wild beasts pose a serious threat. Crocodiles in the river and lions or other great cats attacked them every once in a while, driven by hunger or in the course of some chance encounter, but this very rarely happened. An order of guards was now in charge of protecting the community.

The reason these youths practiced nonstop was to volunteer before Siaais on the Day of the Chosen.

This day.

"It's a great honor to volunteer as a valiant."

"Yeah, some honor."

"I can't talk to you when you're like this."

"What else should I be? Every year the same thing happens. They present themselves. The God chooses three of them to cross the Gate of the Clouds, they enter the realm of Siaais, and we never hear from them again."

"One of them will succeed. One of them will come back and save us all."

"Amos?"

Amelia nodded hopefully. "Well, perhaps he will."

"Cousin, think about it. You're a scholar. Don't let yourself get carried away by false beliefs and hopes. Think with that analytical head of yours."

Amos hit his opponent with his narrow, body-length shield, and the other boy was hurled backward from the impact. The warrior turned his head and saw them. He smiled, and immediately Amelia blushed.

"Well, he might just make it," Ava said to cheer her cousin up, although she did not really believe it herself.

"Yes, he has to. He is so handsome . . . and strong . . ." Amelia blushed.

"Or maybe you can marry him and have clever and strong kids, since you don't stop thinking about him."

"You think of boys too."

"Rarely."

"Don't deny it. We all do. Our lives are very short and we all have desires . . ."

"Marry him, then, and be happy."

"And you?"

"I will control my urges."

"One day you will meet someone and you will change your mind."

"I doubt it."

They continued walking. Nothing but sand surrounded the Great Pyramid. It rose in the middle of the desert, defying time. Staring at so proud and magnificent a structure, immune to the passage of time, Ava felt small, insignificant.

The inconstant river was closer than she remembered, or perhaps it was an optical illusion. The delta and its waters changed, and with them the life of her tribe. They always had to keep a watchful eye on the river and its diversions . . . in the same way Amelia believed that the God Siaais kept his Eye on his tribe.

People were only just beginning to arrive. "We're early," Ava said.

"It's important for us to be here now, to take part in the ceremony."

"Anybody would think you were one of the volunteers."

"Scholars, healers, farmers, and the other crafters may not volunteer, but that doesn't mean they're not willing in their hearts."

"I don't understand why the rest of us have to take part if it's only the valiants who volunteer, along with a handful of lunatics from the other crafts who are never selected."

"Siaais hasn't always chosen a valiant."

Ava shook her head. "It's been a long time since he's chosen anyone but a valiant."

"That's because they're the strongest and best prepared. They have a better chance of surviving the path to the Cure. Our scriptures say it's a path full of dangers, and only the strongest in body and heart will reach the end."

Ava did not want to argue. Amelia had a sensitive heart, and Ava had no wish to see her sad.

Little by little the tribe arrived in front of the Pyramid, like dozens of streams emptying into a great lake. The sun was high in a completely clear sky, punishing everyone there with its burning intensity. Finally, the whole tribe was assembled in front of the Great Pyramid, as they did every year on the same day, the first day of spring, when life broke out in the desert. To Ava it seemed another cruel joke of Siaais to use the same day to send three valiants, the best among her people, to their deaths.

Amelia smiled at her, and these dark thoughts faded from Ava's mind. They took their places at the back. The whole tribe stood in their craft groups to enact the ceremony. Siaais required everyone's presence this day, and death would fall from the sky on anybody who failed to obey.

The last to arrive were the valiants, in tight military formation, with their armor and weapons at the ready. When they took their places, everybody broke into applause, full of pride in such courageous warriors, each of whom embodied the hope of bringing an end to the Curse.

"They'll do it, you just wait and see," Amelia said with conviction. "They'll bring us the Cure and we'll defeat the Curse. We'll live to a hundred."

Ava smiled at her cousin. What a big heart she had.

Ahamon, the leader of the tribe, made his entrance at the moment when the sun reached its highest position. He took his place at the front, facing the colossal Pyramid, dressed as an ancient pharaoh. For a moment Ava thought he had been taken out of the King's Chamber—or no, not from there, but from one of the murals Amelia spent so much time studying. The tribe had adopted the clothing and weapons of the paintings and tombs that had been found inside the temples. Ahamon was twenty-seven years old. He did not have much time left, and he knew it. He was a good, fair leader. Ava liked him.

He turned and spread his arms wide, then greeted his people with a long bow.

"Welcome to all, my beloved people!"

The tribe replied with a bow to their leader.

"Today we celebrate a crucial ceremony for our salvation!"

"The Ceremony of the Chosen!" everyone shouted back as one.

"Let us honor Siaais, our savior!"

The whole tribe began to chant in unison the litany to their God.

As the sun reached its zenith, the moment arrived.

The God Siaais announced his arrival as he always did, with the sky darkening over their heads and bringing night into day. A moment later it was as black as a starless night. It gave Ava the feeling that a dreadful storm was about to descend and kill them all. The scene was so threatening that it made everybody kneel and bow their heads, praying to the God to spare their lives. Ava knelt, but did not bow. She looked at the sky, defiantly unafraid of storm, death, or Siaais. She knew they were all condemned and felt nothing but anger for their despicable God. An anger that was more powerful than the fear she felt.

In the darkness there appeared an intense point of white light, then a bright sphere levitating over the tip of the Pyramid. It looked as though a star had come down from the sky and settled there. It grew brighter still, until its light bathed everybody there.

Many of the Kemet trembled. Some wept.

"We are the people of the desert, the Kemet tribe," Ahamon began in a ritual voice. "Humbly we kneel, Siaais, our only God, our guide, our protector."

The light moved rapidly back and forth over them, then gradually lost intensity. Above the star of light there appeared an image: a huge almond-shaped eye with a silver iris.

The Eye of Siaais.

Ahamon stood up and gave a long, respectful bow. He indicated the people behind him.

"We are your faithful servants. You honor us for another year with your divine presence. Here are our volunteers. They come forth to be chosen, to honor you and to obtain your favor."

"Anyone who volunteers is a fool," muttered Ava.

"Shhhh," Amelia chided her. "You'll offend the God."

The Eye of Siaais gave out a beam of silver light.

"Reveal the Marks of Siaais," Ahamon said, "so that our Father may see them with total clarity."

They all uncovered their right arms, exposing two identical rectangles joined end to end from wrist to elbow, bordered in black. The upper rectangle was silver, the lower one gold and divided into ten sections. The lower Mark measured the progress of the illness, or Curse, indicating how close she was to the end of her days as a human. The upper one was concerned with the Talent: the Blessing of Feeling. The Marks flashed.

"Let the volunteers present themselves before Siaais, to walk the path of the Cure!"

At once the valiants stood up and raised their right arms, showing their markings to Siaais. In the back rows several healers and a few scholars stood up in turn and raised their right arms, offering themselves.

Ava shook her head. "Fools," she muttered.

The Eye began to pass across all the raised arms of the volunteers, back and forth several times. Suddenly Amelia stood up and raised her own right arm.

"What d'you think you're doing?" Ava cried in horror.

"I'm volunteering," Amelia said firmly.

"No! Put your arm down! Kneel!"

Amelia shook her head and neither lowered her arm nor knelt. Ava, in despair, stood up and with her right arm seized her cousin's to pull it down. The light washed over them and went on. Ava managed to lower Amelia's arm and pulled her back down to her knees.

"Let me go! I want to volunteer."

"Stop it!"

The Eye of Siaais emitted three flashes and darkened.

"Raise your eyes," Ahamon said proudly, "and let the volunteers step forward."

At once one of the valiants followed his order. It was Amos. His right forearm pulsed with an intense green. Raising it for all to see, he walked to the front of the Pyramid to stand beside Ahamon.

"Let the others who have been chosen step forward," Ahamon said.

But none of the valiants moved. Their raised arms did not flash.

"Ava . . ." Amelia said. Her voice sounded strange.

When Ava looked at her cousin, her heart skipped a beat. Amelia's arm was shining green.

"No!" Ava cried. She was shaking her head, unable to believe her eyes.

Amelia, white as a ghost, pointed. Ava followed her cousin's finger and saw her own forearm.

It blazed with the same brilliant green.

CHAPTER 2

"We've been chosen," Ava murmured. She was staring at her flashing Marks, unable to believe what she was seeing.

No. It was happening. They would not get out of it. They had been chosen.

"But . . . the odds . . . I can't believe it . . ." Amelia was muttering. She was having trouble breathing. The repercussions of what she had done were only just beginning to take shape in her mind.

Ava continued to stare at her arm, wishing it would stop. She felt stunned, her mind numbed, as though she had sustained a hard blow to the head.

Amelia was trying to recover her poise, but not succeeding. She was as pale as a corpse. "Siaais always chooses three valiants. *Always*," she muttered under her breath.

A murmur, a mixture of surprise and fear, began to ripple through those attending the ceremony as they realized what had happened.

"It's got to be a mistake," Ava cried. She raised her head to look for Ahamon.

The leader of the tribe stared at them in surprise. He turned to the Eye of Siaais and raised both hands in the air, still kneeling.

"Is this the final decision of our Lord?" he asked. "The Chosen are awaiting their chance to honor their God. In no way can a healer and a scholar compare with two valiants. Our tribe offers you strong, well-trained warriors who will confront any challenge to prove their courage and attain the Cure."

Ava was grateful for Ahamon's gesture. She held her breath, awaiting the God's reply.

It came at once. The Eye illuminated them from above the Great Pyramid with two direct beams of green light. One beam fell on Ava's chest. She looked to her right and saw Amelia singled out in the same way. Then the two beams shifted to where Amos was waiting on his knees in front of the Pyramid, indicating to them where they must go.

"Oh no . . ." Amelia moaned.

Ava still could not believe it. Why had the God chosen them? Why a healer and a scholar, rather than valiants who had spent their whole life training for this moment?

Ahamon nodded. The Eye's command was final.

Ava thought of taking hold of Amelia's hand and making a run for it, but then stopped, knowing they would never make it out of the square. It had happened before, more than once. Chosen Ones had tried to escape—too afraid after being selected and unable to handle their dire new reality—and the Eye had shriveled them with a red beam of death that charred the poor wretches mercilessly even as they ran, leaving only piles of ash.

"Our Lord has made his choice. The selection is complete. Let the Chosen Ones come forth." Ahamon's voice trembled, clearly fearing that one or more of the newly Chosen would disobey his command.

The murmurs grew as the crowd parted, making a corridor

for Ava and Amelia. The unexpectedness of what had happened had left everyone confused. These two were far from ideal choices, and everybody knew it. They would surely fail to bring back the Cure. But no one dared to protest.

Ava's shock gave way to rage, and she didn't care who witnessed it. She clenched her fists and looked at the Eye of Siaais, high above, with disgust and fury. She wanted to shout at the top of her voice that she would not accept the judgment—that she did not care if Siaais had chosen her, she would not yield to his twisted, capricious wishes. She would not hide her anger anymore.

"Ava . . . we have to go . . ." Amelia pleaded.

The fear in her cousin's voice made Ava reconsider. "Let me think for a moment."

They could not run or confront the God, because he would kill them instantly. She looked around and saw the expressions on the faces of her people. Where at first they had felt sorry for the two girls, now sadness was giving way to anger. For Ava and Amelia to be among the Chosen Ones meant that the tribe was doomed. Without the Cure there was no hope for any of them. Siaais had promised them the Cure if they could overcome all the obstacles he put in their way and reach it, to prove they were worthy of being pardoned for their sins. The tribe had clung to that hope wholeheartedly.

Ava shook her head. She knew it was all a lie. Nobody would ever attain the Cure for the simple reason that if they did, they would then be free. They would escape the dominion of a wicked God.

"No, no, no," she muttered under her breath.

She was turning it over and over in her mind but could find no way out. She considered whether dying as a traitor to the tribe by refusing to go was the best option they had. They were going to die in any case, but at least it would mean a quick death—even though it would bring shame and dishonor on both of them. She did not mind this for herself, but she didn't wish it on Amelia.

"Ava . . ."

She looked into Amelia's eyes, where her fear and uncertainty shone clearly. She knew Amelia would never betray the tribe. Her heart would never allow her to. And worse still, Ava herself could not refuse to go, because Siaais would consume her in fire and her cousin would be left alone.

"Not right," she muttered furiously.

Ava took a deep breath and seized her cousin's hand. Together they strode forward to join Ahamon and Amos.

"Thank you, cousin," Amelia whispered.

"We'll survive," Ava whispered back.

As they advanced, the tribe began to intone the Hymn of the Chosen: a few voices at first, shyly, but little by little, more of them began to join in. Finally, all voices joined in the litany. Ava and Amelia knelt beside Amos. His face showed no annoyance, and his eyes were bright with determination as he greeted them with a nod. Amelia smiled back at him, and Ava nodded. She knew he could not possibly be happy about any of this, but he hid it well.

"Here are the Chosen Ones for this year!" Ahamon said.

The chanting became livelier.

"On your feet, Amelia, Ava, and Amos! May Almighty Siaais grant you his blessing!"

The three of them rose to their feet and bowed their heads. The Eye of Siaais bathed them in a beam of white light, and after a moment the light turned green and stayed fixed on them.

"Siaais accepts and blesses them!" the leader proclaimed.

The tribe erupted in applause—the excitement and hope of a doomed people.

The beam of light went out.

"Chosen Ones," cried Ahamon, "gaze upon your God! Gaze upon the salvation of our people!"

Amos and Amelia, followed a moment later by Ava, raised their chins high and looked directly at the Eye of Siaais. Then the Eye suddenly vanished from the tip of the Pyramid, and in its place appeared a golden altar. On it was a crystal phial containing a bluish substance.

The Cure!

The God was showing them the prize for which they would have to fight and suffer: the salvation of the tribe.

Give it to us, you cursed, unscrupulous monster! Ava seethed.

The image changed. Now it showed them a glimpse of what they would have to face in order to reach the Cure. In a series of distorted, blinking images which would not allow themselves to be seen clearly there appeared wild beasts, unknown monsters, shadowy beings, strange and distant landscapes, the mysterious Children of Siaais, who defended the Cure—a rapidly changing kaleidoscope of dangers that would freeze the blood of even the bravest.

"Siaais is letting us glimpse the Three Tests of Courage we have to pass in order to reach the Cure," Amos commented.

"He's only trying to make us cower," Ava said, trying to draw strength from weakness.

"I'm scared to death," Amelia said. Her hands were shaking.

"Don't be afraid," Amos said. "I'll protect you, and I'll kill any enemy we come across." He said it so confidently that they both believed him.

Ava sighed. Neither she nor Amelia knew how to kill anything, least of all a person or a monster.

The images came to an end, and the Eye of Siaais reappeared. It turned red, then a moment later it vanished. The darkness disappeared with it, leaving the sky clear and blue once again, with the sun shining brightly.

"Siaais has spoken through his Eye!" Ahamon announced. "The Chosen have been selected!"

The chanting changed, so that now everyone was intoning loudly, forcefully, trying to instill courage in the three Chosen. Ava had never seen them singing like this, with all their heart and soul. She realized that it was for *them*, for the love they felt for Amelia, for the respect they felt for Amos, for their all-but-nonexistent chances of success. She felt the fervor of their support, and her gratitude was heartfelt.

Ava spent the afternoon alone at the oasis, gathering algae and other medicinal plants, and thinking. She wanted to forget everything she had experienced during the ceremony, everything, and concentrate on her duty. She had been chosen at birth to serve the House of Life and become a healer. That was her contribution to the tribe, and she would be faithful to it, at least for one more day. Amelia was a scholar and her vocation was clear. Everybody in the tribe had a purpose: The scholars gathered knowledge, and the valiants honed themselves just for the chance of being selected for Siaais's challenge. They had farmers and merchants, fishermen and shepherds, collectors and craftsmen. Thanks to them, they had garlic, onions, barley, dates, wheat, carob pods, coriander, olives, watermelon, figs, fennel, lettuce, saffron, and other foods she used for her medicines. Today she was looking for coriander and dandelion.

As she searched, Ava's mind went back to the first survivors of the Apocalypse and what they must have had to go through. As far as they knew, practically all the world's population had ceased to exist in the course of two seasons. All man's creations and advances had stopped working. A thousand years later, little remained of that glorious civilization. The first generations had tried to save the knowledge they still had, but little by little, with every new generation, it had disappeared. Now there was barely any knowledge left from the Ancient Ones. The survivors had been forced to live without technology, taking refuge in a tribe that had reverted to the primitive way of even earlier times.

Nature, on the other hand, free of her greatest enemy, humanity, reclaimed the earth and began to flourish, taking over deserted cities and countries, covering everything with her green splendor. Jungles and forests spread, and the seas became clean again. Temperatures went down. Animals repopulated the land and the oceans.

Such was the story told by the relics they had managed to rescue.

But the new order was not complete. The God Siaais came as a punishment to humans for having caused the Apocalypse, and with him his vengeance: the Curse, the abominable sickness for which there was no cure.

The evening went by in the blink of an eye. She stared at Ra, the sun, as he slipped into hiding behind the distant mountains. The day was being used up, like her life.

"One day less . . . and I'm sixteen springs old now . . ." she murmured sorrowfully. More than half her life used up: That had been one of her greatest concerns until today. Now that she was chosen for the tests of Siaais to bring back the Cure, she had a clear presentiment that she was not going to survive. But she would not give up. If this was to be her destiny, she would accept it, grudgingly and distrustfully, and fight to the end.

CHAPTER 3

When she went back, Ava found Amelia waiting for her in front of the Great Sphinx, looking troubled.

"I'm sorry . . ." she began.

"Don't worry. It was a spontaneous reaction, because you have too kind a heart."

"And because I believe there's hope?"

"And because you're a little bit naïve, yes."

The two cousins started walking side by side toward the Great Pyramid. "I don't know what came over me," Amelia said. "I've thought about it a thousand times, but I swear I didn't set off with the idea of volunteering. All I'm any use at is studying and learning. I don't even know how to use a spear, much less a sword or a shield."

"I doubt whether knowing how to fight is going to change the outcome."

"Then you believe we're doomed, that we're going to die?"

Ava nodded. "I'm afraid so. You know I always say what I think, for better or worse."

"I know . . . that's why your words trouble me so much. I've condemned you to death . . ." There were tears in her eyes.

"No, you haven't. Siaais is the one who's condemned us both. Everything that's going to happen to us is at his whim. He's the one who's to blame."

"Or she."

Ava put her head to one side. "Yeah, it might be a 'she,' but because it's so twisted and unscrupulous, I'd say it's a 'he.'"

"Forgive me," Amelia pleaded as she wiped the tears off with the sleeve of her tunic.

"It's already forgiven."

"Thanks, cousin, you're the best."

"I'm not that, but thanks for the compliment."

Ava smiled to make Amelia relax a little. Her cousin looked up at the Great Sphinx and sighed deeply.

"Today's going to be a pretty intense day," she said. Amelia shrugged, and there was resignation in her eyes.

"Two ceremonies in the same day," Ava went on, "the Chosen when the sun's at its highest, and then Accompaniment as it sets. We can skip Accompaniment. We've had quite enough already . . ."

Amelia shook her head. "No, Asmi is my family. We must go."

"She's a very distant relative. She's not close family."

"For me she is. She's got no one else to go with her."

"You're not going to *Feel* her, are you?" Ava asked. "Don't even think about it."

"The God Siaais blessed us with the ability, and I'm going to use it to help her in her last moments if she asks me to."

"You're too trusting. She might turn against you. It's happened before."

"There's still time. It won't happen."

Ava snorted in disbelief. "You're too good."

"Will you come? I know there's no reason why you should, and you don't like it at all . . . but I'd appreciate it . . ."

Ava took a deep breath, then nodded. "I'll be at your side, just in case."

"Thank you, cousin," Amelia said.

They continued the long walk to the Great Pyramid in silence. As they neared it, they saw the guards at the entrance: a hundred of them, stoic, presenting arms. They wore bright armor of steel plate, layered with gold. They stood with spear and shield pointing in front of them, just as the extinct Archaic Ones had done six thousand years ago, in front of this same Pyramid.

Ahamon was waiting in front of the soldiers. He greeted them in funerary garb, much darker than the costume he had worn at noon. Beside him was a group, most of them women, who had come to say goodbye to Asmi in her last moments.

"Welcome," Ahamon said with a slight bow.

They returned the greeting respectfully and took their places alongside the others.

"The Ceremony of Accompaniment is always a sad one. Today we say goodbye to a friend, an honorable member of our people." He made a solemn gesture with a golden staff whose head took the form of a crescent moon.

At Ahamon's gesture, a dozen guards escorted the honored one to them. Asmi's eyes were red from weeping and terror. She could barely stand, and her knees were shaking. Two guards were supporting her by the armpits so that she would not fall.

Amelia looked as if she were trying with all her might not to cry. Ava shook her head, unable to understand why Asmi had chosen such a terrible end of her own volition, fully aware of what it implied. Everybody knew what awaited her. Ava would not have chosen this way. Poison was a much better way out, painless and quick. There was no need to go through the horrible final stage of the sickness. But many clung to the vain hope that perhaps one day the Chosen would come back with the Cure and save them.

"Poor wretches," she murmured. "The sad, crazy hope of those who are doomed to a terrible end."

The moment the words had left her mouth, she regretted them. She did not mean to be cruel. Perhaps Amos the valiant would succeed, even though there was less chance for him in the company of a scholar and a healer instead of two more strong, well-prepared warriors.

She sighed. It was hard for her to be an optimist. Her existence had been marked by harsh experiences that had led her along the path of pessimism—or as she called it, the reality of the life allotted to them.

"Who will accompany her in her last walk?" Ahamon asked, solemnly and rather gently. He was trying to soothe Asmi.

There was a silence. Nobody seemed to have the courage. They bent their heads and stared at the ground. Ava could not blame them.

Amelia stepped forward. "I'll go with her."

Ava looked at the unfortunate victim, and a shiver ran down her spine. Poor woman.

"So will I," Ava said. She was not prepared to leave her cousin alone in there.

Asmi smiled at them, then a moment later burst into disconsolate tears. The guards, who had let go of her, were watching her warily. They were now keeping a prudent distance in a circle around her.

"So be it," Ahamon said. He waved his ceremonial staff several times in the direction of the Pyramid, while he intoned a profoundly ancient hymn.

The entrance was sealed with a great block of stone, just as it had been when it was first built. At Ahamon's signal the guards lifted the block with a massive system of pulleys, pulled by a dozen hefty oxen.

Suddenly Ava had a sense of something ominous. "This is a bad idea," she said, and put her hand on her cousin's shoulder to stop her.

Amelia turned to her. "I've made up my mind," she said. Her eyes gleamed with determination.

Ava knew her cousin would not change her mind. Silently, she cursed the God Siaais.

"The moment has come," Ahamon announced. He led them inside, beckoning Ava and Amelia to follow him. The guards surrounding Asmi motioned her on. Amid sobs, she began to follow Ahamon, Ava, and Amelia.

They went up the ramp leading to the entrance, then under the huge, raised rock and into the Great Pyramid. It was impressive enough on the outside, and no less so within. Ava stared at the millennia-old rock walls that lined the narrow passage and the torches, which burned with a black smoke. The light they gave produced dancing shadows that made her shiver. The place made her skin crawl. Access to the chambers of the king and queen was forbidden, except to the scholars. The lower chambers, on the other hand, were accessible, and these were where they were going: the final place where they took their people when their time was nearing its end and the sickness was about to consume them.

By her side came Amelia, looking at the walls and the hieroglyphs that decorated some of the corners. Ava did not know their meaning, because they had been sculpted by the Archaic Ones, but she knew that Amelia did. Her cousin loved studying everything about that ancient, now-extinct civilization. Amelia always insisted that the Kemet were descended directly from the Archaic Ones. Ava, on the other hand, argued that they were descended from the Ancient Ones who had caused the Apocalypse. They never came to an agreement. Maybe they were both right.

Ahamon was leading the parade at a ceremonial pace. Behind them could be heard Asmi's sobs, amid the heavy footsteps of the guards. They went slowly, respectfully, as though at a funeral—since that was what the Ceremony of Accompaniment really was, a living funeral, even if they did not like to call it that openly. Ava was not deceived. They were leading one who had been condemned by Siaais to her end.

With such gloomy thoughts they arrived at the forking chamber. Three scholars were waiting there, those in charge of safeguarding the contents of each chamber. Inside the Pyramid only the scholars worked, protected by the guards.

Ahamon announced: "The Ceremony of Accompaniment for our comrade Asmi."

"May she be welcome in her last wish," came the response from the scholar on the left.

Originally the Pyramid had only contained a single underground chamber. This had been kept intact, but two more had been added: two enormous chambers, each with an anteroom. Each of these had an elevator that went down to the underground chamber several yards below, which was the only means of entry. The first chamber was used to store all the knowledge and relics they had rescued from different temples. The intention was to safeguard everything and study it, which was what the scholars did. The other chamber was used as the last resting place for all those who so chose when Siaais's Curse claimed them.

They went down the last stretch of the rocky passage and came to the anteroom. When the scholar operated a metal lever, the stone door slid to one side and revealed a small chamber which led to another, deeper one.

"The moment of farewell has come," Ahamon announced.

"No, please!" Asmi cried in terror.

Amelia tried to calm her. "Don't worry, Asmi, we're here with you."

For a moment she stopped sobbing and seemed to calm down.

"You must go in," Ahamon said.

The calm was broken. "No! I want to live. Check my golden Mark again, please, I beg you."

"We've already done that," Ahamon told her, calmly but firmly. "You know this."

"Please," she pleaded.

"I'm sorry. It shows nine and half bars out of ten. The moment has come. It's about to reach ten out of ten."

"Noooooo!"

"There are only two ways," Ahamon said calmly. "This, or else a quick death now, before you reach the final stage of the Curse and become a danger to the tribe. I can grant you the quick death if you so wish."

"No!"

"You're still in time to choose a gentle death. It's your decision. If you wish to leave now, I can grant you that." He showed her the container of poison.

Asmi looked at him, and her eyes flooded with doubt. She was shaking her head. "No . . ." She glanced at Ava and Amelia. "They'll bring the Cure, I know it, they'll save me, I can't kill myself, I can't, I just can't . . ." She began to sob again.

"If you choose the chamber, they might come back with the Cure, that's true," Ahamon said. "That's always our hope."

Asmi made her decision. "I'll go into the chamber."

"Very well," Ahamon said. He put the poison away.

Then Asmi suffered another panic attack. "No! I don't want to! No!" She tried to run away, but the soldiers stopped her and pushed her with their shields back inside the anteroom.

"Don't hurt her," Amelia cried. "I'll accompany her."

Amelia joined Asmi in the anteroom, and Ava rushed in after her.

Asmi was shaking, unable to stop crying. She was terrified.

"Don't worry, Asmi," Amelia said, "Let me Feel you. It'll help."

"Yes . . . Feel me, please," she muttered amid sobs.

Amelia rolled up her right sleeve, revealing her forearm with the Marks of Siaais. With the index finger of her left hand, she touched the upper Mark, the one that gave out a faint silver glow. Then she put her hands on Asmi's head and closed her eyes.

There was a silver flash on her forearm.

"I can feel . . . your fear . . . your pain . . ." Amelia said, concentrating deeply.

Asmi was shaking from head to foot.

"It's horrible, I know . . . I can feel you . . . I can feel your terror, your panic."

As she watched, Ava was growing increasingly restless. She strongly suspected time was running out, and she and Amelia would be in great danger.

"I'll help you," Amelia went on. There was another silver flash. "Easy . . . Do you feel my calm? There's no terror, there's no pain. There's only calm, immense calm. Infinite, as wide as an ocean. Think of the sea, becalmed. That's how you'll feel."

There was another flash, and Asmi stopped shaking. A moment later she stopped crying.

Amelia withdrew her hands. "Are you feeling any better?"

"Yes . . . I'm not afraid any longer . . . I feel calm . . ."

Amelia nodded and smiled.

"She has to be lowered down now," Ava urged her.

Amelia took hold of Asmi's arm. "Now we have to go."

They went with her to the elevator. It was a roofless metal box that looked like a cage for great predators. Amelia gave her a hug and kissed her on both cheeks.

"We'll see each other again," she said.

Asmi nodded. "Come back with the Cure," she begged them, and went into the elevator.

Ava hastened to maneuver the lever on the wall. The chains started to turn on the mechanism of pulleys, and the steel elevator began to descend with a rickety metallic creak. It would lower her to the bottom of the chamber, thirty feet down, and there her journey would end, entombed with others like her, for whatever time they had left.

Suddenly Asmi's gaze turned to the ceiling. Her eyes widened. She opened her mouth in an agonized scream and put her hands to her throat as though she were choking.

"It's starting," Amelia said with immense sorrow in her voice.

"Only just in time," Ava gasped.

Asmi went into convulsions.

"Poor thing . . ."

A new spasm, the worst yet, left her stretched out on the platform. Her body began to turn a darker shade. Suddenly she opened an unhinged mouth as though in a silent scream of agony. A black substance, like a cloying mist, issued from her open mouth. It was as if an evil spirit were leaving her body.

The mist enveloped her completely.

"Siaais's poison," Amelia said as Asmi descended toward the great chamber.

"If it had touched us, we'd both be doomed, like her."

"I couldn't leave her. You saw her. She was suffering terribly."

"Even more terrible if we'd ended up like her."

"Don't be like that. Look at her."

Ava watched her descend, but by now it was no longer Asmi. The transformation always happened very quickly, as though it had been gestating all these years, to hatch in a single moment of utter brutality. All her hair had been consumed in an instant, and her skin had turned a brilliant black. Her eyes had swollen and enlarged, and their irises had now turned completely white, as if blind.

They heard a horrifying hiss coming from Asmi's mouth, and the hisses of an unknown number of others like her replied from the bottom of the great underground chamber. They were welcoming her.

Ava shivered again.

"I've had enough. Let's get out of here."

"We'll bring you the Cure," Amelia promised. "Not everything's lost. You'll be Asmi once again."

A hiss was her only reply.

"You shouldn't promise what we can't deliver," Ava said.

CHAPTER 4

The next morning, with the first light of dawn, the tribe went to fetch the three Chosen from their homes. With barely time to get used to what was happening, they were led to the Farewell to the Chosen. The great journey awaited, and they had to start at once. So Siaais had ordained, and so it must be.

Ava thought it was for the best. Thinking about their fate for days on end would not achieve anything positive, so the sooner they set off and met their fates, the better. She had hardly slept a wink, and her head was full of cotton. The purple circles under Amelia's eyes and her pallor showed that she had slept even less. Amos, on the other hand, appeared calm, even relaxed.

They were led forward amid chants of joy, good wishes, smiles, and a scattering of flowers. At that moment there was nothing and no one more important than the Chosen.

The ardor, the tribe's clinging to the unlikely hope of a miracle, was beyond Ava's comprehension.

Ahamon welcomed them at the Temple of Hope beside the great river. The temple was one of Amelia's favorite places. No one knew exactly when it had been built, but it had belonged to the Archaic Ones. They had found its ruins and rebuilt it. Or so it was believed. It served as a site for prayer to the great river upon which they were so dependent for water, for crops, for life itself. But its main function was the Farewell to the Chosen. It was also where the Kemet would wait for them to return with the Cure—a thing which had never happened. And yet everyday people came to show their respect and beseech the sacred river to bring the Chosen back.

"Welcome to you all," Ahamon said with outspread arms. "It is an honor and a privilege for me to begin the ceremony of the Farewell to the Chosen."

Amelia, Ava, and Amos went up the stone steps to the entrance. Ahamon bade them climb up to where he was standing, and then, in deference, he went down three steps and bowed to them. The people followed their leader's example, and all bowed long and deeply.

"Behold your people," Ahamon said with a wave of his hand, "who are here to bid you farewell, with the respect and honor you deserve."

From the entrance to the temple, the three Chosen had a view of the entire plain, with the whole tribe singing and cheering their farewell.

"The mission you are now setting out on is for them, for your tribe. Never forget that. When you come face-to-face with difficulty, remember who supports you, who awaits your return—all of us." He spread his arms wide to encompass the crowd.

Amelia was so moved, she wept.

"Come back victorious. Come back with the Cure!" Ahamon cried.

The shouts of support and good luck were now coming from the crowd in their hundreds. The sound was deafening, with everybody applauding and cheering at the tops of their voices.

"As if we could possibly fail," Ava said dryly.

Amos burst out laughing.

"Don't be like that," Amelia reproached her. "Can't you see they're putting all their hopes on us?"

"Yes, I can see that. They're making it very clear."

Ahamon joined in the chanting, and the doors of the temple opened.

"Before you leave," he begged them, "look upon your people one last time."

As they did so, Ava had a very strong feeling that this really was the last time she would see them.

They followed Ahamon as he climbed the steps and went into the temple. It was a rectangular single-story building, flat-roofed and made of solid rock. One side faced the plain, the other a small quay. The inner walls were decorated with paintings of ancient pharaohs from the time of the Archaic Ones. On one wall were hieroglyphs which, Amelia explained, showed funerary rites. Ava was sure that the temple had been used for farewells to the dead.

The back garden led to the harbor, where an impressive ship with a single sail was waiting for them. It was a beautiful craft, following the Archaic design.

"A ship for pharaohs," Ahamon explained. "It will take you to your destination, upriver, to the great delta." He embraced each of them in farewell. "You'll be successful. I'm sure of that."

"Thank you," Amelia said.

"You can count on us," Amos replied confidently.

Ava decided to keep her thoughts to herself. Ahamon had said the same words to last year's braves, and they had never come back. Nor those from the year before, or the year before that . . .

When they embarked, they met their first difficulty: There

was no crew. They would have to man the ship themselves. Luckily Amos had been trained in this, as in many other matters. He told them what to do, and they cast off and trimmed the sail to begin their journey. A gentle wind carried them on, away from the temple. In the distance they could still hear their people's chants of encouragement and valor.

Ava relished the beautiful blue of the river and the cooling breeze on her skin.

"I'll take the helm," Amos said.

"What else is there for us to do?" Amelia asked.

"For the moment you can rest. It's going to be a long journey."

Amelia nodded and sat down near him. Ava continued to watch the great river, relaxing to the gentle rocking of the vessel and the wind on her face.

She fell asleep to the swaying of the boat. She dreamed that they were free of the Curse and that they had all lived into old age, to long and full and joyful lives. She dreamed she had reached her eightieth spring and was happy with her grandchildren at her side, and even a great-grandchild in her arms. Then suddenly a shock ran through her body, and she began to feel that something was not right. She became aware that she was in a dream and she wanted to wake up, but she could not get out of it.

"Ava, wake up!"

She followed her cousin's voice back to the waking world. Her eyes opened wide and she inhaled a great mouthful of air, filling her lungs as if it had been withheld from her. She put her hands to her throat.

"Thanks."

Amelia stroked her arm and smiled as she helped her to her feet.

"Did I sleep much?" Ava asked.

"You've slept all day. It'll be dark soon."

"That's strange . . ."

"It must be exhaustion, everything that's happened, anxiety . . ."

"Must be," Ava agreed, though without much conviction, since she was not the kind of person who tired easily, least of all because of anything to do with feelings. As Amelia often reminded her, she was "cold."

Amos smiled at them from the helm. "Night's coming," he said. "Bring out the blankets from the supplies we brought with us. We're going to need them. The temperature's going to go down very soon."

"Right away," Amelia said with a smile.

"How many days will the journey last?" Ava asked him.

"Three days to the gate."

"And then?"

Amos shrugged. "Nobody knows. We'll need to go very carefully and be prepared for anything at all times."

Ava nodded. Amos was clearly more than just a hunk of muscle trained to kill. He seemed to have some brains too.

He stayed at the helm all night. Ava offered to take over, but he said it would not be necessary. The current was gentle and the breeze light, which meant that they would have no trouble. According to Amos, even a blind man with one arm could sail the great river. So she and Amelia went below deck and slept in a luxurious cabin among silks and delicious foods which had been left ready for them. They were being treated to a pleasant journey, at least until they reached the gate.

Amelia indicated all the luxuries they were not accustomed to. "Can you believe it?" she said to Ava.

Ava gave her a huge smile. "No, but I'm certainly going to enjoy myself for as long as I can."

"Me too!" Amelia exclaimed. She, too, was smiling, which cheered Ava up. Watching her cousin smile always delighted her.

Amelia took some food and drink up to Amos, and (as Ava had expected) did not hurry back down again. But she did not mind. She decided no good would come of brooding endlessly about their situation, and once she'd eaten her fill, she drifted off to a peaceful slumber.

—

Ava and Amelia woke to a sunny day with a gentle breeze, and Amos was waiting for them, looking serious.

"Is everything all right?" Ava asked.

"Yes . . . I did a lot of thinking during the night."

"And . . . ?" Amelia prompted him.

"You ought to learn how to fight."

"I think it's a bit late for that."

"It's never too late to learn."

"I agree with him," Ava said.

"You do?" Amelia said in surprise.

"However little we might learn, it will be useful to us," Ava went on. "And I'd like to know how to defend myself."

"I'm very clumsy . . ."

"Don't worry, I'll teach you," Amos assured her. "It'll be very basic, but it could help us in a dangerous situation."

They both nodded: Ava with conviction, Amelia resignedly.

"Are you both right-handed?"

They nodded.

"Good. That'll make things easier. If you want to live, and our people to have a chance, from now on you're going to do whatever I tell you."

"Excuse me?" Ava protested.

"You don't know how to fight, nor are you prepared for survival out there."

"I'll wager we've got better brains and instincts than you," Ava retorted.

"And I'll wager your brains and instincts won't stop something killing you."

"We'll see."

Amelia intervened. "What I think Amos means is that in moments of danger, he'll tell us the best thing to do."

Amos looked at her for a moment. "That *is* what I meant," he corrected himself.

Amelia turned to Ava. "He knows how to react in the face of danger. We ought to listen to him."

Ava looked at her cousin. Amelia was very intelligent, quite apart from having a heart of gold. She gave Ava a pleading look.

"All right," Ava sighed. "But only in the event of danger. The rest of the time I can manage very well on my own, and I don't need anybody ordering me about."

Amos nodded, although his eyes showed that he did not agree. He was obviously quite sure he was the right person to lead the expedition.

"It's settled, then," Amelia said, closing the argument.

"I'll be right back," Amos said and vanished belowdecks.

"He's only trying to help us," Amelia told her cousin soothingly.

"He'd better not let it go to his head." Ava folded her arms. "No muscle-bound oaf is going to give me orders."

"You're impossible."

"And you're too trusting."

Amos came back up, loaded with two shields, two spears, and two sets of armor. Amelia picked up a shield with a worried expression. Ava hefted a spear experimentally.

"As long as the journey lasts, we'll practice every morning."

"I think it's a good idea," Amelia said. "The spear is heavier than I expected . . ."

"So is the shield,"

"That's the gear of a javelin-soldier, the lightest we have," Amos explained. "It's the best thing, considering you haven't developed your physiques enough to wear armor and heavy weapons." He went back below and quickly returned with his own gear. His long shield would cover his whole body, and must have weighed three times as much as theirs.

"Wouldn't a sword be better? Lighter?" Ava said. She was getting the feel of her javelin.

Amos burst into hearty laughter. Ava did not know why he should be laughing so loudly.

"The sword," he began, trying to contain his laughter, "requires years of practice."

Ava wrinkled her nose and made a face at him.

"Put your armor on. I'll help you with the fastenings."

"Thank you," Amelia said. Immediately she began to put on the golden breastplate, seeking Amos's help with a smile that was rather too friendly.

Ava snorted. Out of all the valiants, it had to be this one . . . what luck.

Once they had finished dressing, they felt the weight of the armor straight away, however light Amos might say it was.

Amos showed them his own enormous breastplate. "This part is the cuirass," he explained. It was gold, engraved in silver. "These are the armbands." He indicated the protectors on his arms, which were the same color, with similar engravings. "These are the shin guards." He tapped the matching leg protectors. "And finally, this is the helmet." He put it on. Although its use was to protect the head, it had been made in imitation of one belonging to a pharaoh instead of one of his soldiers, and it was very elaborate.

"Perhaps a little too much?" Ava commented.

"It serves to protect the head, and it marks us as Chosen."

"I like it," Amelia said. "It looks very good on you. You look like a warrior god."

Amos shrugged. "It's our equipment."

"Didn't the Ancient Ones have anything lighter than this heavy Archaic armor?"

"Yes, but we lack the knowledge to duplicate it. We're limited to what the Archaic Ones could make. Let's start your training."

"How do you use the spear—I mean the javelin?" Amelia asked.

"No, we'll begin with the shield. It's the easiest, and the most important. Defense first, then attack."

"All right," Amelia said. She seemed delighted, despite her earlier reservations.

Amos gave them their first lesson on the deck. It was one they would never forget. They both ended up with their bodies aching from the weight and the blows they sustained. Ava did not mind the light beating, because she understood that it might save their lives someday. In fact, when they stopped, she felt rather regretful. She would have liked to go on a little longer.

With the addition of the training, the remaining days of the journey went by quickly. They moored at the delta, following Amos's instructions. He studied a scroll which turned out to be a map from the Ancient Ones, and pointed north.

"A day's journey. You'll be wearing your armor and carrying your weapons," he ordered them, military-style. "One bag each, with water and dried meat. Nothing else."

"But there's a whole cabin full of supplies," Amelia protested.

"They're useless if they can't be carried. They're a gesture of gratitude from the tribe."

"Amos is right," Ava said. "Let's do what he says."

They disembarked and went into the delta, their gold-and-silver armor fastened over linen tunics. On their backs each of them carried a large waterskin and a bag of food, with spears and shields in their hands. Amos inspected them to make sure his two novice warriors were ready.

"Good," he said when he was satisfied. "Follow me."

The landscape was much greener in this area, which pleased Ava. Used to the discomfort and harshness of the desert, seeing plants and lively greens and browns raised her spirits. Lost in contemplating the beauty of the landscape watered by the great river, she did not even notice that the day was over and night was beginning to fall. She was about to ask Amos whether they were going to camp when the warrior raised his fist and stopped.

In front of them they could see a construction of shining metal. It was an enormous silver arch.

The Gate of the Clouds.

It was the entrance to the kingdom of Siaais.

CHAPTER 5

As she stared at the gate, enthralled, Ava saw that it had a cold beauty, metallic and very different from her tribe's world of stone and adobe. The colossal arch, more than sixty feet high and twelve more than that across, shone against the sun. Its feet were robust hexagons twelve feet square, narrowing delicately as they rose. Within the arch was an eerie blue mist, like clouds, giving the whole gigantic structure a mystical quality. It had an air of something divine, as though it belonged to a God and only those chosen by him would be able to cross it.

They stood in silence for a time, staring at the great arch, lost in their own thoughts, their wishes, and their fears.

"It's amazing," Amelia said as she stared at it open-mouthed.

"It certainly is," Ava agreed. "Enormous and strange."

"At last we can begin our journey through the realm of Siaais," Amos said, eager to press forward.

"The metal flashes every now and then," Ava pointed out. "How odd."

"The gate always shines, even at night," Amos assured her, "so that the Chosen can find it and carry out our mission."

Amelia was watching the flashes with great interest. "The flashes have a strange rhythm. But if it shines at night, that must be because it reflects the moonlight."

"The arch shines all by itself, day and night," Amos insisted.

"The Archaic Ones didn't have such things . . . but perhaps the Ancient Ones did. That might explain it."

"The Arch wasn't built by the Ancient Ones or the Archaic Ones," Amos corrected her. He seemed amazed that they didn't know these basic points. "All valiants know this. It's the path we must walk in search of the Cure."

Ava and Amelia exchanged glances and shrugged. "I think we've lived very different lives among our people," Amelia said gently, almost as though she were apologizing. "Scholars and healers haven't had the training you and those of your profession have enjoyed."

Amos nodded. "That's true. I sometimes forget we're not all valiants," he said with a smile, and this time it was apologetic rather than vain.

Ava was surprised that Amos was capable of admitting his mistakes and apologizing. It wasn't usually the case among the valiants, who were always chosen to go in search of the Cure. But it hadn't turned out that way this time. Ava sighed, wishing she and Amelia had not been chosen. They would have to play this grim game of fate against the God and try to come out alive and victorious.

"And what about those clouds trapped inside the arch?" Amelia asked. "I've never seen or read about anything like it. It's unnatural."

Ava shrugged. "Not a clue, cousin. Amos, any idea?"

"It's the Gate of the Clouds," he answered. "What did you expect it to be like?"

"Let's go and have a proper look at it," Amelia suggested.

There didn't seem to be any risk involved. There was only the strange structure in the middle of a wide expanse of moorland, with no life around it. Still, Ava was uneasy. She didn't altogether trust things that were apparently harmless.

Amos went forward to the center of the arch and prostrated himself, letting his muscular warrior's body sink to its knees. "The Chosen present themselves!" he shouted at the top of his voice.

The shock made Amelia jump, but Ava was simply annoyed. "What on earth are you doing?"

"We beg to be allowed through, that we may begin our journey and gain the Cure."

There followed a long moment of silence. Amelia and Ava exchanged puzzled looks.

Suddenly the two hexagonal bases of the arch lit up, with intense and decidedly unpromising flashes. Amelia stared at the yellow one on the left, Ava at the red one on the right.

"Your humble servants ask permission to pass through," Amos went on, with his arms held high.

A lifeless metallic voice issued from both bases of the arch, echoing strangely.

"Unidentified subject. Put the implant to the screen reader."

Amelia looked at Ava. She in turn looked at Amos, who stood up. None of them had any idea what this meant.

"Implant?" Ava asked. "What's an implant?"

Amos was scratching his head. "And what's a screen reader?"

Amelia was squinting up at the sky, as she tended to do when she was puzzling out some difficult concept or deep idea. Ava was trying to understand the situation, but without success. The voice had sounded so impersonal, so empty, so steely . . .

"Is it ancient Kemet language?" Ava asked Amelia, who shook her head.

"I think it must be . . . the language of the Ancient Ones, from the time of the Apocalypse."

Ava shook her head. "That's not much use to us."

"Amelia's a scholar," Amos said optimistically, and looked into her eyes. "She'll be able to interpret the meaning."

Amelia blushed. "My knowledge is mostly about the Archaic Ones, not the Ancient Ones . . . I'm sorry . . ."

"Don't worry, we'll find the answer," he said. He was looking up at the arch, and his expression said clearly that no trivial obstacle was going to discourage him.

"I can't see past the gate," Ava said. She stepped toward the clouds. As she felt no great sense of fear—at least beyond what would be usual in a situation like this—she decided to act.

She reached out to touch the mist . . .

"Ava!" Amelia shouted. "Don't do that. We don't know what could happen. It might be dangerous."

Ava knew that her cousin was right. On the other hand, they had come here to cross this gate. She put her hand inside.

"Ava!"

To her surprise Ava saw her hand vanishing before her very eyes, as if the clouds trapped there had made it invisible. She felt an odd tingling, but no pain. She brought it out again, very slowly, and saw that nothing had happened to it.

"It's a mirage, like the ones you see in the desert when the sun's affecting your head," Amelia reasoned.

"*Subject unidentified. Put the implant to the screen reader. Second warning,*" came the screeching metallic voice.

"That didn't sound too hopeful," Ava said uneasily.

Amos clutched his spear and shield and stood there on guard, staring at the structure and the luminous flashes coming from its base.

"We're at the gate, there's no doubt about that," Amelia mused.

"But it won't open for the Chosen," Amos said, looking puzzled.

"It doesn't seem to recognize us," Ava said. She tilted her head as she studied the two bases with the red lights and identified the round openings the voice was coming out of.

"We're the Chosen," Amos insisted. "We humbly beg that the gate may open for us."

"*Unidentified subject*," the metallic voice said. "*Put the implant to the screen reader. Third and final warning.*" It spoke in the same jarring tone, but much higher in pitch this time.

"Final warning . . . I don't like this," Ava said.

"But it's the gate," Amelia objected. "It ought to recognize us . . ."

"Shields to front," Amos ordered.

Ava and Amelia exchanged puzzled glances.

"Follow my orders! Shields to front, left leg flexed, defensive position."

"But—" Amelia began.

"Do it, same posture as me!"

They did as Amos commanded, standing with their shields in front of them in their left hands, spears in their right, legs slightly flexed.

There came a long whistle. Next, a short beam of light, two handspans in length and an intense, lethal red, shot out of the base on the right and headed straight to Amos's torso. The warrior spun round instantly and protected himself behind his shield. When the beam hit this, there was an explosion and he was hurled backward. He was left stunned.

"Amos!" Amelia shouted in terror.

Now the left-hand base was blinking.

"We have to let it know somehow that we're the Chosen," Ava exclaimed. "Or else it's going to kill us."

Amos came to their side and shook his head. "I'm fine, the shield held."

As Amelia stared at him in concern, there came another long, ominous whistle.

"Look out!" Ava shouted.

"Take cover behind me," Amos ordered. "Shields up."

A new beam, intense red, issued from the base. Amos put his shield forward to block it, and there came another explosion. Amos and Amelia were thrown back and sent rolling across the ground from the terrible impact.

I've got to do something, Ava thought. She ran to the base, which was now blinking in flashes of yellow light. Here she searched desperately for some kind of mechanism, anything that could stop the attack. All she could identify was a rectangle of glass on the metal surface, which was giving out a faint blue light.

Amos got to his feet and helped Amelia, who was completely stunned. At the same moment, there came a new whistle.

"No!" Ava shouted.

Amos seized his shield with one hand and Amelia's with the other. The beam struck them, and the explosion was so strong this time that it left them unconscious on the ground.

"Hell!" Ava muttered, hammering impatiently at the base of the arch. "Open up, you wretched gate, open up."

The whistle sounded again.

The beam's going to come next. We're going to die!

She put her hands on the blue-illuminated glass. "Open up! For heaven's sake, open up!" she cried in desperation.

A silver flash came from her right forearm. *What's happening? What's this?* An idea came to her mind, and immediately she rolled up her sleeve. She saw the Marks of Siaais, and the upper one was shining.

She put her forearm to the rectangle of blue glass.

Her forearm shone silver once, the glass twice in blue.

She turned back to her friends, fearing the worst, but the murderous beam did not come.

"*Subject identified. Access one granted,*" came the jarring voice.

The two bases changed color to green. Ava breathed out heavily in relief and let herself fall to the ground. "That was close . . ."

It was a while before she managed to wake Amos and Amelia, using water from their supplies.

"What happened?" Amos said as he got to his feet and picked up his spear and shield.

"I managed to stop the attack."

"How?" Amelia asked. She was trying to clear the dizziness from her mind and stand up.

Ava helped her. "The Marks of Siaais. I put them close to one of the blue glass squares and the attack stopped. Look, both bases are green now."

"You saved our lives," Amos said.

"You weren't bad yourself," she admitted with a smile.

Amelia giggled. "He behaved like a great guardian warrior."

The compliment utterly confused Amos, who was clearly not used to such things. "Well then, now what?" he asked quickly.

Amelia was looking at the left-hand base. "Ava presented herself, but we two haven't. I think we ought to."

"Okay then. Stay behind me in case something happens again."

Amos held his spear with his shield hand, so that his right forearm was free. When he put it to the blue glass, his forearm flashed silver once, and the glass did the same twice in blue.

"Subject identified. Access two granted."

Amelia brought her own arm close, and it, too, was recognized.

"Subject identified. Access three granted."

The clouds within the arch vanished as if they had been a mirage, leaving all three staring. They heard an abrupt sound, as if a great tree were splitting, then rock grating against rock. It was coming from the center of the arch, on the ground, between the two bases.

"What's happening?" Ava asked in surprise.

Amos shook his head and took up a defensive stance.

The sound went on, growing stronger. It was followed by a strange hum, then suddenly the ground opened at the central point beneath the arch. A metallic cube the size of a small hut came up to the surface, apparently from the depths of the earth.

"What is that thing?" Ava asked, wide-eyed.

"No idea . . ." said Amos.

Suddenly a door opened in the center of the square. They all jumped in shock. Nobody came out. They waited, but nothing happened.

"I think we have to go inside," Amelia said.

"Into that thing? It's come from the bottom of the earth!"

"I think that's where we have to go."

Ava and Amos looked at her in surprise. "I thought . . . we'd cross the gate . . . to the clouds," Amos said, sounding annoyed.

Ava shook her head. "It seems not."

Amelia went to the object warily, and Amos followed. They looked inside. It was empty.

The hum became stronger.

"Come on, Ava, we have to go into the metal box."

"Are you sure? I don't like enclosed spaces."

Amelia gave her a smile of encouragement. "Trust me."

Ava saw that the box had risen to the surface when all three of them had been recognized. It made sense to go in. But the door must lead them to some other place. She hesitated. *Is this the path we have to take? Into the earth?* But she had to make a decision.

"Fine," she said resignedly, and went in.

Once the three were inside, the door slid shut.

Ava shook her head. "I don't like this at all."

"We'll make it," Amos said. He was clutching his shield and spear tightly.

Darkness surrounded them. There was a click, and the box began to descend into the depths of the earth.

Ava felt fear creeping over her. They were being buried alive.

CHAPTER 6

The darkness they were now descending into was so complete, they couldn't even make out their own outlines. All they could hear was a disconcerting hum as the metal box went down, accompanied by a clanking that was not in the least reassuring. It smelled of metal and damp, of wet soil. The farther they went down—and they seemed to be descending into an endless abyss—the colder it became. When Amelia reached out with her hand, feeling in the dark, she found Ava. They grasped each other's hands, finding comfort in that small gesture. All the same, the impenetrable darkness and their certainty that there was no way they could escape were eating at their stomachs.

Amos moved around blindly, slamming the four walls of the box with his hands, searching for something he couldn't find. He went on trying until he bumped into Ava and Amelia.

"Sorry," he said.

"What are you trying to do?" Ava asked.

"I'm looking for a way out, or some way to stop this descent."

"I doubt you'll find either," Amelia said. "I have a feeling this thing was designed to keep us inside until it stops moving."

"We've been going down for too long," Ava said. "This steel box is taking us down into the abyss. I don't like it at—"

"I don't like it either," Amos interrupted. His voice was anguished.

Ava turned toward the warrior's voice in surprise. Amos never showed anything except total confidence.

"Are you all right?" she asked him.

"Yeah . . . it's just that . . . I'm a valiant, a Chosen . . ."

Amelia reached out. "Give me your hand, Amos."

Amos hesitated. But in the end, he groped for Amelia's hand and held it.

"Let me Feel you. I'll help you. The Blessing of Siaais is strong in me."

"That won't be necessary . . ."

"Warrior," she said in a soft voice, as though she were a wise, kind old woman, "you're not well. Don't let pride guide your heart. Pride is a bad friend."

Ava could not see them, but she knew what Amelia was going to do. She had some idea of what was going on in Amos's mind and why he felt so terrible in this enclosed box that was on its way down into the depths of the earth. Unfortunately, as a healer she knew there was no quick cure for an irrational mental fear.

There was a silver flash on Amelia's forearm, on the upper Mark of Siaais. Ava was able to make out her cousin's hand as she put it on Amos's forehead, which glistened with sweat.

"I'm beginning to Feel you now."

"I . . . there's no need . . ."

"There's nothing to be ashamed of."

"Yes, there is," Amos said furiously. "I'm a valiant. I shouldn't be afraid of anything."

"Your fear . . . it's turning into terror. What are you afraid of?"

"This place."

"I know. I can tell what it is. It's fear of this small space, of being trapped. I can feel it growing."

"I don't know why this is happening to me."

"Shhhh . . . I'll make it go away."

There came a new silver flash on Amelia's arm. "There it goes. It's leaving you."

"Yeah . . ."

She withdrew her hand. "How do you feel now?"

"Better. The terror's gone away. How did you do that?"

"She has a special talent," Ava said.

"Nonsense," Amelia replied. "We all have it. It's just that I use it more than most of us."

"I can't do what you just did to me," Amos admitted. "I can only pick up certain powerful feelings in other people like rage, hate, fury . . . I can't relieve them the way you just did."

"If I can, then we all can. Our people are blessed with this talent, everyone in our tribe. But most of us are afraid of it because it comes from Siaais, so it goes largely undeveloped except by a few."

"They're right to be afraid," Ava put in. "Nothing that comes from that capricious, soulless God can be good."

"I don't agree. This Blessing is one of the few good things we have. That's why we ought to use it. The more it's used, the more it develops. That's what the scholars believe."

"We valiants are only taught how to fight, to survive. We hardly know anything about the talent of *Feeling*."

"That's easily sorted out. Just as you're going to teach me how to fight, I'm going to teach you how to use our talent."

"Oh . . . I don't know . . . I don't think . . ."

"There's no reason to fear it. You'll be able to help others.

Me, for instance. If the situation were reversed, you could make my fear vanish."

"In that case . . . all right, then."

"Remember," Amelia said, "it only works on other people, not on oneself, unfortunately."

"I understand."

—

The descent came to an end with a slight jerk, startling them. All three fell silent and tensed, listening very closely. A moment later the humming stopped, but the darkness was still impenetrable. They waited tensely, trying to glimpse some movement, some light, some sound, but there was only darkness.

The door slid open with a screech, and an intense light revealed a long corridor. After so much time in the dark, they had to cover their eyes against the brilliance.

"Get ready," Amos ordered. "Shields in front, spears at the ready."

They waited for a moment, ready, holding themselves rigid, while they tried to adjust their eyes to the light. Nothing happened. The corridor was lit with strange lights above, in a long line.

"We're underground," Amelia muttered. "That light's not natural. Besides, it's too bright . . ."

"Well, they're certainly not torches," Ava said suspiciously.

"It's the light of Siaais," Amos pointed out enthusiastically, "not more darkness. It'll guide us to the Cure."

Ava was not in the least convinced. It would be better for them to keep their eyes open and remember that no Chosen had ever returned from their journey.

"Let's get going," Amos said firmly.

No sooner had they gone out into the corridor than the door slid shut behind them.

Ava spun round. "No!" She heard the humming of the box as it disappeared upward. "Hellfire! We can't go back up."

"Don't worry, let's follow the corridor," Amelia said. "We're sure to find a way out."

They set off down the corridor. It was completely white, walls, floor, and ceiling. It looked as if nobody had been this way for a very long time—and yet it was spotless. Ava nervously wondered how this was possible.

At the end of the corridor, they found a closed door. On its right was a square of blue glass.

"Hold the Marks of Siaais up to the glass," Ava suggested.

When Amos did so, the glass gave out a green flash. The door slid open to one side and disappeared into the wall. They crossed the threshold warily and found a flight of white stairs leading down to a rectangular platform of the same color. At the end of the platform was a pedestal, and behind it an enormous crystal cylinder. Inside the cylinder, in its center, rested what appeared to be a capsule shaped like a metal spearhead, with a rectangular window along its structure. The cylinder and the capsule inside it were nearly three times the height of a person, and they ran the entire length of the platform.

"What's that?" Amos asked.

"No idea," said Ava.

Amelia was driven on by her innate curiosity and her desire to learn. "Let's go and see," she said, and set off toward it.

"Be careful," Ava reproached her. At the same time, Amos hastened to protect Amelia.

Amos looked around with his spear at the ready. Amelia was staring at the cylinder and the spearhead-shaped capsule inside it with great interest. She was barely able to restrain herself.

"The pedestal is another of those 'readers,'" Ava pointed out.

Amos saw that she was right: On it was a glass square that gave out a faint blue light. He bared his forearm, and when he touched it to the reader it gave a green flash.

Suddenly a semitransparent door in the cylinder, which they had not noticed, slid to one side. A moment later another one behind it, inside the capsule, did the same.

"It looks as if we're being invited to get in," Amelia said and, in her eyes, there shone the excitement of someone who is discovering new worlds.

Ava wrinkled her nose. "I'm not sure that's a good idea . . ."

Amos did his best to encourage her. "We have to keep going. The Cure's there waiting for us at the end of the path."

"And so is death, at each step along it . . ."

Amelia gave her cousin a pleading look. "Even so, we have to go, for the sake of our people . . ."

Ava sighed and looked around her. The underground hall seemed to have only a single exit, in the form of the cylinder which penetrated the rock wall on her left. The rest of the great chamber was pure rock, and the platform seemed to be white marble. Everything was very solid, and there was no other way out.

"All right, then," she muttered reluctantly.

They went in, with Amos in the lead and their spears and shields at the ready. The doors slid shut behind them, first that of the capsule, then that of the cylinder.

"What are these weird seats?" Amos asked. He jabbed the tip of his spear into a kind of chair that was elevated on top of a pedestal and covered in some solid-looking material which was unknown to them.

"There are three of them," Ava pointed out. "Together, facing the tip of the capsule."

"They must be for us," Amelia said.

"Well then, let's sit down," said Amos.

Amelia took the one on the left. Amos took the middle one. They were wide, even for someone as big as the warrior.

Nothing happened.

Both of them relaxed and left their shields and spears on the floor in front of them, beside their travel bags. Ava sighed and did the same. She left her things at her feet and sat down.

Suddenly she felt something sliding around her waist. There was a click.

Something had trapped her in the seat.

"What? What's this?"

She looked down at her waist and found that a metal belt was restraining her. She tried to stand up, without success. On her left Amos was trying to tear the belt apart with his strong hands, equally unsuccessfully.

"We're trapped," the warrior muttered.

All three did their best to free themselves, but it was impossible. Another strange sound reached them, a low hum gradually rising to a sharp whistle.

"What's going on?" Amelia asked uneasily.

The capsule rose and hung there in the middle of the crystal cylinder, floating.

Amos struggled with all his strength to get loose. "By Siaais!" he shouted.

Blue spirals began to surround the capsule, as though bright celestial spirits were coiling around it. The hum was now penetrating and uncomfortable.

"I think it's about to do something," Amelia said.

She was not mistaken.

The capsule shot forward at an incredible speed inside the glass tube so that the three of them were flattened against their seats. The capsule left the platform and went into a tunnel. Only the crystal cylinder now separated them from the rock. They were traveling at an amazing speed, leaving behind leagues of rock in the blink of an eye.

Suddenly they no longer felt the pressure of acceleration, even though they were still traveling at enormous speed. The belts around their waists loosened. Amos jumped out of his seat and searched for his weapons, which had flattened themselves against the base of the seat.

"It's like we're flying," Amelia exclaimed, puzzled and thrilled at the same time.

"But what's pushing it?" Amos said in bewilderment. "I can't see any camels or horses."

"I think this is technology of the Ancient Ones," Amelia said.

"And that?" Amos asked. He pointed to the blue spirals that coiled around the capsule from time to time.

"I have no idea," Ava said. "But it's all really weird."

Amos was looking around. The capsule was not very big, with room for the three of them, but little more than that.

"We don't seem to be in danger right now," he said.

Amelia was so excited she was almost clapping her hands. "Look at the speed the rock's going past us. It's awesome."

"We must be a really long way away from the platform where we started," Ava said.

"If there's no danger, we could have something to eat and rest," Amelia pointed out. "We don't know how long this journey's going to last, and all this excitement has given me an appetite."

"That's a good idea," Amos agreed enthusiastically. "I could eat a whole cow."

Amelia smiled at him. "You've got to keep that strong body of yours going."

Amos threw his head back and blushed. "I . . . well . . . and you have to feed that quick brain of yours," he mumbled.

Ava rolled her eyes. She could not believe what she was seeing between those two. She was about to say something, but thought better of it. The situation was strange enough already without adding to it.

They sat down in a circle on the floor in front of the seats and ate from their supplies. Amelia and Amos talked about the differences between a valiant and a scholar in the tribe. They were like night and day, a strong warrior as opposed to a frail scholar. Until that moment their lives, too, had been totally different. But it was obvious that they attracted one another as the moon attracts the tides, and Ava couldn't help feeling a little envious. Amos, usually full of confidence and determination, was looking at Amelia with a timidity in his eyes that made him seem a lost child. Amelia was looking back at him admiringly, smiling every time he spoke to her.

Ava sighed. Deep down, she was glad for them. It would help them to bear this horrible situation they were in. She was glad she was not here with a couple of strangers. At least she was with her beloved cousin, and that helped her to keep her spirits up.

The journey went on for several days. Since they were locked inside the capsule, they rested and practiced as much as they could. Amos made a great effort to teach them to fight, and little by little they made small advances, which they celebrated as if they had won a battle. The girls were grateful for his efforts, and especially for his patience with them. Amos never grew annoyed, but took it in stride and simply repeated the lessons and exercises.

On the fourth day they left behind the rock which had surrounded them, and to their enormous surprise they found they were now traveling underwater. The crystal cylinder that carried the capsule was supported by pillars anchored to the seabed. It was amazing to watch fish of different kinds and colors zigzagging beside them, while the light of the sun filtered by the water made them gleam. The undersea vegetation around them was both captivating and unreal.

Amelia was enjoying every moment of the journey. Not only did she find it all deeply interesting, but she was trying at the same time to understand how it was possible. Amos was more concerned with crocodiles, the possible appearance of some other marine creature, or some other unexpected danger. He could not relax, but was always on the alert. Ava, on the other hand, was wondering how the Ancient Ones had built that underwater viaduct and trying to understand this miraculous method of transport. But unlike her cousin, who was fueled by curiosity and the desire to learn, Ava was driven by the instinct to survive. That was Ava's goal: to come out of this alive.

For two more days they went on underwater before they finally surfaced. The light of day shone on them. Wonderful green landscapes spread out before them. They passed through valleys and over rivers, crossed mountains dense with trees, and raced across flat pasturelands. The leagues of crystal tubing the Ancient Ones had created so that the capsule could travel were impressive, as was the distance they must have traveled from their home. Ava wondered whether they would find a way back. With each league of their journey, the possibility seemed more remote.

While she watched the landscapes go by, she thought about what she had left behind: the tribe, the Curse. She wondered whether the Curse would reach them, even though they were fleeing far away. She glanced down at her forearm, at the lower Mark of Siaais. No, there was no escape, no matter how far they might go. They were already infected, and it was only a matter of time before the illness transformed her. If only there were some way out—and yet something inside her told her there was none. She remembered Ahamon explaining it, succinctly and clearly. There were only two options when the marker reached its end: either a quick death, or the descent into the Chamber of the Cursed. At first, long ago, it had not been like that, and it had cost them dearly. Healers and scholars had tried to heal the Cursed ones after their transformation, but it had been a terrible mistake. The Transformed Ones infected those around them with their illness, turning them at once into those creatures that were half human, half nobody-knew-what horrible-monstrosity.

Those first times had been disastrous, with the tribe on the brink of annihilation. The families and healers who had tried to help the first Cursed ones had been transformed, and soon had infected a quarter of the population. Those who remained, when they realized what was happening and that it could not be stopped, had escaped upriver in barges. The Transformed Ones had chased them on land. The desperate survivors, seeing that they could neither reason with their pursuers nor escape them, had sought somewhere to hide in safety, finally finding shelter among the Great Pyramid and the Sphinx. In this way they managed to flee the Transformed Ones. They armed themselves and decided to fight, to finish off the monsters before the monsters could finish off the tribe.

For fifty years they did this. Those who were transformed among them were locked up so that they could be studied. They tried to analyze them and find a solution, to create a cure, but nothing worked. In the end, seeing the number of casualties and the danger they posed, they decided to build the great chamber underground and banish them there. All those who did not wish to end their own lives, those who kept the hope that one day a cure would be found, went down there. A solution which, even though it might not be a final one, was in some way merciful.

Ava shook her head. *Wishful thinking.* She was determined that she would take her own life before she was transformed into an abomination. Unfortunately, she knew that Amelia would do the exact opposite and keep up her hope of a cure, her hope that her state would somehow revert to what it had been before. If, that is, she did not end up transformed before her time because of some moment of distraction which she was led to by her own good-heartedness. She had to look after Amelia. She would never forgive herself if anything happened to her, not after what had happened to her own mother.

A solitary tear ran down her cheek.

Don't let yourself wallow in your feelings, she scolded herself.

Amid these dark thoughts, the capsule reached its destination, a structure directly ahead. The three glanced at one another for a moment and silently returned to their seats. The belts tightened around them at once. With an enormous deceleration that tugged their bodies forward, the capsule slowed down until it stopped beside another platform, identical to the one they had left behind when they had boarded.

Ava stared at a marble staircase that led up to the door at the top.

She was certain that things were about to go really wrong.

CHAPTER 7

Once they were on the platform, Amelia began to take a close look at the vehicle they had arrived in, trying to understand how it worked.

Ava watched her cousin fruitlessly pressing the unlit panel. "I don't think you're going to be able to start it," she said.

"We've got to go on," Amos said softly, gesturing to the stairs.

"I know . . . I wish I had the time."

Ava rolled up her sleeves and checked the Marks of Siaais. She shook her head regretfully. "No, unfortunately, we don't have time. Don't forget that even though we're here, the Curse goes on stealing what's left to us with every passing moment."

Amelia sighed resignedly. "You're right . . . I know . . ."

They went up the stairs and through the door, then along a long white corridor that ended at still another door with a screen reader.

"Ready?" Amos asked, pointing his spear at the door.

"I'm very nervous," Amelia said, "but yes, I'm ready to find out what else is waiting for us out here."

Ava wrinkled her nose. “Let’s go very carefully. I’ve a feeling things are about to turn ugly.”

Amos nodded. “I agree. Stay close to me the way I taught you, one on each side, and if there’s any danger, we take up a defensive position, shields to the front, creating a small defensive wall.”

“All right,” Ava agreed. “You give the orders, and we’ll follow.”

Amos held his Marks of Siaais up to the reader, and the door slid to one side. To their enormous surprise, they found themselves outside again, in what appeared to be a rainforest. Its tropical green assaulted them with its freshness.

“What a landscape,” Amelia exclaimed.

“I was looking forward to getting out and breathing some pure, fresh air,” Amos said. He spread his arms wide, breathed in deeply, and looked up at the blue, almost cloudless sky. “How I loathe enclosed spaces and the dark.”

Ava made no move from the door. She was looking in all directions with narrowed eyes, looking for possible danger.

“Come on, Ava, step outside,” Amelia called.

Ava was reluctant. She knew that stepping out meant entering Siaais’s realm, and that sent shivers down her spine, because in his realm death awaited her. Still, however little she might want to go on, she could not turn her back on Amelia.

“I’m coming,” she said, and crossed the threshold.

Ava took a few steps toward her cousin, the jungle plants brushing against her legs. The door closed behind her. She turned and saw that it was chiseled into an enormous vertical formation of rocks. She stared at the door for a moment, and to her great surprise it faded, melting into the rock, until it had vanished.

“But . . . that’s impossible.”

And of course, it won't reopen, she thought as she passed her forearm over the rockface.

"The way is always onward," Amos said.

"That's what they might have taught you. Life has taught me always to look for an escape route."

"A valiant always faces the dangers ahead of him."

"A healer runs away when she meets a lion or a crocodile," Ava retorted. "However brave she might be."

Amos, not knowing what to say to this, blushed a little.

Ava could see no way of going back. She knew that this was deliberate. It was part of the macabre game the merciless God was forcing them to take part in. She joined her friends, who were watching strange birds with eye-catching plumage and strange calls that could be heard from the forest canopy. The vegetation was very dense and varied, and seemed to have several layers, from moss and ferns at the foot of the trees to lianas climbing up branches.

"We're a long way from home," Amos said.

"We certainly are," Amelia agreed.

Ava spread her arms wide, to better feel the air. "It's warm here . . . but humid."

Amelia nodded. "Very different from our arid land," she said.

"I'm just glad it isn't cold," said Amos.

Amelia looked down at her armor. "But in this heat and humidity, wearing armor is going to make us sweat like pigs . . ."

Ava bent over to inspect a vivid yellow plant that was totally unknown to her. She shook her head.

"What's the matter?" Amelia asked.

"I don't know these plants. My knowledge of healing is going to be handicapped here if I can't find the plants and roots I know to prepare my compounds with. For the moment, don't eat or touch any plant, no matter how pretty or appetizing it looks. The last thing we need is serious indigestion or poisoning. I've brought some antidotes with me, but I don't know whether they'll work against the poisons here."

Suddenly they heard a whistle: long, high-pitched and annoying. Amelia grimaced and put her hands over her ears. "What's that noise?" she asked.

Amos went a little way into the jungle, parting the leafy plants with his shield in search of the origin of the sound. He pointed with his spear.

"It's coming from over there."

Ava and Amelia went over to see what it was, and Amos parted the vegetation so that they could see. In the middle of a clearing a hundred paces away, beside a stream, they could see a bright metal post, perhaps fifteen feet tall.

"Let's go and see, but very carefully," Amos said.

"Don't get too close," Ava warned him.

They approached it slowly, trying not to make a sound, until they could see it clearly. The whistle was coming from a spherical metallic object on the top of the post.

"What's that, and why's it whistling?" Ava asked.

Amelia half-closed her eyes and examined it thoughtfully. "I'd say it's because of us. The metal is well looked after. The structure is from the days of the Ancient Ones, and it's been maintained."

"Well, if it has been, it wasn't by the Ancient Ones," Ava commented.

Amos shrugged, though the whistling sound was clearly irritating him. "What shall we do?"

"Can you reach it?" Amelia asked.

"Of course I can." He looked almost insulted that one of them would doubt a valiant like himself. He left his shield and spear on the ground, then with two powerful strides and a huge leap he climbed the post in no time at all.

"See if you can loosen it," Amelia called. "It must have some kind of fastening."

Amos, his legs hugging the post like a snake, inspected the sphere, but could not find any kind of fastening. He tried unsuccessfully to pull the sphere off by force but nearly fell.

"Be careful! Hold tight!" Amelia shouted.

He made another attempt, but signaled to show that it was impossible. By now the whistling sound was deeply unpleasant.

"Try turning it to the left," Amelia said suddenly.

Amos did so, and after applying all his strength, to their surprise the sphere unscrewed. The whistling stopped. He threw it down to Ava, who caught it effortlessly. It did not weigh much, was the size of a melon, and appeared to be hollow. Amos slid down to the ground, and all three of them took a good look at it.

"Knife, please," Amelia asked Amos, and he handed it to her.

Amelia introduced the knife deeply into the hole where the sphere had been screwed in, and there was a hollow *clack*. The sphere split in two. Inside it was another one the size of an apple.

"What do you think it is?" Ava asked her cousin.

Amelia handled the object for a long moment in silence. Suddenly, a beam of green light three feet long came out of the sphere. Startled, Amelia let it go. It fell to the ground, and the green light went out.

Amos picked up his weapons in alarm. "What on earth is that thing?"

Amelia placed the sphere on the palm of her hand. When she did so, the sphere once again gave out the beam of green light, pointing north.

"Interesting," she said. She moved her arm to the east, and the sphere rotated in her hand. The light went on pointing north. She tried again, this time to the west, with the same result. The sphere rotated, and the beam of green light indicated north once again.

"Why does it move?" Amos asked.

"Because it's an indicator. I think it's telling us where to go."

"In that case, it was Siaais who put it there," Ava reasoned, and Amelia agreed.

"If that shows the way we have to follow, then that's what we'll do," Amos said.

"First we'd better fill the waterskins from the stream," Amelia suggested. "It could be a long journey."

Ava sighed. As far as she was concerned, this boded ill. The God was indicating the way, but it was one from which nobody had ever returned. She thought of trying to escape, and looked over her shoulder. All she could see was a huge vertical wall of rock, impossible to climb, which was lost in the distance to both east and west. There was no way back. This was a carefully prepared trap. She sighed heavily. They would have to keep going and face whatever might come.

All day they made their way on through the jungle, taking every possible care. For them, walking among the tropical vegetation was like walking on the moon. They were used to the desert, and this environment seemed to them the nearest to the complete opposite that they could imagine. Ava warned them not only about the plants but about poisonous creatures such as snakes, spiders, or even insects, which they might come across in this new world. They went slowly, since the forest was thick. Amos went first, cutting branches and underbrush with strong diagonal sword thrusts to the right and left. He was sweating as never before. Amelia followed, and Ava brought up the rear, constantly looking back as she went. She and her cousin were both sweating almost as much as Amos.

When night fell, they camped in a small clearing, and Amos prepared a fire.

"My whole body's aching," Amelia complained as she massaged her legs. She was not used to so much physical activity.

Ava smiled. "You scholars aren't much used to the rigors of the outdoors," she said half-teasingly.

"And on top of that, wearing this armor and carrying a shield and spear plus the satchel of supplies. My body's begging me to throw them all into the first gully we see in this jungle."

"I don't think that would be a good idea. And Amos wouldn't think it was funny at all."

"He certainly wouldn't. How are we going to practice every dawn? I've still got bruises from those sessions in the capsule. And a lump on the back of my head when it bumped against the seats."

"Yeah, there wasn't a lot of space, was there?" Ava said with a laugh, remembering the knocks they had suffered.

"Amos made us practice just the same," Amelia said sadly as she touched the lump on her head.

"You know that as far as he's concerned, there's no valid excuse to skip training."

"Yeah, and I've tried them all," Amelia said mischievously.

"Ever onward. For the prize," Ava said, imitating the warrior's deep voice and looking as serious as he did.

Amelia laughed. "You've got him to a T." Then she groaned as she pulled off her leather boots. "Ufff . . . I don't remember ever having walked so much at a stretch in my entire life."

"Healers are used to covering a lot of ground searching for medicinal plants, but I have to admit, we use camels most of the time. I'm tired too."

"He isn't," Amelia said. She nodded in the direction of Amos, who was searching for dry wood to feed the fire.

"He's trained for this since he was a child."

"I know, but I'm impressed all the same," she said admiringly.

"Focus on staying alive, cousin. Remember where we are. Remember that nobody's ever returned from here."

"I know, I'm focused."

"Yeah, on him."

"Don't be like that," Amelia said. She threw the waterskin at her.

With a smile, Ava tossed it back to her. She took out an ointment and handed it to her cousin.

"Put some of this on. It's an insect repellent. We don't want you being bitten by some disease-carrying mosquito."

"Ugh, this smells awful."

"That's why it repels insects."

They both smeared their arms, legs, and faces with the revolting repellent. Before long Amos came back with firewood, and all three enjoyed rest and the comforting warmth of the fire.

"The fire'll keep animals at bay," Amos assured them.

"Animals?" Amelia repeated.

He put a finger to his ear. "Listen," he said.

For a moment they fell silent, letting the hundreds of strange sounds of the jungle at night reach their ears.

"There are so many . . . unfamiliar sounds," Ava said uneasily. "Not all of them sound harmless."

"This is a jungle, I don't know what kind of animals there are in it, but there must be predators just as there are in the desert. The fire'll keep them at a safe distance. The important thing is to keep it going, just in case . . ."

Amelia swallowed and looked up into the treetops. They could hear noises and glimpse moving shadows that did not bode well.

Suddenly Ava caught sight of something in the sky between the treetops. "What . . . ? What's happened to the moon?"

Amelia and Amos looked up through the branches. "What's that in the center?" Amelia asked.

Amos half-closed his eyes to see it better, and let out his breath suddenly.

"It's the God Siaais."

Then Ava recognized it. Against the moon, an image was being projected, a huge almond-shaped eye with a silver iris: the Eye of Siaais.

"That despicable God. He's spying on us."

"Ava! Don't talk like that." Amos lowered his voice as if he worried the God was listening to them. "Especially if he's watching."

"Of course he's watching. We're his toys. He must be having the time of his life."

"We're in his realm," Amos pointed out.

"Fine. Let's change the subject."

They chatted for a while as they ate from their supplies, ignoring the eye.

"Shhh!" Amos said suddenly. He was looking around him with all his senses alert.

Amelia and Ava, too, looked around, but could see nothing in the darkness of the night outside the circle of firelight.

Amos got to his feet, peering into the darkness. Very slowly, he picked up his spear and shield. Ava felt a sudden sense of danger, and her stomach contracted. Carefully, she followed Amos's example and picked up her own weapons.

The warrior took a step forward, keeping up a defensive stance with his spear and shield at the ready.

There was a rustle to his right, barely noticeable. Something moving among the bushes. Ava tensed and gestured to Amelia to pick up her shield and spear. Something big and heavy was slowly making its way toward them. Nearby plants stirred. Ava caught the sour taste of fear rising into her mouth and clutched the shield and spear tightly.

Amos made a sign that they recognized at once. Ava took up a defensive position as the warrior had taught them, on his right and a little behind him. Amelia did the same on his left, so that all three now formed a compact defensive triangle.

The sound stopped.

The movement in the vegetation did the same.

The three kept their formation. Ava felt such a level of tension that for a moment she thought she was going to snap her javelin, she was holding it so tightly.

Big cat eyes shone amid the foliage. With a prodigious leap, a great cat sprang out and hurled itself at Amos. The warrior tried unsuccessfully to bear the impact, but was hurled backward between Ava and Amelia.

A majestic, lethal tiger roared in defiance, showing its deadly fangs. They gleamed in the light of the fire.

Amos, meanwhile, was trying to get up. "Hold your position!" he yelled at them from the ground.

The tiger gave a violent swipe with one paw, and there came the sound like that of metal striking against metal. Amelia moaned as she was hurled to one side.

Ava shouted her name.

The tiger roared again and clawed twice at her, and both shield and javelin flew out of her hands. She fell backward onto the fire amid a cloud of sparks.

The tiger, which seemed poised to finish her off, leaped back from the explosion of sparks and fragments of burning wood. By now, Amos was on his feet again.

"To me!" he yelled at the great cat. "Come and fight me,

you evil beast!" It hurled itself at him, clawing at him with all its strength. Amos stood his ground, sheltered behind his shield, but the animal's weight and momentum were so great that he was forced to take several steps back.

Ava recovered, and when she saw Amelia on the ground, unconscious, fear exploded in her heart. *I've got to do something.* In an act of desperation, compelled by terror, she threw the javelin just as Amos had taught her. To her surprise she caught the animal in one of its hind legs, and the javelin penetrated deeply.

The tiger roared in pain and limped back, allowing Amos to act. The wounds the tiger had left were deep—his right arm and side were bleeding—but he took up his weapon and leaped forward, trying to thrust his spear into the animal's open jaws in mid-roar.

At the same time, Ava noticed something strange about the tiger: Its front legs shone in the light of the fire, when there was no reason for them to. Ava grabbed two burning logs and ran at the beast, waving them over her head and shouting at the top of her voice. The tiger shrank back at the sight of the fire, and Amos seized his chance.

He leaped forward and speared it in its side. The animal clawed at Amos, catching him in the shoulder. He staggered back in pain while Ava went on shouting and waving the burning logs at the beast, which retreated once again, ears flattened against its head, roaring fiercely. Amos aimed his spear and ran with all his might at the tiger, which turned to face him. The spear buried itself in the tiger's mouth and went through its head.

The beast staggered and fell to the ground, dead.

Amos fell to his knees.

Ava dropped the logs and rushed to help him. The moment she held him, she realized for the first time that her hands were burned. Intense pain swept over her, but she clenched her mouth and eyes and bore it as best she could. At that moment she wished she were able to use her people's talent to banish the pain from her mind. But even if she were as adept as Amelia, she could only do that for others, not for herself.

She knelt beside Amos. "Let me have a look. You're losing a lot of blood."

Amos shook his head. "Go and see to Amelia. My wounds are nothing."

The wounds were deep, but Ava could see in the warrior's eyes that he would not accept any help until she had gone to Amelia.

"Hold on, I'll be right back," she said, and ran to her cousin.

She found that Amelia had been hit hard on the head and was bleeding from a tear in her thigh. Ava hurried to fetch her satchel and took out a suture needle and thread to sew the wound, together with a preparation against infections. She worked with the skill of an experienced healer, disinfecting and closing the wound, then checked the contusion. It was not serious, although her cousin's head would hurt for a few days.

She patted her cheeks. "Wake up, Amelia."

Amelia came to all of a sudden, her eyes staring. "The tiger!"

"Relax, love, we're out of danger."

"Amos . . ."

Ava ran to the warrior, who was putting pressure on the deepest of his wounds to stanch the bleeding.

"I'm going to make a tourniquet."

Amos's color was far too pale. "All right."

Ava tied on the tourniquet and began to suture the wounds there and then. Amos made no protest. She worked with total concentration until she had made sure the bleeding was under control. Amos fainted and fell to one side.

"Help me carry him to the fire," she begged Amelia.

Together they dragged Amos to the fireside and tried to make him as comfortable as possible. They rekindled the fire with the embers that had been scattered around.

"Is he going to get better?" Amelia asked. Her eyes were moist.

"I'm going to prepare a couple of ointments against infection and a strong tisane for him. He's lost quite a lot of blood, but he's as strong as a horse. He ought to recover."

"Thank you. You're the best."

"I'm a healer, it's my duty. Besides"—she winked at Amelia—"I kind of like this valiant."

Amelia hugged her.

When Ava had finished looking after Amos, she finally relaxed and collapsed, exhausted, by the fire. As she was resting, she noticed the big cat lying dead a few paces away, and something caught her attention again: a gleam. She rose with an effort and warily approached the tiger's body. She knew it was dead, but even so, it awoke so much fear in her that she approached it with the greatest care.

She crouched down beside it and examined the body. At once she realized what was odd.

The tiger's legs were metal!

CHAPTER 8

Ava shook her head, unable to believe it. She was about to tell Amelia about it when she saw something even stranger: On the back of the tiger's neck, something was giving out a red flash. Amazed, thinking it might be dangerous, she hesitated, but curiosity got the better of her and she went to look more closely at it. Embedded in the back of the tiger's neck was a metal artifact, which was giving out an intermittent red light.

She clenched her fists. "Hell! This is the work of Siaais, for sure."

The tests had begun. The merciless God had sent them a creature that was half animal, half steel: the sheer perversity of it. Why was he playing with them like this? Why did he not kill them once and for all and spare them the suffering? Was this some form of entertainment for him?

Amelia, too, was staring at the monster. "It's a horrible thing," she muttered.

"What do you think?"

"From what I've read, the Ancient Ones had things called

machines, metal creations that worked for them, making valuable things and doing work for them."

"I don't think this *machine* could make anything of value or do any kind of work."

"It depends on what it was for. If it was for attacking and killing human beings, maybe it was useful. The Ancient Ones had machine-soldiers. This machine-tiger may be a variation on that concept."

Ava gaped at her cousin. "Well, once you look at it like that, you're probably right. That must have been what it was for."

"Although combining machines with living creatures seems to me a bit beyond the reach of the Ancient Ones. I don't know . . . maybe they managed it before the Apocalypse, but we haven't found any tomes that refer to it."

"In that case it was Siaais."

Amelia was thoughtful. "Maybe. That makes sense."

"Yeah, plenty. He's created them to stop us from getting to the Cure."

"Luckily we defeated it."

"Yeah, but it almost killed both of you. I don't suppose we'll be so lucky the next time."

Amelia was looking down at the ground. "I'm beginning to think the same," she said despondently.

For several days Ava attended to her patients. Amelia recovered swiftly and helped her with water, fire, and the search for food, which was limited to a few berries they had seen some animals eating. There had been no further encounters with strange beasts of the half-animal, half-machine kind, although they had heard bloodcurdling roars. Two days earlier they had also heard shouts which sounded human, but in the depth of the jungle everything was magnified and distorted, so they were not sure what they were hearing.

Amos was better, but though he tried to make it look as though he were already almost fully recovered, it was not really so. The wound in his side was deep and had not yet healed, but at least it had not become infected, as Ava had applied all her knowledge and skill to avoid this. They had built a small camp with large leaves tied to trees, creating a jungle roof to shelter them from the rain, which came from time to time, without warning, fell with great intensity, only to vanish as suddenly as it began.

As night fell, Amelia went to the nearby stream for water. Ava tried to find some dry wood, but it was impossible. Everything was soaking wet, and they would have to sleep without a fire. Luckily the weather was warm, and they knew that they could shelter from the rain and damp. Ava was worried about her medicines and bandages. She could not allow their wounds to become infected, and excess water and humidity were the enemy.

"Ava . . ." came her cousin's voice. She turned. The smile she was ready to greet her with froze on her face.

Amelia was at the edge of the clearing. There was a man at her back, holding a knife to her throat.

Another man was aiming at Ava with something like a horizontal bow, thick and heavy, which he was holding in both hands.

"Amelia . . ." was all she could utter, petrified by the shock.

"Both of you stay where you are, or I'll cut her throat," shouted the man behind Amelia.

"You stay still, don't move a muscle," the second man said threateningly. He was aiming his bow at Amos, who already had his spear in his hand and was trying to get up.

Ava looked out of the corner of her eye for her javelin. It was a few paces further back, beside Amos, who had only managed to get as far as his knees. She did her best to gain time and think of some way out of this.

"Who are you?" she asked.

The two attackers exchanged looks of surprise. "Who are you lot?" said the one who was threatening Amelia.

Ava saw that the two of them were older, apparently in their twenties. They were wearing strange clothes, and over them what she guessed was some kind of armor, because it was very thick and well-padded. They also wore broad belts in the form of leather sashes two handspans across, from which hung dozens of differently shaped containers. Their heads were covered with helmets whose visors had an Archaic look, so that all they could see of them was their eyes. In these she saw a mixture of fear and hatred which left her feeling distinctly uneasy.

"We're from the Kemet tribe. We come from the deserts."

"Let me guess—you're here for the Cure."

Ava was silent for a moment. What did these people know about the Cure? Would she give too much away if she spoke about the Cure? Or of their own purpose here? Perhaps, but they seemed to know about these things already. They might know something interesting, or else they themselves might be able to reach some kind of agreement with them if they cooperated.

"What do you know about the Cure?"

The young man with the bow laughed. "Look at her. Even in this situation she's trying to get information out of us. You'd better tell us everything you know, or else we'll kill your friend, then you, and we'll leave the big guy for last. It'll be fun."

Ava saw in their eyes that the threat was not a vain one. They were ready to kill all three of them. But why?

"Has Siaais sent you to kill us?"

At the mention of the God's name, the two attackers tensed. They feared him.

"Answer my question or he dies," said the one who threatened Amos. His voice was cold and cutting. He would not hesitate.

"We were chosen by Siaais at the Ceremony of the Chosen. We're here to get hold of the Cure for our people. We were attacked by a beast that was half tiger, half machine. We're recovering from that so that we can go on with our quest."

"In search of the Cure?" asked the one who was holding Amelia.

"Yes, and are you another of Siaais's tests? Like the machine-tiger?"

The two attackers burst out laughing.

"You've got no idea where you are or what's going on here."

Ava didn't know what to say. With the knife still at her throat, Amelia's eyes were full of fear and her forehead beaded with sweat.

Amos was motionless as a rock, but his eyes never stopped icily observing their attackers. "Let her go and leave," he said firmly. "Go on your way."

"You're not in a position to demand anything, so just shut up and listen. You have an Indicator. The sphere that marks the way. Hand it over to us."

Ava nodded. She went over to her satchel, slowly and with her hands visible, then took it out and showed it to them. "This?"

"Yeah, bring it here to me," the bowman said. "Slowly, and don't do anything stupid, or your friends die."

Ava did as she was told and left it at his feet. The young man with the strange bow was watching her every move.

"What's your Power?" he asked suddenly.

"Power? What do you mean by Power?"

"Your talent."

Ava realized what he meant, but played for time. "I don't understand . . ."

The one with the knife put his right arm around Amelia's shoulder. He was covered in armor. With his knife he patted the upper part of his forearm. Ava understood that was where they bore the upper of the Marks of Siaais.

"Our people have been blessed with the talent . . . the Power . . . of *Feeling*."

The two youths exchanged a look. "Feel? What's that?" asked the one with the knife.

Ava tried to explain, although it was difficult. "What other people feel. Their pain, their joy, their suffering, their love, their sorrow . . ."

"What a waste of Power," the bowman said disdainfully.

"It doesn't seem to be either useful or effective here," said the one with the knife.

"It helps others," Amelia muttered.

"You shut up and don't move or I'll cut your throat." Her captor pressed the knife harder.

"Can you affect . . . what other people feel?" the bowman asked with a twist of his head.

Ava hesitated and looked at her cousin. Amelia could do exactly that, and it made her a valuable asset. Ava saw a way to escape, or at least, to negotiate.

She indicated her cousin, "She can, so don't hurt her."

The one who was holding Amelia grinned. "Yeah, valuable. And if she can do what you say, dangerous too."

"No, she's not dangerous," Ava hastened to say. "She could help you, make your suffering and pain disappear."

The one with the knife laughed. "Yeah, and she could make me die of pain too."

Ava was horrified. She had never thought of using the talent in that way, but it was not impossible. And if so, then Amelia would represent a danger for them. Telling them about it had been a mistake.

"They're very primitive," the bowman said. "They don't even know what they are or how to use their Power here."

"All the better for us. They might be a problem later on, though I doubt it. The warrior looks dangerous, but these two . . . I don't understand what they're doing here."

"Making things easier for us," his partner said.

Ava hastened to reassure them. "We don't want trouble; we don't want enemies."

"And you won't have them, kiddo," said the one with the knife in a tone of voice she did not like at all.

"We could help each other."

"I'm afraid that's not possible," the bowman said.

"Why not? We could join forces. That way we'd have more chance of surviving in the realm of Siaais."

"Maybe," the one with the knife began, "but then you see, we're here to find the Cure too."

"Then all the more reason to help one another."

The two attackers laughed again.

"They don't want our help," Amos went on. His voice was very serious. "They're Chosen, like us, only from another tribe. They want the Cure for themselves. They wouldn't share it with us."

"Well, what d'you know. The hulk here has a brain," said the one with the knife, with a sinister chuckle.

Then Ava understood. How could she have failed to realize? *How stupid I am, they're here for the Cure, and we're the competition. They're going to kill us.*

Then the one who was holding Amelia threw something

over her head. Ava saw the movement of his left arm and was afraid they were going to kill her cousin, but instead the object fell between her and Amos. When it touched the ground, it shattered with the sound of broken glass. Ava realized that it was one of the containers their attackers carried at their waists. A green smoke with a horrible smell came from the broken container and spread to envelop both her and Amos.

The two attackers lowered the visors of their helmets and stepped back, taking Amelia with them. Ava felt she was about to faint, and when she tried to stop them, she succeeded only in falling to the ground. Amos stood up and took two steps, spear in hand, but was unable to do more before he, too, pitched forward.

"Ava! Amos!" Amelia shouted in terror.

"Shut up," her captor muttered, his knife still her throat.

Ava made a massive effort to keep her eyes open, but the substance they had breathed was affecting her head. She fought to stay conscious, but at any moment she was going to faint.

"Finish them off," said the knife-man.

Ava made one last effort to move, but failed. The gas had paralyzed her muscles. Amelia was screaming desperately and trying to free herself, but the attacker was holding her tightly, still threatening her with the knife. She saw a silver flash behind her and thought that Siaais was coming for her. The blade at Amelia's throat began to move.

Suddenly there was an explosion. Short, powerful. The attacker's knife arm was suddenly shaken, and blood spurted out.

"What the hell?" he shouted. He had lost both his weapon and the use of his arm. He spun round.

Ava could make out someone else, further back, aiming a strange, extended weapon. He lowered it, reached out his arm, then suddenly moved it to one side. Amelia's captor was thrown in that direction.

"Hell!" the bowman said. He aimed and released. The arrow flew toward the stranger's chest, but he raised his weapon at the last moment and the arrow hit that instead with the sharp sound of metal on metal. Ava thought the stranger had been hit, but he was still standing there looking at his weapon.

At that moment Amos moved to one side and speared the bowman in the ribs. Caught by surprise, he dropped the weapon with his eyes gaping wide, then gave a grunt and died. His partner ran for his life, holding his useless and bleeding arm as he went.

Ava saw Amos let go of his spear and then faint.

Amelia ran to them, and at the same moment Ava lost consciousness.

CHAPTER 9

Ava was trying to wake up, but without success. She felt a charge run through her body. She knew what was going to follow, and began to feel queasy. There followed more jolts of intense pain throughout her body.

"Don't worry, Ava," came a voice. "Rest now, everything's all right."

But she could not rest; the pain was too intense. She had to wake up. Her friends needed her. In the midst of the pain, a blurred image appeared in her mind. It was distorted, unfocused, and she could not quite see what it was. Against an infinite blackness, something circular began to take shape. Pain assailed her again, and she lost the image. She clenched her jaw and eyes, trying to force the pain to pass. The image came back: It was a sphere of fire. Now she could see it better: a sphere surrounded by flames. The pain intensified, the flames filled her mind and the sphere vanished.

She opened her eyes wide and cried out in agony.

"Easy, girl, it's over now," the voice said soothingly.

Ava looked around her and recognized her cousin. It took

her a moment to free herself from the nightmare so that her mind could get used to what it was seeing.

"Amelia . . ." she muttered. She was trying to remember what had happened and where she was.

"You've woken up at last. I'm so glad. You had me really worried."

Suddenly she remembered the two attackers, and sat up suddenly, like a spring. "We're under attack!"

"Relax, the danger's over," Amelia assured her.

Ava looked around her and saw a waterfall. She did not recognize her surroundings. They seemed to be inside a cave, but that was impossible. She began to feel nervous.

"Where are we?"

"It's a safe place. The camp wasn't safe any longer, so we had to move."

"Where to?" Ava asked blankly.

Amelia smiled. "Behind a waterfall. We have water and shelter from the rain."

Ava stared at the waterfall from inside the cave. It seemed to be the only way in or out.

Ava's eyes widened as she looked at the cave around her. "How did you find this place?"

"It wasn't us. It was Liam who found it."

"Liam? Who's Liam?" she asked uneasily.

"He's the one who saved us."

At that moment Amos and a stranger came in through the waterfall with a powerful leap, to avoid getting too wet in the spray.

Ava's gaze was immediately caught by the stranger. He was tall and athletic, with very white skin. His blond hair was worn in a ponytail, which seemed strange to her. In her own tribe, men would never wear their hair like that. The stranger, meanwhile, watched her with an indigo-blue gaze, observant and analytical. He was handsome, with fine features, albeit rather too pale. A terrible scar that ran down his right cheek marred his beauty. He came forward determinedly and offered her his hand.

"Hi, my name's Liam," he said.

Ava looked at him in puzzlement. Who was this person? Why were Amos and Amelia not on the defensive? They had just been attacked, and they had almost died.

"Just Liam, and that's all? I need you to explain a bit more."

"I'm not the talkative kind," he said, and moved back a little.

Ava was feeling at something of a disadvantage on the ground, so she got up.

"Liam saved us from the attackers," Amelia said.

"And we trust him already?" Ava said.

"You've been unconscious for a whole day," Amelia said apologetically. "Liam offered us shelter . . . and you needed it . . ."

Amos nodded toward the stranger. "Don't worry, Ava, I'm keeping an eye on him. If he tries to play any tricks on us, he'll pay."

"Well, I don't trust him. I don't trust anything we come across here. It might be a trap, to win our confidence . . ."

"Don't be like that," Amelia said. Her eyes were pleading. "He saved us from certain death."

"It's okay, I understand," Liam said. "In her place I wouldn't trust me either." He sat down on a rock to one side, took out a huge knife, and began to sharpen it with a whetstone. From his waist hung a short axe which looked light and smooth, not like the rough weapons they were familiar with.

"And he's armed. Are you out of your minds? We don't know anything about him."

"Well, we know he saved us," Amelia pointed out. "He

carried you all the way here, and he can hunt." She indicated a roast that was cooking over the coals of a fire.

The smell of roasting meat made Ava's stomach rumble, and her mouth watered. "That's not enough reason to trust him. Amos, disarm him."

Amos looked back at Ava. His expression was serious. "If I had to, I would, but I don't see any reason for it. In any case, his Power is pretty formidable. Not that I wouldn't be able to defeat him . . . but I'd rather not attack him without good reason."

Liam gave a slight nod of respect, which Amos returned.

"He must be an agent of Siaais."

"Yes, I could be," Liam said, "except that I'm looking for the same thing you are."

"The Cure?"

He nodded, without stopping sharpening his knife. "That's right."

"What tribe are you from?"

"From the Colonists."

Ava said, "We didn't even know there was another tribe. We thought they were all extinct and that we were the only survivors of the Apocalypse."

"Well, you were wrong," said Liam.

"How's that possible?" Ava could not understand how it could be that after such a long time they had not been aware of the existence of another tribe.

"My tribe used to think the same, that there was nobody else left on Earth. The attempts to find other people were fruitless. The expeditions never came back . . . we thought there was nobody else left, and that leaving our region meant dying. So the search was abandoned."

"The same happened with us," Amelia said. "It's a logical

conclusion. It didn't make sense to keep sending young people to their deaths."

Liam nodded.

"The attackers!" Ava broke in suddenly, sounding excited and tense. "Were they with you? Are they from your tribe?"

"No, they didn't come with me. They're not from my tribe."

Ava looked questioningly at Amos. She wanted to be sure Liam was telling the truth. Amos nodded in confirmation.

"Then . . . there are other tribes," Ava cried. This was something which so far had been inconceivable.

"I think it's clear by now that there are other tribes," said Liam, "and they're here for the same reason."

"You say that because of what the attackers said?" Amos asked.

"Yes . . . and because I'm here for the Cure as well, just like yourselves. I have to assume that others are too."

"That makes things difficult," said Amos.

Ava was remembering the attack. "What do you know about the other tribes? How many of them are there? How dangerous are they?"

"I've no idea. Until a few days ago I thought, like you, that my tribe was the only one. But since I arrived here . . . everything's changed."

"What do you mean?" Amelia asked.

"I've already come across four different tribes—counting yours."

Ava and her cousin looked at one another uneasily. That could certainly make the whole situation very dangerous.

"If you're one of the Chosen, show me your Marks of Siaais," Ava demanded, still distrustful.

Liam rolled up his sleeve slowly and showed her his right arm, with the two markings.

"How long do you have left?"

"I'm eighteen. I still have some time."

Ava was thoughtful. If he was a Chosen from another tribe, which made sense after what he had told them about the attackers, then they were competitors. And if what he had said was true, there were at least five tribes competing for the Cure. This was very bad news. Now they not only had to fight against the environment, Siaais and his monstrosities, but against other desperate wretches like themselves.

"And your two partners?"

Liam tensed at the question and paused in his sharpening of his weapon.

"Dead."

Amos, Ava, and Amelia exchanged worried looks.

"I'm sorry . . ." said Ava.

"Thank you. They were good lads."

"How did they die? If I may ask."

"I'd rather not talk about it."

"But did it happen here? Was it members of another tribe?"

Liam nodded heavily.

There was a tense silence. Ava wanted to go on asking questions, but she could read in Liam's face that he had had enough, so she changed the subject.

"Amos, how did you kill that attacker? I thought you'd been overcome by the gas."

The warrior had gone to check the roast, but he looked back. "Almost, but not quite. I held my breath as long as I could after the container broke, then I improvised and pretended to faint. I almost didn't make it."

"Our warrior isn't just brave, he's pretty clever," Amelia said. She ran to sit beside Amos, gazing at him proudly, and he blushed.

"Going back to your tribe," Ava said to Liam, "how many of you are there?"

"Not many. There are only a few thousand of us left."

"We ought to try to contact our own tribe," said Amelia, "now that we know we're not alone. It might change our future a lot."

Liam shook his head. "We're in the realm of Siaais. We're not allowed to go back or contact our people, and here there's nobody who can help us."

"How do you know that?"

"I guess it."

"What—?"

Liam raised his hand to interrupt her. "Enough questions for now, if you don't mind."

Ava was taken aback. She shut her mouth and thought about it, then decided it would be better to wait a little before she interrogated him any further.

"All right."

He lowered his gaze. "Thank you."

She continued watching the stranger as he went on sharpening his knife, his blue eyes fixed on the steel. There was a touch of sadness in his eyes, which intrigued her. All the same, she decided that she could not trust him. She would watch him closely, and at the first suspicious move she would go for him.

Suddenly her stomach rumbled, and she realized how hungry she was. The roast looked amazing. They ate and then rested. Ava realized how close to dying they had been, and a shiver ran down her spine. That wretched God was far more twisted than she had supposed. They were not the only tribe he had promised the Cure to, which meant that he also had other tribes under his evil control who were suffering from the Curse of Siaais just as her people were. She was beginning to see that the Curse was a punishment for all who had survived, whichever tribe they belonged to. This left them with no hope of finding a safe place to escape to, which saddened her immensely. There was less and less hope for her people.

She stretched her legs and tried to get comfortable by the fire. Out of the corner of her eye she watched Liam, who was now sleeping easily, as if he were among friends and had no worries. Amelia, too, was sleeping beside Amos. She caught his eye and made a sign to him to keep an eye on the stranger. The warrior gestured with his thumb across his throat, and Ava understood; at the slightest suspicion, he would kill him.

Knowing that allowed her to rest a great deal easier.

CHAPTER 10

In the evening Amos and Liam got ready to go hunting, and also to reconnoiter the area.

"Hey, wait a moment," Amelia said suddenly. She was looking puzzled.

Amos tensed and grasped his spear. "What is it?"

"Liam and us, we're from two different tribes . . ."

"Yeah . . . and so?" Ava pressed her. She suspected that something bad was coming.

"Well, as we're from two different tribes and two obviously different races, not to mention different regions, we shouldn't share a language."

Ava was amazed. This had not occurred to her.

Amos realized what she meant. He stared at Liam in surprise. "Oh . . . that's true . . ."

"I'll tell you why," Ava interrupted. She jabbed her finger at Liam. "Because he's part of Siaais's sinister game. He's working for him!"

Amos got ready to attack, and Liam raised his hands.

"I don't work for the God. I'm here for the same reason you are."

"Why should we believe you?"

"I don't know why I can understand you, but I could accuse you of the same thing. Why are you able to understand me?"

"I've just realized something even stranger is going on here," Amelia said. "What language are we speaking?"

"Kemet, of course," Ava said confidently.

Amelia turned to Liam. "Is that the language you're speaking?"

Liam shook his head. "We're all speaking English."

"English," Amos repeated. "What language is that?"

Now it was Liam's turn to stare at them in amazement.

"What's going on here?" Ava asked. "This doesn't make sense."

"I think . . . it doesn't. But on the other hand . . ." Amelia said. Her eyes were on Liam.

Ava raised her arms in bafflement. "Now you've lost me completely."

"I think what's happening is that both of us are using our own language. We speak ours and he speaks his, and in some very strange way we all understand one another perfectly well. We don't even notice the difference. Well, to be precise, our minds don't notice the difference."

Amos was frowning. "That's crazy."

Ava was shaking her head. She could not see it either.

Amelia looked around. "It's not something in the environment," she reasoned aloud, "it's something in us . . . yes, it must be something in us that's creating this effect."

"In us?" Ava repeated. "But the only thing in us that could do something like that is . . ."

"The Marks of Siaais," said her cousin, finishing her thought for her.

Amos grimaced and looked down at his own right forearm.

"Liam," Amelia asked him politely, "would you mind showing me your markings?"

"Sure," he said, and rolled up his sleeve slowly.

Amelia did the same. "We're going to do a test," she said. "We'll count to ten, both at the same time, then see what the markings do."

Liam nodded.

"Cousin, can you give the signal?"

Ava raised her arm and let it fall.

"One," Amelia and Liam said at the same time.

"Two." They looked down at their markings.

"Three," they said together, and were able to make out a faint gleam coming from the edge of their markings.

"Four." The gleam was whitish now, barely visible.

"Five." Now they could all see it.

Ava went to stand beside her cousin.

"Six."

Amos went to stand beside Liam and looked at his arm.

"Seven . . . eight . . . nine . . . ten."

"That gleam . . ." said Ava.

"We're each speaking in our language, but the Marks translate it as we speak. When it reaches our minds, it's already translated. That's why we don't notice the difference."

"But why?" Amos wondered.

"To help us understand one another?" Liam suggested.

"I doubt that very much," Ava said. "Siaais doesn't want to help us. What he does is set obstacles for us."

"There must be a reason, because this isn't something trivial," Amelia said.

"I hope this makes it clear I'm not a threat," Liam pointed out.

Ava folded her arms and stared at him. "We'll see."

Amos turned to Liam. "Come on, let's go hunting."

They both set off, leaving Amelia and Ava talking about this new, rather worrying discovery. How many more things were they going to discover? What dangers would they represent for them?

They came back at dusk with several hares and squirrels.

"How did you catch them?" Ava asked. She was surprised and delighted.

"He's an expert hunter," said Amos. "He used traps, we didn't have to use our weapons."

"Is that your profession?" Ava asked.

"Yes, I'm a hunter. That's my job among my people."

"You're not a warrior like Amos?" Amelia asked.

"No." He shook his head as he sat down and began to skin the catch. "My two companions were. My job was to hunt for them, feed them."

"Well, you seem to be very skilled with that knife," Ava commented suspiciously.

Liam smiled. "Yes, and with this as well." He indicated a long metal object inside a leather case he was carrying slung across his back.

"What's that?" Amos asked.

Liam looked him in the eye, as if he were calculating whether or not to tell him. "It's a musket, a weapon."

"What kind of weapon?"

Liam unrolled it and showed it to him.

"Do you hit with the wooden part? As if it were a long-handled axe?"

Liam smiled. "No. This is the butt. You use it like this." He set the musket in position, with the butt on his shoulder and the sight set on Amos.

"Watch it, Amos," Ava warned him. She knew instinctively that he was in danger, and he tensed.

"Don't worry, it's broken, it doesn't work," Liam explained. "The firing mechanism's damaged. I stopped an arrow with it in the confrontation, and it broke. I don't think I can fix it, but just in case, I carry it with me."

Amos was intrigued. "And how does it work? I've never seen a weapon like that."

Liam nodded. "It's like a bow, only instead of using arrows it releases these balls." He displayed a handful of metal pellets.

"These little steel balls? You couldn't kill anything with them, they're not even sharp."

Liam gave an honest guffaw. "Believe me when I tell you it can kill a man perfectly easily. The weapon launches the ball at great speed, then it hits whatever's in its path, penetrates it, and makes a big hole. It can go through metal."

Amos shook his head. "I don't want to call you a liar to your face, but I find that hard to believe."

The hunter did not take this badly, merely shrugged.

"What kills isn't the arrowhead," Amelia explained, "it's the strength it's fired with, so that it's able to penetrate flesh and bone."

"That's right," Liam said. "This weapon can throw the ball ten times faster and with a lot more force than a bow does with an arrow, and that's what kills you."

Amelia nodded to show she understood the concept. Amos, on the other hand, was not entirely convinced.

"Without my musket, I'll have to rely on my knife and tomahawk . . ."

"Tomahawk?"

"My axe," Liam explained, and went on preparing the catch. "I'll see if I can make a bow. I'm not too bad with that either."

The mention of the bow brought a question to Ava's mind. "The man Amos killed . . . he had a very strange bow. Do you know what it was?"

Liam stopped his preparations and looked at her. "Yes. But I'm not sure you're all going to like what that weapon means for you."

The three looked at each other, intrigued and worried.

"Whatever it is, it'll be better if we know it," said Amelia. She sat down by the fire and looked up attentively.

Amos nodded. "Let's hear it, then."

"That weapon is called a crossbow. It's a bow, but with a shorter range and more power. It can pierce metal armor, and at only a few paces, a man."

"Oh . . ." said Amelia.

Ava was looking a little confused. She tilted her head to look at Liam. "Why do you say we might not like it?"

"It means that even though it's an ancient weapon, it's more advanced than yours."

"I still don't understand," Ava admitted. She was staring at her javelin and shield on a rock.

But Amelia understood, and her eyes gleamed. "It means that the tribe we met was technologically more advanced than ours. The crossbow and the compounds they used against us are more sophisticated than our own weapons."

"Exactly. The compounds are the result of something called alchemy, and they were most likely enhanced by their Power."

Amelia was beginning to be fascinated. "Do you think their Power allowed them to create powerful compounds?"

"I think so. It would make sense."

Ava made light of this. "Well . . . the fact that one tribe's more advanced than ours isn't too much of a worry."

Liam's face had turned more serious. "It's not just one tribe."

"What do you mean?"

"I'm afraid you're probably the least advanced tribe . . . of the ones I've seen so far . . . I'm sorry."

Ava frowned. "Are you insulting us?"

"No. It's not an insult, it's a judgment."

"And what do you base that on?" Ava asked. She crossed her arms.

"Your weapons, your armor, your knowledge. They're . . ."

"Archaic?" Amelia put in helpfully.

"Yes, that's it, Archaic. I'd calculate something like thousands of years before the Apocalypse. Maybe four thousand years before."

Ava frowned. "Oh, really? And what about yours?"

"Mine are around seven hundred and fifty years before."

"I don't understand this," Amos said, his expression troubled. "Didn't everyone start over from scratch after the Apocalypse? Why's your tribe more advanced than ours?"

Liam sighed. "That's a good question. I don't know. I'm finding these things out myself as they come up. I don't have an answer . . . But I've come across four tribes, and each of them was at a different level of technological advancement. Look at my clothes. Have you ever seen anything like them before?"

Amelia went over to him, touched them, and studied them with great interest.

"You're dressed in leather, the skin of some animal. The boots and the belt I get, but . . . the shirt and pants? Don't you have linen? Don't you find it unpleasant, wearing the skin of a dead animal?"

He smiled. "You get used to it in time, the only drawback is the smell. I wear leather because it's the most suitable for the forests my people live in. We eat what we catch, and we wear it too. And yes, we do have linen and other fabrics, but hunters like me don't use them, for practical reasons. The point is that my people have certain technologies that are more advanced than yours."

"Let's see if I understand this," Ava said. She stood up and began to pace the cave. "Are you saying that the tribes who survived the Apocalypse have evolved at different speeds?"

Liam nodded. "It looks that way. I think every tribe has prospered up to a particular period of time, which might mean one or another might even have reached the era of the Ancient Ones. I don't know this for a fact, but after what I've seen so far, I don't see why it couldn't be true."

"I don't believe it," said Ava. "We're no dumber than the others." She launched a furious kick at a stone.

"It's not that, cousin," Amelia put in. "How much a tribe progresses depends on the level of knowledge and technology that it rescued. All we saved were a few tomes, and we went back to the times of the Archaic Ones. We never tried to get hold of the Ancient Ones' knowledge and discoveries. We made a choice not to do that, because we didn't want to repeat their mistakes, cause another Apocalypse, and bring more curses on our heads. That's our culture, our way of life. We chose what we are now."

"If we're some of the least advanced," Amos said thoughtfully, "we're at a massive disadvantage."

Liam nodded. "I'm afraid that's true."

"They may be more advanced, but that doesn't mean they're smarter," Ava said.

Liam gave a snort. "The problem is that they have better weapons and armor than you do. And they know more advanced techniques of war. If I hadn't acted to save you, you'd all be dead. And that's the reality you're immersed in. The next time you come across another tribe, you won't survive."

Ava had to bite her tongue. She knew Liam was right, but

she did not want to admit it, refused to believe they were the least advanced and with the worst chance of survival in this infernal world Siaais had condemned them to.

"I think we've talked enough for today," Amelia said, to give feelings a chance to settle. "We'd better rest."

"I agree," said Amos.

Liam nodded, but said nothing.

Ava took another turn around the cave, finding it impossible to rest. There was too much to think about. The situation was growing stranger and more complex than she had first thought.

"I'll take the first watch," said Amos.

"And I the last," Liam added.

Ava realized that the last one was at dawn.

"You're not going to leave, are you? You're not going to abandon us?" Amelia pleaded. She had come to the same conclusion as her cousin.

"I'll decide at dawn," Liam replied, and turned aside to sleep.

If he left it would mean one less risk, because they could not trust him. He was not one of them, and he might be putting on an act to gain their trust and then kill them all. It was also possible that this was not so, that he was a good person. Liam was someone who knew more than they did, and he shared his knowledge. He was also an excellent hunter, and had used his skills to their benefit. Trusting him might help them succeed in their quest . . . or it might be the last mistake they ever made.

Ava stared at the fire. Amos had mentioned that Liam's Power was a significant one. What could it be? Whatever it was, the decision to stay with them or leave was his alone, and whether he stayed or not, they would still have to survive . . . and find a way home.

CHAPTER 11

When they woke up at dawn, Liam was gone. Ava sighed. It seemed that he had given them his answer. She gave Amos a questioning look in case he knew something else, but the warrior shrugged, looking regretful.

"What do we do now?" he asked.

"Now," Ava said, "you're going to let me check your wounds and change the bandages. Then we'll decide what to do."

Ava worked until she was sure the wounds had been given proper treatment. Amelia was already fully recovered, but Amos still needed another week—as long as he avoided any sudden movements, the sutures should hold. She thought about how bad their wounds had looked, remembering the monster that had attacked them their first night in the realm of Siaais, and the men who had threatened to kill them. Danger was everywhere.

Ava put her medicines back in her satchel and tried to calm herself. She didn't want to upset her friends, who had enough to bear already with the pain of their injuries.

Suddenly Amos put his finger to his lips in warning. He

picked up his spear and shield and stood at the ready, facing the waterfall.

Amelia and Ava stayed silent and motionless. They were too far from their weapons to reach them quickly.

A figure stepped through the waterfall, carrying something over his shoulder.

"Liam!" Amelia cried. She sounded surprised but happy.

He indicated his shoulder, where he was carrying a dead fawn. "I brought breakfast," he said nonchalantly.

Ava folded her arms. "You didn't leave, then?" she said reproachfully.

Liam set down the deer by the fire. "I decided to stay."

Ava wanted a fuller explanation. "Oh, really? And how's that?"

"I think the more of us there are, the better. By myself I don't stand as good a chance of surviving out there." Liam took out a large knife and set to work on the deer. "If it's okay with you, of course," he added, with a glance at Amelia and Amos. He did not look at Ava, whose face showed a growing anger.

"I think it's a good idea," Amelia said.

"Amos? What do you say?" Liam asked.

"A hunter who knows how to use weapons and defend himself will come in handy. As far as I'm concerned, it's fine."

"All right then, it's a deal."

Ava exploded. "What d'you mean, it's a deal? I don't agree." She was carried away by her fury, not really thinking what she was saying.

Liam looked at her as if he had only just noticed that she was there.

"Two out of three's a majority. They win. I stay."

"What's a majority got to do with it?" Ava protested furiously.

Amelia stepped in. "Liam's right. Amos and I agree that he stays. There are two of us . . . and one of you."

"Amelia! You have to stand with me."

Amelia shook her head. "Yes, and generally I do. But now you're making a mistake, and I don't agree with you at all."

Ava's mouth dropped open in shock. Her cousin always supported her. Amelia openly speaking out against her left Ava with a pang of pain in her chest.

"It'll be good to have an ally," Amos said reasonably. "We're short of warriors."

"Then it's decided. I stay," Liam said, and went on working on the carcass.

Ava was debating between the shock of her cousin's opposition and her anger at Liam's determination. She was part of the group, and he was not. She clenched her fists and screamed in rage and frustration.

"Hell!"

Amelia, Amos, and Liam turned to look at her.

"This is a mistake, you just wait and see," she said, feeling like a child throwing a tantrum.

—

Once they were ready to press on, they left the cave and set off through the thick tropical vegetation. They went on without stopping for half a day until Amos, seeing that Amelia was very tired, called a halt. The warrior had offered to carry her spear and shield, or at least her satchel, but she had refused. Ava, too, was very tired, but she admired her cousin's courage. She was a brave little scholar.

While they rested Ava went over to Liam, who was on watch duty a few paces away from the group. She needed to make sure he was trustworthy, so she tried to catch him out in either a lie or a contradiction.

"Where are you from?" she asked impulsively. His skin was the whitest she had ever seen, and his blond hair and blue eyes were not from anywhere near her own tribe.

"I'm not much of a talker," he said.

"I'd noticed that already. Don't worry, I am."

Liam sighed resignedly. "I come from a region which in the time of the Ancient Ones, before the Apocalypse, was known as the United States of America."

"America . . . the north, right?"

"Yes, that's right, from the northeast. My tribe survived in a small territory near some enormous waterfalls that used to separate two countries."

"Are you all one tribe, or are you divided?"

"We're divided into twelve colonies."

"Oh . . . that's interesting. We stay united, all in the same place."

"Different cultures, different views," he commented, as though he found this perfectly normal.

Ava looked carefully at him again, intrigued by his features. Liam, conscious of her scrutiny, lowered his gaze.

"We're so different, you and I," she said.

"That's normal enough. From what Amelia told me, if you're near some pyramids in the desert, you're from what was once known as Egypt. We're on continents that are separated by thousands and thousands of leagues."

"How do you know about continents and peoples?"

"I like to read."

"You have tomes?"

"Yes, we saved some books, among them some on history and geography. They're my favorites. Now they're worthless, because everything's changed and we're living in a new era, postapocalyptic. The countries and the peoples that once existed have vanished now. It seems only a few of us survived, and from what I'm finding out here, in small groups at different ends of the world . . . That's only a guess. I can't be sure of it. I often wonder . . ."

"About what?"

"Why us?"

Ava nodded repeatedly. "I see what you mean. I'm starting to wonder about that now. Before, I wondered: why me and my cousin? We're not like Amos, who's been prepared for this all through his short life. Now I'm going a step further: Why my people? How come we're still standing? Why has Siaais brought three representatives of the desert people here?"

"There must be a reason. If you think about it . . . why, out of all the world's population, are we the only ones who've survived? Our peoples? And more than that, only a tiny fraction of our peoples. My country was huge at the time of the Ancient Ones, with hundreds of millions of people. Why have only a few of us survived?"

"I think it's got something to do with Siaais."

"That's probably true."

"That capricious God is the one who controls what's left of the world. He decides who lives and who dies. I don't know his reasons, but I'm sure they aren't good ones."

"I see you don't have a high opinion of our savior."

"Savior? He brought us the illness, the Curse."

"Among my people, he's thought to be a savior who managed to ensure that the illness that began after the Apocalypse wasn't deadly to us all."

Ava stared at him in disbelief. "My people believe the illness is his punishment for the Apocalypse. I don't think Siaais is any savior, far from it."

Liam was thoughtful. "Interesting, how different our points of view are."

She smiled sarcastically at him. "It must be because of the distance. Or because some people aren't very bright."

He smiled but said nothing. Ava, meanwhile, was staring at the musket he was carrying on his back.

"A warrior who breaks his weapon . . ." she teased him, seeking to annoy him and see his reaction.

"I'm not a warrior, I'm a hunter. There's a big difference."

She went on prodding him: "Then you don't know how to fight?" She wanted to test his patience and see if he would give something away in a moment of bad temper.

"I can look after myself," he said curtly.

"Well, isn't that just wonderful, because we need a warrior a lot more than we do a hunter."

"Are you sure? You've hardly got any supplies left. How are you going to survive if I'm not here?"

Ava shrugged this off. "We'll manage."

"I'm sure you will," he replied.

Ava made an impatient noise under her breath. She could not succeed in making him angry. And not only that: For some reason Liam made her nervous. The worst thing was that there was no clear reason for it, or at least if there was she could not see it. But there had to be one.

"I agree with you about one thing. We're rather short of warriors."

Ava looked at him in surprise. "That's obvious. The other tribes'll have fighters trained to kill. To kill us."

"Yes, I can vouch for that. But what we do have is a warrior, a hunter, a healer, and a scholar. That's not a bad combination."

"Against three warriors, or more? We have to assume that several tribes might join together, just as we did."

"I'm not saying that our chances are very good, but if we use our heads, we might just make it."

Ava agreed, but she had no intention of putting him in the right. She went on questioning him. "Is your tribe's Power any use?"

Ava felt victorious. The comment had touched a vein.

"It's not something trivial to be talked about lightly."

"No? Isn't that because it's not a very useful Power?"

"My tribe's been developing the Power for a thousand years, and I can assure you it's both useful and powerful."

"The fact that your tribe's proud of it doesn't mean it's valuable, especially here in the realm of Siaais," she taunted him.

Liam sighed. "Maybe a small demonstration might teach you not to laugh at what you know nothing about." He stared into Ava's eyes, challenging her.

Ava held his gaze. "Let's see what you can do."

He nodded and stepped back ten paces, slowly, counting them aloud as he went.

"You're supposed to show me your Power, not run away from me," Ava said sarcastically.

Suddenly he touched the upper part of his right forearm with the palm of his left hand. There was a silver flash. Ava realized that he was invoking his Power by activating the upper Mark of Siaais. She was not too worried. He was ten paces away from her, and her own people's Power only worked in close proximity.

Liam brought his wrists together and spread his palms: first upward, then pushed forward.

Then something extraordinary happened.

Ava felt her body rising two handspans off the ground, as if an invisible force were lifting her. A moment later she felt a push which shifted her several paces backward. When both forces vanished, she fell, and the momentum kept her rolling backward over her head several paces further until she came to a halt in the middle of a tangle of undergrowth, which scratched her all over.

Liam gave a short guffaw.

"Very funny!" Ava shouted furiously as she got to her feet and came out of the bushes.

"You challenged me. This is the result."

"Moron."

Liam smiled, and she left in a fury.

A while later, a little calmer, Ava saw Liam coming back to the group after he had gone to fetch water. She glared at him with loathing, but he was untroubled. *Does nothing affect him? Is there no way of making him lose that calm of his? There must be, I just need to find it. And I will. I don't trust him and that calm of his, not one little bit. That Power of his really is useful and powerful. All the more reason to keep an eye on him.*

Suddenly Amelia let out a muffled scream.

"What's the matter?" Ava asked her uneasily. "Are you all right?"

She was pale and silent, her gaze distant. Ava hastened to her side and took her by the shoulders. "Come on, what's the matter?"

"It . . . can't be . . ."

"Can't be what?"

Amos and Liam looked around, suddenly alert, but everything seemed quiet.

Ava stroked Amelia's cheek, feeling her skin for fever. "Stay calm and tell me what's wrong."

"The Curse . . . the illness . . . it's coming closer . . ."

Amelia's skin was cool to the touch. She seemed to be in a state of shock, but Ava couldn't understand why.

"Don't worry," she said, "it's coming for all of us. That's why we're here, to find the Cure."

"It'll be too late for me."

"Too late? Why do you say that? You're at six out of ten. You've still got plenty of time."

Amelia heaved a deep sigh, and with moist eyes, almost in tears, rolled up her sleeve. With her left index finger, she touched the golden upper Mark of Siaais. There was a golden flash, and the scale which measured the advance of the illness in their bodies appeared on the surface. The scale, in the form of golden bars, began to fill from the wrist upward with black, the black of death. It reached the middle of the scale, crossed it, and went on rising. Three golden flashes indicated the final result: eight out of ten.

"Oh, no!" Ava cried. She put her hands to her mouth, unable to contain her horror.

"What's happened?" Amos asked. His expression was one of pure fear: they were losing her.

"I don't understand it," Ava said. "It should be showing six out of ten."

Amos knelt beside her. "When did you last check yourself?"

"At . . . at the gate, before we crossed. It was showing six out of ten."

"It must be a mistake," said Ava. "It must not work properly here."

"No, it's not a mistake," Liam said. He had rolled his sleeve up to his elbow to show them his golden Mark. The scale was also showing eight out of ten.

"It's Siaais. He's condemning us. He's stealing what little life we have left!" Ava yelled at the sky, full of rage.

CHAPTER 12

At once Ava and Amos checked their own golden Marks. Ava rolled up her right sleeve to reveal the two identical rectangular marks that ran from wrist to elbow. Liam's Marks were identical to her own, as were those on the corpse of the attacker Liam had killed. This led Ava to believe that they must work in a similar way. She would have to talk about this with Liam and try to find out more.

She sighed and put her left index finger on the golden Mark, and it lit up. It reached halfway up the scale, passed it, and went on rising until it had almost reached the top. She waited for a moment until, with three flashes, the Mark revealed the result: eight out of ten.

"Hell!" she cried in frustration.

Amos snorted and frowned.

"You too?"

Amos nodded. "Eight out of ten," he said resignedly.

"That evil God. He's playing with us."

Amelia was looking at them sympathetically. "I . . . I thought it was just me . . ."

"No, it happens to all of us," Liam said. "It probably

happened the moment we entered the realm of Siaais."

Ava was pacing around in circles, furious with the God, the situation, and their bad luck in being here. Surviving in this world was going to be difficult enough, and the fact that their end was fast approaching foretold a future with no escape.

Ava raised her fists to the sky. "Of course no one ever came back!" she yelled. "Either they died or they were transformed in this nightmarish place."

Amos lowered his gaze. Amelia became aware that his face, for the first time, showed defeat.

"It might be a trick, to see how tough and determined we are," Amelia suggested. "Maybe the illness hasn't really advanced as much as the Mark shows."

"You really believe that?" Ava asked. "Knowing how merciful he is, all the great miracles our beloved God has worked?"

"He's not the one, and he hasn't done the other," Liam said in his usual laconic way.

Ava looked at him in surprise. He thought like her, at least as far as this business was concerned. This made her reconsider him. She might have been mistaken in judging him so harshly and not trusting him at all. She reconsidered this: No, she had been right not to trust him. Maybe he was just trying to get her to lower her guard.

Amelia was shaking her head, trying to make sense of what was happening. "There's no explanation for why the illness has advanced so quickly."

"You're wrong, cousin. An illness can advance ten times faster if it finds the right conditions to propagate itself and develop. An infection can kill you in a month or a week, depending on what condition the body is in."

"So . . . does the nature of this jungle speed up the illness?" Amos asked.

"That's what I think. Once we set foot in this place, the illness began to advance a lot faster than it ought to. If it's the same for Liam, it's because we're here in this jungle."

"That makes sense," Liam agreed.

"But why?" Amelia asked.

"Because Siaais is a twisted God who enjoys toying with us, the way a cat plays with a mouse before she kills it."

Amelia shook her head. "I don't want to think that . . ."

"No? Then why doesn't he give us the Cure? He says it exists and he has it in his possession. So why's he making us go through this? Why's he playing with our lives?"

Amelia was looking defeated. "I don't know," she said. "I don't understand."

"There's something curious about what's happened," Liam pointed out.

"What's that?" Ava asked.

"He's left us with a time score of two out of ten, and if this has happened to us, from two different tribes, we can assume he's done it to all the tribes who are here in this jungle now."

Amos was not sure where he was going with this. "So . . . ?"

"We already know it's a competition between the tribes. But Siaais has added a time limit. We have to reach the Cure before we're all transformed."

"It's cruel and inhumane," Amelia protested with a frown.

"That's why it's the most likely explanation," Ava said. "I think Liam's absolutely right."

There was a long silence while the four of them digested what they had just found out.

Amelia was still staring at her forearm. "So what do we do?"

Ava half-closed her eyes. "We run for our lives, and we get hold of the Cure before our time runs out."

"And what about the other tribes?" Amelia asked fearfully.

"We try every way we can to avoid them. If we run into them and they attack us, we fight back and run away. What I'm absolutely sure of is that we're not going to let them kill us. We're not going to die here; you have my word on that."

The other three stared at her. She clenched her fist. "Are you with me?" she asked.

"We are!" said Amos, and Amelia and Liam joined in.

"All right then," she said, "let's pack our things and be on our way."

They went on through the jungle, following the strange indicator they had found. At Amos's suggestion Liam went first, since he was a more gifted tracker and a better explorer than the warrior.

Moving through that vegetation, which was so thick that it made walking difficult, while at the same time keeping alert for any sign of danger, was truly arduous. Since Amos was walking beside Amelia, trying to help her as much as he could, Ava decided to move forward and walk with Liam, who was now following the course of a river they had come across.

"May I ask you something?" she asked him, after she had walked in his shadow for a very long time.

He looked at her and nodded.

"I'd like to know whether—"

"Keep your voice down," he interrupted her.

". . . whether you arrived here the same way we did?"

"I arrived with my two companions after we'd reached the Gate of the Clouds," he replied, without stopping, alert to everything around him.

"Did you go down into the depths of the earth in a metal box?"

"Yes, an elevator."

"Just like us, then."

Liam glanced aside at her, nodded, and went on walking,

clearing a way through the vegetation with his knife and tomahawk.

"Did you get into a very strange carriage that went at enormous speed under the ground, and then along the bottom of the sea?"

Liam stopped. "Yes, it was a very advanced conveyance."

"That means that we both got here in the same way from our respective tribes. I think that's very significant."

"Is it?"

"Why do you enjoy opposing me all the time?"

"I don't."

"Do you have any other theory?"

"No," he said and went on walking.

"Then do you accept mine?"

"For now."

Seeing that she was not going to get any more information out of Liam for the time being, Ava dropped the subject. If she antagonized him, it would only make things more difficult. So she smiled, hoping it looked genuine.

"All right," she said.

Liam looked back at her with one eyebrow raised. He said nothing and went on.

She thought her smile must not have been as convincing as she would have liked. She fell back a few paces until she was back with Amelia and Amos, with whom she felt safer.

Suddenly Liam held up his hand in a fist. Instinctively, although they did not know the sign, they stopped where they were. With his other hand Liam gestured to them to crouch down among the greenery, where they would be safe.

Amos, very slowly and silently, moved forward to where Liam was. The hunter pointed to something, and Amos nodded. Ava wondered what was happening. Amelia looked at her questioningly, but she could only shrug. They could see nothing from where they were.

Unable to hold back her curiosity, Ava began to crawl forward. Amelia followed her, and when they reached Amos's side, he glared at them reproachfully.

Ava ignored him and craned her neck to look ahead. She had to muffle a cry. A yellowish-green snake was hanging from a thick branch. It was huge, as long as five men and as thick as three arms. Its long tail was coiled around the branch, and its head was sliding down to the ground. A cold gleam attracted Ava's attention, and to her horror she saw that the snake's head and tail were of metal.

In its eyes she saw red lights, which were flashing.

She froze.

"We've got to do something," Amelia whispered urgently in her ear.

The snake was climbing back up to the branch, very slowly.

Imprisoned in its coils was a human being, either unconscious or dead.

CHAPTER 13

Amos shook his head. "That snake's unnaturally large . . ."

Liam put his finger to his lips, warning his companions to silence. "Yes, it's colossal," he whispered.

"We have to save her," Amelia said softly. "She might still be alive."

For a single moment, Ava was able to see the victim's face. It was a girl like her, of around the same age, although she seemed to be from some other ethnic group. Her skin was lighter and she had fewer folds in the skin surrounding her eyes.

"Amos, please," Amelia said. "We can't just let her die."

"It's too dangerous," Amos answered. "Besides, she's dead by now. The snake had to have strangled her so it could eat her later, and now it's taking her away."

Amelia turned to Liam for support.

"I'm sorry, it's too risky. If she's dead, we risk dying for nothing."

Suddenly the girl kicked out in an attempt to free herself. The colossal snake stopped its ascent and began to coil tighter around her body, which shook in a spasm.

"She's alive," Amelia pleaded, her eyes moist. "Save her. Please!"

Ava knew, just as Amos and Liam did, that to intervene here would be a mistake. The girl was lost, and in any case she was from another tribe. There was no sense risking death for someone who might later betray them—and even kill them. But Amelia saw none of that, only a poor girl whose horrifying end was unfolding before her very eyes, and her heart screamed for her to be saved.

Liam and Amos exchanged glances. Amos bowed his head, as though considering it.

"We've got to help her. We can't just let her die."

Amos breathed out resignedly and made his decision. He turned to Amelia and nodded.

"I'll help her. You stay here. I'll take the risk by myself. Is that understood? There's no point in all of us taking an unnecessary risk. I'm a warrior. I'll fight the beast. And I'll win."

"Thank you!" Amelia said. She put her hand on his arm lovingly.

Amos crept forward through the thick undergrowth toward the snake. Ava held her breath, awed by his courage. It took the heart of a true valiant to face that monster, and she watched him full of both pride and fear for his life.

The girl was kicking, trapped in the coils of the snake, fighting against death. Her arms were trapped tightly against her own body by the snake's deadly grasp. The monster hissed, and the sound made Ava shudder. Now the snake exerted more pressure with its scaly body, and she feared the poor girl would be crushed. Suddenly the girl stopped struggling, and it seemed that her time had run out.

The snake saw Amos approaching and hissed threateningly. Its red eyes flashed, and its mechanical jaws opened to reveal the deadly blades of its metal fangs. It was an image to instill fear in any warrior.

None of this had any effect on Amos, who leaped with a roar and came down hard, thrusting his spear into the snake's body, where it was gripping its prey. Ava saw it open its mouth and hiss in pain. Blood stained the scales of its fleshy body. Amos gave a second leap and buried his spear in the same spot a second time.

The snake spun to attack him with its two great fangs, but Amos brought up his shield just in time. Sparks flew from the clash of metal on metal. Unable to bite its intended victim, the snake lashed at him like a whip, knocking him backward to the ground.

The snake tried to bite him again, but luckily for Amos he was a couple of paces too far away and the steel fangs failed to reach him. Seeing that it could not reach the warrior from the tree, the snake slid down without letting go of its prey. It began to slither toward Amos, who was still stunned but clambering to his feet.

"Amos, no!" Amelia cried in terror.

The reptile rose on its body, opened its mechanical jaws, and lashed twice with its head. Amos defended himself without fear, blocking the first attempt with his shield and the second with his spear. But the colossal machine-snake then reared up, and its jaws came down on its victim with enormous power. Amos took cover under his shield and received a massive blow, but by making use of all his strength and training he managed to avoid falling.

The beast had the upper hand now. It was attacking from above while Amos tried to stab its body. He succeeded twice, the deep wounds driving the serpent into a frenzy. It hissed and attacked again, ramming the shield with such force that it sent the shield flying from the warrior's grasp.

Amos thrust his spear into the snake's body, which was already bleeding from several places. With a swift sideways movement, the snake struck his head, knocking him to the ground once more. The monster rose to deliver the final blow. Its silver fangs flashed in a mouth that was entirely metal. Its red eyes gleamed.

"No!" Amelia sobbed.

Ava stood up to try and help Amos, but Liam beat her to it. Five paces away from the snake, his outstretched right arm flashed silver as he used his Power on the monster's head. The head suddenly froze in mid-dive, straining against a powerful, invisible grip.

The monster gave a threatening hiss as it pushed down to reach Amos. Liam struggled with all his might, his jaw clenched as he pushed the beast's head upward, and its head began to move away from Amos.

The beast continued to fight with all its massive strength, and slowly it began to gain the advantage. Liam was standing rigid, his legs flexed, sweating profusely. His face, distorted by the effort, showed that he would not be able to hold the monster back for much longer.

Ava, aware that at any moment he would collapse and Amos would die, took her javelin and without stopping to think ran toward the snake. Her eyes were fixed on the beast's red eyes, which flashed at her approach.

Liam realized what was happening, and opened and closed his hands while he stared fixedly at the snake. The monster's head seemed to be left trapped in the air. It tried to move toward Ava, but he pressed both his hands together, straining to direct his Power. It was as though he had the snake's head trapped between his hands. The snake fought to free itself, pulling in all directions.

"I can't . . . go on . . ." Liam muttered.

Ava heard him, and knew she had to act. She raised her javelin. The snake hissed again.

Suddenly a sword struck the creature's neck and penetrated deeply into the flesh. It tried to free its head to counterattack, but without success. Liam, with a colossal effort, was still managing to hold it.

Out of the corner of Ava's eye, she saw Amos hacking with his sword in both hands, like taking an axe to a tree.

Finally, Liam faltered. The snake broke free as he fell, exhausted and overpowered. Ava seized the moment and attacked, flinging her javelin into the gaping maw of the monster, This seemed only to enrage the snake, which was now staring at her with its gleaming red eyes. Ava readied herself for the killing bite.

It never came.

Amos, with one last extraordinary blow, decapitated the snake. The head and part of its body fell to the ground, while the remainder stayed rigid.

Ava felt that she had been reborn. "Thanks, Amos."

Soaked in sweat, Amos waved his hand wearily in acceptance. But the girl was still trapped in the snake's deadly embrace.

"Help her!" Amelia shouted.

Amos moved and tried to free her, but in his exhausted state he was forced to call the others. "I need help," he called.

Ava and Liam ran to help him, and between the three of them they tugged at the snake's body. It was some time before they finally managed to free the girl.

Ava examined the stranger and found that she still had a pulse, but she was barely breathing. She pinched the girl's nose and blew air into her mouth several times in long draughts.

The girl showed no reaction. The purple tinge on her face was a very bad sign.

Ava began to press down on her heart. "Come on! Don't die on us now," she muttered.

Once again she blew air into the girl's lungs, and finally there was a reaction. The girl opened her eyes very wide, took in a long breath of air, then exhaled and inhaled again until her lungs were full at last.

"She's alive!" Amelia cried. She was smiling broadly.

The girl looked at them with horror in her eyes and gasped: "Don't . . . don't . . . kill me."

"We're not going to hurt you," Amelia assured her.

"Who are you?" Ava asked.

"My name's Emma."

"Where did you come from?" Ava asked.

There was no reply. The girl had fainted.

CHAPTER 14

"Wake up," Ava said to the girl. She splashed a little water on her face.

Emma came to suddenly and looked up at them from the ground with terrified eyes.

"Don't hurt me, please," she begged, and Amos and Amelia exchanged a look of relief. She was alive.

"We're not going to do anything to you," Amelia assured her.

Ava glanced over her shoulder to see how Liam was doing and saw that he was still unconscious.

"Amos, I'm going to see what's wrong with Liam. Keep an eye on her."

Amos nodded.

Liam had no wounds that were readily apparent. She checked his pulse, which was normal, and his breathing, too, seemed to be steady. She searched for any other sign that something strange might be happening to him, but found nothing. She tried to wake him.

Liam did not react.

"What's the matter with him?" Amelia asked.

"I don't know, and that's what's worrying me. I can't find anything wrong with him."

"It must have been because he made use of his Power."

"Yeah, I agree."

"Do you need help?" Amos asked.

"No, you watch the girl. Don't trust her. She might be dangerous."

Amelia looked at the huge dead snake on the ground and gave a gasp. "That was very close," she said to Emma.

The strange girl sighed, still looking terrified. "Yes. Thank you very much. I thought I was dead. If you hadn't come along, it would have eaten me. I owe you my life. I'll do whatever's in my power to help you."

"There's no need," Amelia said. "We're glad we were able to save you."

"Yes, there is. I owe you a debt and I'll repay it, even if it takes me a lifetime."

Ava was searching under Liam's clothes for some sign of a blow, a sting, or a bite, but there was nothing. She checked his head, but found nothing wrong there either.

"I hate to say it, but this may be beyond me."

"We've got to do something," Amos said. He was scanning the jungle around them. "We can't stay here, we've got to keep going. We've got to get him to wake up."

Amelia said, "I'm going to Feel him."

"Do you think that's a good idea, with him unconscious?"

"The only way to know is to try it."

Amelia had rolled up her sleeves and touched her upper Mark of Siaais. As she activated her Power, there came a silver flash. Then she put her hands on Liam's head, closed her eyes, and concentrated.

"I can feel a void . . . blackness . . ."

Ava could see a faint silver luminosity around the two of them. "Don't take too long about it, cousin. I don't like this."

"I can feel him. He's fallen to the bottom . . . he doesn't see me trying to reach him . . . Liam, wake up, it's Amelia. I'm here with you." She fell silent for moment, then: "The blackness is beginning to surround me."

"Get out, Amelia! We mustn't lose both of you!"

"I can't . . ."

Amelia's head fell to one side. Ava seized her arms and drew them away from Liam's head. Her cousin collapsed, unconscious.

"Hell!" Ava exclaimed angrily.

"What happened?" Amos asked uneasily.

"She's unconscious, like Liam."

"What are we going to do?"

"I don't know . . . let me think."

"Can I help?" the prisoner asked.

Amos looked at her and grimaced. "What did you say your name was?"

"Emma."

"Listen carefully, Emma. This is no time for nonsense. If you try anything stupid, I'll run you through." The warrior put the tip of his spear to her chest to underline his threat.

"I won't try anything, I promise," she said in her soft, gentle voice.

"Good. Stand up."

The girl breathed out heavily as she got slowly to her feet. Ava took in the strangeness of her clothes for the first time. She wore a jacket and pants of a very bright metallic gray. She also wore black boots and gloves with metallic ornaments. You could see her gleam a league away.

Amos gestured to her, and they both walked over to Ava

and the two convalescents. "They'll come to soon, right?" the warrior asked uneasily.

"I honestly don't know. This is outside my experience, and we can't stay here in the middle of the jungle with time against us."

"Excuse me, but I know what's wrong with them," said Emma.

Ava and Amos looked at her in surprise. "Sure you do," Ava said. "And you'll want something in return for telling us."

Emma nodded.

"If you don't speak right now, you'll regret it," Amos assured her, the threat in his tone unmistakable. Even Ava was taken aback.

"All right, I'll help you, but afterward I'm going to ask for something in exchange."

"So talk."

"The state they've fallen into is the result of excessive use of the Power, when you go over the threshold that body and mind can bear. This state usually lasts about a day, but in some more severe cases it can be up to three. At least, that's what happens with my people."

"A whole day?"

Emma nodded. "It also depends on the type of Power and to what extent it dominates, which isn't the same for everybody. Your Power is different from ours, so I wouldn't know what to tell you . . . but at least a day, I'd say."

"Well then, we have a problem," said Ava.

"Can't they be woken up somehow?" Amos asked Emma.

"Their minds are in a very fragile situation. Trying to force them into waking might do more harm than good."

Ava stared at the two unconscious bodies. Things were getting more complicated. They were in a very vulnerable situation, unable to defend themselves against attacks with Liam and Amelia unconscious. She could not understand any of this. Among her own people nobody had collapsed in exhaustion because of the excessive use of the talent, since the link would break and they would stop Feeling.

So why had Amelia fainted like Liam? Incomprehension and worry were making her anxious.

"May I ask for what I need now?" Emma asked.

Amos narrowed his eyes. "What do you need?"

She pointed toward the east. "My partner fell there, very close to here. I think he's dead, but I need to check."

"There were two of you, then?" Amos asked.

Emma nodded. "The beast buried its fangs in him while we were resting. We didn't hear it coming. Then it caught me."

"You'd better check her story," Ava said to Amos. "I'll stay here keeping an eye on them. Search her. I don't like her clothing. She might be hiding a weapon somewhere. We don't know where her people come from or how advanced they are."

Amos searched Emma thoroughly, but found nothing. "She's unarmed. At the first sign of trouble, shout my name, Ava."

"I will."

He gestured to Emma with his spear to lead the way, and they disappeared into the dense vegetation of the jungle. Ava heaved a deep sigh. Seeing her cousin unconscious, so fragile and vulnerable, filled her with a horrible combination of fear and impotence. Normally she could always help people. It was what she most enjoyed in her profession, to help the sick to heal. It gave meaning to an existence she knew was doomed. She had intended to devote the short time left to her on this earth to helping heal wounds and illnesses. But everything had changed.

She heard a strange sound to the north and spun round, her heart racing. She recovered her javelin and listened for a little longer. Nothing. Just the sounds of the jungle.

A seeming eternity went by—although it could not have been very long at all—and then Amos returned with Emma. The girl was looking deeply sad, and she had obviously been crying. Beside his spear Amos was carrying a curved sword in its sheath.

"What did you find?" Ava asked.

"She was telling the truth. There were two of them. Her partner's dead, about twenty paces from here."

"And your other partner? There were three of you, right?"

"Yes, there were three of us. He died a few days ago. The men of the snows captured him."

Ava exchanged a look with Amos. "The men of the snows?"

"Can you describe them?" Amos asked.

Emma nodded. "The leader's a big man, broad-shouldered and strong-armed. He's blond, almost silver-haired. His skin is very pale. His hair's tied in two braids and his eyes are the color of ice. With him are two other boys, also blond with light eyes, big and strong. They wear chainmail armor, and they carry axes and wooden shields. I think they're from the north. From the snows."

"Why do you say that?"

"They wear bearskins over their backs, like cloaks."

"Interesting . . ." said Amos.

"They captured Arata, who was lagging behind, and killed him with a single axe-blow, not far from here." She gave a sob.

"That must have been horrible," Ava said.

Amos was frowning. "We'll have to steer clear of them. And they won't be the only ones. I'm afraid it's going to get even more dangerous . . . every step we take toward the Cure."

"So what are we going to do?" Ava asked.

"I can only think of two things. Wait for them to wake up. Or you could use your Power to wake them up."

"I don't think the second option is a good idea. Besides, it's been a long time since I've used my Power. It's not a good idea."

"You've abandoned the gift of Siaais?"

"I have my reasons," Ava assured him.

"But you *have* used it," Amos insisted, "and that means you've developed it. You can Feel them."

"You were born with the Power too. You use it."

"I'm a valiant. We haven't developed the Power. It's damaging to us." He recited this as though it were a dogma: "Feeling what the enemy feels is the path to defeat. We don't Feel."

"You really want me to risk falling unconscious, like them?"

"You asked me, and I told you the two possibilities that occur to me. Waiting for them to wake up on their own is very dangerous, especially after what she's just told us." He nodded at Emma. "Here we're completely exposed to an attack. We wouldn't be able to defend them, and there are only two of us . . ."

"Three . . ." whispered Emma.

Amos and Ava stared skeptically at her.

"You saved me, I owe you my gratitude. I'll help you. On my honor. I can help. I can wield the katana." She indicated the weapon Amos had in his hands.

"For the moment, stay put," Ava said. "Amos, keep close watch on her. She could be lying."

Ava considered the situation. There were not many options open to them, but she did not want to use the Power. She hated it after what had happened . . . to her mother . . .

She looked around. They were in the middle of the jungle, with Amelia and Liam lying unconscious on the ground, a gigantic, half-mechanical snake a few paces from them, and the corpse of its last victim a little further away. Monsters and murderous tribes were lurking everywhere. And with Liam and Amelia unconscious, Ava was certain none of them would survive.

"Hell!" she cried. "All right, I'll try."

CHAPTER 15

Ava knelt down beside her cousin and closed her eyes. She always felt nervous when she was about to use her Power: the Blessing, as it was known among her people—although for her it was really a curse, because it reminded her that they lived under the yoke of a merciless god. She could not remember the last time she had used it, but it had been a long time ago.

She opened her eyes again and rolled up her right sleeve. With the fingers of her left hand, she touched the upper marking and activated her Power. There was a silver flash. She shut her eyes and concentrated. Unaccustomed to using her Power, her control was poor. Everyone in the tribe was taught how to use it when they were very young, but only some developed it fully, She had used it only to calm the patients she treated. Then had come the business with her mother, and since then she had not wanted anything more to do with the Power.

Take it easy, relax, and don't be too hasty, she told herself, trying to remain calm and focused. She placed her hands on Amelia's head and tried to Feel her, tentatively. Everything around her blurred, began to vanish, until only she and Amelia were there. She started to Feel what her cousin was feeling, but something was wrong: She found no feelings at all. No joy, no love, no fear.

Only emptiness.

It hit her suddenly and flooded her completely, a void so intense that she began to shake. She felt that the blackness wanted to trap her, to take her away with it.

Ava knew this feeling. She had experienced something like it once before, at the fateful moment of her mother's death . . . and with that memory came an immense rage.

You're not going to take me!

Ava fought back against the pull of the void with all her being, but the emptiness would not relent.

I've got to control the intensity of this, or it'll drag me along with it.

Little by little, she began to push it back. Her whole body was sweating, but by sheer force of will, she managed to resist the gravity of the emptiness until she no longer felt its pull.

I've got it under control now. But how do I bring Amelia back?

She concentrated again, now a little calmer. *I need to send her a powerful feeling so that she reacts.* Making another person *Feel* was a lot more complicated than *Feeling* herself. It was something she had not attempted very often, and when she had, she had not been very successful.

I can do this.

Ava sent Amelia a feeling of worry, the worry she herself was feeling at that moment. Nothing.

Ava sighed deeply and tried again. She changed the feeling and sent her cousin love. She loved her cousin more than anything in the world.

That didn't work either.

Rage flooded her, and without being able to control it she

sent it to Amelia: everything she was feeling at that moment because she was unable to bring her back.

Amelia opened her eyes wide, and her face took on a look of fury. “Noooooo!” she cried.

Ava took her hands off at once, cutting the union with her cousin. She backed away in amazement. “Are you all right?” she asked tensely.

Amelia sat up and stared at her without recognition. She looked like she was about to scream again.

“Don’t let her shout,” Amos hissed, worried about attracting danger.

Ava clamped her hand over her cousin’s mouth. Amelia began to writhe violently, and Amos had to help Ava hold her down.

“What’s the matter with her? Why’s she screaming and fighting us?”

“I think it’s because I transmitted a strong feeling of rage to her, and that’s what she’s experiencing now.”

“So how do we calm her down?”

“I don’t know!”

Amelia struggled for some time, then suddenly went limp. Her eyes, which had been rolling in every direction, were now focused, and she seemed to recognize them. Ava uncovered her mouth.

“Ava . . . Amos . . . what’s happening?”

Amos kept hold of her, just in case.

“What’s the last thing you remember?” Ava asked.

Amelia stared at her blankly. “I was helping Liam . . . I started to feel emptiness, blackness . . .”

“And then?”

“Then . . . well, nothing . . .”

“You were unconscious. I had to bring you back,” Ava said.

“We need to bring Liam back too,” Amos interrupted.

Ava grimaced. "I don't know if I can go through that again."

"You've got to bring him back, Ava. We need to get away from here. Amelia's in no state to do it, and you've already done it once. You can do it a second time."

Ava gave in reluctantly. She sat down beside Liam and activated her Power, then placed her hands on his head and focused. *Concentrate*, she told herself. *Let's get this over with and get out of here.* Once again she felt a wave of emptiness and blackness, but this time she was able to control it much better.

She tried to summon the rage she had used to bring back Amelia . . . but felt empty, exhausted. *I can't believe it. I get angry all the time. Now when I need it most, I'm spent. What do I do?*

The thought of her mother's face, of their final moment together . . . and with it came a feeling of immense rage. *Ah, there it is. I hope you appreciate this, Liam . . .*

Liam gave a start and bolted awake and leaped to his feet before she could restrain him. He clenched his fists, and there was bloodlust in his eyes. Amos moved to seize him, but Liam gave him a powerful kick to the chest that sent him sprawling.

"Liam, no!" Amelia shouted. But he only stared back at her without recognition.

Suddenly Emma hurled herself at Liam's feet with a well-practiced movement and brought him down to his face. Amelia and Ava seized their chance and flung themselves at him, clutching his arms and legs with all their might. Amos, now back on his feet, ran to help hold him down.

Finally, the fight went out of Liam. "What happened?" he asked.

"Ava brought you back," Emma explained.

Liam stared at Ava in surprise. "Did I use too much Power?" he asked. He was staring at them in surprise, apparently not remembering any of it.

"You fainted," Amos explained, "and we couldn't wake you up."

Liam was trying to catch the direction of the sun through the forest canopy. "But . . . how long has it been?"

"Not that long, thanks to Ava," Amos said. He gave her a small smile and a nod of appreciation.

Amelia winked at her cousin. "You have to teach me how to do that."

"Sure. But not today," Ava said. She was shivering, still shaking off her experience.

"I'm glad you used the Blessing," Amelia told her.

Ava's mouth twisted in distaste. "That makes one of us." Wanting to change the subject, she turned to Liam. "Do you remember anything after the fight with the snake?" she asked him.

He thought for a moment. "No . . . not a thing." He indicated Emma. "Is she the one we saved?"

Ava introduced Emma, and the girl greeted him shyly.

Liam returned the greeting, "I'm glad you survived."

She gave the trace of a nod and lowered her gaze. "Thank you."

"And now?" he asked.

"Now we get out of here," Amos said urgently.

Following the light of their Indicator, they picked up their things and left as fast as they could, making their way into the dense jungle. They went in single file with Liam first, followed by Ava, then Emma in the middle with Amos behind, and Amelia bringing up the rear. The arrangement was not by chance. Amos was watching Emma. Ava had insisted that they still could not be sure of her.

They walked all day, hardly taking a break to rest. Emma walked on in silence, now and then glancing over her shoulder to find the tower of muscles which was Amos directly behind her. It was clear that the girl was growing uncomfortable with her new situation.

Night was beginning to fall when they reached the end of a long gully, which followed the course of the stream they had been walking along. Without leaving the cover of vegetation, they surveyed the plain which opened out before them . . . and were in for a great surprise.

They saw a huge arch.

"Another Gate of the Clouds!" Ava exclaimed.

The beautiful metal structure rose in the middle of the plain, with nothing more than grass around it. It looked exactly like the one they had passed through after they had left their tribe.

"That really is strange," Amos said uneasily.

Liam suddenly crouched down among a group of tall plants further on. "We've got problems," he said.

Amos hastened to his side, spear and shield at the ready. "What's wrong?"

Liam picked up a bow in one hand and a quiver of arrows in the other. "I found these." He pointed through the foliage. "There are several dead men just up ahead."

CHAPTER 16

Amos and Liam examined the bodies. They were from the same tribe, judging by their appearance, clothing, and weapons, but there was no clue to their origin. They were all broken and bloody.

Amos shook his head. "Something beat them to death . . ."

"Another group of Chosen?" Ava asked.

"If so," Amos said, "then what we're facing is a very savage one."

Liam gathered up one of the bows and a quiver of arrows. "Yeah, there are easier—and less brutal—ways of killing. "

"We should keep moving," Ava said. "We're obviously meant to go through the arch. Let's get to it and put this place behind us."

"I agree," said Liam.

When they came to the new Gate of the Clouds, Amelia tried to activate the gate. Nothing happened. She held her Marks of Siaais against the screen reader a second time, then a third. Still nothing.

"Does anyone know why the gate isn't opening?" she asked.

"Let me try," said Emma. "We're pretty good at this sort of thing."

"When you say 'we're pretty good,' you mean your tribe?" Ava asked.

"Yes, my people."

"Is it connected with your Power?"

"Yes . . ."

Amelia, too, was curious. "What kind of Power is it? How does it work?"

"It's hard to explain . . . For some reason my people can identify and interact with the technology of the Ancient Ones." She touched her arm, the upper Mark of Siaais, and there came a silver flash. She laid her hand on the reader, and suddenly threads of an intense blue appeared around it. An instant later they began to appear along the entire metal structure, as if Emma were lighting them up. These were followed by other threads, in different shades of yellow. Thousands and thousands of luminous threads, spreading out across the whole arch, seeming to show every single point where pieces of ancient technology were activating. The arch seemed to be made up of thousands of conduits of different lengths that lit up, one after another, flashing in blue and yellow.

"This is . . . unbelievable," Amelia murmured, open-mouthed.

Ava, too, was staring at it in awe. "They look almost like veins . . ."

"Hurry up with the gate," Amos urged them. "I have a bad feeling."

And as if that warning was a portent of terror, they heard a rumbling sound.

"Look out!" Liam shouted. At the same time, he nocked an arrow in the bow and aimed it east.

The rumbling grew louder, and the foliage began to stir. Something large and heavy was approaching.

Emma continued to use her Power on the arch, trying to find some way to activate it.

Suddenly there came a brutal growl, and a moment later a huge gorilla broke through the vegetation and ran toward them on all fours across the plain.

Ava froze. The creature was ten feet tall and almost six feet wide. It stopped in front of them and beat its chest, roaring. Its arms and legs were all metal and wires.

Amelia cried out in terror.

The animal charged at Liam, but the hunter remained calm as he loosed an arrow at the monster's right eye, but missed, then rolled to one side to avoid the brute's charge.

The gorilla roared in fury and attacked Amos, who was unable to dodge it. He managed to shelter behind his shield, but was knocked down and thrown to one side. He rolled away as the creature's enormous metal fists tried to crush him against the ground.

Liam sent another arrow at the beast to drive it away from Amos. He hit it in the neck, so that the gorilla turned to him and roared in fury. Amos took the opportunity to get to his feet and move a few paces away, but the gorilla leaped aside and delivered a blow with its arm that sent him flying.

"Emma, hurry!" Amelia cried. "It's going to kill Amos!"

"I'm trying," Emma muttered under her breath. Her fingers were moving in strange patterns, as if she were sifting through which threads she should activate and deactivate, and when.

The huge ape now turned to Liam. The hunter lowered his bow and activated his Power. With impressive calm, he concentrated as the gorilla charged, raising both arms to deliver a massive blow from above. Liam put his arm forward with his palm open, and the metal fists came down on his head with enormous force. At the same time there was an explosion of energy and the beast was thrown backward.

Liam looked at his arm in astonishment. "What the—"

Amos leaped on the gorilla before it could recover and drove his spear into its chest in search of its heart. A metallic sound told him that this part of the beast, too, was mechanical under its hairy hide.

"I can't reach its heart!"

"Go for its eyes! Blind it!" Liam shouted at him as he launched another arrow.

The beast roared angrily and shook off Amos with a tremendous blow. The warrior was left lying on the ground unconscious, his head bleeding. Amelia cried out and ran to help him.

"I've nearly got it," Emma shouted. "I just need a little more time." She was moving her fingers as fast as she could, pressing with their tips, activating and deactivating luminous threads around the screen reader.

Liam released another arrow and pierced one of the gorilla's eyes. It roared in pain and rage and went for him, and this time he was unable to dodge it. It knocked him down, threw him into the air, and left him lying on the ground a few paces away, groaning in great pain.

Ava joined Amelia in helping Amos to his feet, but the beast saw them. With a roar it hurled itself at them.

"Run!" Amos shouted.

Amelia and Ava raced toward the gate. The beast came to a halt and turned, churning up earth and plants in its abrupt change of direction. Amos managed to recover and leaped onto its back, where he clung to its neck with all his strength. The gorilla tried unsuccessfully to shake him off amid roars and grunts, but could not reach him with its metal arms.

Liam picked up his bow again and ran at the beast. He released an arrow at a run against its good eye and hit his target. Finally the beast managed to grasp Amos and throw him violently on the ground, where he lay still. The beast then raised its right arm to crush him.

Seeing that the warrior was out of action, Liam used his Power again, directing it with his hands to hold back the animal's metal arm. The beast heaved downward with all the strength of its machine body, while Liam countered with the strength of his Power. The monster roared in rage, not understanding what was happening. The struggle between opposing forces intensified, and Liam clenched his jaw as he held the beast's fist and pulled it upward.

He was suffering agonies in his attempt to hold the beast back, and he knew he wouldn't be able to keep it up much longer. He would go beyond his limit again, and feared that if he did so he would fall unconscious.

The upper Mark of Siaais on his arm had begun to flash silver . . .

Suddenly, with a grimace of enormous pain, Amos got to his feet. He picked up his spear, clasped it firmly with both hands, and buried it in the wounded eye. The beast gave a great bray of pain. Liam, meanwhile, held tight and went on pulling at its arm. He was at the end of his tether; he could feel it. The creature was too strong.

"I've got it!" cried Emma.

There came a deep sound, like a huge rock splitting, then another of stones and earth grating against rock. The ground under the arch shook. Next came a strange but familiar hum. The ground opened in the center of the arch, and a metal box reared up from the depths of the earth. A door opened in the center of it.

"Come on! Inside!" Ava shouted.

Emma and Amelia followed Ava into the box. Amos ran to join them, and Liam released the beast, its fist striking the ground where Amos had just been. Blind and furious, it lashed out again, but struck only air. Liam ran after Amos and caught up with him quickly.

Guided now solely by its hearing and sense of smell, the monster followed with great strides, roaring, on all four metal legs.

"Don't let the box close!" Amelia cried. "They have to make it . . ." She and Ava held the doors back with their bodies.

Liam and Amos arrived at that moment, pursued by the monster. Ava and Amelia released the doors. The gorilla was almost on them, roaring and displaying its fangs. It reached them the moment the doors closed. They felt a terrible blow, which dented one of the doors, and Emma jumped back. The elevator began its descent, amid swaying and loud creaking. A second blow sent a shudder through the structure and Liam staggered back against the rear wall. They heard a roar of rage above their heads. The beast had been left behind.

"Phew . . . that was close . . ." Ava gasped.

Darkness enveloped them.

"Is there any light?"

"I'll get it," Emma said, and began to manipulate the wiring of the box. Shortly afterward, an intermittent series of amber lights illuminated the interior.

"Fantastic," said Ava.

"Cousin, Amos and Liam are both wounded," Amelia warned her.

The men were both sitting on the floor, panting. They looked as though they were exhausted, and both were bleeding. She examined their wounds.

"What a battering you took," Liam panted. "He certainly left his mark on you."

"Speak for yourself," Amos muttered.

Ava grimaced as she examined the wound on Amos's head. "You need stitches."

"Go ahead."

"Let me see what other wounds you've got."

"Take a look at Liam's."

"There's no need," Liam said. "They're nothing."

"I'm the healer, and I'll be the judge of that," Ava snapped. "Keep quiet and let me have a look at you in peace."

"I've got to rest . . ." Emma whispered. "I've used my Power a lot." She slid down with her back to the wall until she was sitting on the floor, and a moment later she was fast asleep.

The descent was a long one, and nobody spoke. They all used the time to rest and regain some of their strength. Liam and Amos fell asleep. At last the box—*the elevator*, Ava reminded herself—stopped with a hum and a shudder, but only the undented door opened. Emma did not wake up, even when Ava tried to rouse her.

"Has she fallen unconscious too?" Amos asked.

"No, it's not like what happened to Liam. She didn't push herself that far, but her mind's exhausted from using her Power and she's deeply asleep."

"What are we going to do with her?" Amelia asked. "We shouldn't wake her up until she's rested and recovered."

"I'll take care of her," Amos said, and slung Emma over his shoulder.

They set off along the long white corridor, and as they went, the lights came on with strange irregular blinks. When they came to the door at the end of the passage, they put their Marks of Siaais to the reader, and this time it worked.

Warily, they went onto the platform. It was identical to the one they had found under the first gate, with the pedestal and the enormous glass tube and the capsule-like carriage within it.

"Another railroad," Liam commented.

Ava, Amelia, and Amos looked at him blankly.

"It's a means of transport of the Ancient Ones," he explained. "Only this one's very advanced, I think, even for them."

When they went down to the pedestal they heard a hum, and the lights glowed more brightly.

"Something's happening," Liam announced.

Ava pointed to the pedestal. "Let's get past the screen reader."

Liam showed his Marks to the reader. There came a green flash, and the semitransparent door of the cylinder slid to one side. A moment later another, which gave access to the carriage, opened behind it.

The doors slid closed as Liam, who was the last, stepped inside. A red light in the ceiling began to blink.

The carriage was bigger this time, with a dozen rows, each of three seats.

They settled in the seats, and the train shot off at enormous speed. Once it had accelerated enough, the speed steadied and they were able to leave their seats safely. There wasn't much to see, since they were traveling underground.

Emma woke up at last, and looked around apprehensively. "Where . . . where are we?" she murmured.

"In the underground carriage," Amelia told her.

"The train?"

"Train? What's a train?"

"A mechanism for transport on rails, although this one isn't exactly on rails but using a more advanced system."

"It's like a cart without horses," said Amelia.

"That's oversimplifying it." Emma indicated the glass cylinder and began to explain to Amelia as much as she knew about the subject.

Ava sat down on the floor and opened her satchel to check her supply of medicines. Amelia and Emma had sat down in front of her at the other end.

Eventually, Amelia changed the subject. “What do you call what you do?” she asked Emma curiously.

“We call it ‘hacking.’”

“I’ve never heard of that. Is that a name you made up, or did you get it out of some tome or other?”

“We got it out of books. There were people before the Apocalypse who spent all their time ‘hacking’ AI systems to fight against evil. That’s why we call it that.”

“AI systems?”

“Artificial intelligence. They’re like artificial minds that are capable of thinking and acting on their own without any need for humans. They were put in control of most of the technology that ran the world . . . I don’t know whether you’re following me . . . It must be very difficult for you to imagine, much less to understand it.”

Ava glanced at Liam.

“There’s no knowledge of that in my tribe,” he said. “She must be talking about a technological development we know nothing of. Her tribe’s definitely more technologically developed than mine.”

Emma nodded. “Computing machines evolved into computers, then into intelligent systems, and finally into systems of artificial intelligence. At least that’s according to what we’ve deciphered. But we only have very basic knowledge of these things. We had enough to do with feeding ourselves and fighting against the fevers.”

“Fevers?” Ava repeated in surprise. In the desert, fevers were very rare.

“Yes. In my land they kill a lot of people. Our knowledge of medicine isn’t very advanced.”

“Amelia,” Ava asked, “how come they know about these things and we haven’t the slightest idea about them?”

"It's what Liam tried to explain," she said, and the hunter nodded. "Each tribe, depending on its location, the technology it was able to salvage, the knowledge it's built up of religion and economy, and all sorts of other factors, is either more or less developed than ours. On the other hand"—she looked at Emma—"as far as I can see, not even you—and you're very advanced—are advanced in every way."

"No, I'd agree that we're not. I saw how Ava healed Amos and Liam, and we don't have either the plants or the knowledge to prepare those medicines."

"That's very interesting," said Amelia.

"Why do you say that?" Ava asked.

"Because no tribe is absolutely superior to the others. They all have their unique knowledges and technologies, but also their deficiencies. It evens things out."

"Yeah," Ava added, "and we also have to take the Powers into account."

"Very true," Amelia agreed. "Judging by what we're seeing, Emma's tribe is more advanced technologically than Liam's, but Liam's Power, at least as far as the ability to attack is concerned, is more powerful than Emma's, however spectacular hers may be."

"That's a good point," Amos said. "I'd like to have Liam's Power."

"What do you call your Power?" Amelia asked Liam.

"We're Psionic. We can carry out physical actions with our minds, without any physical means being involved."

Ava narrowed her eyes. "That's not quite clear to me."

Liam smiled. "You see your satchel?"

Ava nodded. He activated his Power and stretched a hand out toward the satchel. When he raised one finger, the satchel rose from the floor and hovered in the air.

Then Liam moved his arm sharply. The satchel flew toward

Ava's chest, and she was too surprised to catch it. The satchel thudded into her, leaving her breathless.

They all smiled, and Amos laughed. All except Ava, who was glaring murderously at Liam.

He gave her an innocent smile. "Do you get it now?"

"Very funny."

"Our Power's nothing compared to yours," said Amos.

"I don't agree," Amelia said. "You see it from the point of view of a warrior. Our Power lets us feel what others feel, it lets us alleviate their pain and comfort them. For me, that's important."

"You're Empathic," said Emma.

"Empathic?" Ava asked. She had never heard the term before.

"Yes, capable of feeling, perceiving, and influencing the feelings of others. I've read that it was one of the Ancient Ones' areas of study, but we don't know much more."

Amelia folded her arms. "I still think it has its value."

Amos gave Emma back her weapon: the katana. "You're going to need it. I trust you," he said, and gave her a wink.

When Ava thought about what they had been through and what would be waiting for them when they left the train, she felt she would rather have some more forceful kind of Power, like Liam's.

What would they encounter next?

CHAPTER 17

They emerged into the outside world without trouble, following another illuminated corridor. They found themselves on a hill. Behind them the gate closed and vanished, melting into an ochre-orange mountain of granite.

"What is this new world?" Amos said in amazement. He was looking down at a huge plain full of strange constructions, half-ruined buildings, and broken avenues. They were the ruins of a gigantic city that stretched as far as the horizon.

"This world . . . I think it must be a city," said Liam.

"Of the Ancient Ones," Emma added.

Ava and Amelia exchanged looks of amazement. In the desert there lay the remains of a great city, but it was mostly buried in the sand, so that they had only been able to investigate part of what lay beneath it. What they were now looking at was a huge city which had survived the passage of time, at least in part. The buildings of concrete, steel, and glass were still standing, although most were in very bad condition. Many appeared half-demolished. Bridges and roads, too, were in ruins, damaged everywhere by the erosion of time and weather. Some parts hung broken or remained partially standing, leaning one against the other. In the distance they could see tall towers of stone and steel which had not yet fallen.

"How strange," Ava said uneasily.

It had clearly been abandoned very long ago, but the reason was not apparent. No sign of human or animal life was visible, nor the remains of any that might have died here.

Amelia scratched her head. "If this is a city of the Ancient Ones, then those buildings ought to be in an even worse state than they are, practically destroyed by the passage of time, like our own . . ."

"I don't understand," Amos said. "Why?"

"The buildings of the Ancient Ones weren't built to withstand the passage of time without being repaired. These ought to have crumbled ages ago. If they're really from the time of the Ancient Ones . . ."

"This is Siaais's work," Ava said. She sounded angry. "He's kept the city so he can amuse himself with us here."

"I agree," Emma whispered. "This city may be half-destroyed, but it's also too well-preserved. And it shouldn't be, after so long."

"Let's go very carefully," Amos said. "I don't like the looks of this place, and it's sure to be full of dangers, just like the jungle."

"Probably even more so," Ava said, to keep her partners on their toes.

"Why more so?" Amelia asked.

"Think about it. We've survived the first stage. This must be the second."

"The Three Tests of Courage?" Amos asked.

"Yeah, that's what I think. And the tests will only get more dangerous as we go."

Liam nodded. "I agree."

"You know about the Three Tests of Courage as well?" Amos asked him.

"In our culture they're known as the Three Passages."

"In ours they're The Three Environments," said Emma.

"And this is the second test of courage, the second passage, the second environment."

"We'd best stay alert," Amos cautioned.

They set off down a path that led toward a great collapsed bridge with a small stream running underneath it. It was hot and the landscape was arid: not as much as the land of the Kemet, but close enough. The sparse vegetation was shriveled, and there were hardly any trees to be seen anywhere. They caught sight of a forest in the distance, beyond the city.

"This climate's very different from the jungle," Ava said.

"Yes, it's semidesert," Emma agreed.

"We'll have to conserve our water," Liam pointed out.

Amos nodded, and they checked their waterskins. He gestured toward the stream at the entrance of the city. "We'd better fill them now."

When they reached the collapsed bridge, they replenished their water supplies quickly and made their way across it, toward the city.

"Curious bridge," Amos commented. "It's very wide."

"It's wide because when it was in use, a lot of people used it to travel in and out of the city," Emma explained.

"On foot?" Amos asked.

"No, in vehicles."

"What are vehicles?"

"See those rusty metal wrecks on both sides of the road?"

Amos went over to inspect one of them, and Amelia and Ava went with him, intrigued. "Are they like steel carriages?" Amos asked.

Emma smiled. "Yes . . . rather faster and not pulled by

animals, but yes, when all's said and done they were carriages that were used to transport people and things."

"You have them in your tribe?" Ava asked. She was surprised that Emma knew what they were.

Emma shook her head. "No. These are the first ones I've seen, but I recognize them from the knowledge that's stored in our computer systems. I've seen images of cities, with all kinds of vehicles coming in and going out, all the time. They're called cars and trucks, and they came in all kinds and sizes. But we didn't have any ourselves."

"Liam, what about you?" Ava asked.

"We had a few that partially lasted over the years, but we could never make them work. They need all sorts of technologies we don't know about, and things we don't have to repair them and make them run. We don't have access to computer systems like Emma's tribe, though what we do have is a public library that survived and that we look after."

They went along what had once been a great road leading to the entrance to the great city, empty except for dirt and dust-covered ruins. The route was not an easy one. Too many steel skeletons of vehicles littered the road, and several stretches of the bridge had collapsed. The travelers needed great care to not slip through the huge gaps. The bridge was over a hundred and twenty feet above the ground in some sections, and no one would survive such a fall. And there was still a danger that more sections would collapse at any moment.

At last they reached the entrance to the city. It was deserted, or so it seemed, at least. It had a sinister air, with its empty ruined buildings, its deserted avenues, and the metal carcasses of so many different vehicles, in all shapes and sizes.

"We'd better check the Indicator to make sure we're still heading in the right direction," Ava said.

Amelia laid it on the palm of her hand, and the sphere promptly pointed the way with its green beam of light.

"It's telling us to head toward the center of the city," Amos said.

Ava felt a shiver run down her spine, and knew that something was wrong. Not just with their situation, but with herself. *I know what it is. Hell!* She looked down at her forearm and saw the intermittent golden warning flash. She rolled up her right sleeve and touched the lower Mark of Siaais. A more intense golden flash confirmed what she had feared. She had made no mistake; the measurement had changed.

She gave a deep sigh. "Everyone check your lower Mark."

Amelia voiced the bad news. "It's showing nine out of ten."

"So's mine," Amos confirmed.

"All of them," Ava said sourly.

"Dwelling on it isn't going to help," Liam pointed out.

"Exactly," said Amos. "On we go. We can't afford to waste time. We haven't got any to spare."

They went into the great city along one of its main avenues. It was very wide, and the group walked in the middle, looking closely at those structures that were still standing.

No sign of any person or animal. It was a ghost city.

Death had passed through here long ago and swept away all signs of life. What most unsettled Ava was not the fact that it was deserted, but that they could hear nothing, not a sound. Not even the wind brushing against walls of brick or passing through the broken windows of the buildings. They were soon completely surrounded by those suburban houses where the Ancient Ones had lived. Emma explained that the homes were built just far enough from the center of the city to feel separate, yet near enough to reach it quickly in their vehicles.

They stared in all directions as they walked, discovering

an ancient world where long ago thousands and thousands of people had lived. Ava felt like an intruder, a stranger who would be rejected by the ghosts that must still be there, hidden within the abandoned structures.

When night fell, they decided to stop and rest. They were exhausted after walking all day with hardly a break. But Ava felt reasonably well, all things considered. Luckily she had spent much of her life roaming the desert in search of medicinal plants and was used to the rigors of the sun and the harsh terrain of her homeland.

Ava looked for the moon, and to her regret there it was: the enormous almond-shaped eye with its silver iris, the Eye of Siaais, projected on the surface, clearly visible.

She clenched her fist at the moon and cursed under her breath. "He's watching us here too."

"I assume he's watching every step we take," Liam said. "You can't do anything to stop it, so you might as well ignore it."

Liam went to inspect a building that did not look too damaged. He stepped with care to make sure the floor would bear his weight. He felt the walls, which seemed solid.

Ava ventured into the building behind him. "This looks like a good place to spend the night."

"Yes, it's still mostly intact, except for the northern section, which has collapsed."

Amos poked his head in to take a look. "We'd better make sure the surrounding area's safe first," he suggested.

Liam nodded. "Agreed. We need to find out if there are any threats nearby before we set up camp. Amos and I can go scouting. We'll explore the immediate area, then come back."

"It'd be better if Amos stayed with us," Emma whispered, and lowered her gaze.

They stared at their newest companion in surprise.

"Emma's right," said Ava. She turned to Amos and Liam. "You two are the best fighters. It'd be better if one of you stayed here to protect the others."

"Fine," said Liam. "I can go alone, that's no problem."

"Someone ought to go with him, just in case," Amelia pointed out.

"I'll go," Ava said. Without waiting for the group to say anything, she picked up her spear and shield and went to stand beside Liam.

The hunter looked at her like he was about to protest, but Ava gave him no time and started to walk away. He gave in.

They skirted two blocks of half-ruined buildings. Liam went first, in a half-crouch, in silence, taking cover among rusted vehicles and rubble. Ava realized that he was very well trained. He made scarcely any sound when he walked, always chose paths that were in shadow, and stopped now and then to sniff the soft warm breeze that had arrived with nightfall.

They stopped behind the remains of a large vehicle and crouched down. Liam scanned the buildings around, looking for possible dangers.

"Did you always want to be a hunter? And to be Chosen?" Ava asked him impulsively.

Liam stopped his scrutiny and looked her in the eye.

"Yes, and yes," Liam said.

"That's not much of an explanation,"

"You didn't ask for an explanation, you just threw two questions at me, I answered them."

"Why did you want to be Chosen?"

Liam shook his head. "To save my people. To end the sickness."

"I understand, but . . ."

"Isn't that what you want? Isn't it why you're here too?"

Ava looked sharply at him, but he did not flinch.

"Yes, I want to save my people, I want to end Siaais's Curse. And no, I'm not here of my own free will. The Eye of Siaais chose me. I wasn't one of the valiants, like Amos. Neither was Amelia."

Liam was a little taken aback by this. He raised an eyebrow. "Strange."

"What is?"

"The fact that you were chosen without having volunteered. That's not usually what happens." Liam's eyes showed unease. "Let's check one more block to the north, and then go back."

"Fine."

As they walked toward the building on the corner, Liam, who was several paces ahead, stopped suddenly and tensed. He looked at her and put his finger to his lips.

Ava could not help noticing that his lips were very attractive, naturally outlined, but the intense stare he now turned on her brought her back to reality. Something bad was happening. She waited for his signal, and when at last it came, she caught up with him.

"A large group, in the square," he whispered. "They're resting."

"How many can you see?" she asked him very softly. It was night and they could barely see a thing.

"Four in sight, but they've got two scouting." He pointed north. "There, two blocks further on."

Ava looked in the direction he was indicating, but could see nothing. She narrowed her eyes and finally managed to make something out: two shadows, moving.

"I can see them now."

"And two more at the rear, to the south. Don't make any sudden movements, or they'll see us. They're on the lookout in case anybody's following them, and we've passed very close. Too close. They almost saw us."

Ava strained her neck and looked in that direction. She had trouble making them out, but a moment later there they were, between the ruined buildings.

"I see them. One on each side of that ruined road full of holes."

"Yes. I've counted eight in all. From at least four different tribes."

"We should head back as quietly as we can, without being seen. If they see us, we're dead."

Liam started to go back, but stopped halfway, his eyes fixed on something new.

"What's the matter, Liam?" she whispered.

The hunter's jaw had clenched, but his gaze never shifted. There was a strange gleam in his eyes, of hatred.

"There, to the right of the group in the square. Two more are just arriving."

Ava saw two huge warriors appear, with long blond hair. One was carrying a shield and axe, the other an axe in each hand.

"Who are they?"

"The one in front with the two axes: He's the leader. His name is Sven."

"How do you know?"

"He's the one who killed my partners."

CHAPTER 18

At Liam's signal they withdrew very stealthily to avoid the lookouts and quickly made their way back to the camp.

Amelia and Emma were sleeping side by side inside the building. The silent, starlit night gave everything a deceptive air of calm. Amos was keeping watch by the door, and without waking the girls Ava and Liam told him what they had seen.

The warrior looked troubled at the news. "Should we hang back?"

"Time must be running out for them, too, just like us," Ava said. "Their Marks must be showing nine out of ten, like ours. I don't think they'll retrace their steps and waste time when the goal, the Cure, is in the opposite direction."

"Ava's right," Liam said. "They'll keep going. We need to be careful not to let them find out about us."

Amos nodded. "Very well then, we'll stay back. No fires, and absolute silence."

"Right. Let's rest. Tomorrow's going to be a complicated day."

Ava and Liam exchanged glances. She could not say whether it was because of his eyes or the scar that ran down his cheek, but she was afraid of what he might do if he came face-to-face with his partners' murderers. Afraid of what was in store for them, of what she was going to find.

They lay down to fitful sleep, full of nightmares. Once again she felt an intense pain that ran through her whole body like a series of discharges, as if she were suffering intense cramps. The image of the sphere of fire, which she had seen before in her dreams, returned. The pain increased, and the flames with it, as if they were consuming the sphere. Suddenly she saw the flames seeming to burn the outer rim of the sphere, leaving a smooth surface. The sphere began to spin and move away, turning from light brown to white as it receded into the distance. She felt another massive discharge of pain from her head down the length of her back and down to her feet, and the sphere changed again. Now it was surrounded by a huge flat circle.

What were these visions? Why was she having them while she suffered? Gradually the pain subsided, and she was finally able to shake off the nightmare and rest a little before waking up to the new day.

They all rose at first light, troubled and tense. Amos had explained to Amelia and Emma what Liam and Ava had discovered, and Liam went out to explore for himself. When he came back he told them he had found an alternative route heading north, and they set off. He chose narrow streets with easy access to adjacent buildings so that they could hide quickly, rather than wide avenues like those they had previously followed. He led the group, with Amos bringing up the rear.

The city was a graveyard without bodies. Thousands and thousands of people must have populated those streets. Whatever had happened to them? The more they saw of this wasteland of concrete and steel, the greater her feelings of emptiness and fear.

When they reached a crossroads, they heard voices from a street that opened to their left. Liam raised his hand, and they stopped and crouched down. At a signal from the hunter, they ran quietly to hide in the nearby houses.

Liam went to stand on one side of the street and Amos on the other. Ava, anxious to see what was going on, hid behind the remains of a nearby vehicle to watch what unfolded. She saw three boys. One, at the far end of the street, wore a strange four-colored coat. In front of him were two colorful warriors with feathers decorating their heads. They were speaking loudly and waving their hands, standing ten paces apart, giving the impression that they were staying at a prudent distance from each other.

The boy with the strange coat was staring grimly at the two warriors. He was tall and slim, with dark shoulder-length hair, fair skin, and intense gray eyes. He and his rivals must be from some other race that they did not know. She had no knowledge of people who wore feathers in their long black hair.

The young man with the gray eyes glanced back quickly. "We needn't fight," he called, "but if you force me to, you'll die a horrible death."

He was at the end of what looked like a blind alley whose walls and buildings were damaged, with great chunks missing. He could only get out of it by the way the two other boys were blocking. What surprised Ava was that he did not seem to be afraid. He kept his chin up and his eyes fixed on his rivals, and his voice was confident and defiant. But it did not sound like bravado, which she found curious, because he was not carrying a weapon.

The other two boys looked at one another. To judge by their muscles and their stance, there was no doubt that they were warriors. On their chests and legs they wore strips of leather, with a kind of armor over their chests made of pieces of wood. The feathers adorning their hair were strikingly colorful. The one on the left carried a long hunting knife and a short axe, the other a spear and a long knife. On their backs they carried short bows.

"The Cure is only for one tribe, for the winner," said the taller of the two warriors. "For us."

"That's a mistake, and you'll pay for it with your lives," the gray-eyed boy warned them.

The second warrior was defiant. "We'll see about that. The spirit of the animals is with us. You won't be able to defeat us."

Their rival smiled confidently. "I have the elements with me."

The other threatened him with his knife. "You don't deceive us. We're not afraid of you. The Cure's going to be ours. Your quest ends here today." He made a threatening move with his knife.

"We can share the Cure . . ."

"The Cure's not to be shared!" shouted the warrior with the spear.

"There's no law that says it can't be done."

"Siaais forbids it."

"Not explicitly," said the boy with the gray eyes. "We can go together for the Cure."

"That's for cowards. The Cure is for the strongest."

"I see you're very negative about the whole collaboration thing. In fact, I don't understand why you're so angry." It was as if he found the two warriors' extreme aggressiveness amusing.

"We'll rip out your guts!"

"I'm waiting," said the boy with the coat. He spread his arms wide and smiled again.

There was a moment of tension. Nobody said anything.

And the confrontation began.

Almost simultaneously, three silver flashes in their arms signaled that they had activated their Powers. Ava watched in fascination.

The first feathered warrior ran straight toward his rival. As he did, it seemed to Ava that she could glimpse the silver ghost of a large cheetah around his body. The second took a couple of steps forward and gave a massive leap of nearly twelve feet, and around his body there appeared the silver outline of a great puma.

Immediately she realized the Power these warriors had. Their bodies were moving with incredible agility, speed, and strength: the first with the speed of a cheetah, the other with the leap of a mountain lion. It was as though they were possessed by the spirits of those animals.

The boy with the coat stayed calm, and a small metal object appeared in his hand. He flicked it with his thumb and a small flame appeared, giving his face an eerie cast and making his gray eyes glitter.

The two warriors covered the distance between them and their rival in a single moment. The speed of the cheetah had allowed the first attacker to reach his target in the blink of an eye. The puma boy rose to an amazing height to come down hard on his enemy.

They're going to kill him. He's got no way out. Ava saw the cheetah warrior spread his arms, ready to strike with his axe and knife. The puma warrior, meanwhile, was coming down from his leap, his spear already poised to impale his enemy.

When the cheetah warrior was only a step away, the boy with the gray eyes extended his left hand toward the flame, palm out, as if he were pushing it forward.

And then something unthinkable happened.

The tiny flame grew and fanned out, multiplied a hundred times in intensity. It hit the first warrior squarely and he caught fire. He was burning so rapidly that he was consumed on the spot. He gave a single cry of pain and died.

The boy then quickly dodged the attack of the puma warrior

who was descending on him. The spear brushed his scalp, but he didn't even flinch. The warrior landed on his toes only a step away from his enemy and turned to attack, but the gray-eyed boy had already launched another tremendous burst of flame. The puma warrior was instantly engulfed by fire and burned to a crisp. He hadn't even had time to scream.

Ava was staring in open-mouthed disbelief. *What a Power!*

The boy with the gray eyes contemplated the remains of the two charred warriors on the ground. "I warned you," he told them.

With a swift movement of his hand he snapped the metal object closed, and the tiny flame went out.

Ava tossed a pebble at Liam's back. The hunter gestured to her to keep quiet, but she shook her head and went up to him. He stared at her in disbelief.

"We've got to talk to him," she whispered. She gestured toward the street, where the boy was still staring at the ashes of his defeated enemies as though he were praying over them.

"That's a bad idea," Liam said.

"You've seen his Power. It's incredible. We need him."

Liam shook his head.

"Come on! We've only got two warriors, and there are groups here with ten or more. We need him."

Amos crawled across to them and shook his head. "It's very risky," he whispered.

"But—"

Liam was starting to look angry now. "I can't believe we're even discussing this, Ava. You don't trust anybody."

"I know, but—"

"You saw what he just did."

"That's exactly why we have to get him to join our group."

"No," Liam said flatly. "It's too dangerous."

"We have to risk it or we won't survive. I mean that."

Looking at her two partners' faces, Ava could see that their refusal was final. She understood their concerns, but this was too important. She thought for a moment and came to a decision.

Ava got up, went into the street, and walked directly toward him.

"Stop!" Liam called.

It was too late. Ava took a few determined steps, and the boy looked up and saw her. She suddenly felt her knees trembling with the reality of the risk she was taking, especially when the boy raised the metal object in his hand and reignited the tiny flame.

Oh, no!

CHAPTER 19

"Don't kill me!" Ava cried.

His gray gaze was deadly. "You want to try your luck too?" he asked defiantly.

"Not, not in the least. What I just saw's enough for me." She knelt down and set aside her javelin. She raised her hands, palms up, to show that she had no more weapons, then very slowly stood up.

The boy tilted his head to one side and went on watching her with narrowed, distrustful eyes, trying to guess her true intentions.

She smiled at him. "May I come a little closer?" she asked in her friendliest voice.

He thought about it, tilting his head to one side and the other, apparently unsure. At last, he beckoned her toward him.

When she was five paces away, the boy raised his other hand. "You're close enough now."

"I just want to talk."

"Hmmm, that's not the usual thing around here. Most of the people I meet prefer to kill."

"I'm different from them."

"You're different, I can see that," he said with a mischievous smile, "but I'm not so sure you might not want to kill me."

"I swear I don't wish you any harm."

"In fact, it would be a shame to burn up such a pretty girl." He gave her a roguish smile.

Ava felt strange. The boy was staring at her intensely, and she blushed. "My name's Ava," she hastened to say.

"Mine is Logan."

"You're powerful," Ava said. She gestured at the two charred bodies on the ground in front of him.

"Yes, I am."

"And not exactly modest," she added. She was trying to break the ice, hoping the tension of the situation would fade. She was afraid the boy might change his mind and burn her alive.

Logan gave a bitter chuckle. "No, I'm not exactly modest or friendly, though I do have other qualities."

"I'm not over-friendly either."

"Then we'll get along well," he said, and coughed. Ava realized at once that it was not a simple cough. Thanks to the knowledge and experience her profession had given her, she knew there was something more serious behind it.

"Getting along is what I want to talk to you about," she said as she searched his face for other symptoms of illness.

He crossed his arms. "I'm listening."

"I'm with a group . . ."

"I can see them. They're a bit nervous about the risk you're running with me." He nodded behind her.

She turned and saw Liam with his bow at the ready, aiming at Logan from a few paces away, and Amos approaching from the other side.

"Tell them they're close enough. We don't want an accident . . ."

Ava turned again. "Liam, Amos: Stop, please! Everything's fine. Stay still."

Both boys stopped where they were.

"That's better. Tell the one with the bow to lower it. I don't like being aimed at."

"Liam, could you lower your bow?"

He stared at her for a moment, then did as she asked.

"Are you the leader?" the gray-eyed boy asked her, and coughed again. He put his hand to his mouth.

"No . . . not exactly . . ."

"The messenger, then?"

"Not that either. I'm just the most determined."

The boy smiled and nodded. "How many of you are there?"

"Those two boys you can see, and two girls as well."

"And you."

"That's right."

"A total of five. From different tribes, judging by what I can see. The handsome one with the scar isn't like you or the big one."

"That's right. We want you to join us."

Logan gave Amos a long stare, then Liam, and finally Ava. "Why?"

"We're short on warriors, and you're phenomenal," Ava said. She hoped she wasn't being too transparent by trying to appeal to his vanity.

Logan smiled. "You're doing fine. Flattery goes down well with me."

"So you'll join us?" Ava insisted.

"Not so fast. I didn't say that. What do I get if I join you?"

"Safety. In a bigger group, you'll have a better chance of surviving. The two warriors we have are very good."

"I'd imagine they are, otherwise you'd be dead by now. All

the same, as you've seen, I can manage pretty well on my own. I've already killed a fair number, and it wasn't that hard, believe me." He coughed again.

Ava had to think of something she could say to persuade him. And then an idea occurred to her.

"I'm a healer. I can help you with that cough, and with any illness."

Logan seemed to be interested in this.

"What else can you offer me?"

"We have a girl who can communicate with the Ancient Ones' machines."

Logan's eyes went wide. "Now that's really interesting. I lost a partner at the gate because we couldn't activate it."

"So, are you interested?"

The young man thought about it. He scratched his chin and took another long look at all three of them.

"What happens if we reach the Cure? You have people from three different tribes already, and with me there'd be one more. Who gets to keep the Cure if we get hold of it?"

Ava did not know what to say. She had thought about this once or twice after Liam and Emma had joined them. But it was such a remote possibility that she had preferred not to think too much about it and face the situation when it arrived.

"How about crossing that bridge when we get to it?"

Logan laughed aloud, then coughed. "I like you. You've got guts, and you're smart."

"Does that mean you're willing to join us?"

Logan closed the metal object over the flame and offered her his open hand. "I'm willing."

Ava stared at his hand, not knowing what to do, then held out her own as he had done. He smiled and shook it, showing her how it was done.

"This is how you close a deal."

"Oh, all right."

"See? I'm bringing something to your group already. I'll make an awesome addition."

"I'm sure you will," Ava replied, looking amused. She turned to Liam and Amos. "You can come over now, there's no danger. He's agreed to join us."

While Liam and Amos approached, Ava got a better look at Logan's intense gray eyes, which stood out vividly against his dark hair. She had to admit that he was really good-looking.

When the duo reached her side, Ava made introductions, but Liam had only harsh words for her. "Are you out of your mind? He could've killed you." It was the first time Ava saw a crack in his composure. His blue eyes gleamed intensely, his expression showing a mixture of concern and frustration that made his scar more livid.

She made a placating gesture. "Nothing happened, as you can see."

Liam gave a scornful snort. "It was foolish, and you could have died."

She sighed. "It was worth the risk, and everything turned out well."

Liam withdrew into himself once again and resumed his usual air of reticence.

Ava smiled. Strangely, she relished the fact that he worried about her. It seemed . . . tender of him. And if there was anything Liam was not, it was precisely that. It gave her a strange, pleasant feeling in her stomach. Plus, she was impressed. His calm and poise, even when she was doing something outrageous, were admirable.

"I can't believe you decided to join us," Amos said.

"Your friend here is very persuasive." Logan indicated Ava with a wave.

"And no nonsense," Liam warned him. "If you try anything, it'll be the last thing you do."

Logan smiled. "I've no intention of doing anything. Are you the leader?"

Liam narrowed his eyes and shook his head.

"No?" Logan said in surprise. "I thought you would be." He turned to Amos. "You?" The warrior thought about it and shook his head in turn. "So who is?"

Nobody replied.

Logan's smile widened into a grin. "Maybe what you really need is not so much another warrior but a leader. I could volunteer for the job . . ."

"No, we don't need that," Ava hastened to say.

Amelia and Emma, both awake now, walked over to them from their temporary shelter, looking uncertain.

"There's no danger," Ava told them. "This is Logan, and he's joining our group."

"And it'll be a real pleasure after seeing such beautiful maidens," Logan said. He bowed elaborately to Emma and Amelia. Amelia smiled, and Emma giggled.

Amelia introduced herself.

"A goddess, that's for sure," Logan said with a smile, and she blushed.

"A scholar . . . I'm not much of a goddess."

Amos's face was a poem. He was not at all happy with what he was seeing.

"And you?" he asked Emma. "What's your name, my beautiful water lily in a calm lake?"

The girl lowered her eyes shyly. "I'm Emma, and I'm certainly not a beautiful water lily . . ."

"Of course. How indelicate of me. You're a beautiful flower I've never seen before."

Emma's cheeks turned red.

"I see you're quite a ladies' man," Ava said scornfully. "Goes well with the immodesty."

"You wouldn't be upset because I haven't had the opportunity to present myself to you properly, as I did with your partners, would you?"

"Dream on."

"There'll be time enough for that." He smiled roguishly.

Ava rolled her eyes. Logan was not only handsome and dangerous, he was a lady-killer. They would need to be very careful with him.

"We need to get moving," Liam pointed out.

"Yes, all that noise from the fight could attract other groups," Amos agreed.

"Right, let's grab our supplies and go," Ava said. She looked at Logan, who nodded.

When they were ready, Liam took the lead and set off. Ava gestured for Logan to go after him, which he did. There was no need for her to say anything, Amos moved off after Logan, and she followed, with Amelia next and Emma bringing up the rear. They went at a crouch, under cover of the abandoned buildings, along narrow, deserted streets where only dirt and dust were visible. Not an animal, not a sound, nothing.

Suddenly they heard several loud noises, like a sequence of small explosions. Liam gestured that they should crouch down and hide. Ava gave Logan a questioning look, but the new member of the group merely shrugged and shook his head.

They saw two figures running down the street toward them, obviously fleeing from something.

"Inside!" Liam snapped. He went into the building on his

left, and they all followed at once. It was a brick building several stories tall. Liam went up to the second floor and beckoned them to follow.

"Hide," he whispered. "Don't let them see you."

Again they heard the short, repeated explosions.

Liam looked out of a window. Ava, unable to help herself, followed him. The two figures were almost level with their own position. They were from a strange tribe, with turbans and long white robes with wide red belts. They had long black beards and dark faces, but a different shade from those of the Kemet. They were armed with swords and curved knives.

"What tribe are they from?"

"Don't know," Liam said, "but they're warriors."

And then they saw what they were fleeing from. After them appeared six figures, dressed in black from head to foot, carrying strange weapons. They moved forward as one, forming a line across the whole width of the street. Their faces were not visible. They were wearing strange, round, black helmets that covered their entire heads and shone as the sun touched them. Suddenly they stopped and aimed their weapons, which were like Liam's musket, but of a more advanced kind.

The explosions sounded again.

The first of the fugitives fell in front of the building where Ava and the group were hiding, and she saw blood gush from the body. She covered her mouth with both hands to stop herself from crying out. The fallen one's partner was running for his life, and as he ran past them the explosions rang out again. The fugitive gave a cry of pain and fell to the ground dead in the middle of the street. The other unfortunate victim who had fallen in front of them was still moving. He was badly wounded, but not dead. He tried to drag himself away, but could only move a couple of steps.

The six figures in black reached his side and aimed their black metal weapons at him. Explosions rang out, and the poor wretch was riddled where he lay on the ground.

And Ava felt pure terror.

CHAPTER 20

They threw themselves down onto the floor and stayed absolutely silent, not even daring to breathe. Logan was holding something bright in his hand. Amelia and Emma were clasping one another's hands as they lay on the dusty stone floor.

Ava found the tension unbearable. "What are they doing?" she hissed.

Very carefully, very slowly, Liam half rose and stared out through the glassless window. "They're still as statues, just looking at the bodies," he whispered.

"Why?" Ava whispered back.

"I don't know. They're waiting for something."

They waited, but nothing happened, and Ava decided to see what was going on for herself. She quietly crawled to the damaged wall below the other window and looked out through a crack. The figures were still motionless, like black-painted statues. She could see nothing at all of these warriors' faces or bodies under their dark, shining armor. The weapons they carried were long and strange, though she had the strong impression that they were of a kind similar to Liam's, the one that was not working anymore.

Suddenly they heard a hum, then a few broken words:

"Black Terminators . . . *brbrszs* . . . Secure sector six . . . *brbrszs* . . ."

The six figures turned round, changed their position, and formed into a double line, with three of them on each side. They began to walk, all in step, up the street they had come from, toward the north, perfectly synchronized.

Nobody moved, waiting for the threat to depart. At last Liam leaned out the window very carefully and gave a quick glance up the street.

"They're gone, heading northeast."

"Phew . . ." Amelia gasped.

Ava got to her feet. "Who are they?"

"They're not another tribe, that's for sure," Logan said. He was shaking the dirt off his odd coat.

Amos was surprised by his confidence. "How do you know?" he asked.

"There were six of them, all dressed the same and carrying the same weapons. There are only three in each tribe."

"Maybe theirs cheated," Amelia suggested. "Or else they were allowed an advantage."

"Siaais allowing cheating, or one tribe to have an advantage over the others?" Logan said. He sounded as though he did not believe it for one moment.

"I'm actually with Logan in this," Ava said. "I don't think our magnanimous, all-powerful God would allow an advantage to anyone. And he certainly wouldn't allow any of us to cheat."

"So who are they, then?" Amos asked.

"No idea," Logan replied. "But they're obviously very dangerous."

"They're another obstacle, another one of Siaais's tests," Emma said in a whisper, and they all looked at her.

"Why do you think that?" Amelia asked.

"There are six of them . . . with armor and weapons from the time of the Ancient Ones. They're sent by Siaais."

"Are you sure about the armor and weapons?" Ava asked.

"Yes. I've seen them in the information systems. I don't know what type they are, but I recognize them."

"When you say you've seen them," Amelia asked, "what do you mean? You mean you've seen them somewhere in a tome?"

"The information systems have databases where all kinds of information are stored: books, diagrams, maps, and images. I've seen images of those Black Guards before."

"During the Apocalypse?"

"I'm not sure . . . I'd say a little before, but I couldn't swear to it. The knowledge I've seen is only partial, and most of it doesn't have dates we can refer to."

"This is very odd," Amelia said thoughtfully.

Ava nodded. "It certainly is."

"The best thing to do is avoid them," Liam said. "Those weapons are very dangerous. A lot deadlier than my old musket."

"Deadlier?" Amos repeated.

"My weapon only shoots one bullet at a time. Judging by the way the sound of the shots repeated, those fire a whole lot, and very fast."

"Well, isn't that just wonderful," Ava said.

Liam was watching the street. "Let's wait a little till we're sure they're not coming back," he said cautiously.

The group relaxed and sat down on the wooden floor with its covering of dust and debris; Ava was staring at the metal object Logan was turning over in his hand. "What's that thing you use to create a flame?"

He showed it to her, but without letting her take it. "You don't know what it is?"

"It's a lighter," Liam said.

"Exactly."

"How does it work?" Ava asked.

"It has an element inside that creates a spark. My people have learned to make them. We find them very useful, as you were able to see."

"Did you learn to make them from the Ancient Ones?" Amelia asked.

"That's right. From the knowledge and means we have at our disposal."

"Interesting."

"And your Power allows you to create bursts of fire?" Ava asked curiously.

Logan eyed her with a cynical smile. "I'll tell you about my Power if you tell me about yours," he said. Then he looked round the others in the group and paused for a moment. "Well, if everybody talks about their own. It wouldn't be fair if I gave away my greatest secret to you and you didn't give yours away too."

"What do you all think?" Ava asked the others.

"I don't see any problem," Amelia said. She, too, was intrigued by Logan's Power.

Emma nodded, still looking down.

"Whatever you all want," Amos said.

"It's a bit too soon," Liam said. It seemed that he did not yet trust Logan.

Ava looked at him reproachfully. "As the majority's in favor, we'll share information."

"The more we know," Amelia pointed out, "the better our chance of helping each other and surviving."

Logan gave them an inviting smile. "Who wants to go first?"

"I will," Amelia said. "You see, we three, the ones wearing

linen and gold"—she indicated herself, Ava, and Amos—"are . . . Empathic. We're able to feel what other people feel."

Logan looked at her in surprise. "That's a really curious Power. Can you feel what I feel?"

Amelia nodded. "Yes, and even alter it. Calm the pain, the sorrow, the anguish, by transmitting peace, happiness, good feelings."

"That's really peculiar. Most of the Powers I've seen are more . . . aggressive . . . whereas yours is very . . . how can I put it? Harmless?"

"We can also transmit rage, and other less pleasant feelings," Ava pointed out.

"Hmm . . . can you transmit pain?"

Ava looked at Amelia, who shrugged, then at Amos, who shook his head.

"We don't know."

Logan looked puzzled. "You don't know? You ought to. Siaais didn't give us the Power so that we could do good, he gave it to us so that we could fight, to find a way to the Cure."

"I don't agree with that," Amelia replied. "Our Power's always been used for good, and with very positive results."

"It's no use against other Powers, like mine," he said, and there was a threat in his voice. He created a flame with his lighter in a swift, well-practiced movement, and Ava began to feel uneasy.

"I see I've got your attention. If I activate my Power and you activate yours, who do you think'll get out of here alive?"

"Not you," Liam warned him. He had his hand on his bow.

Logan smiled and put out the flame. "It's just a piece of advice. Learn to use that Power to defend yourselves before it's too late. I'm sure there are Powers even more terrible than mine, and sooner or later we're going to have to face them. And if we're going to survive, we need to defeat them. I don't see that working with a Power that's purely . . . benign."

"We'll bear that in mind," Ava said. In truth, the idea didn't sound so farfetched to her. The Kemet had never attempted what Logan was suggesting. Logan and Liam used their Powers to inflict harm when they had to. Why did her tribe have to limit the use of theirs? Were they making a wrong assumption?

"Next," Logan said, shaking her out of her meditation.

Emma raised her head and spoke quietly. "I'm a hacker. My Power allows me to interact with the technologies of the Ancient Ones and manipulate them."

Logan nodded. "Ava told me about you. That's a very useful Power."

He turned to Liam. "And you?"

Liam was evasive. "I'd rather not talk about it."

"He's a Psionic," Ava explained. "He can move objects with his mind without physically interacting with them."

Liam glared at her.

Logan was trying to understand. "You move things with your mind?"

"Yeah, and more," Ava said. "He can hold, squeeze, push, throw, and all sorts of other things without touching them."

"Very interesting. I'm glad we have someone else in the group who's powerful. We'll need it."

"Your turn."

Logan looked from one to the other for a moment, as if considering.

"All right, I'll explain. My tribe has a very useful Power, though it's also very dangerous. You need to know how to use it, or else an accident can kill you—and everyone around you. That's why we practice all the time." He sighed. "I'm an Elementalist. We can manipulate the four elements—fire, air, earth, and water."

They stared at him, not really understanding. "Tell us how it works," Ava asked. She sounded very interested. "How did you create those terrible bursts of flame?"

"Actually, it's simple. To create fire, all I need is a little fire. To create water, a little water, for earth, a little earth, and to create air, a little air."

From the expressions on their faces, it was clear that they were still in the dark.

"I'll show you." He bent down and took a handful of earth from the ground. He activated the upper Mark of Siaais and immediately tightened his hand. The earth was transformed into a rock. With a movement of his hand he threw it. It reached a tremendous speed, impacted against a wall, and embedded itself in it.

Ava was impressed, and she was not the only one.

"Can you do anything you want with the four elements?" Amelia asked.

Logan laughed. "No, not at all. It took me almost a year to learn and perfect what I just did. It takes a lot of practice. There are a handful of things I can do with each element, and that's all. But I'm always trying to experiment and develop new skills."

Amelia was very excited. "That's fantastic! You'll have to show us how you experiment with your Power."

Logan nodded. "Anything else you want to know?"

Emma raised her hand, and Logan looked at her. "Yes?"

"Your coat," she whispered. "I like it . . . four colors for four elements?"

Logan laughed again. "Sharp eye. You obviously have a good head on your shoulders, Emma."

Emma shrugged and looked down again.

"Yes, my four-colored coat is for the four elements of Nature. The front right half is red for Fire. The front left is blue for Water. The back right white for Air, and the back left brown for Earth."

"Right, then," Ava said. "Now we all know about everybody's Powers, let's hope things go better for us."

"We're still alive," Amelia pointed out. "And that's saying a lot in this place."

"That's true," Ava agreed.

"Well then, on we go," Logan said, as if he were now the one who made the decisions. "Time's moving on, and we're not exactly in the lead."

Liam gave him a warning look.

"Well, since you haven't got a leader . . ." he apologized, looking virtuous.

"Liam, could you lead the way?" Ava asked. She gave Logan a warning glare. "We'll follow you."

Liam nodded and set off, and the others followed him.

"And you, smartass, beside me," Ava said to Logan.

The Elementalist gave her a smile of great charm. "Don't get your hopes up. You're not my type."

Ava blushed harder than she had ever done before. Then her embarrassment gave way to rage. "You're an idiot!"

Logan laughed and went on walking with a broad smile on his face.

She shook her head. *If he weren't so handsome and charming, he'd be offensive*, she thought.

They went northward. Night fell on the deserted city, and they suddenly heard a new volley of shots. They stopped to listen. The volley was followed by the sound of screams, of fighting, then more shots. Ava felt a shiver down her spine and had to shake it off. There came more screams, more shots, and then silence.

CHAPTER 21

They sought shelter in a house nearby that was in good condition, or at least did not look as if it were about to collapse at any moment. After carefully checking the house, they found a trapdoor that gave access to a cellar. It was a good place to hide and get a little rest.

"I'll make a fire," Logan said. He picked up a few loose boards and a wooden chair, which he smashed with a couple of blows, and made a pile in the middle of the cellar.

Ava was worried about being found out. "Is it safe to make a fire?"

Liam looked at the four enclosed walls and the trap door. "Yes, as long as it doesn't smoke too much." He was looking at Logan.

"It shouldn't," Amos said. "The wood's dry."

"Good," Liam said. "I'll go upstairs to make sure there's no fire or smoke visible."

"I'll come with you," Amos said.

The rest of the group sat down around the pile in a circle. Emma and Amelia scanned the cellar in search of anything interesting. Ava was watching Logan intently. She knew she ought to be keeping an eye on him, particularly when Liam and Amos were not there. It was not that she was anticipating trouble in that cellar, but considering that they had come across a problem at every step, they had to be on the alert about everything.

Logan took out his lighter and lit it with a swift movement of his wrist, as if he were snapping his fingers. He touched his upper Mark of Siaais, which flashed silver, and with a flick of his hand sent a small ball of fire the size of a plum into the pile of wood. The ball burst on impact and the entire pile caught fire.

"Wow!" Amelia exclaimed. "You have incredible control over your Power."

He was surprised. "Don't you all have a strong control over your Powers?" he asked.

"No," Ava had to admit, "I barely have any at all."

Logan stared at her in amazement.

"That . . . that's terrible. Why? Our Power defines us, it makes us what we are. At least, that's how it is among my people. I don't get it."

"Well, you see," Amelia began, trying to explain, "our Power defines us, it's true, but not everybody feels comfortable using it. It's an invasion of the other person's privacy. A connection gets established between what both people feel, and that isn't comfortable at all. It's very invasive."

Logan looked at Ava. "So, since you're a healer, as you told me, you ought to have a very good grasp of it, right?" Logan asked.

Ava did not know what to say. "I don't . . . I mean I have reasons . . . personal reasons . . ."

"For not using your Power?" He was looking at her with great interest.

"Yes . . ."

She turned her head away, feeling troubled. A sharp pain

flared in her chest. It happened every time she spoke or thought about the reason she did not like to use the Blessing. Her mother's death still haunted her. Tears came to her eyes as Ava remembered her face, her staring eyes, and that final scream.

Perhaps sensing that the subject was too personal and painful to Ava, Logan let the matter drop. He turned to Emma. "And you? You must have practiced a lot."

Emma nodded. "It's different for me. To use it I have to have a machine, a system I can connect to. Without that I can't use it . . . I can't practice . . . I can't get better at it."

"Interesting," Logan said.

"I can show you, if you want."

"Oh, that would be wonderful," Amelia said. She was deeply intrigued. "How? There's no system of the Ancient Ones here."

"The Indicator," Emma said, and held out her gloved hand.

Amelia understood and nodded. "Oh yes, of course." She took it out of her satchel and handed it to her.

Emma took it in her right hand. With her left she touched her upper Mark, triggering her Power with a silver flash. She closed her eyes in concentration. Luminous threads of an intense blue began to run across the surface of the Indicator, then others in different shades of blue, which entered the sphere, then still others in different shades of yellow: hundreds of threads which revealed every component of the device. The sphere now seemed to be made up of an amalgam of blues and yellows, which blinked at intervals and in different places. Emma probed them with her fingers as she sought to understand the Indicator's workings. For a long time she went on manipulating the object, until she finally opened her eyes and quenched her Power.

"That was amazing," Logan said.

"Wasn't it just?" Amelia agreed eagerly.

"Thanks," Emma said. "It's easier to show how my Power

works than to explain it. I've probed nearly all the technology the sphere uses to indicate the right direction. With two or three more tries I'll have understood it, at least at a basic level. But there's a limit. Once I've completed those studies, however hard I try, I won't be able to get any more information than I already have. I won't be able to go deeper and learn, or get better at using my Power . . ."

"Oh . . . now I see," Logan said.

"What a shame," Amelia said sadly.

"Considering that my people have no more than a few hundred machines and systems that use the technology of the Ancient Ones, we can't develop our Power any further than those systems allow us to."

"What about looking for machines and systems outside your tribe's lands?" Amelia suggested.

"We've tried many times . . . but nobody who's gone on an expedition has ever returned."

"Like our explorers," Ava put in.

"Our people sent explorers in search of other tribes," Amelia explained, "but nobody ever came back . . . so we stopped doing it. And we never stray far from our own domains, for the same reason."

"I think that applies to all the tribes," Logan said. "We stopped looking long ago too."

"That accursed Siaais," Ava said angrily. "He kills them."

"Almost certainly," Logan agreed.

"Don't talk like that," Amelia said uneasily, looking up at the ceiling. "He might be listening."

"Let him," Ava retorted. "What do we care? Look at the situation he's left us in."

"Exactly," Amelia said. "This isn't the time to make the God angry." She sounded afraid.

Not wishing to argue with her cousin, Ava said nothing more.

"Now we, on the other hand, practice constantly," Logan said. "It's part of our culture, our way of life. When one of us finds a new way to manipulate any of the elements, we show it to everyone in a great ceremony. It's a time of joy for the whole tribe. But it's strange, because while our Power allows us to manipulate the four elements, it's specific to everyone. Each of us can gain individual skills that the rest may not be able to manage. That's why when one of us discovers a new skill, he or she is rewarded with privileged status."

"Have you gained it?" Amelia asked with interest.

Logan smiled from ear to ear. "Of course. That's why I was chosen to reach the Cure."

Ava could not restrain herself. "How cocky can you get!"

He laughed. "Don't believe me if you don't want to."

Liam came down the trapdoor. "All quiet," he said. "Looks as though the danger's passed."

"And you, hunter?" Logan said.

"I what?"

"You know, those ears of yours don't miss a thing," Ava said.

Liam sighed. "Yeah, I practice every day. My people laid that down a long time ago. It helps us against the dangers, and it also helps us to develop new uses. Very like what he told you. But we don't celebrate. When someone discovers a new use of the Power, it's taught to the others. We try to make sure everyone can do it themselves. We believe that increases our chance of reaching the Cure."

"I'm beginning to feel bad," said Amos, who was on his way down from the trapdoor after Liam. "In our culture the valiants, the warriors who volunteer, hardly develop the Power at all. We spend our days practicing combat and training our bodies. We improve our fighting skills, our resistance, our speed, and of course our strength."

"That's not a bad strategy either," Logan said. "My fire can be devastating, but if you hit me with that spear of yours the moment we met, I'd die before I could get anywhere near my Power. I'd advise you, if we meet other tribes or enemies, to strike first and ask questions later. That's your major advantage."

Amos nodded. "That's what I intend to do."

Logan smiled. "One thing you've mentioned seems odd to me."

"What's that?"

"You say you have volunteers?"

"That's right. The valiants train day and night to be chosen on the day of the ceremony. We volunteer."

"We don't have volunteers," Logan said. "The eye chooses whoever it wishes."

"We don't have volunteers, we have Exceptionals," Emma said. "That's what we call the ones who've managed to develop the Power further than the others. They're the ones who present themselves to the Eye of Siaais, because they're the best among the people. Only them. The others don't present themselves."

They all turned to Liam, keen to know how they did it in his tribe.

"The Eye chooses the ones Siaais prefers that year. We don't have volunteers—everyone has to present themselves to the Eye—but out of all of us we select the best, and they're the ones who present themselves first. It's always three of the selected who's chosen."

"This is all very strange," Amelia said. "We've worked out that all the tribes go through the same selection process, but some put forward volunteers and others don't."

"I'm beginning to think our system of training volunteers might be a mistake," Ava complained.

There was a long silence. They were all left wondering about what they had learned that evening and its many implications. They decided to eat what they had left, after which they would be out of food. Luckily, they had water for three more days or so. But the lack of food and water would become one more serious problem to add to those they already had.

Ava, Amelia, and Emma went over what they had left in the hope of finding something more to put in their stomachs, though they knew they would find nothing. Logan's eyes were on Amos and Liam.

"Who's going to be the alpha male of the group?" he asked them suddenly.

Amos and Liam exchanged a look of puzzlement. "There's no alpha male in this group," Liam said.

"Are you sure? You both look the part." He pointed to Amos. "He's the definition of an alpha."

"We're not wild animals," Amos said. "We don't need an alpha male to dominate."

"Someone's going to have to make the difficult decisions in the group."

"We do that perfectly well already, thank you," Liam assured him.

"But now I'm here too," Logan said. He gave them a virtuous smile.

"So you want to make the decisions now?" Amos asked.

"Well, it would be the most natural thing to do. I'm the most powerful of us three, after all."

Liam and Amos exchanged another look, this time of disbelief. "That remains to be seen," Liam cautioned.

Logan spread his arms and puffed out his chest. "We can see whenever you like."

"That wouldn't be a good idea," Amos warned him.

"I think it is. I'd beat you easily."

"I'm telling you, you're going to regret it," Amos said in a tone so sharp that the threat seemed to freeze in space and time.

There was a long silence. Ava said nothing. She watched the standoff between the three males and wondered who would win. Whether they said so openly or not, she knew that each of them would want to make the group's decisions for them. She found the situation amusing. For the first time since they had come into Siaais's realm, she found that she was enjoying herself a little.

"You three can beat each other senseless and leave the leading to us, that would be entertaining."

The three men looked at Ava, who smiled back with irony. The three of them relaxed a little, perhaps finally realizing that fighting among themselves was not in their best interest.

"Fine," Logan asked, sounding less aggressive. "How are we going to make the difficult decisions?"

Liam and Amos looked at one another. Then they looked at Ava. Logan realized and looked at her too.

Ava saw them staring at her and understood.

"No and no. I will not be the leader."

"It was your idea," Amos pointed out. "It's that or a bloodbath."

"We don't want Logan to lead and he doesn't want us to lead. Somebody else has to do it," Liam told her.

Ava thought about it. She didn't want to lead, but having the three of them fighting all the time to make any decision was going to be disastrous. They would all die. They had to coalesce and collaborate to stay alive.

"Fine, I'll do it. For all our sakes. And I hope that's the end of that silly argument. Let's have no more about alpha males or any more nonsense."

And with those words, Ava took the leadership of the group.

CHAPTER 22

They went on again with a new goal added to that of reaching the Cure: finding food. Liam took the lead. He was a great hunter, and certainly in his own natural surroundings would have been able to find food. But in a world of concrete buildings and deserted asphalt streets, without a single green area in sight, it seemed an impossible mission even for him. He climbed onto the roof of a tall building to search for some area where there might be animals or edible plants.

"Did you have any luck?" Amelia asked him when he came back down.

"I think so. I saw trees a little further on. We'll head there."

But optimism died the moment they came to the place. It was a park with trees, vegetation, and even a small lake in the middle. There was only one problem: There was not a single animal in it. Not a squirrel, nor a bird, nor a dog, and not a single fish in the lake: nothing. They walked around it in silence. The only sound they could hear was the wind in the branches of the trees. Nothing else.

"What do we do now?" Logan asked.

"I could search for another green area," Liam said gloomily, "but I think we'll just find more of the same."

"We're in a deserted city . . . we're the only living beings . . ." Amelia mused aloud, seeking a solution.

"Not the only ones," Logan pointed out. "There are others like us."

"True. What do you suggest?"

"We could take their food away from them."

"No!" Amelia cried. "We can't turn into thieves."

"If we don't eat, we'll grow weak," Amos said from his warrior's point of view, "and we won't be able to fight properly. We won't be able to defend ourselves if they attack us."

"Let's keep looking," Amelia said optimistically. "We'll find a way."

"Yeah, let's keep looking," Ava agreed. "I don't relish the idea of fighting the other groups over food . . ."

With the arrival of night, what little optimism Amelia had managed to inspire in them vanished. There was no food to be found, and pessimism settled in like a black cloud over their heads.

"If we keep on through the center of the city, we won't find any food," Liam pointed out.

"He's right," Ava said. "It's one thing that the animals should have disappeared, although that's strange, because if men disappear, then they ought to be wandering about the city at their leisure, right?" Everyone nodded slowly, puzzling over this. "And it's even stranger that there isn't a single berry or a tuber or a fruit in the whole city. That can only be because in some way Siaais has arranged it like that so we'll die of hunger."

"She's right, you know," Logan said.

"So what are we going to do?" Amelia asked.

"I could go east, out of the city, find some food, and come back," Liam offered.

"No," Ava said. "We have less chance if we separate. We've got to stay together."

"I have an idea," said Emma.

"Let's hear it," Ava encouraged her.

"Liam says we won't find food in the city . . . that's not completely true. We won't find live food, but what we will find is dead food."

They all looked at her blankly. "Dead?" Ava asked, looking disgusted.

"I meant that the cities of the Ancient Ones used to have food that was dead and preserved. We can look for that."

"That's a great idea," Amelia said more hopefully.

"I see only one problem," Ava objected. "Where do we find this food that's dead and preserved?"

Emma smiled. "We look for a food shop."

They spent the whole of the following day searching for the food shop Emma had mentioned, but without success. In fact, she only had a vague idea of what a food shop might be like, so her directions were not at all precise and almost obliged them to look into every building they passed. Hunger began to grow among the group.

At last, with darkness fallen, Ava suggested looking for somewhere to sleep. Liam found a largely intact three-story house on a corner. Here they made themselves as comfortable as they could amid the rubble and dirt. Ava heard her stomach growling and felt the pangs of hunger. She sat down and drank from her waterskin. Opposite her, Logan was writing something in a notebook he carried with him. She wondered what it could be. It was curious that given the situation they were in, he should be taking the time to write notes . . .

"How's the hunger?" she heard Amos ask on her right. She turned and saw the warrior and Amelia talking a few paces away, leaning against the wall.

"I'm not going to lie to you, I'm starving."

"Don't worry, we'll find food, I'm sure of it. Either we'll find one of the shops Emma talked about, or else Liam'll find something to put in our stomachs. Don't worry about it too much."

"Yeah, sure," Amelia replied with a shy smile. Her voice was subdued.

Ava, knowing her cousin perfectly, was sure she did not really believe this.

"You just wait and see, tomorrow with the first light of day we'll be able to fill our stomachs," Amos assured her. He gave her an encouraging smile.

"You don't seem to be so affected by hunger, considering how big you are. You ought to be really feeling it. You need more food than we do."

"No, I can bear the hunger," the warrior assured her.

Amelia was immediately interested. "How's that possible?"

"We train ourselves to put up with extreme conditions like hunger or thirst, heat, whatever. We were prepared beforehand for anything we might come across. Since nobody has ever come back from the realm of Siaais, we didn't know what we'd be facing, so part of the training is preparing ourselves to put up with adverse conditions of all kinds."

"Oh . . . I didn't know that."

"You thought we only trained in combat?"

"Well . . . more or less," she said, feeling rather embarrassed.

"Don't worry, most people think that. And I know that among the scholars we're not very well-regarded."

Amelia's face showed the embarrassment she felt. "You're a lot more than a warrior who only knows how to kill. You're a valiant. A noble person, a fair one, a fighter, a protector. We owe you our lives."

"Thanks. You honor me with your compliments."

"Because you deserve them. If I'm alive, it's thanks to you and your efforts. And don't think I don't notice how you always try to protect me. I see it, and I appreciate it."

"I don't want anything bad to happen to you."

"I know, and I'm deeply grateful."

"You're a scholar. You have knowledge I can only dream of having someday, knowledge that's come in very useful here. You're as important to this group as I am."

"Thanks for saying that, but we both know it's not true."

"I think it is. We complement each other very well, you with your knowledge and me with my training."

Amelia smiled. "If you look at it that way . . . yes, we make a good combination."

"You look after me and I'll look after you," Amos said with a wink and the trace of a smile.

"I'll do that," Amelia replied. She was blushing up to her ears. "Did you always want to be a warrior, a valiant?"

Amos nodded. "Yes, ever since I was a kid. When they told us about the professions in the tribe and their functions, I never had the slightest doubt about what I wanted to be. I was lucky that my body guaranteed acceptance. I know of others who weren't accepted as valiants because their bodies weren't strong enough. What about you? Did you always want to be a scholar?"

"Yes, I think so . . . the other disciplines didn't interest me much, but I don't really know why. Not even healing, which is very beneficial and involves a lot of study." She shrugged.

The warrior nodded. "Well, it seems we both had very clear ideas ever since we were little."

"Have you ever regretted your choice?" Amelia asked, intrigued.

The warrior shook his head. "I was born to be a valiant. I've always thought so. I can't see myself as anything else. And you?"

"Me neither. I always wanted to be a scholar, and I never thought of changing, not for a moment. I love what I do."

"Well, there you are: both the same."

For a moment they were both silent, looking down, until Amelia broke the silence.

"I enjoyed this talk a lot . . . getting to know you a little better . . . finding out more things about you."

"Me too." He bowed his head lower to hide his embarrassment. "We ought to talk more often . . . I mean if you feel like it, of course."

"I'd like that . . . a lot."

"Good . . ."

"Very good . . ."

"Although I don't know how we'll find the right moment in the middle of this almighty mess," Amos said, and shook his head.

"By looking for it at odd times," she replied with a smile.

Amos looked into her eyes, and their gazes locked intently. Time seemed to stop for them. It was as though there was nobody else around.

Ava, meanwhile, was staring at them, spellbound. They were going to kiss, she was absolutely sure. The tension was so palpable that she could almost see it. She held her breath.

"I'm dying of thirst," Logan said suddenly as he came over to them. "Amos, can you hand me the waterskin?"

The moment passed. Their gaze broke apart.

Amos turned his head to Logan. "Sure, here you are," he said, and threw him the waterskin.

"Thanks, pal."

As Logan went past Ava's side, she hit him in the leg. He looked down at her in surprise and confusion.

"What?"

"Dumbass!" she whispered.

"What did I do?"

CHAPTER 23

Ava's recurring nightmare troubled her again that night, robbing her of rest. Pain ran through her in spasms, and no matter how hard she tried, she could not wake up.

Once again, she saw the great white sphere with the flat ring around it, as if it sliced the sphere through its center. The ring seemed to be made up of multiple concentric rings, and the same was true of the sphere. Together they floated in absolute blackness, spinning slowly. The image filled her with dread.

A surge of pain shot through her spine, a convulsion seized her, and agony rose from her stomach, through her chest, and into her throat.

What followed was something she had never experienced before. She was suddenly staring up at the sphere while floating on her back, not in water, but something more viscous. She began to have difficulty breathing. Air was no longer reaching her lungs. Her throat hurt so much that she was about to suffocate. She made one last desperate effort to breathe, but there was no air, only the beckoning blackness.

"Ava!" cried a distant voice.

"Wake up!" came another.

She was shaken roughly. Ava opened her eyes wide and sat up suddenly like a spring. She looked around fearfully as she took in a huge breath of air, then a second and a third.

"Are you all right?" Amelia asked her.

"You were having a nightmare," Emma added.

Ava remembered she was among friends and allies and began to feel a little calmer. "I was suffocating . . . I thought I was dying."

"How awful," Amelia said sympathetically.

"Breathe slowly through your nose," Emma told her.

She followed this advice for a while, during which Amelia told her that Liam and Amos had gone out to scout the surroundings before they all set off again.

Finally, Ava managed to relax. She noticed Logan looking at her with interest.

"Not a word," she warned him. The last thing she needed now was a stream of unwelcome questions or comments.

He smiled and let her be.

Satisfied that she was recovering, and to give her some space, Amelia and Emma began to talk about the technology of the Ancient Ones. Logan had settled back against a wall on the other side of the room and was writing in his notebook again. "What are you doing?"

He looked up at her. "I write things down so I don't forget them," he said, and went on writing.

"What things?"

"Anything I find interesting and want to remember later. I like writing and drawing."

"Are you writing anything about me?"

Logan smiled from ear to ear. "Particularly about you. You're the most interesting thing that's ever happened to me."

Ava stared at him, wide-eyed. Was he sincere, or just teasing her? "You're laughing at me . . ."

"I swear I'm not."

"It must be hunger that's giving you hallucinations."

Logan chuckled and nodded. "Must be."

"Now, seriously, drop the flirting and tell me what you're noting down."

"Mainly things to do with my Power: Every time I use it, the little improvements I attempt, and the differences I experience. Then I study them and try to make sense of them to improve my mastery and control."

"You study it constantly?"

"Yes, and so should you. It gives us advantages, and we need to learn as much as we can about our Powers in what little time we have before we . . . you know . . ."

Ava nodded. She understood. "So, your aim is to be very powerful?"

"One of my aims, yes. I want to be the most powerful among my people. Or rather, I *wanted* to be the most powerful among my people. Now I'm beginning to see things a bit differently."

"Why did you want to be the most powerful among your people?"

"I wanted respect," he said gravely.

"Respect? You're very powerful already, we've all seen that. You already have respect."

Logan shook his head. "You respect me. My people don't."

Ava was taken aback. "How can that be? I don't get it. Is everyone among your people more powerful than you are?"

"No, I'm among the most powerful. I've studied and practiced with the Power ever since I can remember. There aren't many of my people at my level."

"And so?"

"Don't think about it too much. What shocked you most when we met?"

"Your gray eyes."

Logan smiled and nodded. "Well, those same eyes are the things that deny me my people's respect."

"I don't understand."

"My gray eyes mark me as mixed-race, impure, and because of that I belong to an inferior caste."

"Caste?"

"Social class."

"But why? I'm mixed-race too. My skin is lighter and my eyes are green, and both those are uncommon among my people, but they don't discriminate against me because of it. It's just that I'm not as pretty as my cousin. Boys don't find me attractive, but that's all."

"You're lucky. I've been looked at askance, badly treated, discriminated against, even beaten . . . but all that's made me more determined."

"Is that why you're so powerful now?"

"I think it is, partly . . ." Logan considered this for a moment, his gaze distant. "I never thought about it before, but yes, it's possible all that mistreatment led me to make more of an effort with my Power, to try and be better than all those who looked down on me."

"I'm sorry they've treated you badly."

"Don't worry. It's all in the past now."

"Still, they had no right, beating you because you're mixed-race. That's despicable."

Logan gave her a gentle smile. "Not everybody has your pure heart."

Ava scoffed, "Don't imagine my heart is pure or sweet . . . it's not. But I can't stand injustice. It's something I can't deal with. If I see something unfair, I can't restrain myself."

"Ava, paladin of justice."

Ava did not know the word. "What's 'paladin'?"

"A leader."

"Oh yes, I'd like to be that."

"You will be, I'm sure of it. But if you want some friendly advice, never take justice into your own hands. Don't turn yourself into a judge. You'll come to a bad end that way."

Ava looked into his eyes and saw that the advice was sincere. She nodded.

"I think I understand what you mean. I won't be."

"I'm glad."

"Sometimes you talk very strangely, using words I don't know."

"It might be because of my profession."

Ava tilted her head to one side. "What are you?"

"I'm a scribe."

"Someone who spends the day writing down the official events for the chief of the tribe?" Ava said in disbelief.

"That's right. For the chief and the scholars."

"Well, I'm sorry to have to tell you, but I'd never have guessed it. It doesn't seem to suit you."

Logan laughed. "Maybe there's more to me than meets the eye! It's what I was allotted, and I accepted it. I'm not complaining. It's helped me a lot with my Power, and I've learned a lot."

"How come you're here? A scribe despised by his people . . . I wouldn't have thought you'd have volunteered at the ceremony."

"And you'd be right. I didn't volunteer. In fact I never thought I could be chosen. Among my people, warriors learn to use weapons and the Power. They're extremely lethal. Usually, three warriors are chosen. And also . . ." He fell silent. There was something he did not want to reveal.

"And also . . . ?" Ava encouraged him.

"Can you keep a secret?"

"Of course."

"It's not something I'm proud of . . . but nor do I see why I should feel ashamed . . . The Cure, the saving of my people . . . has never been my priority. Call me selfish, say I have a chip on my shoulder—it might be both those things, I'm not saying it's not. I always believed that particular heroic achievement would be someone else's, that I didn't need to concern myself with it. And now, the ironies of life, here I am, the great hope of my people . . . at least for this year."

"I'll keep your secret. Now you can keep mine."

Logan was immediately intrigued. "What's that?"

"That I feel the same way as you. I never thought I'd be chosen, I never wanted to save the tribe, find the Cure."

"What a pair of heroes we are, you and me . . ."

Ava smiled and spread out her hands. "So who did you come with?"

"Two warriors and myself."

"What happened to them?"

"The stupid fools were killed with long-range weapons."

"Firearms?"

"Worse, long-distance bows. They thought they were invincible. They strolled through the jungle as if it belonged to them. Two silent arrows."

"And what about you?"

"I was walking crouched down, and the arrow passed very close to my head. I ran for my life and never looked back."

"You did the right thing." Ava was looking thoughtful. "It's curious . . ."

"What is?"

"That you and I have a lot in common. Much more than I thought."

He smiled. "That's good."

"I'm not a warrior either, and I didn't volunteer. Yet we're both here . . . both mixed-race . . . don't you think it's strange?"

"Strange? You mean as if there must be some reason for it?"

"I'm getting more and more convinced that none of it's coincidence. Everything has a reason, it's just that we can't see it yet."

"I'm not so sure, but I'm not going to contradict you. All this is very weird."

"Mark my words: There's a connection here. The two of us weren't chosen at random. I can feel it."

Logan shrugged. "We'll have to find that connection."

Ava smiled. "I like the fact that you listen to what I say."

"I like the fact that you like it."

"Why do you try to flirt with me whenever you can?"

"Because you're a beautiful rose on the point of blooming. Your splendor will soon come to the surface and delight all our senses."

"I've no idea what you're talking about, and I don't understand you."

"Your face, your hair, your figure, your charm, your appeal . . . You keep them all hidden, ignored, but I can assure you: Once you allow yourself to blossom, you'll be irresistible. All the young men will drop at your feet in surrender."

Ava gave a dismissive snort. "I know you're a womanizer, so don't go on."

"Oh, you do, do you? And how do you know that?"

"It's obvious, not just because of your appearance, but because of your manners and the way you behave. They belong to someone who's confident, someone who knows his charms work."

"My, how you've analyzed me. I thought you weren't interested in me."

"And I'm not interested in you. You can stop playing with me, you're not going to get anywhere."

"Perhaps a poem might soften that character of yours . . ."

"If you come out with a poem, I'll give you a black eye."

Logan gave a guffaw. "If you don't want me to insist, I won't. After all, I'm a gentleman, and the last thing I want to do is offend you."

Ava looked into his eyes to make sure he was serious. Yes, his eyes showed that he was sincere. She was surprised. She had not expected him to be interested in her. He was handsome and powerful, and she was his opposite. She thought about his last words and realized that she would miss his attention and comments if she refused him. Not that she wanted anything with him . . . or perhaps she did? She was thoughtful. *Do I like him? Really? He's only a ladies' man, and cocky at that, and he knows it. He only wants to flirt with me, and I'll end up being another of his serial conquests. No way. Nobody's going to conquer me. No way!*

"No paying me compliments. Treat me as if I were Amos."

Logan raised his hands. "I give up. If you want it that way, so be it. No gallantry or attempts at seduction from now on."

"That's better."

"But that won't make me stop liking you."

"You had to have the last word, didn't you?"

"Always."

Ava shook her head and moved away from him.

Liam and Amos came back to tell them that the area was clear. They would be able to set off at once. They picked up their equipment and got ready to leave.

"Today we'll find food," Liam said to cheer them up.

They all nodded, but none of them was in the least convinced that it would be so.

CHAPTER 24

They walked all morning, alert to any possible danger. Toward noon they passed a building that stood out from all the others. It was very large, built of granite, with great round columns at its entrance. There were small green areas in the front and back, with grass and trees.

"What a huge temple," Amos said as he stared at it. It was enormously tall, with several stories inside it.

Amelia was studying the complex with great interest. "I don't think it's a temple."

"It must have been important, to be so large and imposing," Ava reasoned.

"Not a place of worship either," Logan said. "I wonder what it was for. Buildings as splendid as this were usually for a specific purpose, because they must have cost so much to build."

"Let's go inside," Emma said suddenly.

They all looked at her in surprise. "You want to go in?" Ava asked.

"Yes."

"Why? We need to go on north. It's what the Indicator says, and time's running out."

"It'll only be for a moment," Emma insisted.

"Why do you want to go inside?" Ava asked.

"It's a library."

"Liam used that same word earlier," Ava said. "What's a library?"

"A place that stores knowledge, usually in the form of books, although it could also be in the form of electronic or digital media."

Ava looked to Amelia for help in understanding this explanation.

"I think it's like our archives, where we keep the tomes of knowledge and wisdom we rescue." Amelia guessed. "But what makes you think that's what this building is, Emma?"

Emma pointed to the words chiseled on the granite above the great main door. "*Public Libra*—The rest has fallen off. It looks like ours, that's why it caught my attention."

"I don't know if it's a good idea to go in," Liam said.

"We might find information that could help us," Emma countered.

Amelia nodded. "I agree, we should investigate. We don't know what kind of knowledge we might find in there. It might help us to sort out the mysteries around us."

Emma unsheathed her katana decisively. "Wait here, I'll go."

"No way. Either we all go in, or else no one does," Ava said. "But you can lead the way."

"Then come on," Emma said, and started toward the door at a determined pace.

Liam gave Ava a disapproving look. He didn't like the risk they were taking, and he was letting her know.

She shrugged. "Maybe we'll find something that'll help us

get out of this nightmare," she said, and followed Emma and Amelia.

The doors, when they reached them, would not open.

"I could burn them," Logan offered.

"I don't think that would be a good idea," Amelia said. "The smoke would be visible from a distance."

"There's no need," Emma said. She pointed to a panel on the wall to the right of the door.

Emma touched the upper Mark of Siaais on her arm. There was a silver flash, and she pressed the palms of her gloved hands on the crystalline surface of the reader. She closed her eyes and concentrated. Both gloves lit up, one in yellow and the other in blue. The strange threads formed by the two colors extended to penetrate the reader. Emma began to direct them, moving her fingers at great speed as she probed the panels to interact with the device's systems, testing each in its turn as she searched for the one that would open the door.

While Emma worked, Liam kept watch on the east side of the great building, hidden behind one of the columns. Amos was doing the same on the west side.

"Got it," Emma announced at last.

The door opened with a loud crack. With Ava's help, Logan pushed the door until it was wide enough to allow them to slip through. They went in one by one, first Amos and then a reluctant Liam, who was still concerned about what they might find inside. Once they had given the signal that everything was okay, the others followed. They found themselves in a large hall with massive paintings on opposing walls.

Everything was covered in dust, and there was a funereal silence, which made each step they took echo against the walls.

Logan used his Power to create a small flame in his hand to light their way. The enormous arched windows had been boarded up, so there was no natural light in the building. Amelia was looking up at the lofty walls as she went, when suddenly she sneezed from the dust. She put her hands to her nose and mouth to stop a second sneeze, and Emma raised her hand. They all stopped at once, looking around with their weapons at the ready in case someone had heard the sound. The sneeze had sounded ten times louder than normal in those gloomy surroundings. For a long moment they waited, but everything remained silent and deserted.

They went on, now even more carefully, and came to a great space where the walls were covered with huge, faded frescos and the columns were covered with ornately carved but warping wood. On the vaulted ceilings were flaking paintings amid crumbling decorations in wood and gold. The floor, under its layer of dust and dirt, was tiled in two colors of marble. In a far-off, long-gone time, it must have been both beautiful and imposing. It was still the latter, but its beauty had decayed with the passing of countless years.

Beyond this, they came to a vast hall. Logan intensified the flame in his hand, and they were now able to see it more clearly. On both sides of a long aisle were wooden tables, one after the other, over thirty on each side. There was room for more than twenty people at each of those tables. Against the walls and under the windows they could see shelves containing hundreds of books, if not thousands.

Amelia muffled a cry. "Look at all those books," she whispered.

"So many of them," Emma said, wide-eyed.

They moved down the aisle between the rows of tables, staring at the books. Above the tables there hung thirty or so very elaborate lamps, each with hundreds of glass ornaments.

Amelia went to one of the shelves to look at the books, and Amos followed her at once.

"Don't get separated," Liam whispered. He was looking around the hall as if the characters painted on the immense ceiling were about to come to life and fall on them.

The lofty stone ceilings, the domed nave, the decorative woodwork, and the paintings all seemed unreal to Ava. None of these things were like anything in her native land. To her they seemed almost divine.

Emma beckoned them to follow her. She had seen something at the far end of the hall. Amelia returned with several books and a look of immense excitement on her face. Amos followed her with an expression of concern.

Emma led them to an elaborate table with two vertical panels on it, bigger than any they had seen so far. On the table were several rectangles, with writing on each one. Everything was covered with a thick layer of dust, but when Emma blew hard, it flew aside. The black rectangles had letters and numbers on them.

"Systems!" Emma cried, and her eyes gleamed.

She put the katana back in its sheath over her back, then sat down in front of one of the panels. She activated her Power, then carefully placed her gloved fingers on the black rectangle. She concentrated, and her fingers lit up once again in blue and yellow, sending their luminous threads to take possession of the black panel and whatever was behind it.

A moment later, the vertical panel lit up.

"This is getting interesting," Ava murmured.

Line after line of letters and numbers began to appear on the panel, flashing dizzyingly up and down. Ava stared wide-eyed, trying to understand what was happening. The lines of letters and numbers came and went in a continuous cascade. Emma followed them, eyes narrowed, while her fingers moved incredibly fast. The more her fingers moved, the more luminous threads appeared, and the faster they seemed to react with the lines that appeared on the panel.

"Do you know what she's doing?" Logan whispered in Ava's ear.

"I've no idea. All I know is that she can interact with the machines She must be accessing information. She said 'system.' I think that's where the Ancient Ones stored things. That's what she told me. We'd better let her do her thing and see what she finds out. It could be important."

Suddenly the lines stopped moving, and one appeared in red. "CONDITIONING PROGRAM BY ERA," Emma read aloud.

"What's that?" Amelia asked.

"I don't know, but it might have something to do with us."

"Do you think you can manage to get access?" Liam asked.

"I can try. I can't guarantee anything, though. And also, we have to bear in mind that it might trigger an alarm."

"An alarm?" Logan asked. "Why?"

"Because I'm going to use my Power on the part of the system that's protected. If I can't, it probably means it knows I'm trying to get in illicitly."

"Have you done this before?" Ava asked.

"Yes. I'm breaking through the safeguards of a protected system, so as to gain access to the information stored inside it."

"Hmmm . . ." Liam said, and to judge by his expression he did not like the idea.

"I think we ought to risk it," Ava said.

"So do I," Amelia chimed in.

Emma nodded. "Me too."

"The three girls say yes. And the three boys?" Ava asked.

"Too risky," Liam said.

"I agree with Liam," said Amos.

The girls looked at Logan, who grinned from ear to ear. "All this feminine attention! I'm with the girls. I want to know what it means."

"Go ahead, Emma," Ava said.

Emma's fingers moved with shocking speed. The lines of text and numbers came back. Then Emma's arm gave a flash. She gasped in surprise, but went on working. Ava could see the perspiration on her forehead. She was fighting the system, trying to get ahead of it, to outsmart it. There was a second silver flash on her arm, but in her concentration she did not even notice.

A red light went on under the table. Ava bent down to see what it was with an ominous feeling unsettling her stomach.

A siren went off, and a circular red light appeared in the ceiling.

CHAPTER 25

Ava put her hands over her ears. The strident noise of the siren was piercing her eardrums. The light in the ceiling was spinning angrily, illuminating the whole room in an intense red: the red of Siaais, the red of death.

"Stop it!" Logan called to Emma.

"I can't! The alarm's gone off! I've got to go on till I break the code, or else it won't stop!"

Logan brought his hands up to cover his ears. "Do whatever you have to, but make it stop! The whole city's going to hear this racket!"

Suddenly a door-sized panel between two bookshelves on the far side of the room flew open. "Unauthorized access. Intruder alarm activated," came a metallic voice, monotonous and inhuman, and a metal being emerged from a hidden alcove.

Ava stared at it open-mouthed. The upper part of this machine resembled a man. In its head were large round eyes, shining with a white light that illuminated the space in front of it. The mouth was a long slit, and it had no nose. Its torso and arms were like those of a man, but made of metal. The lower part was conical, giving the impression of a steel skirt that reached down to the floor. Three small wheels allowed it to glide across the room toward them.

Without thinking twice, Liam raised his bow, aimed, and released an arrow. It struck the machine in the chest and bounced off to one side. Liam nocked another arrow, and at the same moment the machine turned toward him and raised both arms. At the end of each was a firearm. Liam hastened to seek cover.

"Look out!" Ava shouted.

Liam leaped behind a table at the same moment the guardian fired. There were two shots, and part of the table broke into flying fragments.

"Everybody take cover!" Liam ordered. He hurled himself over another table and took cover behind it.

The guardian focused on him, ignoring the others. "Unauthorized intruder. Eliminate threat," it said as it set off toward Liam. It was unexpectedly agile on its three wheels, spinning around and turning sharply when it met an obstacle. But it had trouble maneuvering through the narrow space between the long, heavy tables as it tried to keep its two arms aimed at Liam.

Ava and Amelia took shelter beside the table where Emma was still struggling against the system to gain access. Her fingers were a blur of motion, but she still had not succeeded in deactivating the alarm.

"We have to protect Emma," Ava said to her cousin, who nodded in agreement. They both held up their shields to give Emma cover, leaving their javelins on the floor.

Logan seized the moment when the machine was taking another shot at Liam to attack it. He activated his Power and lit his lighter in one swift motion.

"Burn!" he said, and created a fireball which floated in front of him for a moment before he launched it at the guardian. The machine was engulfed in flames and within a few short seconds it stopped moving and ceased firing at Liam. Logan smiled. It had been a bull's-eye.

The flames eventually died down, but to his horror Logan realized that the fire had failed to consume the guardian. When the flames had vanished, the thing suddenly spun round and aimed its weapons at Logan.

"Second intruder identified. Action: eliminate," it announced.

Logan stared at it open-mouthed. The fire had damaged parts of the machine, but had not penetrated the thick metal shell that covered it. The guardian was about to shoot, and he would not have time to use anything against it.

Amos came forward at a run and hurled himself on Logan, pushing him down. They heard two blasts and knew the machine's weapons had not been damaged by Logan's flames either.

Amos groaned in pain.

Liam got to his feet. Leaving his bow aside, he activated his Power by touching the upper Mark on his arm, which gave out a silver flash. He stretched out his arms and seized its head. He tugged with all his might, trying to topple the machine without success. It must have weighed tons.

The guardian fired once again at Logan and Amos as they dodged behind an overturned table. The noise of the detonations echoed off the walls. Pieces of the table flew into the air, and they were forced to cover their heads with their hands amid a shower of broken wood and splinters.

The machine attempted to move around the table toward them, but Liam had gotten a grip on it with his Power and was pulling it backward. He fought with all his strength, sweating and grimacing with intense effort, but the machine held firm.

"Emma, get a move on," Ava called.

"I'm doing my best," Emma called back.

The guardian turned toward Liam and aimed. He released the machine and threw himself to one side. Two shots whizzed past him and buried themselves in a bookshelf. Pages and other fragments of books flew into the air.

Logan moved behind the table and pulled a small bottle from a pocket on his belt. He activated his Power again as he opened the bottle and poured out some of the contents into the palm of his hand: water. He flung it at the guardian and the water suddenly turned into an icy jet, which began to freeze the machine the moment it reached it.

The guardian turned to Logan and tried to aim with its half-frozen arms, but it could not raise them high enough.

"Eliminate . . . threat . . ."

Logan conjured with the water once again, sending more Power. The machine's arms froze solid, and the guardian became encased in ice and frost from its head to its wheels. But though it was unable to raise its weapons, it still managed to shoot, hitting the table Logan was crouching behind, so that he was forced to take cover again.

Now, instead of attacking the machine directly, Liam used his Power to lift one of the heavy tables and hurl it at the half-frozen guardian. The table impacted on its upper half with such force that the wood shattered, but it hurled the machine backward and left it stretched out on the floor.

"I've got it!" Emma said suddenly.

"Seriously? Now?" Logan complained with a look of disbelief on his face.

The alarm died. At the same time, the red lights stopped spinning and went out. Amos went up to the guardian and used his shield to hammer its arms until he'd bent the metal to uselessness.

Liam was looking down at his arm, which was shining an intense silver. He said nothing, but his expression was worried.

"What's the matter?" Ava asked as she went to his side.

"I don't know . . . it started when I lifted the table."

He showed her his arm, where the upper Mark was still shining. Ava sensed that something odd was going on. This was not normal. She put her hand on the Mark, which gradually faded.

"I don't know what it is, but something odd's happening to you," she said. "Do you notice anything off?"

Liam shook his head. "No, quite the contrary, I feel better in some way . . . I can't explain it."

Ava examined him, searching for some indication that what was happening to the Mark might also be affecting his physical well-being, but she found nothing.

"Ava, come here quickly!" Logan said suddenly. "It's Amos. The machine got him, he's bleeding."

"I'm fine," Amos said, trying to reassure them. "It's nothing." He was holding his side.

"You're bleeding. That's not nothing," Amelia said. She looked terrified.

"Let me see," Ava said as she knelt down beside him, and Amos drew his hand back.

"The shots went through the armor, but I don't think it's serious. They haven't gone deep enough to reach anything vital."

"Thank heavens," Amelia gasped in relief.

"I told you it was nothing . . ." Amos said, waving it aside.

Logan patted him on the shoulder. "Thanks for saving my life, hulk," he said gratefully.

"You're welcome. Next time don't just stand there trying to use your Power when something's about to kill you."

"I wasn't expecting that machine to survive the fire . . . it caught me by surprise. Nothing normally survives my fire."

"It looks as though you're not that invincible after all, almighty lord of the elements," Ava chided him as she worked on Amos's wounds.

Logan laughed. "It's never happened to me before, that's true, but I don't see myself as almighty, particularly after this. These machines are more difficult to kill than men or animals. I'll bear that in mind for next time."

Ava finished tending to Amos's wound. "The bandage should hold, but try not to make any sudden moves, or you'll start to bleed again."

Amos nodded. With Logan's and Liam's help he got to his feet, and they went over to Emma, who was still intent on the screen.

"Are we safe?" Ava asked.

"Yes, I managed to disconnect the alarm and the guardians."

"Were there more of them?" Amelia asked uneasily.

"Yes, two more, one in each adjoining building. Their function is to protect this place."

"Did you manage to find anything out? Was it worth risking our lives?"

"I managed to gain access to information about a secret project. A Conditioning Program by Era."

"That sounds like a good start," Ava said, "but I don't understand some of those words. What's a project, and what's a program?"

"Don't worry about the terms, they're not important. The important thing is that the Ancient Ones, from what I could make out, were studying human behavior and conditioning in different eras of history."

"Studying how?" Amelia asked with interest.

"There's a mass of information I'd need a lot of time to understand. Too much. There are thousands of files. From what little I've managed to examine and make sense of, a group of scientists theorized about the reactions of people in extreme situations across different historical periods. How they'd behave, and what their reactions would be."

"What for?" Ava asked in puzzlement.

"I think the goal was to prepare the population for a possible global catastrophe."

"Like the Apocalypse?" Amelia asked.

Emma nodded. "That could be."

"That would make sense," Amelia reasoned. "They were preparing to confront a catastrophic event, which we know finally occurred."

Logan was scratching his chin. "Well, I don't think that would have been much use . . . if those eras are over now . . ."

"Yeah, it's rather strange," Ava agreed. "Who cares how someone in the past would react in the face of a cataclysm?"

"It'd be better to concentrate on how the present population would react—well, the present one at the time it happened," said Liam.

"Still," Emma said, "whatever it might have been, this is what it looks as though they were studying, and it was a secret government program."

Ava raised one eyebrow. "How do you know that?"

"By the way the access key was coded. It's a strong cipher, created shortly before the Apocalypse."

"Who created it?" Amelia asked.

"One of the governments of the Ancient Ones. There was great concern among them about protecting secrets from rival nations."

"All this is a massive tangle, and it doesn't get us any nearer the Cure," Amos said unhappily. He was quite clear about their goal, and all this was leading them astray.

Liam nodded. "Amos is right. We can't allow ourselves to become distracted. Getting hold of Cure is what matters."

"That's not completely true," Emma pointed out. "This secret program we've just uncovered does have something to do with us. And I also think that if it has something to do with us, then it also has something to do with getting hold of the Cure."

"Why do you say it has something to do with us?" asked Liam.

"Don't you see the connection?" she said, looking very serious.

There was a long silence as the three boys looked at one another and shook their heads. Amelia and Ava were looking thoughtful. Then suddenly Amelia's eyes widened.

"Emma's right. There is a connection."

"What?" Logan said blankly. "I don't see it."

"It's us," Amelia said. "Think about it, about where we're from. Don't you notice anything strange?"

"We're different . . . we come from different places . . ." Liam ventured.

"That's right, we're from different places, different tribes. But there's something else."

Logan shrugged. "I still don't see it . . ."

"We're not only from different places, but from different times," Amelia explained. "We're from different eras."

The three boys exchanged glances, then turned back to the girls. Liam nodded.

"Okay," Logan said, "I think I see where you're heading . . . their society had developed as far as the Bronze Age." He indicated Amelia, Ava, and Amos. "So what about my society?"

Emma looked him up and down, studying him with her analytic gaze. "You, judging by your clothing and the knowledge you've showed us: I'd say you come from a society that had developed up to the Middle Ages, approximately. I don't think you got any further than that. As for your place of origin, I'd say England, am I right?"

"Wow!" Logan cried in surprise. "Yes, I come from England, near London."

"And judging by your features, descended from someone from India, probably."

"And Liam?" Ava asked Emma. "What can you say about him?"

"From what he's told me, I'd say he's from the north of the US."

Liam nodded. "Yes, that's right, near the old border with Canada."

"And your tribe is modeled on the frontiersmen of the Industrial Age."

Amelia tilted her head. "I'm very intrigued by your origin and era," she told Emma.

"I come from Japan, near ancient Tokyo, from the Information Age. Which means we have four different eras in this group. That's rather strange and significant, it seems to me."

"That's what I think too!" Amelia cried excitedly. "This is really interesting."

Ava was shaking her head as she looked up at the domed ceiling. "More like really complicated."

Emma went on analyzing the situation. "If you think about it, we've seen other tribes, also from different eras. Which leads me to believe this isn't random, it's by design."

"That's my belief too," Amelia agreed. "More than that, we started off thinking that the way our tribes developed was because of their individual circumstances. Now, seeing all this, I'm beginning to think there might be more behind it than that."

"What do you mean?" Ava asked uneasily.

"After what we've found, I don't think it's coincidence that groups based on different epochs of human history should be wandering about this place for no good reason. It's not a coincidence. There's intention behind it."

Ava was shaking her head. "I'm beginning to like this less and less."

Amos, too, was shaking his head. "I don't believe any of this. Things in our tribe are what they are because that's the way they happened. Nobody designed anything."

Liam and Logan were frowning, apparently not completely convinced.

"I think Amos's way of looking at it fits better," Ava said, trying to simplify the situation. "Our tribes have developed at different speeds because of the different circumstances they found themselves in."

"Are you sure of that?" Amelia said, hoping to prod her into thinking about it more carefully.

Ava waved her arms. "Of course I'm not sure! I'm not sure of anything here. What I want is that it should all have followed naturally from being in the desert, from having the knowledge we had at hand, from our culture, from our religion. You said it yourself, cousin. It's a less complicated solution."

"Yes, but I don't think that any longer. I'm beginning to think that all our tribes have been manipulated, their development controlled in some way, for some end."

"But why?" Ava asked.

"Perhaps those aren't the questions that need to be answered," Amelia suggested. "There's another, more crucial one."

"What's that?" her cousin asked.

"By whom . . . ?"

Ava nodded.

"By that wretched Siaais!" she shouted.

CHAPTER 26

Emma went on checking the files she had found in the information system, while the others decided to investigate the other areas of the library in search of water and food. It was an unpromising place to find these things, but they would lose nothing by trying.

"I'll check the east wing," said Ava.

"I'll come with you," Logan offered. "It'd be better to go in pairs, just in case." He offered her a seductive smile.

Instead of replying immediately, she looked at Liam out of the corner of her eye to see his reaction. There was none, at least no obvious one. The hunter had bent down to examine the guardian machine they had defeated. Clearly, he did not seem to be interested in her, or to care about the interest Logan was showing in her. For some reason she could not put into words, she did not like this.

"Great. Let's go," Logan said, and led the way with his lighter held at the ready.

Ava followed him. They needed to find food, that was the important thing. To think about anything else was pointless in the complicated situation they were in. She was angry with herself for worrying over something as trivial as Liam's feelings about her.

He was still examining the guardian machine when he announced, "I'll go check the western wing."

Amelia glanced shyly at Amos. "We'd better go together . . ." she said.

"Yes, of course. We'll search the northern area."

Amelia thanked him with a smile and turned to Emma, who was still absorbed in the terminal. "Are you sure you're not in any danger?"

They waited for a moment for Emma's reply, but none came. Her mind was focused on the computer system, eyes closed in concentration, fingers dancing rapidly.

"Come on, let her get on with it," Amos said with a wave of his spear. Amelia nodded, picked up her javelin and shield, and followed the warrior, who was carrying his weapons as if they were a bunch of feathers. To her they might have been two sacks full of stones. What really worried her when she felt the weight of her own burden anew was that she was feeling weaker and weaker for lack of food, and she did not know how much longer she could bear carrying them.

They passed Liam, who was still on his knees studying the weapons at the end of the machine's arms, which had begun to thaw.

"I put them out of action," Amos said, seeing his partner's interest.

Liam gave a wave of his hand. "I know. What I'm trying to do is understand how they work. It might come in handy later on."

"This type of weapon's totally strange to me," Amos said. He held out his own shield and spear. "I'll stick with what I know."

"I know what you mean, these are very advanced. And yet"—Liam scratched his chin—"they're firearms, after all . . . the working principle must be the same as, or similar to, my old musket."

"Emma comes from the most advanced era of all of us," Amos said.

Liam watched her for a moment while she worked, then stood up and shook his head. "I don't suppose she'll know much about this type of weapon either, even though she's from a tribe with more advanced knowledge."

"Why's that?" Amos asked in surprise.

"Because she doesn't carry any firearms. She has a sword, which I guess is special to her culture."

"You could be right," Amelia said. "It makes sense that if her people had more advanced weapons, they'd have brought them."

Liam got to his feet. "We should all go looking for food. Anything else can wait."

While Liam went in search of the west wing, Amelia and Amos set out for the northern part of the building.

"Thanks for coming with me," she said as she and Amos entered an enormous hall which contained armchairs and long shelves full of books.

"It's my duty to protect you," Amos replied gently, and gave her a firm smile.

"I know . . . and I'm deeply grateful for your protection." She gave him a warm smile.

"I can't help it. You're a scholar . . ."

"A little slip of a thing, and without much flesh on her bones, you mean." She tilted her head in amusement.

Amos shook his head. "We need you, because of that head of yours and all the knowledge in it. Look around here: all these tomes full of wisdom, and I wouldn't know what to do with them, but you would."

"Unfortunately books won't protect us against murderous machines, and they won't fill our stomachs either. Sometimes . . . I feel as if I don't contribute very much to the group . . ."

"Of course you do, you contribute a lot. I need you beside me . . ." Amos took a book, opened it, and showed it to her. "I don't even recognize the language it's written in," he said with a flush on his cheeks. "I feel stupid . . ."

"Stupid? Don't say that." Amelia wagged a finger at him. "You're intelligent, quite apart from being strong, and a great warrior. And I can't read these books either."

"Thanks, but compared to you or Ava or Emma I don't think I'm particularly intelligent . . ."

Amelia closed the book. A small cloud of dust issued from it and she sneezed. "You undervalue yourself. You're worth a lot. Don't feel you're any less just because we're here in this place full of books. Out there, you're the one who's really valuable."

Amos smiled and went on looking around the hall with interest. "What is this place?" he asked.

"If I'm not mistaken, it's a reading room."

They searched the whole room, but found nothing. There were only books and more books: nothing remotely edible. They went on up a flight of elegant marble stairs with banisters of elaborately ornamented oak. This led to another large hall full of tall wooden shelves. A long corridor ran from one end to the other, and on one side a row of huge and dirty windows let the light in.

"Don't be afraid," Amos said suddenly, as if he were worried that she might be inwardly suffering.

"I am, I can't deny it. Even here, among all these shelves of books in this place that delights me so much."

"It's good to feel fear, it keeps us alive."

"You're not afraid, though."

"Of course I feel fear in the face of danger. I'm human. We all are, and we all feel fear."

"I thought the valiant didn't know fear, that you'd been trained not to feel it."

Amos shook his head. "They teach us to control fear and use it to confront danger. That doesn't mean we don't feel it."

They searched the hall and again found that there were only books, along with furniture to help with reading. By now Amelia was worried and rather downhearted. She opened a cupboard beside one of the great windows in the hopes of finding something, whatever it might be, however little, something that would give them hope. Suddenly a pile of books fell onto her. She screamed and fell on her backside.

Amos ran to help her. "Are you all right?"

"Yeah . . . they just fell on top of me."

Amos offered his hand and helped her back to her feet. Amelia shook off the dust and sneezed a couple of times. Facing one another, their bodies nearly touching, they looked into one another's eyes. A powerful feeling rose from the pit of her stomach, as if she were floating, and a wave of heat filled her cheeks. She could not take her eyes off his, and a desire to hold him in her arms, to kiss him, came over her with an intensity that took her completely by surprise.

Amos leaned in, his face very close to hers as if drawn to her by magnetism, drowning in her eyes. Their lips came closer, almost to the point of touching.

She pulled him a little closer to her, and their lips touched.

They melted in the kiss.

CHAPTER 27

Ava and Logan were being careful to make no noise as they searched the eastern wing of the great library, in case they ran into another surprise attempt to kill them. It was deserted, and everywhere they went they found the same thing: decaying furniture and shelves full of dusty old books.

They found a rectangular hall with tapestries on the walls and a very high ceiling with an eye-catching fresco of angels seated on clouds. Logan took a book from an ornamented shelf and began to leaf through it.

"What on earth are you doing?" she asked him, in some annoyance.

He showed her the book he was holding. "What d'you think?"

"This is no time to start reading," she snapped. "We've got more urgent things to worry about."

"You're absolutely right, but I couldn't resist it."

"You couldn't resist reading?" she asked with a gesture of disbelief.

"Some of us like books."

"I can't believe you like books that much."

Logan laughed. "Don't forget, I'm a scribe. I've lived all my life among books and scrolls."

"I remember, I'm just having trouble picturing it. You're so vain, I can't see you among books, especially if you aren't obliged to be."

"The words that best describe me are *conceited* and *smug*. Terms which probably weren't in your vocabulary."

"Don't treat me as if I were dumb, because I'm not," she fired back. "I may not have spent my whole life among tomes and papyri like you, but I've had to learn a lot to become a healer."

"I'd imagine a lot of that learning was practical. The theoretical side was probably lacking."

"The scholars have found tomes from more advanced ages that have allowed us to improve some things."

Logan nodded. "My tribe works in the same way. We also have scholars who study all the knowledge we find. I've worked with them my whole life, making copies and creating new books of knowledge for our people."

"Don't you think that's curious?"

Logan looked at her blankly. "What is?"

"That your tribe and mine are similar, when our people's development has put us in different times and parts of the world?"

"It might be important, I'm not denying that. It could also be random."

"Well . . . maybe . . ." Ava wrinkled her nose and was thoughtful.

"I've always lived among books, because of both obligation and devotion. My profession required it, true, but I've always loved them ever since I was little. The fact that I'm charming, handsome, and irresistible doesn't stop me liking books."

She raised her eyebrows. "It doesn't stop you being arrogant."

"Not to mention smug," he agreed with a smile.

"You're not easily offended."

Logan shrugged. "Why should I be? I'm attractive, and I know it. There's no need to pretend otherwise, particularly with someone who interests me."

"And who you'll never get."

He chuckled. "Touché."

"What does that mean?"

"It's from another language. It means *hit.*"

"You speak other languages?"

"It is an expression."

Ava rolled her eyes. "I can't believe it."

"You're finding me more and more interesting and irresistible all the time, aren't you."

"More like irritating and unbearable," she snapped back. Unfortunately, that was not what she really felt. In fact, she found Logan increasingly interesting and attractive, which was confusing her and making her angry. She hadn't fully reckoned with just how scholarly and cultivated he was—or how attractive she found those qualities. Which irritated her even more. "You're obnoxious."

Logan burst out laughing. "Let's go on searching," he said, and put the book he had been leafing through back on its shelf.

For hours they searched a variety of halls, on the upper levels as well as the lower ones, but found nothing to eat. Finally, they decided to go back to the others and see whether they had been any luckier.

When they returned to the hall where they had left Emma, they found Liam on guard by the door. He had just come back. Amelia and Amos, too, had returned and were resting on a sofa. Emma was still in front of the terminal, exactly as they had left her.

"Any luck?" Liam asked.

Ava shook her head. "Nothing at all. You?"

Liam sighed. "I didn't find anything either," he said. He looked more somber than usual. Ava wondered whether it was because she and Logan had been together, alone. Deep down, she hoped this was so.

"You two?" she asked Amelia and Amos.

"Nothing. We didn't find a thing," Amelia said sadly.

"This isn't the place for finding food," Amos said mournfully.

"Liam? Do we keep going?" Ava asked, and the hunter simply nodded.

"Right, so we go on," she said. She glanced at Emma, who still seemed intently focused on the library's machines.

"I tried talking to her," Amelia said uneasily, "but she's not responding. You'd better have a look at her, Ava."

"This can't be good," said Ava, as she looked at Emma more closely. The girl's eyes were closed. Her fingers had stopped moving and there were no luminescent threads connecting her to the machines. She was no longer using her Power.

"Emma? Can you hear me?" Ava asked.

There was no reaction.

"It's like she's somewhere else," Amelia said.

"Yeah, I'll need to examine her. Liam, can you bring her to the couch?"

Liam began by gently pulling Emma's hands away from the terminal. Nothing happened. A moment later she slumped, unconscious. Liam picked her up in his arms and carried her over. Ava spent a few minutes checking her pulse, her breathing, the condition of her eyes and skin.

"How is she?" Amelia asked Ava.

"She seems okay. It's probably just overuse of her Power."

"She was connected to the machine for a long time. D'you think it might have affected her mind?" Amelia asked.

"We'll have to wait till she wakes up to find out. I'm going to make her a reinvigorating tisane of medicinal herbs. I'll need fire and a pot . . ."

"No problem about the fire," Logan said, and held up his lighter.

"We don't have any pots, but we might be able to use part of the guardian machine," Amos suggested. "It's metal."

"Let's get to it, then," said Logan. He fetched one of the more rickety chairs, pulled it apart for kindling, then used his Power. A moment later he had a fire going.

Amos wrenched off the guardian's head and battered it against the wall until the dome on top came loose. He soon had a rudimentary pot, which he handed to Ava.

"Nice bit of work," she said gratefully. She began to prepare the medicine. "We'll have to spend the night here," she told the group.

"Okay," Liam said. "I'll keep watch at the northern door."

"And me the southern one," Logan added at once.

Night arrived, adding to the already oppressive gloom of the library, Amos broke a couple more chairs and kept the fire going.

"She's so fragile," Amelia said, and stroked Emma's face.

Ava touched her cousin's arm. "Don't worry, she'll get better."

"Do you think so?"

"Yes, her pulse is strong, and so is her breathing."

"That's a relief."

"Go by the fire and try to rest a little. I'll take care of her."

The hours went by slowly, and Ava had trouble keeping her eyes open. She hadn't realized how tired she was. Unable to stop herself, she fell asleep beside Emma and fell back into her nightmare.

There came a strong surge of pain at the nape of her neck and down her spine, all the way to her toes. She cried out in her dream, but nobody could hear her. She was utterly alone. She saw herself floating face up in some viscous liquid. There was something in her mouth and on her head, but she could not puzzle out what it was. She was experiencing something unheard-of: She was looking at her body from the outside. Had she died? Was her spirit looking down on her body stretched out somewhere? Suddenly another jolt of pain shot through her, and she screamed in agony.

She woke up suddenly. Emma was sleeping placidly. Liam was on guard at one door, Logan at the other. Everything seemed quiet. She saw that Amelia had sat down beside Amos, very close to him, and watched in shock as they came together for a long, passionate kiss. She stared at them in open-mouthed wonder. In this accursed place, half-starved, with terrible enemies round every corner waiting to kill them, the two of them had found love.

She realized, too, that she was losing her greatest and only friend. They had been together ever since they had been able to walk. And though Ava knew she would never lose her completely, Amelia was drifting away from her a little. She sighed. Perhaps she was a little jealous. It was laughable.

To find love, you have to be looking for it, or at least be open to the possibility of finding it, and I've just turned down a suitor who's handsome, intelligent, and powerful. Maybe I should lower my defenses a little . . . No! I've got enough problems as it is without getting into a relationship. We've got to get out of here alive, with the Cure. Nothing else matters.

With the morning light coming in vividly through the dirty windows, Emma opened her eyes wide.

"What? Where?"

"Relax, you're with us," Ava said. She grasped the girl's arms to stop her from making any sudden move.

Amelia and Amos came over to them at once. Emma looked all around, and it looked as though she was beginning to recognize them.

"Yeah . . . the computer system . . ." she stammered.

"Are you all right?" Amelia asked.

She put her hands to her head. "I think I am . . . I have a terrible headache . . ."

"I can help you with that. I've been brewing you a tisane of healing herbs that'll take it away."

"Thanks . . ."

"Did you find out anything interesting in the machines?" Logan asked Emma.

"No . . . but I learned that my Power can kill me if I'm not careful. That goes for all of us."

CHAPTER 28

Once Emma had recovered, they left the library and continued north. The streets were deserted, but all the same they walked warily.

As they went along a wide street, keeping close to the walls on their left, Ava moved forward to join Emma. “What you can do with the machines is amazing,” she said.

Emma lowered her head. “Thank you.”

“My people don’t have machines. At least, not like those.”

Emma nodded. “It must seem a little overwhelming.”

“It’s a nightmare,” Ava said furiously. “Sometimes I feel as if I’m dreaming and can’t wake up.”

“I know what you mean.”

“What was your life like among your own people before you were chosen for this?”

Emma hesitated. “I . . . well . . .”

“Sorry. You don’t have to tell me if you don’t want to.”

“No . . . it’s nothing . . . my life was ordinary for a hacker. Among my people the Power isn’t highly developed in everyone, only in a few.”

"Ah, like among my people. You see? We have things in common."

"The reasons are different . . . your people don't use it much out of consideration for privacy, and a desire to do no harm. In our case . . . it's a lack of resources."

Ava looked at her blankly. "What resources?"

"The Ancient Ones' computer systems. We've only got a few terminals with access to the ones that still work, and so not everybody can use them. That's why there's a selection at the age of twelve. Those who show a range of aptitudes with the Power and are exceptionally good at interacting with the systems are given the rank of hackers, and can go on practicing and improving their Power. Unfortunately, the rest aren't given those opportunities, so their Power doesn't develop."

"Oh . . . I hadn't thought that you might only have a few machines. What about the others? What do they do with their time?"

"Many of them maintain the systems we have. We need to generate electricity and manufacture components that are very difficult to make. We put great care and emphasis on this. If we lose the systems, we won't be able to develop our Power. The rest of us occupy ourselves with the survival of the tribe: food, water, clothing, and other basic necessities. And then of course there are the warriors who make sure they're prepared to come here in search of the Cure. They train in the art of the katana"—she indicated her curved sword—"and unarmed combat."

"With skills like yours, you must be treated like a goddess among your people, right?"

"Envy is a strong enemy," Emma said suddenly.

Ava stared at her. "So it is," she agreed, but said nothing more. She let Emma go on speaking at her own pace, without forcing her.

"Not all our people look on us kindly. The warriors especially. They think we're wasting our time and resources on maintaining the machines and training hackers."

"Let me guess; they'd rather all the effort was focused on creating and maintaining warriors."

"Exactly. Our society is primarily warrior-centric. They prepare themselves for the day they'll be selected to come here, to the realm of Siaais, and get hold of the Cure."

"It sounds very familiar . . . we have warriors like Amos, too, who are dedicated to the same goal."

"Yes, but in our case, they're the ones who control our society. They don't feel that this Power Siaais has granted us is a priority for them. The Power is a secondary thing, something warriors might come to need as a support."

"I see . . ."

They turned a corner, and Liam gave the signal to halt. As they waited, they heard shots. Of two different kinds: some slower, others in volleys. Ava felt a chill. These were the Black Guards they had seen earlier. Fear began to clutch at her stomach, and Emma did not look much better. Crouching beside Ava, behind the rusted skeleton of what had once been a large vehicle, Emma's eyes showed the same fear. They waited until they were sure they were not in danger. At last Liam gave the signal, and they set off again.

Ava patted her on the back to encourage her. "I think you're amazing."

She smiled gratefully. "I'm good with the Power. I like it and I understand it. I've practiced a lot. Whenever I was allowed to."

"That's pretty obvious."

"But . . ."

"But?"

Ava wanted her to trust her, to tell her what was troubling

her. She liked the little hacker, and she wanted to be her friend.

"I don't know . . . whether I'll be good enough . . . when the moment of truth comes."

"You are. I'm telling you so."

"I'm not so sure . . ."

"You'll do it," Ava said, projecting confidence in her tone and her expression. She wanted Emma to believe in herself.

"Thank you. It's what I most want. Not to fail. To get hold of the Cure and save my people from that horrible end."

Their way took them by a long, desolate avenue, where they had to avoid piles of debris from a building whose façade had collapsed onto the road. They had already crossed more than half the city, which was a real achievement in Ava's eyes. When she glanced back, she was encouraged to see that Amelia had fallen back to walk beside Amos. They walked together whenever they could, sharing glances and smiles . . . which was extraordinary considering the situation they were in.

Suddenly, from around a corner, there appeared a person. They froze in their tracks.

A boy came toward them.

Liam activated his Power at once. Logan did the same, igniting his lighter in one fluid move. Amos moved in front of Amelia and Ava, covering them with his shield and strong body. Emma took a step back and drew her katana.

"Stop!" Liam called out.

But the boy carried on toward them. He was half-naked, with a kind of loincloth at his waist. He was carrying a short bow in his right hand, and was covered in paint and blood.

Without stopping to think, Liam used his Power. On the boy's right, a piece of metal which looked like an old post had fallen onto the road. Liam gestured, then moved his arm and hips in an abrupt swing and launched the post at the boy, who was already raising his bow in readiness to attack. There was a hollow sound. The metal post hit the boy on his side and knocked him over, so that he was left lying in the middle of the road.

Liam and Amos went to the corner to make sure no one else was coming, while Logan went over to the wounded boy.

"Looks pretty bad," he announced.

Ava hastened to get a look at him. The blow had left him stunned and breathless, but his injuries were not mortal. What was mortal, unfortunately, was a knife wound that had pierced his stomach. He was beyond help.

Amelia knelt beside him. "Tell me, where are you from?"

"From the great jungle . . . with the great river . . ."

Ava looked at him closely. His skin was reddish, and the paints were made out of a mixture of roots and flowers. He was neither very tall nor very strong.

Emma looked at the boy. "Judging by his features, and because he's from a jungle region with a great river . . . I'd place him somewhere in Amazonia, in South America."

"What happened to you?" Ava asked.

"Another tribe . . ." he stammered, and pointed at Emma, at her face and eyes.

Amelia was surprised. "Were they . . . like her?"

"Yes . . . three . . . firearms . . . and swords . . ."

Emma said nothing. She was looking thoughtful.

"Have you seen any more tribes?" Amelia asked.

"Yes . . . big group . . . and other smaller group . . ."

"What's that smaller group like?"

The boy tried to answer, but he began to cough blood.

"I don't want to die here!" he cried suddenly.

The dying boy looked at Ava, his eyes staring, full of terror and suffering. She recognized the feelings, had known them herself. She couldn't bear seeing the boy's anguish in the face of death. Something within her took pity on him. If she couldn't help him with her healing, then she would do it with her Power, even though the idea was hateful to her. She didn't want to use her Power, but neither did she want to let this poor wretch die in pain and fear among strangers, in a nightmare world.

She touched the upper Mark on her arm and activated her Power with a silver flash, then put her hands on his head and concentrated. As she had expected, she felt his despair. The boy's terror and pain flooded into her. The feelings were so strong, so intense, that for a moment she thought they'd consume her.

Ava shut her eyes, clenched her jaw, and made a great effort, seeking to modulate the boy's feelings, trying to reduce them and dominate them.

At the same time, she felt something on her upper Mark. She did not know what it was, but something had happened to her Power.

She breathed deeply through her nose, exhaled through her mouth, and calmed down: a little at first, then completely. With enormous effort she concentrated on sending that feeling of calm, of peace, back to the boy. Gradually his expression changed. His eyes lost their fear. Ava continued her efforts to ease his suffering. The boy sighed, his face showing absolute calm and inner peace. He breathed out and died in her arms.

"Poor thing . . ." Amelia said. Her eyes were moist. "You did that very well."

"Thanks. I may not like to use my Power, but my control felt less unsure that time."

"That makes me happy."

"Did you notice the flashes on my Mark?"

"Yeah, that's something new."

"D'you know what they could be?"

"No. It never happened back in the tribe. Only one flash when you activated your Power, maybe one more in difficult situations, but I've never seen three in a row like that."

"Me neither . . ."

Logan searched the body, but found nothing useful. "He wasn't even carrying food or water," he reported.

Liam came over with Amos. "Better keep going in case whoever stabbed him comes to finish him off," he said, and pointed north.

They set off, leaving the dead boy behind, and Ava wondered what was happening to her. She was at once mournful and at peace. There was so much death and pain in this accursed place, but her small act of compassion had felt like an act of resistance. She was sure that if Siaais was watching—and she was sure he was—he would not have liked her helping a rival, which made her feel even better.

She went over to her cousin and took her hand.

"If my time comes, promise me you'll Feel me. Don't let me die afraid."

"Don't say such things," Amelia said, shaking her head. "You're going to live. I'm sure of that."

"Promise me."

Amelia sighed. "I promise."

"I love you, cousin."

"And I love you, too, a lot."

They stopped and held each other in their arms, and Ava savored the moment. Then they went on walking down a narrow, ghostly street, and unease crept back into her soul.

CHAPTER 29

Night was getting close, and with it the need for shelter. Liam had gone to explore the area ahead, so they hid themselves as best they could and anxiously awaited his return.

He returned at a trot, with night following at his heels. "I've found a building on a corner that looks like a good place to spend the night," he told them.

"Lead the way," said Ava.

Ava was grateful for the rest. Crossing the huge city on empty stomachs was turning out to be a harder task than they had initially thought.

"Anything new?" Ava asked Liam as they pitched camp inside the house.

"We'll finish crossing the city tomorrow."

Nobody reacted. Hunger was wreaking havoc on their bodies, and their water was soon going to run out. The food shop Emma had suggested looking for was nowhere to be found.

They all made themselves as comfortable as they could for the night. Nobody felt very talkative, except Amelia, who could always find something to talk about.

"What d'you think caused the Apocalypse?" she suddenly asked aloud, and they all looked at her in surprise.

Logan turned to face her from where he was stretched out in a corner. "That's a curious question."

Ava guessed that this had not been asked simply out of curiosity, but to give them all something to talk about so that they could stop thinking about how hungry they all were.

"There are different theories," Logan went on. "Among my people, these are the two main ones: Some think it was war between the large, powerful nations. Others think it was a great plague that decimated most of the population. I don't know . . ." He gave another shrug.

Ava decided to join in the conversation, if only to forget her rumbling stomach for a moment. "Our people believe that as punishment for causing the Apocalypse, the God Siaais brought the Curse upon us. There's no theory about what caused the Apocalypse, except that it was the fault of men, of the Ancient Ones. My belief is that Siaais himself unleashed the plague that finished off humanity, then blamed us men. I think the Curse is nothing more than the consequence of the original plague Siaais used to put an end to humans." She crossed her arms.

"Ava!" Amelia gave her a look of fear, then pointed to the sky.

"It's what I believe. I don't care if he hears it."

"Liam?" Amelia prompted, to stop Ava from going on with her hostile opinions about the God.

"Among my people there are several different theories as well," Liam said. "One involves a natural catastrophe, an enormous meteorite which crashed into the Earth and killed most of the population, leaving only a few areas where humans could survive. Another theory talks about weapons of mass destruction, which either were used during a world war or went off by accident. And finally, a plague like those you've already mentioned. Those are the main ones. There are other, stranger ideas, such as a hostile invasion by beings from some other planet." Liam shrugged. "We don't claim to know which of those theories is right. It might have been any of them. Or none of them."

"What about your people, Emma?" Amelia asked. "What do they believe?"

Emma sighed. "My people decided it was because of a war between world powers with weapons of mass destruction, chemical weapons to be precise. They killed billions of people and, as a consequence of this, we were left with the illness we all now suffer from."

"That sounds very much like my theory," Ava said, "except that it's not humans who are to blame but the God."

"In my culture Siaais is seen as a merciful God, because he gives us a chance to get hold of the Cure every year," Emma said.

Ava threw up her arms. "Are you joking?"

"No . . . in our culture it's humanity who is to blame for the Apocalypse. Siaais gives us a chance . . ."

Ava turned to the others questioningly. "Do any of you believe this about Siaais?"

Logan threw his head back. "My people view Siaais as a warrior God. He's not a God of peace. He's a God of War and Death. This place is proof of that."

Liam nodded. "My people accept the mandates of Siaais as an omnipotent being who deals out his justice. They fear him. And judging by what we're finding out, they're right to fear him. But there is a group that questions his behavior, and his origin. They do it in secret, trying to work out where he came from, and why. They call themselves the Seekers of Truth."

"I like this group," Ava said. "I'd love to join them."

Liam smiled. "Be careful what you wish for. I've heard several of its members have been burned by the Eye of Siaais."

"See?" Amelia said reproachfully to Ava. "It's what I always tell you!"

Ava's determined expression made it clear that she would go on with her convictions.

"What about you?" Logan asked Amelia. "What do you think caused the Apocalypse?"

"I think . . ." It was hard for her to speak, as though she were unsure. "I think there are other possibilities. It could have been a great volcanic eruption, a gigantic tsunami, or some other natural disaster . . ."

There was a silence as they each considered the possibilities.

"It could be . . . that Mother Nature got tired of her bad treatment at the hands of Man," said Logan.

"Still," Amelia said, "I think the most common theory, the one we've all mentioned, is that of an illness, from one cause or another."

Ava looked out the window and saw the eye of Siaais projected on the moon in the sky. She was sure it was watching them with a deadly stare.

"One day we'll manage to get rid of you," she whispered.

She saw Amos keeping watch at the other window, alert to the night sounds and to any movement outside that might mean danger.

"Go and get some rest, it's my turn to watch," he told her, and winked.

Ava nodded and went to lie down between Liam and Logan, who had each curled up in a corner. Emma and Amelia were together, and seemed to be asleep. She managed to get reasonably comfortable, and although the place was full of dust and dirt, the fact was that she no longer cared, she had gotten used to it. They were all very dirty, and as they could not spare any drinking water, they were not washing. She would have given anything to be at the oasis near her home and to bathe in its clear water. But home was a long way from here.

Ava became aware of movement. It was Amelia, who was getting up and silently making her way to Amos.

Amos smiled. "Why aren't you resting?"

"I can't . . . my stomach won't let me . . ."

"You're hungry. Don't worry. Eventually it'll pass, and then exhaustion'll let you sleep."

"D'you mind if I stay here with you until I do?"

"I don't mind." He made room for her by his side so that she could get comfortable.

Amelia gave him a grateful smile, and he smiled back at her tenderly. Then he turned back to the window to go on with his watch. This tender scene gave Ava a feeling of well-being, of warmth.

"D'you think we'll make it?" Amelia asked Amos.

He turned to look into her eyes. "We'll make it. Never doubt that."

"You're not just saying it to make me feel better?"

"You heard Liam: we're almost out of this forsaken place . . . and besides, he told me he found out something interesting."

"Food?"

"No, not that. He spotted a new gate a little further north, just like the two we've already crossed. That's where the Indicator's directing us."

"Another gate?"

"It must be the third test. If we cross it we'll have survived two, and we'll only have this last one before we get to the Cure."

"But we don't know what's waiting for us on the other

side . . . or rather we do: danger, suffering, and death, the same things we've faced since we started this journey."

"Probably . . ."

"No, it'll be worse, because we're getting near our goal. Siaais will send us new obstacles, he'll use any means he can to keep us from reaching the Cure." Amelia heaved a deep sigh. "But I feel protected, safe, being with you . . ."

Amos dipped his head shyly. "I'm glad," he said. "I won't let anything happen to you."

"Don't hide that handsome face," Amelia said gently, and raised his chin lovingly.

"Handsome? Me? Not that, for sure."

"Don't pretend. D'you think I didn't see you in the square when you were practicing with the valiants, and how the girls looked at you?"

Amos raised his eyebrows in surprise. "They weren't looking at me, it would have been Isop or Oscus, who were always with me. They were the ones for the girls."

"Not for all the girls, not for me."

Amos, left with no idea what to say, stared at the ground again. Amelia smiled at him and stroked his muscular arm. He met her eyes again, his gaze was intense.

"No matter what happens, I'll stay with you until the end."

Amelia looked into his eyes and came closer to him until their bodies touched.

"What do you feel for me?" she asked softly.

"I . . . I love you . . ."

They kissed passionately, and still Ava didn't look away. They held each other in defiance of hunger, danger, and the dark of night, two young souls who had come together at the worst of times and gave each other hope for something more than mere survival. While the others slept, Amelia and Amos joined themselves, body and soul, in a moment that would unite them forever.

Ava smiled, and with a pleasant feeling in her heart, fell asleep.

That night she had no nightmares.

CHAPTER 30

Ava woke a little before dawn and, for once, she felt rested. The others were asleep, except for Liam, who was on watch duty by one of the windows, scanning the street with his intense gaze.

She stood up noiselessly and went over to him.

"Beautiful," said Liam, who had already heard her approaching.

Surprised, Ava blushed. "Beautiful . . . ?"

"The night," he said, pointing at the sky beyond the dirty windowpanes.

"Yes, it is." She felt a little ashamed of having thought that he meant her.

"The stars have always stopped me sleeping," he admitted.

"Really? Why's that?"

"I've always wondered whether somebody would reach them one day."

"I've never thought it possible," Ava said, shaking her head. "But Emma told me that the Ancient Ones had technology so incredible and advanced they were able to go to the moon, and much further, to other distant worlds. She mentioned Mars, and even Jupiter and Saturn."

"Those planets are a long way from the Earth. It seems unbelievable to me that the Ancient Ones could have done it, quite honestly."

"I sometimes wonder whether to believe everything Emma tells us."

"If she tells us, it's because she believes it. She's either read about it or seen it in the information systems she's been able to access."

"Yes, I know. I don't doubt her, it's just that I wonder whether it's another of Siaais's evil games to confuse us."

"Do you think he puts false information in the world?"

Ava shrugged. "Why not? For him it's all a game. Don't you get the feeling he's playing with our minds?"

"Yeah . . . I sometimes have that feeling . . . as if what's around us wasn't completely real . . ."

"That's it. This world was created by Siaais, and he's put us in it so he can toy with us."

"I'm not saying you're not right, but I want to believe that Emma isn't mistaken and that the Ancient Ones really did go to Mars and beyond. I'd have liked to experience those planets."

"Let's make a deal," Ava said.

"I'm listening."

"If we get out of here alive, let's search for the Ancient Ones' technology and go to the moon. And even further, if we can."

Liam smiled. "I think that's a fantastic idea."

Ava laughed. "We have a deal," she said, and when she offered him her hand, he took it.

For a long moment, they both stared thoughtfully up the stars in the clear sky. Then Ava asked: "Suppose we find some unknown being on one of those distant planets?"

"You mean an alien? Well, in that case we'd have to make friends with that being."

"With our luck, he'd probably want to kill and eat us."

"Yeah, probably."

"What d'you bet he'd not only want to kill us, but to get rid of the whole human race? You just wait and see."

"That could happen too. But let's hope he's peaceful and intelligent, a lot more advanced than us, and willing to help us prosper and build a better future."

Ava looked into his eyes. "You're an optimistic dreamer. I think it's more likely that this being would capture us, find out how to get to Earth from our minds, then come here and invade us."

Liam shook his head. "Let's . . . hope for a better outcome."

Ava was about to say something else, but let it pass. She didn't want to go on with her pessimism. She concentrated on the idea of spending plenty of time beside Liam on a long journey to another planet. Just the thought of it was enough to lift her spirits.

One by one the rest of the group woke up. By now they were used to rising before the first rays of light reached them. As he had come to do, Liam went out to scout ahead while dawn was still some way off. The rest of the group went outside, meanwhile, to breathe fresher air, since inside the building it smelled rank, of damp mingled with dirt. Everything was quiet, and the sun had not yet risen. Nobody spoke, for fear of attracting some unsuspected danger. Amos kept watch from the crossroads at the end of the street. The others sat down on the sidewalk to wait.

Suddenly Ava saw a shadow moving in the gloom down the street to the south. It would not be long before the sun rose, but for the moment they were still shrouded in darkness. She tried to catch a better glimpse of this dark shape, which seemed to be moving in their direction. The hair on the nape of her neck stood on end, which was a very bad sign.

"There's something, or someone, coming this way," she told her partners unsurely, and assumed a defensive stance with the javelin and shield at the ready.

Logan got to his feet and came to her side. Amelia, too, got up and took up her weapons. Emma's katana was already in her hand.

Logan squinted in the direction Ava was watching, searching for the threat. "Are you sure you saw something?"

"Pretty sure."

He turned to Emma and Amelia. "Can you see anything?"

They both shook their heads. Ava's gaze scanned the deep shadows around her, but she could make out nothing in the pre-dawn gloom.

"Can't you create some light?" she asked Logan.

With a swift movement he brought out his lighter, but it refused to catch.

"What the—"

Suddenly, in front of Logan, there appeared a face. It was completely black. Two white eyes without pupils stared back at him, and the creature gave a shrill scream that pierced his eardrums.

"For heaven's sake!" Logan cried as he leaped backward. He was so startled that his lighter fell to the ground.

"A Corrupted One!" Emma cried out. Logan took two quick steps back, his eyes wide with fear. He tripped and fell on his backside.

The creature took a step forward as the first rays of dawn touched its blackened skin, revealing it to Ava as a Transformed One. Its skin was shining black, and hairless. Its eyes were enormous, their irises white in a sharp face where in place of nose and ears there were only long, dark holes. Its mouth opened wide, lipless and toothless, as though it were trying to scream, Instead, a black mist began to issue from its mouth.

"It's Siaais's poison!" Ava shrieked.

"Don't let it touch you!" Emma yelled.

"Move, Logan!" Ava urged him.

Logan started to crawl backward, then got onto all fours and moved as fast as he could.

The creature took two steps forward, tracking Logan as the toxic mist continued to direct its contagious mist at Logan. It was starting to look as if there was no way he could avoid being engulfed by it.

Suddenly a silver flash caught a beam of sunlight for the briefest moment, followed by the sound of a sharp blow. The creature's head fell to the ground. A moment later, before the shocked eyes of Amelia, Ava, and Logan, its body did the same.

When Ava looked up, she saw Emma holding her katana with both hands, its blade stained black.

Instantly they all moved back from the creature and saw that the feared black mist which was still issuing from its mouth was beginning to fade, until it had disappeared completely.

"I don't think there's any more danger," Amelia said as she stared at the lifeless body.

"Are you sure?" asked Logan.

"We'd better keep away from that thing," Emma said. Its viscous black blood was dripping from the blade now.

Logan got to his feet and shook the dust off his coat, then bent to retrieve his lighter. He picked it up without realizing how close it was to the creature's severed head and immediately took a couple of paces back. He activated his Power, and this time the lighter produced the spark he needed and burst into flame.

"So now you're working? Why not before?" he snapped

at the lighter in annoyance and used the fireball he'd created to incinerate the remains of the Transformed One. When the flames went out, there was nothing left of the being except a pile of black ashes.

"D'you think it was one of us?" Ava asked her partners thoughtfully. "One of those who came here, I mean, from some tribe?"

"Probably," Logan said.

"I think so too," said Emma. "It was one of those others who ran out of time."

"Well," Logan said, "this one got what we keep for those who are transformed."

Amelia looked at him in horror. "You're not so barbarous as to burn them alive?"

"It's the safest way to avoid infection."

"You mean you kill them when they're transformed?" Ava asked in surprise.

Logan nodded. "It's either them or us. You know that very well. One of them can infect all of us. My people decided over a hundred years ago that anybody who was transformed would be sacrificed for the good of the others who were still alive."

"But that's inhuman," Amelia objected. "They're alive too. They're human beings too."

"They might be alive, but they certainly aren't human beings."

Ava turned to Emma. "And you?"

Emma sighed. "We cut off their heads the moment they're transformed. It's a safe way of stopping the infection. It's quick, and the vapor of death is extinguished."

"Horrible!" Amelia cried. She put her hands to her eyes to stop the tears. "Suppose one day we find the Cure? And suppose one day we can go back and cure everyone?" she snapped accusingly.

"If that day comes," Logan said, "we'll all celebrate, because we won't have to kill again."

"And all those you've killed?"

"They're the price that had to be paid for the survival of the rest."

It took Ava a while to calm Amelia, but once she did, she left her with Emma while Ava pulled Logan aside.

Logan spoke first, "Your people don't kill them, do they?" the Elementalist whispered. "That's why Amelia's so upset."

Ava shook her head. "We lock them up in an underground chamber, in the hope that someday we'll find the Cure and be able to restore them to their human state."

"You know that's a fantasy, don't you? The Cure might prevent new infections, but it certainly won't be able to undo the damage the illness has caused in those who've already been infected."

Ava sighed. "My rational mind tells me you're right, and yet—maybe because of all the time I've spent with my cousin—my heart wants to believe that in the end the Cure will heal those wretches who may have been transformed, but haven't yet perished. Call me a dreamer, but I'd like to think it's so."

Emma heard her and smiled. Her expression suggested that it was a pleasant dream, but her eyes said that when all was said and done, it was nothing but that: a dream.

CHAPTER 31

When Amos returned and saw the pile of ashes, he gave Ava a questioning look.

"A Transformed One," she told him.

Amos frowned. "Here too?"

"We think it might be one of the Chosen of another tribe," Amelia said.

"We're running out of time."

"I'm afraid we are."

"As if we didn't have enough problems already," Logan said dryly. "This adds an extra note of excitement to the situation."

At that moment Liam returned as well. They told him what had happened with the infected person.

"We'd better get going, then," he said.

"Yes," Ava said. "Have you picked up any danger?"

Liam shook his head. "The way north seems to be clear. I saw another gate of Siaais."

"At least that'll get us out of this place," said Ava.

Liam shrugged. "I don't know about that . . ."

"If it's the third gate, it'll lead us to the third test of courage,"

Amelia pointed out. "And we'd better be prepared for new dangers. However hard it's been for us so far, the last part is likely to be the worst of all."

"Everyone stay alert," said Liam.

Amos gave him a nod. "Lead the way."

It did not take them long to lose themselves among the tall buildings of concrete and steel. Liam chose clear streets where there was good visibility to avoid being caught by surprise.

Around midday they stopped to rest in a circular plaza with a huge fountain in the center. There wasn't a trace of water in it.

"I can't believe he's even dried up the fountains," Ava complained.

"He's making it very difficult for us," Amos agreed.

"He does it on purpose. It's just a macabre game for him."

Amelia and Emma sat down by the fountain, and Logan came over to inspect it. "There's no water," Liam pointed out to him.

"Hmm," Logan said. "I've just thought of something. I don't think it'll work, but on the other hand there's nothing to be lost by trying one of my crazy ideas."

"Go ahead."

Ava was immediately interested, and went to see what Logan was going to do. Amos joined her.

The Elementalist climbed into the great fountain and went to the pipe from which water was supposed to emerge, looked at it for a moment, and scratched his head thoughtfully. Logan activated his Mark of Siaais. He placed both hands on the dry pipe, closed his eyes, and concentrated.

"What's he doing?" Amos whispered to Ava.

She shrugged. "I've no idea."

Logan began to move his hands upward as though he were tugging at the pipe to dislodge it from the floor, except that he was doing so with his Power. A few pearls of perspiration appeared on his forehead from the effort he was making. Suddenly there came a strange sound, part metallic, part earthy. It was followed by a slight tremor which was perceptible across the whole plaza. They all stood up and watched him uneasily.

A new noise, louder than the previous one, came from under the fountain, followed by a stronger tremor. Logan nearly fell to the floor, but went on with his eyes closed, concentrating deeply.

Suddenly there came the sound of a small, muffled explosion, and he was thrown backward out of the fountain. From the spout issued a huge jet of water, which rose more than fifteen feet into the air.

"Water!" Amelia cried as the jet fell on them like rain.

"He found water!" Ava shouted delightedly.

Amos went over to help him to his feet, while Liam tried the water.

"It's fresh," he announced. "I don't know if it'll be drinkable, though. We'd better boil it."

Amelia clapped her hands enthusiastically. "Well then, let's do it."

Logan got to his feet and shook his coat.

"How did you do that?" Amos asked.

"My Power manipulates the four elements. It occurred to me that if there was a well under the fountain, or something like that with water in it, then my Power might be able to reach it and get it to come up to the surface. And what do you know, I was right!"

They boiled water on the spot, using Logan's Power once again. They worked fast and as a team, because they had no idea how much water there was under the fountain or how much time they had left before it ran out.

Afterward they sat down, feeling refreshed and much more cheerful. Finding water had bought them a few days more.

Ava sat down by Logan, beside the fountain. "Can I ask you something?"

"Of course, how could I refuse?" The ghost of a flirtatious smile appeared on his face. "Is it about the water?"

"No . . . it's about the Transformed One. What happened to you?"

Logan's expression turned serious. Ava thought she saw fear in his eyes. "He nearly infected me."

For the first time, Ava saw that his usual arrogance and self-confidence were gone.

"Why didn't you incinerate him with your Power straight away?"

"That's what I was trying to do, believe me, but the lighter failed. The flame didn't take, and I don't know why. Now it seems to be working properly again." With a quick movement of his hand he clicked it open and lit it, then showed it to her to prove he was not lying.

"I believe you. What worries me is that you almost died because of that lighter."

He smiled sourly. "It worries me, too . . . a lot . . ."

"I know. I didn't mean—"

"To use my Power, I rely on my elements." He showed her his belt with its containers under his coat.

"What do you carry in that belt?" she asked, intrigued.

"The lighter for fire, a little bag of earth, a small bottle of water, and a small bellows." He pointed them out to her one by one.

"Do you mind?"

"Not at all, but don't break them, or else I'll be in serious trouble. I don't think I'd be able to find substitutes for them here."

Ava picked them out one by one and studied them carefully, then gave them back to Logan, who stowed them away in his belt. "I'm at the mercy of the elements," he said. "I live and die by them." Once again, he lacked his usual bravado.

"What's the matter?" Ava asked him, a little concerned.

"I'd rather not talk about it . . ."

She put her hand on his arm. "Come on, you know you can trust me."

Logan looked up at the sky, then at her, and breathed out heavily. "My greatest wish, my greatest aspiration is to be able to use my Power without the physical presence of the elements." He bowed his head.

"Has anybody among your people done it before?"

He shook his head and sighed. "Nobody's ever done it. We don't even know whether it's possible. The scholars say no, that our Power manipulates the elements, but isn't capable of creating them. I like to think it's possible, it's just that we haven't found the formula yet. I try every day and I fail every day. But I'm not going to give up. One day I'll manage it. I know I will. I've dreamt it."

Ava smiled. "If anybody can do it, it'll be you."

"Thank you," he said, and bowed his head.

"How's that cough doing?"

"Fine. Your care has cured it."

"You need to be careful with illnesses."

"Why d'you say that?"

"Because even though you're so powerful, your body, your health, is fragile."

He shrugged. "Yes . . . my health has never been good. I get sick easily."

"That's because your body finds it hard to fight off illnesses."

"You're a healer, you know these things. What can I do?"

"People are different in many ways. The human body, its health, is still a great mystery to my people, but I have a few answers. In your case, you need to be very careful not to fall sick. Changes of weather, rain, cold: You need to be careful to avoid them. And above all, stay away from sick people. Your body may not be capable of fighting off illnesses from outside."

"Would you rather I hid underground and avoided human contact altogether?"

"No. I'm just telling you that's what would be best for you."

"I prefer human contact, contact with you."

Ava blushed and shook her head. "You're hopeless. Put a scarf over your mouth. That'll help to stop you falling ill."

"But then you won't be able to see my handsome face, my irresistible smile."

"That's a bonus," she teased, and moved away, leaving Logan with his retort unspoken.

CHAPTER 32

Their spirits were much higher when they set off again. Finding water had raised their morale considerably.

Unfortunately danger had not gone away. Once again they heard shots from nearby, so they had to hide in what seemed to be an ancient church. Liam and Amos forced a window and sneaked inside, and the others followed. They stayed quiet, crouching inside the building, hoping to avoid fighting any other groups.

After some time in hiding, and since for the moment they did not seem to be in any danger, Amelia began to inspect the whole interior of the church. It was a subject that fascinated her: ancient religions, those of both the Archaic Ones and the Ancient Ones.

Ava looked around for Liam and found him on watch duty at a window with part of its glass broken. He was sitting on the floor, looking out through the window from time to time.

She sat down beside him.

"You're very quiet. Is everything all right?"

"Yeah, everything's fine. You know I'm not much of a talker."

She smiled. "You do talk when you want to, at least to me."

Liam nodded. "Yeah, some of the group are very talkative." He glanced at Logan.

Ava caught the acid tone in his voice. "Don't you like Logan?"

"It's not that. I just don't trust him too much."

"And do you trust me?"

"You enjoy making my life impossible, which inspires a certain trust in me." The smile he turned on her was a sincere one.

Ava nodded. "That's true. Sorry. I didn't trust you at first . . ."

"And now?"

"Considering what we've been through . . . yeah, now I do."

Liam relaxed a little. He let his shoulders droop and made himself more comfortable. "If I'm honest, I'd rather be hunting in the forests of my own land than in this maze."

"And I'd rather be in my favorite oasis, gathering plants."

"I understand you perfectly. D'you miss your home very much?" he asked, sounding genuinely interested.

"Well, quite honestly, even though I'm reluctant to admit it, yes, I do. It's not much, just a hut with adobe walls, two rooms, no luxuries. But I've always felt safe there. I used to believe I was safe from the Eye of Siaais. I always imagined that he couldn't see me there, that he couldn't control my destiny. I can't bear the idea of that evil God watching and controlling us all the time."

"Is that what you think he does?"

"Don't you?"

Liam moved his head in a gesture of doubt. "Most of my people think our God is omnipotent and omnipresent. On the other hand there are others who don't think that, or at least not so much. He controls us, it's true, but he isn't everywhere at every moment."

"Which group of thought do you belong to?"

"You like to know everything, eh?"

"About you, yes," she said with a playful smile.

"Because you don't entirely trust me and you want to know what I'm hiding?"

"That's right," she said, although it was not true. She wanted to know so that she could get to know him better, to know what he thought, because he interested her.

"I'm with the second group. I think he watches us, but not every moment."

Ava was thoughtful. Thinking about Siaais gave her the shivers.

"Are you all right?" he asked with concern.

"It's nothing. I always get angry and rather sad when I think of the fate we have to endure. D'you think we'll survive this? That we'll get hold of the Cure?"

Liam shrugged, then sighed deeply. "I have to believe we will."

"You don't sound very convinced."

"My heart tells me to keep going, that while there's life there's hope."

"And what does your head tell you?"

"That the odds are against us."

"Because of the other tribes? Because of that Sven, who's the leader of the big group?"

Liam was silent at the name, and there was pain in his eyes. "Partly, but mostly because of all the obstacles Siaais is putting in our way. They worry me more."

"I see. And suppose we meet the big group, Sven's?"

"Then I'll kill him."

Ava looked at him in surprise. There was pain and rage in his eyes. Liam was always calm, it was impossible to make him angry, and yet at that moment he was furious.

"What happened? How did your two comrades die?" she asked. Her voice was gentle, sympathetic.

"Sven is very dangerous," Liam said suddenly in a tone heavy with frustration.

"What's his Power? It would be handy to know it. We might find some way of countering it and defeating him."

He shook his head. "The problem is that I don't know," he said sadly.

"You don't know? Didn't you fight him?"

Liam shook his head, and his face revealed the sense of failure he was feeling. "I was hunting," he said bitterly. "I didn't see what happened. I heard the shots of two muskets in the distance. I ran there as fast as I could . . . and I found . . ."

"Don't worry, take your time."

"I found Mike dead at the camp. He'd been hacked to pieces with an axe."

"Oh my goodness. I'm so sorry . . ."

"They'd tied Pete to a tree. He was wounded and bleeding. They were having fun with him. The three Nordic ones, in their bear cloaks, with their axes in their hands, were mocking him. *Hack him to pieces, Sven*, one of them was saying. *Let's have some throwing practice*, said the other. Sven, the leader, was laughing with them. He hit Pete with the butt of his axe and broke his nose."

"Cowards!"

"There were people from at least three other tribes with them. The leader of one of them, a big, muscular man, with skin as dark as night, asked him to stop wasting time. *Shut up, Ashib, if you travel with me you do as I say*, Sven said to him. There was a moment of tension between the three Nordics and the three Black men, who I guess must have been from somewhere in Africa. Now that I think about it, it's strange . . ."

"What is?"

"The Africans were as big and strong as the Nordics, if not more so."

"So?"

"They weren't armed."

"Yeah, that's weird . . . unless they're like Logan . . ."

Liam stared at her, his eyes very wide. "Yeah, that might be it. That their Power's so strong it doesn't need weapons."

"Well, that would make our very limited odds even more so," said Ava.

"Yeah . . . it would." Liam looked worried. Ava didn't want to ask him to go on, so she decided to wait.

At last he gave a deep, prolonged snort. "They decided to play at throwing axes at Pete's head. To come as close to it as possible. The first one who threw came so close that Pete had to shrink away as far as he could, but he was tied up and could barely move his head a couple of inches. The second one buried itself in the tree, but sheared off part of his scalp."

"Oh, how horrible!" Ava put her hands over her face.

"Amid roars of laughter, it came to the turn of the leader, Sven. I was in position by now. I charged my weapon and aimed. Blood was running into Pete's eyes, I don't think he saw me. The leader raised his hand to throw, and I shot."

"What happened?"

"The shot got him in the head, he should have died at once. But it didn't even wound him."

"Are you sure you hit him?"

"Yeah. He put his hand to his head, so he must have felt the hit. He turned and gave the alarm. His two men came after me."

"Did you get away?"

He shook his head. "I tried to save Pete. I used my Power against the first one who was running at me swinging his war axe. But it didn't work."

"What do you mean?"

"My Power didn't work. The warrior reached me and tried

to split me in two with his axe. I dodged the blow and brought him down with the butt of my musket. I tried to use my Power against the other one as he came for me, but I failed at that too. At that moment I realized something was going very wrong. I saw Sven was sending more men against me, and I had to get out of there fast. The last thing I heard was Pete's death cry as Sven killed him."

Ava stroked his arm. "That's horrible. I'm so sorry."

"They were good men, devoted warriors."

"How come neither your weapon nor your Power had any effect on the Nordics?"

"I've no idea, it just doesn't make any sense to me."

"We've got to avoid them at all costs."

"We'll do our best, but the moment will come when it'll be unavoidable."

"Why d'you say that?"

"We're all following the same route, toward the same goal. It's inevitable that we're going to meet . . ."

Ava felt a great void in her stomach. The few hopes she had were rapidly vanishing with every day that went by in that accursed place. They were never going to get out of there alive, and she was beginning to see that more and more clearly.

Liam noticed how upset she was and took her hand. "We'll survive," he told her with determination in his eyes.

"Thanks . . . for the encouragement, for the support."

"You're welcome."

Ava felt good in Liam's company. More than that, she felt happy. A pleasant warmth rose from her chest, and a feeling that was simultaneously exciting and good fluttered in her stomach.

CHAPTER 33

After another long trek through the city, they finally reached a bridge, at the end of which awaited the great metal arch of the next gate.

Crossing the bridge would not be an easy business. It was in far worse condition than the one they had crossed to enter the city. The lanes were damaged, with massive sections collapsed, creating enormous holes and cracks high above a canyon. The remains of many vehicles were not going to make their passage any easier.

They went very slowly, careful where they put their feet. Liam kept his eyes glued to the road, carefully navigating the junkyard maze while being careful to avoid leading the group onto a section that looked too unstable.

When they reached the middle of the bridge, Liam signaled them to stop, stay low, and take cover. The group hid behind the remains of a number of vehicles and the concrete barrier that split the road into two sections.

Liam readied his bow, and the others armed themselves. Ava craned her neck to see what was happening.

And then she saw them.

A dozen dead bodies lay scattered amid the rubble of the road a little further ahead. Judging from their clothes, they seemed to belong to different tribes. They had died recently, because the blood they lay in hadn't dried yet. Reaching the gate was going to be even more difficult than they had expected.

Liam pointed east, and Ava followed his finger. Beyond the corpses, behind the remains of several vehicles, she could make out half a dozen people. All she could see were their heads and shoulders. They were lying in wait.

Liam drew back. "We're in serious trouble. There's a group waiting for us to move forward so that they can ambush us."

"Who are they?" Logan asked. "D'you know them?"

"Sven's group, the Nordics and Africans."

"How many are there?" Amos asked.

"Six. Three from each tribe."

"What are we going to do?" Emma asked. "We can't just stay here. Time's running out."

Suddenly they heard a hoarse but powerful voice. "Hey! You! We want to talk with your leader."

Ava swallowed.

"What do we do?" Amelia asked nervously.

Logan tilted his head to one side. "Let's see what they want."

Ava let out a long breath. "All right. I'll talk to them."

"Be very careful," Liam said. "Stay low. Don't give them an opportunity to hurt you."

Ava took up a position that allowed her to see the other group through a window of the vehicle, but she kept her body well-hidden so that no shot or arrow could reach her.

"What do you want?" she asked at the top of her voice, doing her best not to sound intimidated.

"My name's Sven," the hoarse voice said. There was authority in it, as if his mere name ought to be respected.

Ava craned her neck to see him better. He was just as Liam had described him. He oozed danger.

"What do you want?" she repeated, keeping her tone as harsh as she could, although she found it hard to do so.

"This is the end of the journey as far as you're concerned."

"We're going to cross that gate, and neither you nor anybody else is going to stop us," Ava replied with a vigor whose source she could not have explained.

Sven gave a loud, disdainful guffaw. "If you try to reach the gate, you're in for the same treatment as those wretches lying on the road. At least they won't turn into infected ones. I think we did them a favor."

"Some favor."

"You must know we're all running out of time. They'd have ended up being transformed. So we helped them. That's what good people we are," he added in a voice full of irony and malice.

"There's no need for bloodshed," Ava said. "We're all here searching for the same thing. We can work together and help one another."

The Nordic laughed. "No way, little one. The advantage is ours. The Cure's going to be for us. Nobody else is going to get it. I'm not thinking of sharing it. We'll be the first and only ones to cross the gate. You only have two choices: Turn back now, or die."

Ava turned to Liam. "They're not going to let us through," she whispered.

"I was expecting that."

Ava turned to the rest of her comrades, who were watching from their hiding places. "So what are we going to do?" she asked in a whisper.

Logan spread his hands wide. "I hate to say it, but Sven is right: Either we retreat, or we fight."

“There’s nothing I’d like better than to tear Sven’s head off for what he did to my partners,” Liam admitted, “but I don’t think confronting them here is a good idea. ”

“I’m not afraid of them,” Logan said, and his eyes showed that he meant it.

“Nor I,” Amos added.

Ava sighed. “It’s not about being afraid, it’s about the fact that if we fight them, some of us will probably die. I’m not ready to risk that. Liam is right. Fighting them on this bridge is a bad idea.”

“We should withdraw before they decide to attack.”

Slowly, they began to retreat without losing sight of the enemy group. Sven began to laugh in great disdainful guffaws. Luckily Sven and his group did not move. It seemed strange to Ava that they were not pursuing them.

Then a group of figures appeared at the entrance to the bridge.

“Oh no,” Liam muttered.

They all stopped. Ava felt the blood freezing in her veins.

Siaais was sending his sinister Black Guards.

CHAPTER 34

"Everybody take cover!" Liam shouted.

The six Black Guards formed themselves into a line at the entrance to the bridge. For a moment they stayed still, as though they were waiting for something.

"We're in a tight spot," Amos said. He kept turning his head to keep track of the guards on one side of the bridge and Sven's group on the other.

"Once again, we have two options," said Logan. "Either we attack the guard or Sven's group. But we're going to have to do one or the other if we want to get out of here alive."

Ava looked at Liam, whose eyes showed deep worry. "I don't agree," he said. "The best option is not to attack either of them. Our odds are slightly better if we force them to come to us."

"Ava, what do you think?" Logan asked her, and by his voice she understood that he was looking for her support. She thought for a moment. Logan's suggestion would probably give them a chance to escape, but it was also risky. She looked at her cousin, then at Amos, then at Liam, and finally at Emma.

"If we attack, it seems certain that some of us will die."

"But not all of us," Logan said.

"There's no guarantee of that."

"What's certain," Logan said, "is that if both groups attack us, we'll all die, trapped in the middle."

Ava heaved another deep sigh. "I get that," she said, craning her neck to take a quick glance at both enemies. "Even so, I can't condemn some of us to death, even if the others are saved. We'll wait to be attacked, and make a stand."

"Sometimes leaders have to make difficult decisions," Logan said with a gleam of determination in his eyes.

"And this decision is mine," Ava shot back. "Not yours. We won't attack."

"Fine," Logan agreed resignedly. "I hope it won't be your final decision—and our final act."

Ava bowed her head. She knew she might be condemning them all to death for lacking the courage to charge against their enemies.

"Amelia, Emma, Amos," Liam ordered, "keep an eye on the Nordic group. If they move, let us know. The rest of us'll keep an eye on the Black Guards."

Suddenly the Black Guards began to move. They came in a line, keeping the same pace, perfectly synchronized.

"They're coming," Ava said, and grasped her javelin firmly.

"Sven and his people aren't moving," said Amelia, who was looking toward the other end of the bridge.

"They must have seen them," Liam guessed. "They're going to let them deal with us."

The sinister Black Guards stopped a short distance away and began to fire their weapons. The shots sounded like a chain of high-speed thunderbolts. The bullets pelleted the vehicles and concrete barriers they were hiding behind, some ricocheting with whistles that were almost more frightening than the din of the shots.

"Hell, now the party's getting started," Logan cried as he activated his Power.

Amos and Ava hid behind a pile of rubble and raised their shields to protect themselves. There was nothing they could do until the enemy came closer. Except the guards weren't moving, but instead firing at them from a distance. Bullets were flying everywhere, and sooner or later they were going to find their targets.

"They're going to tear us to shreds," Ava muttered. She was beginning to think that they were lost.

"They're too far," Liam complained. "I can't reach them with my Power."

"I can't reach them either," Logan said.

"What do we do?" Ava asked, trying to stay calm.

Logan arched an eyebrow. "It's like they know that at this distance we can't use our Powers against them."

"That would make sense," Ava said from the ground. "They're Siaais's guards, they must know everything about us."

The guards went on firing. The noise was unbearable.

Liam was watching Sven and his followers. "We can't go back. The other group is waiting for us to do that, so they can finish us off."

Amos stood up suddenly. "Follow me to victory!" he shouted, and began to move forward behind his shield. Several bullets struck it, but were unable to pierce it. To everybody's surprise, he moved five steps on, then hid behind the remains of a truck. The Black Guards focused their fire on him.

"Let's take the opportunity he's given us!" cried Liam. "On we go!"

The Black Terminators saw them advancing, and opened fire on them. Logan and Liam hurled themselves on the ground. Carried on by their own momentum, they slid until they found cover behind a car.

There was a pause in the firing. The six Black Guards were reloading their weapons simultaneously.

Amos, realizing that they had a moment until they had finished reloading, seized his chance. He rose from behind the truck where he was hiding and threw his javelin with all his strength against the guard on the far right.

Something surprising happened.

The spear hit the guard's chest, but instead of piercing his torso, it flew off to one side with a metallic ring. However, Amos had thrown it with such force that the guard fell backward and lay still on the ground.

"Amos! Take cover!" Amelia yelled.

Amos crouched down at once to hide from the other five guards, who by now had finished reloading their weapons. They opened fire again. The bullets brushed past the heads of Liam and Logan.

"Can you reach them?" Liam asked Logan.

Logan smiled in satisfaction and nodded. "I think I can, from here. What about you?"

"Yes, now I can deal with them. My Power'll reach far enough."

"The two in the center—the left-hand one for me and the other one for you."

"Right. On the count of three."

"One," Logan began.

The shots broke out like a vibrant chant of death.

"Two."

Liam had his eye on his target. "Ready."

"Three. Now!" Logan called.

Their heads appeared on either side of the car. Before the Black Guards could aim, Liam made his target fly backward with such force that the guard fell over the bridge into the canyon.

Logan, meanwhile, made the other guard in the center burst into flames. The burst of flame he created was so massive that it caught the guard on his left, and they both caught fire. As the bullets continued to fly, they both hid behind the car.

Ava risked a glance, and was left staring wide-eyed. The two burning guards were still firing. There was no fear in them, and they knew no pain.

"It's impossible . . ." she muttered.

Emma was watching from further back. "They're not human!" she shouted.

"What d'you mean?" Logan asked in puzzlement.

"They're machines," said Emma. "Machines in the form of men."

"Do you know what they are?" Ava asked her.

"I think I do. We'll see in a moment."

Bullets passed over their heads again, bouncing and ricocheting against metal and stone.

"Sven's group," Amelia warned them agitatedly. "They're heading for the gate."

"The wretched cowards," Logan muttered. "They're leaving us here to our fate."

"More than that, to our death," Ava corrected him.

One of the bullets suddenly grazed Amelia's arm, and she cried out.

"Amelia!" Ava cried. She rushed to help her. "I'll bandage it."

When Logan put his head out for a moment and checked the damage, the two guards no longer looked human. What was left of each was a skeleton entirely of metal. It seemed that their bodies were made of polished steel. They were still firing, and two pairs of bright red eyes in metallic skulls were seeking them out to kill them.

"They're called robots," Emma explained. "Like the guardian

machine we fought in the library, only these are more advanced. They were created by the Ancients to help them with their domestic tasks, in factories, and in war."

"These look very much like they were made for war. I can't picture them knitting," Logan said with a sarcastic gesture. He had crouched down again to avoid the bullets.

One of the robots he had burned stopped firing. Its weapon had jammed. Suddenly the others, too, stopped firing.

"What are they doing?" Liam asked Amos.

From where he was lying on the ground, Amos had raised his head to see what was going on. "They're moving forward and reloading at the same time."

"This is our chance," Liam muttered to Logan. "Now or never! If they reach us, we'll be dead!"

They rose together and unleashed the full force of their Powers. Liam hurled one robot against the one beside it with such brutal force that there was a tremendous metallic clang. Both robots were left on the ground, with various parts of their bodies buckled. Liam imprisoned them between his psionic hands and hurled them against a metal guardrail with all the strength of his Power. The robots crashed against the barrier and ended up as a tangled heap of bent, broken limbs. They tried to get back up, but without success.

Logan tried a different strategy, exchanging fire for wind. He took out his bellows and turned the air it produced into an impressive gust of wind which struck two more guards, hurling both backward, rolling over and over, until they crashed into the cars behind them. Before they could get up he sent another strong gust of wind, and this time he hurled them up into the sky. Both robots shot up to a great height, and when he withdrew the flow of air, the machines fell with the force of their own weight and crashed against the ground. They did not move again.

There was only one robot left now. This one had finally managed to get its weapon un-jammed, and it began firing again. Liam and Logan got down instantly, but a bullet grazed Liam's left arm.

"Are you all right?" Logan asked.

Liam held back a grimace of pain. "Yeah, I'm fine. It's just a scratch."

"There's just one to go," Logan pointed out.

Suddenly they heard a war cry. Amos came out at a run with his shield in front of him and ran to the final guard. The murderous machine turned to him and fired. Protected by his shield, Amos hurled himself at the robot and pushed it over with the momentum of his run and the strength of his massive body. Both human and robot rolled across the ground. The first to get up was Amos, who used his shield to smash the robot's metal skull. Sparks flew with each blow, and at last, after one final massive blow, the red lights of the eyes went out for good.

"Well done," Logan said.

Amos was breathing heavily. He looked back to his friends and grinned. "That's what I've spent my entire life training for."

CHAPTER 35

They went on toward the gate of Siaais, with Liam and Logan leading the way. There was no trace of Sven and his group. They must already have crossed.

Emma went to the screen reader to open the gate. She used her Power and started to interact with the mechanism.

Amelia had lagged some way behind. Her hands were on her thighs and she was bent over. She did not look well. Amos was trying to comfort her. When Ava saw them, she went back to them.

"Is everything all right?"

"Amelia isn't feeling well," Amos replied. He was holding her by the waist. Ava saw that her cousin's face was extremely pale, and her legs were unsteady. She gestured to Amos to let her down to the ground, and the huge warrior did so with great care.

Ava set about examining her. "Say something, Amelia. Tell me what's wrong."

"I'm fine, don't worry . . . it's just . . . I get dizzy now and then, but it's nothing."

Ava gave her water from the skin she carried and examined her thoroughly. "She's exhausted, and weak from hunger," she explained to Amos, who was staring at Amelia's face with great concern.

"The elevator's here," came Liam's warning from the great gate.

"Amelia needs a few moments to recover," Ava called back.

"Maybe it'd be better if you went down and made sure Sven and his group aren't waiting to ambush us while Amelia recovers," Amos told the others.

Liam and Logan looked at one another and then nodded. "We'll go first," Liam agreed. "We'll be back shortly."

"I'll come with you to operate the machines," Emma offered.

There was little Ava could do to restore Amelia's strength in these circumstances, except prepare a mixture of water and herbs to help her regain some energy, meager though it was.

Amos watched, deeply worried. He took Amelia's hand and tried to encourage her. "Don't worry," he told her with a smile. "You'll be as good as new in no time. Ava's treatments are infallible."

"What would I do without my great warrior to protect me?" Amelia said from where she was lying on the ground, and blew him a kiss. Amos smiled and blushed.

"So much love is going to melt my heart," Ava said jokingly.

"I'm better already," Amelia said. "Help me up, please."

Amos helped her, but the moment she got to her feet her knees gave way and she collapsed. Luckily the warrior was holding her tightly and he caught her. He lowered her gently to the ground and looked at Ava in search of help.

"She needs nourishment."

"Why don't you use your Blessing and trick her mind? If

you can make her believe she's just eaten, it might help us to get her as far as the gate."

Ava blinked. "You know, considering you're a big hulk of a warrior, you're really quite brilliant. You're absolutely right. I don't know why that didn't occur to me."

She activated her Power, concentrated, and placed her hands on Amelia's head. The first feeling she received from her cousin's mind was one of great weakness, and she had to fight against this. *I'm not going to be beaten by those feelings*, she thought, and countered them by sending a feeling of physical strength into Amelia's mind.

As she was trying this, they heard a strange humming above their heads.

Amos looked up and immediately went into a defensive stance, shield and javelin at the ready.

A humanoid robot was descending from the sky. On its back were four spinning blades which allowed it to move through the air, parallel to the ground. This machine looked even more advanced than the Black Guards.

"Ava!" Amos shouted in warning.

Ava looked up and saw the threat. "I need more time to help Amelia."

"Don't worry, I'll protect you both."

Ava closed her eyes again, concentrating her Power and seeking to infuse Amelia with a feeling of great fortitude, as if she had just gotten up from a long, invigorating rest after a great banquet. She had to trick her cousin's mind into believing that she was bursting with strength.

The robot landed a few paces away. Its legs, hands, and body were covered with sections of red armor that revealed cables and steel components. Its face was a scarlet mask with gleaming purple eyes. The appearance of that face was partly human, but the machine visible under the surface was frightening. It was armed with a strange-looking spear with a long white shaft and a blade made of red light.

The robot spun the spear between its hands at great speed. It used it to hit the remains of a vehicle and sliced through the rusty metal as easily as it sliced through air.

Amos narrowed his eyes, looking troubled, but he knew he needed to keep the robot's attention focused on him. He assumed a more aggressive posture and waited unflinchingly for the robot to attack him.

The spear sought Amos's head, and he crouched very quickly to avoid the strike. He counterattacked with his javelin, landing a sharp, massively powerful blow to the robot's torso. Sparks flew with the sound of metal striking metal. The machine took two steps back, managing to keep its balance.

It attacked again, stabbing at Amos's chest. He raised his shield in time, but the blade of red light pierced it and struck Amos in the shoulder.

Amos grunted in pain and took a step back. The robot attacked again, this time with a horizontal slice aimed at the warrior's neck. Amos raised his shield reflexively, and the top of it, sliced off by the spear, fell to the ground. The spear missed his jugular by a finger's breadth.

Ava finished tending to Amelia and helped her cousin to her feet. "We have to leave, Amelia. Quickly."

Amelia, who was on her feet by now, saw that Amos was dodging another blow of the deadly spear. "I'm not leaving without him!" she cried.

Amos realized that Amelia was already on her feet. "Run to the gate! I'll keep this murderous monster distracted."

"I'm not going to leave you here."

"Ava! Take her with you, don't let her stay here."

The warrior saw the robot coming and counterattacked by beating it with his javelin and what was left of his shield. He managed to hit the robot's face, forcing it to retreat several paces in order to maintain its center of gravity.

"We've got to go, Amelia!" Ava pleaded.

Her cousin shook her head. "I can't leave him, Ava. I love him."

"He needs to know you're safe. If we stay we'll only distract him or get in his way. We're putting him in danger. We've got to get to the gate."

Once again Amos shouted: "Run to the gate! Get to safety!"

Ava tugged at her cousin's arm. "We've got to do what he says. Come on!"

Amelia glanced at her dear Amos, then at the gate. She didn't know what to do. Ava dragged her away at a run, while Amos launched blow after blow at the robot in an attempt to crush its armor. It counterattacked, and he defended himself as best he could, losing his shield completely after a few more strikes of the spear. Amos did not give up, but struck the robot's head again and again until the mask which covered it fell to one side, revealing a face of metal and cables and a violet eye which now hung grotesquely down its cheek at the end of several wires.

Amos launched a powerful kick, and the robot fell over backward. Amos dropped his spear and picked up a large rock, then moved behind the robot's head, ready to smash it.

From the ground the robot tried to pierce him with its spear, but missed. Amos raised the rock above him, then with a tremendous blow smashed the robot's head against the ground. Sparks and smoke issued from its metal skull.

He raised the rock for the final blow as Ava and Amelia watched from the gate. The elevator reached the surface and the door opened. Liam leaped out to see what was happening.

Amos brought his rock down with all his strength and crushed the robot's head completely.

Suddenly Amos's eyes opened wide, and he looked down at his stomach. In its death throes, the robot had caught him with its spear. His armor was useless against the weapon, which had penetrated his stomach and come out through his back. He looked toward the gate, toward Amelia.

"I love you . . ." and he collapsed onto his knees.

She screamed his name in horror. She tried to run to him, but Ava held her back with all her strength.

"Amos, no! Nooo!" Amelia kept on screaming, her eyes wet with tears.

Ava, unable to keep hold of her, turned to Liam. "Help me, we've got to get out of here."

Liam seized Amelia by the waist and dragged her inside the elevator with Ava close behind, and the doors closed after them.

Amid Amelia's cries of despair over the loss of Amos, the elevator headed down into the depths of the earth.

CHAPTER 36

The journey on the high-speed train was torture for everyone. Not only because they had lost Amos, but because they had to witness Amelia suffering his loss. She wept and wept, and nothing Ava or the others could say or do would ever console her.

Ava's heart was broken. Amos had given his life for them, to give them another chance to get hold of the Cure and save their people. There was nothing she could do to ease her cousin's sorrow. Ava had offered to use her Power to help her feel better, but Amelia wanted nothing of it. She didn't want to feel better, she didn't want her pain eased, because what she was feeling was real and it was all she had left of Amos.

But for the sound of Amelia's weeping, their underground journey was silent. Everyone was lost in their own thoughts.

Ava was very worried. She went to Liam's side and whispered in his ear: "I may need your help."

"Whatever you need, just ask me."

"In Amelia's current condition, her grief could be fatal. She'll end up killing herself." She looked back at her cousin. "I'll have to do something, I can't let her die. She's all the family I have."

"Just let me know what you need and I'll help you."

"Thanks, I knew I could count on you."

When they reached the end of the line, the train decelerated as it had before. Liam and Logan checked the underground station and made sure it was deserted. There seemed to be no danger.

"On we go," Liam said.

Logan helped Ava to get Amelia off the train. She was no longer in tears, but her eyes were red from so much weeping.

The station was practically identical to those they had seen before. After making sure there was no danger, they went up the marble stairs to a metal door.

Amelia collapsed.

Ava stroked her head.

"No, let me be. Don't do that to me," she said, and shook her head to avoid the touch. "I want to remember him. I want to feel!"

Ava gestured to Liam. The hunter held Amelia down to prevent her struggling, and Ava put both her hands on her cousin's head.

"No! Don't make me forget!"

The terrible despair and pain that Ava felt as she entered her cousin's mind almost made her give up. But she took courage and drew strength from what had happened to her mother. She remembered that. She felt the pain, the fear, the panic of that day. *It won't happen again, Never. I'll fight. I'll resist. I'll never fail a loved one again. I'll help Amelia whatever happens, whatever the cost. I won't let her suffer. However strong those feelings of pain and suffering may be, I'll fight them and I'll win.*

For a long time, she fought against the feelings flowing through her cousin's mind and succeeded in doing what she had not been able to do with her mother: She controlled them without them overpowering her. With a great effort, she began to send feelings of peace and well-being into Amelia's mind.

The pain was almost overwhelming, hard to conquer, but she went on trying, until at last she managed to overcome all resistance and make her cousin feel what she was transmitting to her. Amelia stopped sobbing and was left lying on the ground. She fell asleep.

Ava withdrew her hands and looked up at Liam. "Thank you," she whispered.

The hunter nodded. "I'll carry her," he offered, and took her in his arms.

"Emma, the door," Ava said.

"I'll take care of any threats," said Logan. He activated his Power and lit his lighter, and Emma opened the door.

—

They looked out at the new world they had come to and were lost for words. It was a spotless city, with shining white buildings of steel and glass. Avenues, buildings—everything their eyes could see—all shone as if someone were there to clean it all day and night. It was perfect: clean, well-tended, and bright. But something was out of place in that image of perfection, which Ava recognized immediately. There was not a soul in it. The streets, squares, buildings: Everything was empty, absent of any life.

Nor was there any trace of Sven's group.

At the far end, against the horizon where the city touched the blue sky, stood a slim tower, white as snow, which seemed to reach as far as the sky. Its base was wide and rectangular. As it rose, the building's profile tapered gradually, and at the top of it the Eye of Siaais watched over everything eternally.

Ava shivered.

"I think that's where we're supposed to go," Logan said.

She couldn't shake off her unease. "I don't like this place."

"It's too clean . . . too well-preserved," Emma said. "It's as if there were still people living here."

"Except that there's not a soul to be seen," Logan pointed out.

"Let's be very careful," Liam said. He was still holding Amelia in his arms.

"Is it me, or is the temperature here very low?" Ava asked. "I'm freezing."

"That makes two of us," Logan said. He was flapping his arms to warm himself.

"Look," Emma said, and her breath was a white cloud.

"We'd better get moving," Liam said. "In these conditions we won't last long in the open."

They began to walk in the direction of the tower. Nobody spoke. The loss of Amos was like a heavy weight on their spirits. Carrying on without him would never be easy.

Liam carried Amelia over his shoulder and did not say a word, but Ava caught him glancing back behind him to where Amos had always been, covering his back. He must have been deeply affected by the death of their friend.

Logan was in the lead, but he was far more unsociable than usual. He might never admit it, but Ava suspected Amos's death was weighing heavily on his heart. She, too, had a huge void in her chest, a sorrow and emptiness so great that it seemed to her she would never fill it.

They stopped to rest under an elevated walkway, which afforded them some protection from the gusts of cutting wind. They had managed to make their way forward past a couple of blocks of immaculate buildings. The sky was gray, the sun had disappeared, and the snow was beginning to fall in the midst of a squall.

"We're going to freeze," Emma said, shivering. She was looking up at the sky, which was becoming more threatening by the moment.

"If hunger doesn't kill us, the cold will," Logan said, hugging his stomach. His teeth were beginning to chatter.

"We're very near. Let's keep calm. We need to drink," Ava said. She handed them the waterskin they had filled from the fountain they had left behind.

As they drank, Logan activated his lower Mark of Siaais. He was left staring for a moment, wide-eyed, at the golden reflection.

"Hell!" he said bitterly, and kicked a stone so that it flew into the air.

"What's the matter?" Ava asked.

"My damn Mark is indicating ten out of ten."

Ava activated her lower Mark and saw that it, too, was now showing ten out of ten.

"Ten out of ten," Emma confirmed.

"Me too," said Liam.

Amelia, awake now, said nothing, and did not even try to check. She was lying in the fetal position with her gaze distant.

"The Cure's in that tower," Ava said, trying to raise their spirits. "We just have to cross this last stretch and reach it. Stay calm. Don't lose hope. The odds against us are colossal, I know that, but we're not giving up. We've come too far, lost too much. If Siaais kills us, so be it, but we're not giving up. We're going on."

Liam nodded in agreement. "Well said. I'm with you, Ava."

"That infected one we saw was a clear warning," Logan pointed out. "We'll soon begin to transform, all of us."

"We still have time," Ava insisted. She felt more motivated now that she could see the tower in the distance. "We'll get the Cure."

"Once the Mark shows an infection level of ten out of ten, how long until we change?" Logan asked.

She sighed. "There's no exact time. Each person transforms at a different rate. The Mark of Siaais will begin to give out golden flashes when the transformation begins. The faster the flashes, the closer to the end."

"How long do you think we have?" Liam asked.

She hunched her shoulders and bowed her head. "Until sundown at the most."

"That gives us a chance," Liam said. "We can get to the tower in that time."

"I don't want to be transformed," Logan said. "I'd rather you all killed me."

"Right now, you're still you. Right? Well then, let's go on."

Logan smiled at Ava's courage. "You're right, let's go on."

And with those thoughts they set out toward the great white tower, which rose, shining, against the horizon.

From its pinnacle, the Eye of Siaais watched their approach.

CHAPTER 37

They went on several blocks further through deserted, snowy streets. The storm was worsening, and the icy winds continued to lash them with a cutting intensity.

"We've got to find shelter!" Ava said. She could see that although Amelia was now walking on her own, she was still in a state of shock and freezing.

"There, ahead," said Liam, pointing toward a huge building with an arched entrance.

The door of the building was metal. Liam tried to force it open, but it was impossible.

"Allow me," Emma said. "It has an access panel on the right, under that metal cover. I'll use my Power and see if I can open it."

Emma put her hands on the access panel. The yellow and blue threads of her Power flowed from her fingers. Ava watched her working, entranced, still unable to grasp how her Power worked.

Suddenly Liam, who had started keeping a lookout once he stepped aside to Emma work, sounded the alarm. "Something's coming!"

"Sven's group?" Ava asked.

"No, it's something else. I heard a hum and I saw something in the sky. It looked like some kind of . . . mechanical bird . . ."

"A what?" Ava asked blankly.

Liam pointed to the sky with his bow. Ava saw a flying machine coming toward them, floating amid the blizzard. It was black, square, with a red dot in the center. It seemed to be keeping itself in the air with four spinning blades.

Logan shook his head. "I don't like this."

"Logan," Ava said, "look after Amelia."

"Ava, I can help—"

"Right now what I need is for you to protect Amelia. She's in no shape for anything, and I wouldn't forgive myself if anything happened to her."

Logan nodded and took a defensive position with Amelia behind him, his Power activated and his lighter at the ready.

"So what is that thing?" Ava asked Liam when she saw it approaching them, hovering five meters off the ground. Unlike the one that killed Amos, this was smaller, and not shaped like a man. It was boxy.

"I don't know, but I'm not prepared to run any risks," Liam said. Without waiting for a reply, he released an arrow.

The arrow reached the flying machine with such luck that it hit one of the spinning blades and broke it. The machine spun erratically as it tried to stay in the air, then struck the wall of the building opposite and fell to the ground.

"Well done!" cried Ava.

Suddenly they heard another humming noise. Liam looked toward the east and saw something flying toward them quickly.

"Here comes another," he said and nocked another arrow.

"Hurry up, Emma," Ava called back. "We have unwanted company."

Instead of replying, Emma simply nodded. She was concentrating too hard to speak.

At the sight of the new flying machine, Ava was left speechless. It was three times the size of the first.

"The small one must have been a scout, and it's called up a soldier," said Liam. He released another arrow.

This time the arrow hit the metal body of the machine, but did not succeed in doing more than make it wobble from the impact. It regained its balance, then suddenly what looked like a weapon appeared from under its shell.

Liam nocked another arrow and released. This time he hit a spinning blade. The machine lost its stability and also some altitude, but soon succeeded in righting itself. Its weapon suddenly turned to aim at Liam.

"Look out!" Ava shouted.

The weapon fired a red beam and hit Liam.

"Nooooo!" Ava cried, her heart bursting with anguish. She ran toward Liam, expecting to find him dead.

But he was still standing. The beam had hit his bow, which had broken in two. He threw it to the ground and tried to activate his Power. A new beam was aimed at his chest. Without even stopping to think, Ava gave him a hard shove, knocking him to the ground. As the flying machine switched targets, Ava dived for cover just before it fired at her.

At the same moment, Liam used his Power to throw the machine against the side of the building. The crash was deafening. The hunter brought his hands together, leaving a small space between them, then began to squeeze palm against palm as if a press were closing on the metal body of the machine, crushing it until it was completely destroyed.

"I've got it!" Emma exclaimed, and the door opened.

The group ran into the building. Logan appeared to be holding up Amelia.

"How is she?" Ava asked him, deeply concerned.

"She's fine. But she's still unresponsive," Logan replied. His eyes were dull.

Ava saw that her cousin was still withdrawn deep into herself. She stroked her cold forehead, then her cheeks, but she did not react. Ava kissed her forehead tenderly.

Emma managed to shut the door behind them and turn on the lights.

"What is this place?" Logan asked.

"I'd say some kind of military facility or laboratory," said Emma.

Logan scanned the inside, but all he could see was a hall with white walls and a few metallic decorations. The temperature inside was comfortable, and they were safe from the harsh weather outside. They sat down on the floor and rested.

"Machines that fly . . ." Ava murmured thoughtfully.

"The technology of the Ancient Ones," Emma said.

Logan was shaking his head. "This is getting worse. Machine-men weren't enough, now he's sending us machine-birds."

Ava refused to let pessimism overcome her. She looked up at the ceiling and let out her growing rage. "You won't defeat us! Do you hear me, Siaais? We're going to make it! The Cure will be ours!"

Logan smiled at her. "No need to shout, I think he heard you."

"I hope so," Ava said and then concentrated on checking how Amelia was.

"What do we do now?" Logan asked.

"The best thing to do would be to go on to the white tower as directly as we can," Liam suggested, "and take shelter in the buildings as we go, so that we don't freeze to death."

Logan nodded. "Yeah, I think the same. We'd better do it fast. We're running out of time."

"Wait," Emma said. "When I was accessing the entrance panel I saw something that caught my attention . . . something I think we ought to investigate before we go on to the tower."

"What did you see?" Logan asked.

"The name of this place: AGL."

"Why is that important?"

"Yes. It means Advanced Genetics Laboratory."

Logan stared at Emma blankly, then looked at Ava and Liam for help. Ava shrugged.

"It looks as though we don't know what you're talking about," Liam said.

Emma nodded. "This lab has been used to perform experiments with human genes," she explained.

"What are human genes?" Ava asked, looking bewildered.

"I don't know how to explain it. They're like the building blocks of every organism, including us. They specifically control heredity."

"And why would they do experiments with . . . that?" Logan asked, puzzled.

"To alter them, with the intention of creating different kinds of people . . . stronger, immune to diseases, for instance."

"Can that be done?" Ava asked.

"From what I was able to see in the Ancient Ones' files, they were working on it."

"If the Ancient Ones were working on it," Liam said, "and this place is so close to the tower, then it's probably important."

"That's just what I thought," said Emma.

"Okay," Ava said, "I think you're right. Let's investigate."

Emma went to the door that led deeper into the facility and began the process of unlocking it with her Power.

"It's going to take me some time. It's protected by a very complex algorithm."

While Emma was trying to hack the mechanism of the door, Logan sat down beside Amelia and began to write in his notebook.

Liam, meanwhile, sat down with his back against the white wall and began to sharpen his weapons, his long hunting knife and his tomahawk, as was his habit. He flinched and clutched his side, then went on sharpening. Ava sat down beside him.

"How are you?" Liam asked her.

"I've been worse," she replied, trying to hide the sorrow she felt about Amos's death and the state Amelia was in.

Liam nodded. He understood her pain. "We'll get out of this."

"Don't worry about me."

"I do . . . after what happened to Amos . . . I feel responsible . . ."

"What happened to Amos is a terrible tragedy, but you're not responsible," Ava said. "The only one who's responsible is that bloody God who put us here to suffer and die for his enjoyment."

"Even so . . ."

"Don't worry about me. And . . . thank you."

Liam nodded.

"I've always wondered . . ."

Ava leaned in close and touched the scar on his face.

"No . . ." he said and moved back, embarrassed.

"You needn't be ashamed."

"Actually, I am."

"It doesn't make you ugly, it gives you character." She did not say this to make him feel better, it was the truth. Liam's features were delicate, and the scar gave him a masculine roughness which she liked.

"I don't care about that. I don't lose sleep over my appearance.

It didn't matter before this madness we're in, and now it matters even less."

"Is there a story behind that scar?"

Liam nodded, and his eyes dulled.

"It'll change your opinion of me."

Ava hesitated. What story could there be behind a scar that would make her change her opinion about Liam? Her curiosity was too strong.

"I want to know. If you don't mind telling me about it."

"All right," he said, and heaved a deep sigh. He began to take his jacket off and then his shirt. Ava's attention was caught by his well-formed pectorals and chiseled arms. She lowered her gaze to his stomach and saw abdominal muscles that made her jaw drop. Then he turned and showed her his side and part of his back. Two handspans of scars ran along it. Ava knew at once that these were the scars of some terrible wounds. He had barely survived, and the recovery must have been long, very long.

She restrained her surprise and passed her fingertips along the scars. She felt nervous and excited. She wondered whether Liam would notice how flushed her cheeks were. He bent his head. Her desire for Liam surprised her so much, her hand began to shake. Luckily for her, he put his shirt back on, then his jacket. Ava drew her hand back, hoping he had not noticed that delicate moment.

"They still trouble you."

"There are days when they do."

"That's why sometimes you hold your side . . ."

Liam nodded. "It's troubled me less and less with the passing of time."

"One day you won't even notice it."

Liam smiled. "Thanks, but we both know these wounds are always going to trouble me."

Ava wanted to deny this, but she was incapable of lying to him.

"Yes . . . they will . . ."

"I don't mind. They remind me how lucky I am."

"Are you really?" Ava looked at him in puzzlement. His past was full of scars, his present was a hell, and his future would probably never arrive, since they were all going to die.

"I am, because I've been able to live this extra time."

"Since the wounds?"

Liam nodded. "I was fifteen when it happened."

"Those were terrible wounds to leave scars like that on such a young body."

"So they were. I was between life and death for six weeks. Finally I came out of it, they say by the grace of Siaais . . ."

"Perhaps he wanted you to live so that you could be here now, suffering all over again. That's the kind of God he is."

"Anyway, I've enjoyed three more years of life, and I'm grateful for that."

"You're not dead yet. We'll beat Siaais at his own game. We'll get the Cure, and you'll live to be a hundred."

Liam smiled. "I love your fighting spirit and your determination."

"I'm not a quitter, especially in front of him." She pointed up to the sky.

"We'll fight," he promised her, "to the end. You can count on me."

"I do. Without you we won't make it." She smiled back at him.

"You'll make it," he said, took her hand, and squeezed it to give her courage. Ava felt something alight inside her. He was gazing at her with those intense indigo eyes of his. She began to feel hot again, together with a sense of well-being and euphoria. She didn't know where those feelings came from, and it suddenly made her nervous.

"Tell me what happened," she said, to divert her thoughts.

Liam let go of her hand, and his face darkened.

"Among my people, we hunters normally go out in pairs. It's an ancestral habit that's become the rule. One winter morning, my partner John and I went out hunting. It was a gray day and snow had covered the forest. Winter's hard for all the guilds, and it's when hunters are most in demand. Food is scarce, and fresh meat is greatly appreciated. We headed to the eastern mountains, the highlands, the Misty Peaks. It's an area we know well, we hunt there all year round. So, with hunting bag, traps, muskets, and our knives and axes, we set out. John and I grew up together. Later on, it happened that we were both selected to be hunters. We didn't find it strange—after all, his father and mine were both hunters too. I don't know what it's like in your tribe, but among my people families stick to tradition when trades are handed out. It doesn't make much sense if your father's a hunter, then you become a farmer. You won't know anything about the trade, because in your home they don't have the necessary knowledge to pass on to you . . . There are exceptions, obviously, and adjustments at particular times of need, but in most cases the trade's passed on from father to son. We made the journey to the highlands at a good pace, in spite of the snow. When we reached the highlands, we checked our traps. You may not believe it, but you catch more animals with traps than with weapons."

"I believe you," Ava said, nodding even though she had no experience whatsoever with hunting.

"The forests were covered in snow," Liam went on, and his face darkened again. "There were only a few birds and small animals looking for food that morning. We got to one of the traps and saw we were in luck. A sizable white hare had fallen in. John had just started to pick it up when we heard a noise to the north. Some animal was making its way toward us, and going by the noise and the shrubs it was disturbing, it must have been a big one. I signaled to John to get ready, and we'd go for it. He signaled back that we already had enough for the day. The traps were half-full. The noise sounded from closer at hand, and I made the sign for a boar to John. He nodded. We got ready and loaded the muskets." Liam sighed. "What came out of the thicket wasn't a boar, it was a brown bear. Huge. For some reason it had woken up from hibernation, it was hungry and angry. There was a moment's hesitation, of fear, and then John and I fired. I was closer, and the bear fell on me. I had no time to move away. I saw the claws that caught me in the face and side, and I fell to the ground in agony. The bear clawed at my back and I thought that was it for me. I saw John activate his Power to help me, and I passed out." He paused.

"What happened? Did John save you?"

Liam shook his head. "A search party found me at nightfall. When we didn't return, they came looking for us."

"John?"

"They found John's body beside the dead bear. The beast had torn out his throat before it died." Liam bowed his head between his knees.

"It was my fault. I told him we should make one last kill."

"You had no way of knowing it was going to be a bear. You can't blame yourself."

"I should have known, and of course I blame myself. I should have realized we were close to the caves where the bears hibernate and that one of them could have woken up. But my greed for more meat, my mistake, cost him his life. Every day these scars, this pain, remind me of the mistake I made, and that my best friend paid for my stupidity with his life."

"Liam, don't say that . . . it wasn't your fault, it was an accident, bad luck . . ."

Liam took a deep breath and fought back tears.

"Is that why you weren't always interested in leading the group? Because of what happened with John?"

Liam shrugged. "I don't want anybody else's life on my conscience."

Ava understood. But she knew that Liam was a natural leader, with a good head and common sense when it came to making difficult decisions.

"I trust you. I trust your ability to lead," she said, hoping for his agreement.

"You don't need me, you're doing it very well. We're in good hands with you in charge. You have fixed ideas and you're very clever, which is a great combination. Even Logan hardly questions your decisions, because he respects your leadership, as I do."

"I'll admit I'm stubborn about my opinions. It's difficult to make me change my mind. But I'm not clever. Amelia and Emma are clever."

He shook his head firmly. "No. They're intelligent, and that isn't the same thing."

"What's the difference?"

"Intelligence has more to do with the ability to understand concepts. Clever is about overcoming obstacles. Here we need more of the latter than the former if we want to get out of here alive."

"I'd never looked at it that way . . ."

"And not only are you good at it, you like it, which is doubly good."

"It's not that I like it . . ."

"Deep down, yes, you do. You only need to control that force of yours a little."

"Force? Don't you mean my outbursts?"

Liam smiled. "Yeah . . ."

"I know what you mean . . . I'll try."

"With that under control, you'll guide us to the Cure, and we'll get out of here."

"But I need help . . . I won't be able to get you all out of here by myself . . ."

"You have my help, and you'll always have it," he assured her, and his intense gaze left no doubt.

"Thanks . . ."

Liam's words made her feel better. She felt that their chances of getting out of here alive were now slightly greater.

A cry of delight interrupted them.

"I did it!" Emma said. She was in front of the door, which now slid into the wall, leaving the way clear.

"Time to move on," Ava said.

CHAPTER 38

"Go carefully," Liam told them. He was looking ahead as they went down the long, spotlessly white corridor.

Ava went on with her cousin at her side. She had her arm over Amelia's shoulder, not wanting to leave her for a single moment. Amelia looked dazed. Ava had managed to get her walking, and for the moment that seemed to represent enough progress. She would soon be herself again. Recovering from intense trauma was something that took its time, as Ava knew very well from her own experience. She had never truly gotten over her mother's death. How long would it take Amelia to overcome the loss of Amos?

Even if they found the Cure, Amos would still be gone.

Logan went forward as he always did, with his lighter in one hand, ready to act, confident in his Power.

"Everything'll be all right, I'm here," he said with a wink and a mischievous smile.

From his behavior and his self-confidence, he gave the impression that nothing could defeat him. Ava knew it wasn't true, but she liked the fact that the dark young man was so daring.

Liam, always quiet and wary, led the group, flanked by Emma.

They reached a locked door at the end of the main corridor, with an access panel. Emma activated her Power and went to work getting the door to open.

"How's my beautiful cousin?" Ava asked Amelia.

Amelia did not answer, but simply lowered her gaze to the floor.

Seeing Amelia so despondent broke Ava's heart. She was always so happy, so full of life, so full of light, whose mere presence gladdened everyone around her. Now Ava barely recognized her. She was like a ghost, left to wander with the group, allowing herself to be led without aim, without life.

"Security controls disabled," Emma said.

The door opened wide, its panels sliding back into the walls. Another long, spotlessly white passage appeared in front of them, with many doors on either side.

The first doors they passed opened into rooms filled with strange medical equipment, crystal tubes of blood, and machines with other tubes resting in them, ready to be analyzed. There were access panels, and screens displaying images that none of them understood.

Further on they reached a room with noises coming from it. They readied their weapons and activated their Powers.

"Be careful," Ava warned Liam. "I don't like this place at all. I have a really bad feeling."

The hunter nodded. When he opened the door, they saw a huge hall of cages filled with animals: monkeys, dogs, cats, and rabbits of different varieties, sizes, and ages. At the sight of them coming in, the animals began to scream, bark, and howl until the noise was deafening.

"What's the matter with them?" Ava asked Liam. "Why are they so agitated?"

"Don't know, but it's not a good sign."

"Poor things . . ." Ava went over to one of the chimpanzees in a metal cage. She put her face closer to see them more clearly.

The chimpanzee lunged at her face with its mouth open, revealing enormous teeth. Ava fell backward, terrified.

Liam went up to it and saw that though its body was that of an ape, its jaws were more like those of a tiger.

He shook his head. "Something's been done to this poor chimp."

Logan went to the cages where the cats were kept, As he got closer the cats tried to hurl themselves at him amid growls more like those of a bear than of a cat. As with the apes, the cats' jaws were far larger than they ought to be.

"This is very strange. I've never seen cats with fangs like that. Apart from wanting to eat me, which I can understand up to a certain point, seeing as I'm so delicious. But it puzzles me."

Liam went over to the dog cages and immediately noticed they were not normal dogs. Their bodies and limbs were overdeveloped. But they did not look aggressive, approaching him and whimpering for affection as soon as he came near them. He kept his distance, because the bodies of those dogs looked more like those of a lion or a tiger. Their heads, on the other hand, were of normal size.

"This is really weird . . ."

Emma found an information system at the back of the room. "I'll see what I can do," she said, and began hacking the machine.

"Poor animals, they're doing terrible things to them," Ava said when she managed to get back to her feet.

"They're experimenting on them," Logan said.

"People cross different breeds of dogs to get new kinds with particular characteristics," Liam said. "I think they're doing something like that . . . but much more advanced."

"And on a much larger scale," Logan added.

"You're not wrong," Emma said suddenly. "From what I can see here, what they're doing is manipulating and splicing genes, and injecting highly advanced experimental drugs in order to get stronger, faster, more powerful specimens."

"I don't understand much of what you said," Ava confessed.

"What she means," Liam explained, "is that they're experimenting with these apes and dogs to make them into something more like gorillas and lions."

"What I understand her to mean is that they're creating genuine monsters," Logan countered. He was still staring at the animals with great interest.

"I'll see if I can find out more," Emma said.

"Let's get away from these animals," Logan suggested. "I don't like the look of them, or the way they're looking at us. For once I don't feel like being wanted," he added with a grimace.

As they all moved away from the cages, the animals made a ferocious attempt to attack them. The creatures were not only excited, all of them were extremely aggressive. Luckily the cages held.

"I don't even want to imagine what would happen if one of those cages opened accidentally," Logan said.

"Got it now," Emma said. "It's true, the experiments being carried out in this lab are to modify the subjects in order to make them more aggressive."

"That's awful, an appalling thing," Ava said. "Poor animals."

"Let's get out of here," Logan said. "This place gives me the creeps, more so every moment."

They all felt the same way. They continued on their way down the corridor to the end, glancing uncertainly into the other labs they passed. They did not stop again until they came to a closed door at the end of the corridor.

"Do we go in?" Liam asked the others.

"I don't fancy finding any more experiments," Logan said with loathing.

"We've come this far," Emma pointed out. "This room seems to be the key one. We ought to find out what else this place is hiding. It might help us to find out what's in store for us in the tower."

"She's right," Ava said. "Let's see what this hall's hiding and whether it can help us get out of this horrible world."

It did not take long for Emma to deal with the door. They found a large hall full of machines of different types, test tubes, and all kinds of containers and measuring instruments they did not recognize.

And yet it was not the technology of the laboratory that left them speechless. It was the room's sole occupant.

It took Ava a moment to control the horror she felt.

A person was hanging above the floor, legs and arms outspread, against a silver wall. His entire body was well-developed, as though every single muscle in his body had been inflated. But the really striking thing was the man's face, which was grotesquely deformed. Its mouth and jaw were exaggeratedly large, with four huge protruding fangs.

"This is a nightmare!" Amelia screamed suddenly. "It's all a nightmare!" She began to sob. Ava hastened to put her arms around her, trying to soothe her.

Emma saw another access panel and went to get information from it.

"Poor man . . . to end up like this . . ." Ava said. She was still doing her best to calm Amelia.

Emma gasped suddenly. "I've got it now. It's the program for genetic improvement. The experiments that are carried out in this laboratory are in search of genetic improvement of both animals and humans . . ."

She nodded and went over to the terminal, activated her Power, and began to type on the scorched keyboard.

Ava looked again at the poor man they were experimenting on. What was Siaais trying to attain with all this? Why these genetic experiments on animals and humans? She had no idea, but she was sure there was some deeply unpleasant answer.

"System hacked," Emma said.

Ava came out of her reverie and turned to her friend. "What did you find?"

"The robot's activated an emergency procedure. I was able to follow it. It sent a mass of data to another, more critical system."

Ava looked around. "Which one is that?"

Emma shook her head. "It's not in this facility. The robot's sent it all to another building."

"Do you know where it is?"

Emma concentrated. After a moment she opened her eyes. "I've found the location. It's a slightly bigger facility, five hundred meters north."

"Then we'll go there. I want to find out what Siaais is up to. Perhaps it'll finally give us an advantage."

"Yeah, I feel the same," Emma said. "The more we know about what's going on, the better."

"This poor man looks very bad," Logan said suddenly.

"What's happening to him?" Ava asked Emma.

The hacker lowered her gaze. "When the robot activated the emergency procedure he not only sent all the experimental data, he also terminated the experiment."

"We should go," Liam said.

"Yeah, we'd better," said Emma. "The emergency procedure must have set off an alarm. They're sure to send a team to find out what's going on."

"What? Humans, too?" Ava said incredulously.

"That thing isn't human," Amelia said with great sadness.

Suddenly the door behind them opened and someone wearing a long white robe came in.

"Stop right there and don't move!" Liam said threateningly, with his hunting knife at the ready and his Power activated.

The newcomer stopped dead.

"Try anything and I'll torch you," Logan warned him. He was holding his lighter at the ready and had activated his Power.

The stranger showed them his hands. In his right he held a portable access panel, in his left a strange pencil that shone with a blue light.

Liam was studying him with narrowed eyes, ready to attack. "Who are you?"

"I'm a scientist, a doctor."

"What are you doing here? Who do you work for?"

"I'm carrying out an experiment of the greatest importance," the man replied in a monotonous voice. He did not sound alarmed.

Logan moved closer to him. "Who's that poor wretch hanging on the wall?"

"That's research subject SI50328. I'm monitoring his progress."

Logan was getting angry. "What are you doing to him?" he snapped.

The doctor did not flinch. "The subject is making satisfactory progress. The results so far are very promising." He activated his pencil to make a note on his access panel.

"Don't do that," Liam warned him.

"I have to note any deviation or anomaly that comes up during the process of incubation," he replied calmly.

Ava noticed something odd in the man's eyes. They were dim, appearing to have no life in them, and this puzzled her.

"I think this doctor isn't human," she said.

Logan gave the man a glare. "We can find that out right now," he said, and moved the flame of his lighter in front of the doctor.

"No, wait," Emma said. "That won't be necessary."

"Are you sure?" Logan asked distrustfully.

"I've just thought of something. Procedure for acting when confronted by an emergency?" she asked the doctor.

"In an emergency, the procedure is to send all information to the main system immediately."

Emma nodded. "He's a robot," she concluded.

"It doesn't look dangerous," Ava noted. She walked up to it and stared into his eyes, almost nose-to-nose. Seeing him close up, she realized that although he looked human, she could see from his eyes, skin, and hair that he was not. "Who's your creator?"

The robot did not look back at her, but went on staring at the back wall where the subject of the experiment was hanging. "My creator is Siaais."

"I guessed as much. What kind of experiment is this?"

"That information is classified, and access to it is restricted."

"Who are you authorized to reveal that information to?"

"Siaais."

"Anybody else?"

"The chief of the clinical investigation. The one in charge of the AGM project."

"More of those blasted initials," Logan grumbled.

"What does AGM stand for?" Ava asked.

"Advanced Genetic Modification."

"Right. I want to know what you're doing in the advanced genetic modification project."

"Authorization denied. Access to information denied," the robot replied without even glancing at her.

"What d'you mean, denied?" Logan asked threateningly. "Talk, or else I'll burn your head to ash!"

"I don't think that'll help," Liam said.

"He's a robot," Emma pointed out. "He's guided by a predetermined program, and he won't answer our questions unless he gets authorization."

Ava turned to the robot for the last time. "What are you all doing in the AGM program?"

The robot scanned Ava's face again, then looked away. "Access denied," he said, and turned round.

"You bloody pile of scrap with the face of a man," Logan muttered.

"Fine," Ava said, "we'll try it your way, Logan."

"Okay. Move back."

With a huge burst of flame, Logan set fire to the robot doctor. Its outer layer began to burn, but the robot within stood there unflinching. The flames grew fiercer, burning the robot's cables and metal parts. The heat it now gave out was scorching, and Ava and Emma took a step further back. The robot was enveloped in flames now. It did not move.

"Emergency," it said suddenly.

The robot turned and moved across to one of the systems on the wall. It activated a terminal, and a keyboard appeared.

"Critical emergency," it said again, enveloped in flames.

It typed a series of commands into the terminal with its burning hands, then stepped back and collapsed onto the floor.

"Crit . . . ical . . . emer . . . gency . . . save information . . ."

"Logan, please put it out."

"As you wish," the Elementalist said. He took out his water container and activated his Power. An instant later a large wave hit the robot and put out the flames.

"Emma, could you see what the robot's done to the system?"

CHAPTER 39

They left the laboratory behind and went outside, where the icy wind and snow welcomed them with their embrace. Emma went ahead with Liam. Ava followed, looking in every direction as she went on, expecting to be attacked by some new evil of Siaais. She could not get over how different this world was from the previous one. All the buildings were a shining white, with large glass and steel windows that shone as if they were of polished silver, even in the midst of the storm. The avenues were of a polished gray, without a single imperfection anywhere. The snow piling up on the ground only added to the beauty of the environment. But there was one thing both worlds had in common: They were utterly devoid of life.

To the north the great white tower with the Eye of Siaais above it seemed to be controlling everything that was happening there. Ava looked at it for an instant and felt such shudders that she had to shake them off. *Siaais is watching us, he knows we're near, he'll never let us reach the Cure. But I won't give up, never. We'll find out your secret and reach the Cure. For Amos, for all of us.* Her eyes turned to Amelia, who was walking beside her with her head bent, lost in her own thoughts. Lost in her immense loss.

Suddenly two of the small flying machines appeared, skimming one of the cross streets.

"Look out!" Liam called.

At once the group hid under the arcades of one of the buildings. Because they were glass and steel, they had to crouch and seek the shadows to avoid being seen from above. The two scouting machines flew past without detecting them.

Ava gasped in relief, turned to her cousin, and gave her a hug.

"We're a lot smarter than those machines. We'll manage to fool them and reach the Cure, just you wait."

The ghost of a smile appeared on Amelia's face. This small sign filled Ava with happiness and gave her hope. It was the first time her cousin had smiled since Amos's death. It might be a long way from her usual broad smiles, but it was a victory.

They continued on as soon as Liam gave them the all clear, and turned east into an avenue between buildings that appeared to be completely of glass, with huge windows. Suddenly they heard shouts and strange sounds echoing against the buildings, distorted and amplified. Liam raised his arm, and they all flattened themselves against the wall and crouched down. Liam took a quick glance round the corner, and Ava followed him.

"What is it?" she whispered.

"It's Sven's group . . ."

Ava poked out half her face and took a look with one eye. She saw the group of Nordics and Africans fighting against what she recognized as robots. Robots in the form of men, but with some parts made of bright gray metal and others of some white material that covered faces and torsos. They had weapons like the Black Guard's rifles, but these shot red beams which made no sound, only a short, muffled hiss with every shot. Ava hid behind the corner again and turned to Liam.

"What do you think?"

Liam shook his head. "They're our enemies. We're not going to help them. Let's wait and see what happens, and then we'll act."

"Agreed," Ava said.

Logan came over to take a quick look.

"Those cretins are getting what they deserve," he said with a venomous look. "There are two dead on the ground, one Nordic and one African."

"Those robots must be pretty dangerous if they've managed to kill two of them," Liam said.

Ava shuddered. "We'd better keep a very close eye on them."

The three peered round the corner at different heights, and watched the battle that was taking place. Ava could see two Nordics, followed by two Africans, confronting five robots. Sven and his comrade were brandishing axes and shields against the robots and their red-light weapons. The two Africans, unarmed, were hiding behind them. The situation was definitely strange. Ava took it for granted that all four were going to die.

The robots were very agile, not keeping still for even a moment. They moved, attacked, and moved again. They were the very opposite of the Black Guards, who barely moved, and when they did, they did so in unison. These robots were totally independent from one another, and looked almost human.

"This is going to get interesting," Logan commented. He sounded as though he was enjoying the fight.

The robots hit Sven's comrade's wooden shield, which shattered into a thousand pieces. The other blows hit the Nordic in the chest, and Ava gave him up for dead. Despite this, the Nordic did not fall. He reached for a second axe to accompany the one he was holding in his other hand. The robots changed position with great leaps, rolling on the ground, then shot again, this time at Sven. The Nordic spread his arms wide and took the shots in his chest and face. The rays hit him squarely, but still he did not fall.

"Is this all you can do, you damn brainless machines?" he shouted.

"We're going to tear you into metal shreds," the other Nordic said.

Ava could not believe they were still on their feet. They ought to be dead by now. How was it possible that they were unaffected by the robots' attacks? It must have something to do with their Power. Ava could see their right arms shining bright silver. Yes, that had to be it. Their Power was protecting them.

While the robots were focused on the Nordics, the two Africans took cover inside a building by crashing through its glass entrance.

Both Nordics launched an attack, axes in hand. As they advanced the robots went on shooting to no effect. When the Nordics reached the first two robots, Sven landed such a blow that the machine's head flew off and rolled across the pavement. Its body stayed standing and kept firing until Sven gave it a massive kick. It fell on its back and didn't rise again. The other Nordic hacked at the right leg of the next robot and tore it off. The robot, unbalanced, failed to stay upright and sank to its remaining knee. It didn't stop firing until Sven and his comrade finished it off with their axes.

The three remaining robots moved in circles around the Nordics, bombarding them on all sides, but the two huge warriors remained unaffected. When the Nordics advanced, the robots moved back, staying out of range with massive leaps and agile sidesteps, and went on firing.

"Damn cowardly machines! Fight!" Sven yelled.

Suddenly a new robot entered the battlefield. Ava had no

idea where it had come from. It looked like the others, with gray coverings instead of white. But it was considerably larger in every dimension. It moved with a slow, heavy tread. Mounted on its massive shoulder was what Ava guessed was a very large weapon.

"What on earth is that?" Logan whispered.

The moment the two Nordics saw the new robot, they launched themselves at it. The new arrival did not waste a moment and fired its weapon. The discharge was so massive that the glass outer walls of the nearby buildings shattered. Pieces of the road shot off in different directions, with rocks crashing into everything around them. Ava's ears were ringing so loudly in the aftermath that she was deaf for a moment.

As the smoke cleared and her hearing returned, Ava saw the Nordics lying on the ground, unmoving. The three white robots came to inspect them. They surrounded the two fallen Nordics and fired their red-light weapons at them simultaneously, and they did not get up again.

"This is the end of the road for them," Ava said.

"We'd better move back so the robots don't see us," Logan cautioned.

No one disagreed. But as they started to retreat, Ava caught movement out of the corner of her eye and stopped.

Sven had leaped to his feet, and his partner now did the same.

She was struck dumb. It was simply impossible. There was no way they could still be alive.

Sven and his partner hacked with their axes at the three robots like madmen. They brought them down and went on hitting them until the machines were completely destroyed.

There came a click and hum from the heavy robot reloading its weapon. Ava and her friends realized what was about to happen and covered their ears to protect them.

Just at the moment when Sven and his partner were turning

to attack it, the huge robot fired again. There was another great explosion and a terrible roar. Once again glass and rock flew everywhere, covering everything with a thick cloud of dust.

They can't have survived, Ava thought, but once again she was wrong. Sven got up slowly, shook the dust and dirt off his body, and picked up his axes. One of them was completely bent, so he threw it away. He waited for his partner to join him, and the two of them hurled themselves at the remaining robot. With deafening war cries they attacked, using their axes like hammers, battering the robot's legs until the huge machine toppled like a falling tree.

Once it was lying on the street, they went to work on its head until it stopped moving.

When they were done, the two warriors collapsed, exhausted, over the remains of the robot's body, panting and sweating from the effort and the fury they had fought with.

To Ava they looked weak, half-defeated, sitting there in the middle of the road, unable to stand. She noticed that both men's arms had stopped shining silver at the upper Mark of Siaais.

She turned to Liam and Logan. "Now's our chance to get rid of them."

"That's a bad idea," Liam whispered. "You've seen what they're capable of. Nothing seems to hurt them."

"I'll burn them," Logan said.

"Do you really think that'll work? Bullets and beams have no effect on them. What if they're immune to fire too? It's too risky."

"Lasers," Emma threw in.

Ava looked at her. "What?"

"The robots' red-beam weapons," Emma explained. "They're called lasers."

"Whatever," Logan said. "If fire doesn't work, I'll use water, or air, or earth. They can't be immune to everything."

"Suppose they are?" Ava asked. "Suppose that's their Power?"

"We'll have to take the risk," said Ava. "They're ahead of us and following the same path, and their goal's the same: the Cure. They'll kill us before they let us get past them. Right now we have a small opportunity. Later, we won't."

"I'm with Ava," Logan said. "Better now than later. They're alone in the middle of the road. They look weakened. We have a chance against them."

Liam did not seem convinced, but he nodded.

"Right, then," Ava said. "We'll deal with them now. Emma, can you stay here and protect Amelia?"

The young woman nodded. "Don't worry, I'll look after her."

The three crept around the corner and advanced slowly toward the two Nordics. Logan and Liam touched their arms to activate their Powers. Logan was confident of his, while Liam was troubled. Ava's nerves were tingling. The two Nordics saw them, but did not move. They looked beaten . . . although they had looked that way before and had survived.

"Our paths cross again," Ava said as she and her companions stopped ten paces from the Nordics.

Sven looked at them with a cold, lethal smile. "Seems like fate."

Ava glanced at Logan and Liam and signaled them to attack. Sven and his partner activated their Power.

Logan attacked at once, launching a ball of flame that exploded above the Nordics, raining fire. Ava watched in disbelief. They ought to have burned to ashes in a few moments, and yet they did not. The flames went out, and the two men were still sitting there. Their gazes were now cold and lethal. They had not liked the attack. They got to their feet slowly.

Liam struck. He gripped the upper part of the fallen robot with his Power, raised it, and hurled it with great force at Sven.

The Nordic was thrown backward from the impact against one of the walls of the building on his right and fell to the ground. He seemed to be stunned. The other raised his axe and began to run toward Liam.

Logan bent down, picked up a stone from the ground, and hurled it at the running Nordic. Mid-flight he turned it into a huge, sharp-edged rock. It shattered on impact with the Nordic, who was thrown backward.

"You got them!" Ava shouted.

But it was not true. Slowly, the two men got up again.

"They're not injured," Logan said in disbelief. "The bastards aren't even bleeding."

"I was afraid of this," Liam said. "Their Power must give them immunity from physical attacks."

"So what are we going to do?"

"I've no idea, but don't let them get close or they'll tear us to pieces."

Ava felt utterly helpless. Her Power was useless against the Nordics, and her javelin suddenly seemed like a ridiculous weapon.

The two men began to walk toward them, slowly but confidently.

Liam and Logan got ready to attack. And then something very strange happened: They could not get their Powers to work. Liam tried to hurl two of the small robots at Sven but could not even move them. Logan tried to make the ground under Sven's partner sprout stakes of stone, but his Power, too, failed.

"What the hell's going on?" Logan exclaimed.

"I don't know, but I can't get my Power to work."

"Me neither!"

At that moment Ava realized that the two Africans had come out of the building in which they'd waited out the Nordics' fight with the robots, and were watching them. Their arms flashed silver.

"It must be them," she said. "Their Power must be interfering with yours."

"That must be why the Nordics find them useful, as a defense against other Powers."

Ava was horribly afraid. They were going to be slaughtered.

Sven attacked Liam, but the hunter dodged and the axe missed his head. Sven turned and delivered a cross-stroke. Liam stepped back and the axe just missed his stomach.

"I'm going to cut you in two," the Nordic said. There was fury in his eyes.

Liam did not answer, but unsheathed his axe and hunting knife.

Sven laughed aloud. "You won't do anything to me with those."

Liam watched him, his eyes filled with a controlled hatred. Sven attacked and blocked him with his axe. He countered with his knife and drove it into the other's stomach. It did not go in.

"Hell!"

"Told you," Sven laughed. He counterattacked, but Liam continued to block.

Logan saw the other Nordic's axe coming down on him and threw himself to one side. The axe went again, ready to split his head in two. Luckily his movements were slow, very slow. By the circles under his eyes, Logan realized he was exhausted. He smiled, knowing what he needed to do: He ran to keep his enemy at a distance. The Nordic tried to chase him, but his steps were slow, weary, clumsy.

Ava, seeing her two friends in danger, knew she had to do something or Liam and Logan would die. She saw the Africans, close by but not too close, and she knew that those two men were the key. She ran at them, javelin in hand.

Ava tried to impale the nearest of the Africans. The warrior sidestepped her attack with ease and landed a blow to her face that made her stagger back. The explosion left her stunned, but the man wasn't finished with her. He delivered a well-practiced kick that sent a shock of pain to her stomach, knocked her to the ground, and left her breathless. She lost her grip on her javelin and it tumbled out of reach.

Now she understood why the Africans carried no weapons. They didn't need them. They were experts in unarmed combat. If they caught her, she was dead.

Ava tried to get up, but the pain held her back. She activated her Power, not knowing what to do with it, but knowing she had to do *something.*

If only I could get up I could run for safety, but I can't even move, it hurts so much. The Power of her people could not be used for oneself—everybody knew that—but she was desperate. Ava tried to focus on her pain, but her Power didn't work. She cursed in her anger for the strength to get to her feet.

The huge warrior swiped at Ava with one leg and gave her such a blow that she struck the ground again and rolled several paces. The pain was terrible. Another kick like that would kill her. She was nearly paralyzed with fear of another attack, but she couldn't give up. She had to try—for herself, for Amelia, for all of them.

Suddenly a voice rang out behind the two Africans.

"Why don't you try it with me, you cowards?" It was Emma, katana in hand.

The two warriors spun around, flexing their legs, their arms at the ready, and their new attacker. Ava feared the worst. The Africans were huge and strong, while Emma was small and slender. Both men attacked with fluid movements. They launched punches and kicks at Emma with great coordination and skill.

She defended herself, fighting with almost the same skill as her attackers, but moving backward. With every move, she was using her katana to keep them away from her. The two men put pressure on her with spinning kicks and swift sidesteps, accompanied by sharp blows with legs and fists.

She went on the attack, moving forward and lowering her center of gravity, and with a precise slash wounded one of the men in the leg. She took a kick from the other and rolled across the ground from the impact. The African hastened to finish her off, but she rose in a flash and caught him in mid-movement. She moved her head to the right, and his fist brushed her ear. She launched a short, precise cut, and the warrior fell to the ground with his throat slit.

Suddenly Logan felt something. His Power was working again. Without stopping to think, he used it against the Nordic, who was chasing him like a lame hound after a hare.

"Maybe I can't wound you, but I bet I can slow you down," he muttered under his breath.

He took out his flask of water, spilled some into the palm of his hand, and sent a blast of frozen mist against his opponent. Frost began to cover the Nordic's skin, building up rapidly. He took a step toward Logan, but could not take the next. His feet had stuck to the ground, with encased in ice. He raised his axe to deliver a blow, but was left frozen in mid-chop. Logan had frozen him from crown to sole.

"Help Liam!" Ava shouted as she recovered her javelin.

Liam dodged Sven's axe and hit his chest with both tomahawk and knife, but the Nordic's skin was impervious. Sven hit Liam on the forehead with the handle of his axe, a sharp, terrible blow that left his opponent numb.

"Gotcha," Sven said triumphantly, with a deathly smile.

"I'll kill you . . . for my . . . partners . . ." Liam mumbled.

Sven laughed. "No, your journey ends here," he said, and raised his axe to deliver the final blow.

Logan sent a gust of hurricane wind that swept Sven into the air. But the axe was already falling. It struck Liam, and he fell to one side.

"Liam! Nooooo!" Ava shouted as she ran toward him.

CHAPTER 40

"Liam, speak to me!" Ava cried as she knelt down beside him.

Liam didn't answer. His eyes were closed and he was not moving. He was bleeding from a terrible wound in his chest, and he looked dead. She searched for his pulse.

A few steps to the left Emma launched two cross-strokes at the wounded African, who took a step backward. The huge warrior took a quick glance at Sven just in time to see him fall, and he suddenly ran off toward him. Emma was about to give chase, but thought better of it and went back to Amelia, who was waiting hidden around the corner.

"How is he?" Logan asked Ava.

Her voice caught in her throat. "Give me a moment . . ." She put her ear to Liam's mouth.

"He's breathing, but very faintly. His pulse is still strong."

Logan gasped in relief. "Thank goodness. That wound looks pretty bad."

"Yeah, we need to see to it as soon as possible, or he'll bleed to death."

Logan, looking ahead, saw Sven at the end of the street,

starting to rise. The African caught up with him and helped him the rest of the way.

"We'd better get Liam out of here. If Sven comes back with the African, I won't be able to use my Power and he'll kill us."

Ava nodded. "Give me a hand. We'll get him away from here."

Logan helped her carry him to the corner, where Emma and Amelia were waiting for them.

"Logan, you keep watch," Ava told him. "I'll try to stanch the bleeding, then we'll get out of here."

Logan nodded and stayed on the corner, keeping an eye on Sven and the African, who were now coming down the street. Luckily Sven could barely walk. He looked as if he were carrying the weight of a mountain on his back, and was exhausted from lack of food, the fight, and the massive use of his Power. He would not be able to go on fighting for much longer.

"That Nordic's on the verge of collapse," Logan said. "We ought to finish him off."

"We tried already, and look what happened. I almost died, and so did Liam. Liam was right, it was a bad idea then, and it still is."

"He can barely walk . . . If he tries to fight, he'll collapse."

"And what state do you think we are in? Liam's at death's door. I'm exhausted, we're all so hungry and weak we can barely fight either. If we go on using our Power with our bodies tired and weakened like this, we're going to die. No, we're not going to fight, it's too dangerous. Siaais can decide their fate. I've learned my lesson, and I'm not going to make the same mistake again."

He sighed resignedly. "All right. We'll take the cautious route. I only hope we won't regret it in the end."

Ava stopped Liam's bleeding by packing the cut with a wad of linen. The four of them then carried Liam to a nearby building, where Emma used her Power on the access door. Once inside, they laid Liam on a counter in the empty lobby and Ava resumed tending to his wound.

"You just hang on and don't you dare die on me," she whispered in his ear. "We can't lose you now, we need you."

Logan was watching from just inside the door with his lighter at the ready. Emma and Amelia joined Ava, helping her tend to Liam. They cleaned the wound, and Ava began to suture it. Liam began to shake, and Ava was forced to stop.

Liam's pain seemed to bring Amelia out of her state.

"I'll use my Power to ease his pain and make sure he doesn't fall asleep," she said.

Ava turned to her with a broad smile. "You keep him calm, I'll keep him alive."

"Yes," Amelia said. She touched her upper right arm and activated her Power, then placed her hand on Liam's head. There was a silver flash, and she entered his mind. A moment later he stopped shaking. His face showed no pain, and his body relaxed.

"Stay with him, Amelia. You're doing really well," Ava said as she worked. It took a while to finish closing the wound. Then she wrapped his chest in strips of linen and let him rest.

Hungry and exhausted, Ava let herself fall to the floor, and Liam fell into a deep, peaceful sleep.

Emma took over Logan's watch. Amelia was still looking after Liam, applying her Power so that he stayed calm and pain-free. Logan came over and sank down beside Ava.

"It's been a tough time," she said, and drank from the waterskin he offered her. Her throat was as dry as the desert of her own land, but the cool water comforted her a little. She was so hungry that her head was clouded and her body lethargic.

"It certainly has."

They were silent for a moment.

Logan touched both his Marks of Siaais, and they flashed gold and silver. "It's blinking," he said. He sounded numb.

Ava stared at the golden flashes and knew what this meant: They would be transformed at any moment. She checked her own Mark, with the same result. It was flickering with intense golden flashes. They were running out of time.

"We can split up," she suggested. "I'll stay here with Liam. You keep going."

Logan shook his head.

"No. We can't split up now. We need to stay together."

"And when one of us starts to change?"

"Well, then, so be it."

"I'm with Logan," said Emma from the door. "We're not going to split up. We've come this far together. Whatever happens next, we should face it together."

"I'm not going anywhere without my cousin," Amelia said from Liam's side.

Logan looked back at Ava. "Then that's decided. We stay together."

Ava smiled. She was grateful for her friends' brave spirit, even though she feared that decision might doom them all.

They rested until Liam woke up.

"How d'you feel?" Ava asked him.

"Alive . . . I'm alive . . ." he muttered.

Ava smiled. "Well, you stay that way. We need you alive."

He groaned with pain when he made an attempt to move.

"Wait, I'll help you. You've got a deep wound in your chest."

"Another scar. That's neat. I didn't have any on this side."

"Don't complain, you'll be better-looking," Logan joked.

Ava smiled. "Yeah, to be sure."

They helped him to his feet, and he managed to keep his balance with a grimace of pain.

"Can you walk?" Ava asked.

"I'll try."

He took a couple of steps with the help of Ava and Amelia.

"I think so, but I feel so weak . . ."

"That's natural," Ava said gently. She did not want to worry him, but the reality was that in his current state, weak from hunger and gravely injured, he wasn't going to live much longer.

"I may be able to fix that," Amelia said.

Ava looked at her in surprise as Amelia activated her Power and laid her hands on his head.

"I'm going to transmit a feeling of well-being and strength to him so that he can keep going."

"That'll work, even in his condition?"

"I think so. I've realized that the feelings I've been transmitting since we've been here are more intense, and they last longer. It's as if my Power had increased."

"Interesting . . ." Ava murmured, wondering what it could mean.

Amelia finished ministering to Liam. "How d'you feel?"

Liam sat up. "Better. Great, in fact."

They all looked at Amelia in amazement. Liam still looked dreadful. His face was ashen and there were black circles under his eyes. And yet he was feeling full of life. It was amazing.

Logan glanced at Ava and Amelia. "Couldn't you do the same to us? I can barely stay on my feet, and I'm so hungry I could eat Emma raw."

"Hey!" Emma objected.

"Of course," Amelia said. She looked at Ava, who nodded, and both of them used their Power to transmit strength and well-being to their two friends. Then they did the same to each other.

"How do you all feel now?" Ava asked.

"I feel fantastic," said Logan. "I'm not hungry, and I'm full of strength."

"No trace of exhaustion, or hunger either," Emma agreed.

"My wound doesn't bother me at all," Liam said.

Ava sighed. "Good, but keep in mind that what you're feeling isn't real. Your bodies are really on the verge of collapse, so don't overexert yourselves, or they'll snap like twigs and there'll be no way of fixing it."

"In other words, if we overdo it, we'll kill ourselves," said Logan.

"That's right."

They gathered together their bags, waterskins, and weapons and went outside. It was still snowing, but the storm had passed.

"Where to, Emma?" Ava asked.

"Northeast."

"Okay, but we'll take a detour so as not to pass the same place, in case Sven and his followers are still there."

Logan nodded, and they went on very slowly. The cold was still intense, and although the wind was no longer blowing so intensely, when it did so it chilled them to the bone.

They arrived at the second lab without further incident. The building was very like the one they had already investigated, but considerably larger. Emma, wasting no time, hacked the entrance. As with Amelia, her Power now seemed to allow her to work faster and with greater ease.

"Let's have a look," Ava said.

They went down another long white corridor. They went through a door on the left, then down a long flight of stairs to a lower level.

"You know where we're going, right?" Logan asked Emma.

"Yeah, I was able to connect to one of the main systems, and I have the map of the building in my head. The labs are on the lower level to protect them from attack or a natural event."

Once underground, they were about to go down another long corridor when Emma halted them.

"It's not here. We have to go down another floor."

Liam took the lead, and they went down to the next level. He glanced along the corridor and saw no one.

"For the moment there doesn't seem to be any danger."

Ava opened one of the doors to take a quick look as they went on. What she saw left her speechless. A dozen strange vertical capsules were fastened to a long wall. Multiple cables and pipes came out of the tops of the capsules and led into the spotless white wall. They were made of silvery metal and transparent glass. Inside them she saw different kinds of animals immersed in some liquid, floating inert, as though in a deep sleep. Or dead.

"Oh no, what new horror is this?"

Liam appeared behind her, then Logan. A moment later Emma came into the room.

"They're experiments," she said.

"Those poor animals," Amelia said. "Are they dead?"

"I'd say they are," Logan said.

But at that moment, a panther reacted and tried to attack him through the glass. Luckily it held.

Logan took a couple of steps back. "It's alive! How can it be alive if it's in that liquid!"

"All this is very weird, and getting weirder by the moment," Liam said.

"It's Siaais experimenting," Amelia said suddenly in an exhausted voice. "He experiments with animals, and he's experimenting with us."

Ava touched her cousin's arm. "Whatever experiments he makes, he won't defeat us."

Amelia lowered her gaze. "He already has."

"What I don't understand is why he does it," said Liam.

"To create guards to watch over his realm and kill anyone who gets in," Logan suggested.

"If Siaais wanted to kill us, he'd have done it already," Liam said. "I'm convinced of that."

"Maybe all this is nothing more than a twisted game," said Ava.

Amelia's eyes were brimming with tears. "A game where innocent, brave, and honest human beings die."

"I still don't understand what he's after," Liam said. He was walking from one capsule to another, taking a good look at the animals inside.

"Whatever it is, we won't give it to him," Ava said.

Emma activated her Power and started typing on a terminal keyboard. Ava stroked her cousin's hair, which was tangled and dirty, and wiped the tears off her cheeks.

"We'll get out of here, I promise."

Amelia nodded.

"There's an armored door at the end of the corridor," Emma reported. "There must be something important behind it. It's the only one made of steel, and it's shut. The other rooms are labs like this one, with animals in capsules.

"I haven't been able to decipher all the data in this system, because there was a complex algorithm protecting it. It'll take me a while to decipher it, but there's something rather suspicious here . . ." Emma closed her eyes and fell quiet, then opened them again. "Interesting . . . I'd never been able to do this before, but it seems that now I can. The data's stored in my memory. It's all in there, and I can see it and access it and it doesn't vanish."

"You mean you have it in your head and you don't forget it?" Ava asked.

"That's right."

"Well, that's not so strange," Logan said.

"It is when we're talking about this much data," Emma explained. "I shouldn't be able to remember a fraction of what I'm retaining now."

"Wow!" Logan said. "This place is going to drive us all crazy."

"Not sure about crazy," Liam said, "but it's certainly true that there's something strange here that affects our Powers."

"Yeah, they're definitely growing," Ava said.

"Is it because we're using them more?" Logan asked.

"Partly, maybe," Ava said. "But maybe also because of this place and the situations we're being caught up in. I think they affect the development of our Powers."

"I agree," Liam said. "But again . . . why?"

"I've just accessed something interesting," Emma called, and they all crowded around her. "I was right about the armored room. That's where we'll find the important part of the study being carried out here. We need to get inside."

"Okay then, let's go," Ava said.

They left the lab and went warily on to the end of the corridor. Emma set to work on the access panel of the armored door.

Liam was restless, looking behind them with a skeptical expression. Logan had his lighter at the ready, which could only mean he was thinking either that they might be attacked, or else that some unknown danger was waiting for them behind the door.

"Got it!" said Emma.

CHAPTER 41

It was an enormous laboratory with gray walls full of machines, terminals, and endless wires, cables, and pipes that ran along the floor and went in and out of the walls. There were green and blue lights everywhere that blinked, each in its own rhythm.

In the center of the room was a large vertical capsule. All the systems seemed to be servicing it. Its back was steel and its front, glass. Inside was a young man floating in a blue liquid. Two tubes came out of his nose and were connected to the top of the capsule. In his mouth was another tube, also connected to the top. A number of cables of different colors were connected to his head, torso, and legs, and joined an odd-looking connector at the top of the capsule, from which extended a large silver pipe that ran to a huge rectangular system filling the whole back wall of the room, blinking with many colored lights.

They went in warily.

"What on earth's going on here?" Logan said.

"No idea," Emma replied. "But it looks important. The resources being devoted to this one subject are even greater than the hybrid experiment in the previous building."

Ava went closer to the capsule to study it and the poor wretch within. She looked at the tubes that came out of his nose and mouth and all the cables attached to his body, and she shuddered.

Emma consulted one of the massive consoles in front of the capsule. What could they be trying to find with those experiments? Who was the poor wretch inside the capsule? Was it one of those who were looking for the Cure, like themselves, whom Siaais had captured? Just thinking about it made her skin prickle. Why would the God want to transform them? What was his true goal? There had to be a reason, and it had to be a very important one. If they wanted to defeat Siaais at his own game, they would have to find out what it was.

Logan was looking disgusted. "What are they doing to that poor man?"

"Who knows what plans Siaais has?" Ava said. "Up to now I thought this was just an evil game he was playing to amuse himself. Now, seeing all this, I think there's something more going on here . . ."

"I've got the information," Emma announced. "I'm surprised by my Power. I think my mind's now capable of storing a massive amount of data, at least for a while."

"How long?" Ava asked.

"I couldn't say . . . the amount of information I've downloaded into my mind is enormous. I doubt I can retain it for long. And there's no guarantee I'll be able to understand it. There's just so much . . . It'll take time for me to process everything."

"Can you do it while we travel?"

"I think so."

"Then let's get out of here. I think we've all had enough of this place."

"Yeah," Logan muttered, "we should go before they send some robot or one of those abominations for us."

Liam was already leading the way, and they managed to leave the building without incident, which greatly relieved them. He scanned the avenue, then the sky, and led the way toward the great white tower with the Eye of Siaais on top of it.

They stopped in a square with a fountain, and Logan set about replenishing their waterskins. There was a large and very elaborate white gazebo, well protected from the wind, and the others sheltered under it.

Emma massaged her temples. "Are you okay?" Ava asked.

"Headache," Emma said. "I'm trying to decipher the data, but it's coming at a cost."

"I'll deal with the pain," Amelia told her. She activated her Power and placed her hands on the hacker's head.

"Thank you," Emma said, and closed her eyes.

Ava sat down beside them and watched her cousin use her Power. She was glad to see Amelia more like her old self.

"Can I ask you something?" Liam said beside her.

Ava nodded.

"Okay . . . what do you want most?"

Ava snorted. "Seriously? What I want most right now, without a doubt, is to end Siaais, to get rid of him. To get hold of the Cure and save my people."

Liam nodded repeatedly. "Yeah, me too. Before, I only wanted the Cure, but this terrible experience in this accursed realm has taught me we can't stay under the God's yoke, his control, with him doing whatever he pleases with us. We need to get rid of him somehow, or else this nightmare will never end."

"I'm glad we agree."

"Whatever it takes?"

"Whatever it takes."

"Good," Liam said. He was quiet a moment, then asked, half-laughing, "So how on earth do we kill a God?"

"No idea, but we'll find a way."

"You sound so sure."

"I am. One way or another, we'll do it."

"You're very brave. Does anything scare you?"

"Who says I'm not scared? But I don't let fear get me down. Fear keeps me awake, alert, and tense, and that's how I want to be."

"And what happens if we have to confront Siaais directly?"

"I'll be scared, very scared, but it'll help me remember what I have to do and why. I'll control my fear and not let it dominate my actions. I'll fight against the God, you just wait."

Liam smiled. "I haven't the slightest doubt of it. What concerns me is that you might not survive it."

"Maybe none of us will," she said gently.

"Well, if I have to die, I'll die, that doesn't bother me. The thought of you dying . . . that troubles me," he confessed.

"Don't let it do that. We're in this together, to the end. We'll live or die together."

Liam nodded and took her hand in his own. A warmth rose from Ava's stomach and went up her chest to her cheeks. She felt so good beside him, so happy, and she was so attracted to him . . .

"There's something else . . ." she said, lowering her gaze.

"What is it? You can tell me. If I can, I'll help you with it. You know that."

"This is something I haven't told anybody. Not even Amelia . . . though I'm sure she's already noticed something, she's very perceptive."

Liam nodded. "She is that."

"Amelia's always been very much in favor of using the Blessing, as it's called among my people, the Power, as you call it.

But I've always felt a great reluctance to use it, because it came from Siaais. I've always mistrusted my Power. The Ancient Ones didn't have it, did you know that?"

Liam nodded. "Yeah, there's no reference to the Ancient Ones having Power in any of the books we've rescued. My people are convinced the Ancient Ones didn't have it, that it's a result of Siaais's arrival."

"That's right. And if an evil God gives us a Power, shouldn't we distrust it?"

"If you look at it that way . . . perhaps you're right . . ."

"And if he really has the Cure . . ."

"You don't believe he has it?"

"I don't know, nobody knows. How can we?"

"Well . . . I don't . . . but it's what Siaais promised us . . ."

"And what nobody's ever attained."

"That we know of. Some other tribe might have reached it in the past, and we just haven't heard of it."

"Do you really believe that?"

"I . . . I want to believe it . . . otherwise, there's no hope . . . for any of us."

"Well, I don't. I clung to that hope for a while, too, but not anymore. I don't believe anything Siaais wants us to believe. I think it's all a big lie."

Liam was silent for a while.

Ava sighed. "Sorry. Sometimes my feelings get the better of me."

"It's okay, don't worry."

"The Power . . . the Blessing . . . Siaais's Gift . . . it brought my happiness to an end . . ."

Liam tensed at the words. "What happened?" he asked her gently.

"I was just a little girl . . . and . . . I killed my mother."

Liam's eyes widened as he tried to cover his surprise. "I'm sure it was an accident; you couldn't have meant it . . ." he said soothingly.

Ava shook her head. "I killed her. It wasn't deliberate, but that doesn't change what happened. I'm responsible for her death."

"Tell me what happened."

Ava took a deep breath. "Ursula, my mother, was a scholar. One of the best. She and her sister Phila, Amelia's mother, were studying a dig full of very important relics, two days' journey or so from the Great Pyramid. My mother took me with her. She wanted me beside her all the time. She used to say our life was too short, and we ought to keep our loved ones always near us so as to spend as much time with them as possible. I don't remember exactly what happened, only fragments. I remember arriving at the dig, and the workers removing the sand to uncover the great tomb. I remember they found a huge buried chamber with Archaic artifacts and relics. My mother spent all day and part of the night working. Her passion for knowledge was incredible. One evening, everyone had stopped working for the day and come back to the tents to rest. Phila begged my mother to leave it, then carry on at dawn. She said she would, in just a short while. I was standing on a rock a couple of paces away from her. She was lying on top of a stone slab with hieroglyphs she was trying to decipher, at the back of the chamber . . ." Ava's eyes moistened at the memory.

"Take your time, I'm here with you," Liam said soothingly.

"Thanks." She wiped her eyes with her sleeve. "Suddenly I heard a crack. That I remember well. I think I knew instantly what was going to happen. I turned and saw the slab my mother was lying on collapsed into a great chamber below. I heard her gasp of surprise and saw her vanish."

She took another deep breath and then let it out slowly. “And then I heard her voice calling, ‘Ava, help me!’ I realized she hadn’t fallen, and I crawled to the hole and saw her fingers gripping the edge. Fear left me frozen. ‘Ava, honey, help me,’ she said, trying to keep calm, though I could see terror in her eyes. The darkness below her was deep. I didn’t know what to do, and I started to sob.”

Liam stroked her back. “You were just a kid in a horrible situation. It’s natural.”

“My mother tried to calm me. ‘Shall I go and get Aunt Phila?’ I said. I was scared to death. She shook her head. ‘The camp’s too far,’ she said, ‘I won’t be able to hold on.’ Sobbing, I asked her what to do. ‘Take my hand and pull me up,’ she said. I did, but she was too heavy for me. ‘I can’t, mother, I can’t,’ I said between sobs. ‘Don’t be afraid,’ she said, ‘hold me with both your hands and pull with all your strength.’ So I did. I grabbed her left hand with both of mine and pulled as hard as I could. I was sobbing with fear, the dark abyss looked unfathomable and she was hanging in the void. ‘Don’t cry, I’ll make the fear go away, I’ll Feel you,’ she said and while I pulled her, with her hand in mine, she closed her eyes and Felt me. She meant to use the Blessing to take away my fear, to soothe me, to send me peace and safety.”

“It didn’t work?” Liam said, already guessing it had not.

“No, that’s not what happened. When she Felt me, before she could modulate her feelings and send me the calm and safety I needed to save her, all the horror she was feeling at that moment passed into me. I couldn’t control it. A horrible terror of falling and being crushed at the bottom came over me. With a cry I let go of her hand, trying to escape that feeling of terror. And I killed her. I saw her eyes open wide as she fell. ‘Ava!’ she shouted. Her eyes will never leave me. The terror left my body and was replaced by despair. I was found the following morning by the hole, with my mother dead at the bottom, several stories down, on a floor covered with the hieroglyphs she loved so much."

"I . . . I'm . . . so sorry. It must've been awful," Liam said, not knowing what to say.

"Now you know why I haven't wanted anything to do with the Blessing."

"I can understand . . . that's a horrible, traumatic experience. I'm so sorry it had to happen to you. But it's not your fault at all, it wasn't you who killed her."

"I let her fall."

"No. You can't blame yourself for what happened. You mustn't. You did all you could, you were a little girl, nobody can blame you for anything."

"Everybody tells me the same thing . . . but I know what I feel and I can't change it."

"I'm so sorry . . ."

"It's okay, and now you know the truth."

"Thank you for trusting me."

Ava looked into those deep indigo eyes and was lost in them. She felt well, unburdened of all the emotional weight she'd been carrying. And for the first time in a long while, that pain she had always carried in her chest vanished. She knew it would only last for a moment, but a moment of peace, of well-being, was all she needed.

She hugged Liam, and he held her in his arms.

"Everything's okay, I'm with you," he whispered in her ear,

It was a wonderful moment Ava would always remember.

Logan came over and held out their waterskins.

"Ahem . . . am I interrupting anything?"

Ava indicated the waterskins, to change the subject. "Are they full?"

"All full," he said.

Suddenly Emma's eyes widened. "We've got to get to the tower!" she cried.

"Emma, what is it?" Amelia asked.

"To the tower, quick, all of us!" she shouted, and she began to run.

CHAPTER 42

They ran without stopping until they reached the tower. There were no other unwanted surprises on the way, which seemed like a miracle to them. The building was immensely tall, seeming to touch the clouds.

"Emma, why such a hurry?" Liam asked. "It's not safe. We don't know what dangers are in store for us in there, and there are sure to be plenty."

Emma, who was searching for a panel that would open the tower door, turned and showed Liam her right arm. It was giving out huge flashes at rapid intervals, warning them of what was about to happen.

"I've run out of time. Either we get to the Cure, or I won't make it. I'll be transformed . . ."

Ava felt her heart shrinking as if a metal hand were squeezing it. "Don't worry, we'll make it. You'll be safe," she promised, although she no longer believed there was a Cure to be found.

"Of course you will," Amelia joined in.

The tower had a door in the form of an arch, very like the gates they had already crossed to get there. Emma looked for a panel that would give access to the door on either side, but without success. Ava and Liam, meanwhile, were looking up at the enormous structure.

"Siaais is up there," Ava said.

Liam's eyes went to the top of the tower and he nodded. "I think so, too. Most likely he's on the top floor of this building. He'll have the Cure with him. We'll get it. We won't leave this building without it."

Ava looked at him with pride in her eyes. "You'd rather die than not get the Cure."

"I still have hope," he told her. "I'll help you kill Siaais to bring this cruelty to an end, but more than that, I want to help my people. And I need to believe the Cure is real. So either I leave this tower with it, or I don't leave it at all."

Ava felt his words were making something stir inside her. The hunter was a man of honor, a man to be admired. She looked into his indigo eyes, noticed the scar on his beautiful face, and felt an explosion of attraction and warmth inside her. She wanted to hug him, to kiss him, to hold him in her arms. But now was not the time.

Suddenly Emma let out a cry of frustration. "I can't see any terminal or panel I could hack! I've no idea how we're going to get in."

Suddenly they heard a click, followed by the sound of moving parts sliding over one another. Above the great door there appeared the Eye of Siaais, but much smaller. It gave out a red beam that tried to sweep across them, but they moved away at once.

"Look out!" Ava called.

Emma, who had also stepped back, was staring at the beam as it swept a particular area in front of the door.

"It doesn't look like a weapon to me," she said. "I believe it's a recognition sensor—a way for the tower to know who to let in."

"You think so?" Logan said, not sounding at all convinced.

Emma took a step forward and put her left hand under the beam, and Amelia cried out in sudden fear.

Nothing happened. Emma took another step and let the sensor examine her from head to foot.

A metallic voice sounded: "Chosen recognized. Access granted."

A moment later the enormous door opened.

The five companions looked at each other with uncertainty, and a little fear.

"The time has come to prove what we're made of," Ava said. "We can't give in to fear, we've got to go on, come what may."

They all nodded. Nothing was going to stop them. Their will was iron. They readied their weapons: Liam, his tomahawk and knife; Emma, her katana. Ava clutched her javelin tightly and glanced aside at Amelia, who was doing the same with fear in her eyes.

"Let's get on with it," she said, and went into the tower ahead of the others.

The whole base of the tower was a huge chamber of white, oval walls. The floor was white, streaked marble. Ava looked up at the high, egg-shaped ceiling, which was translucent. Liam, Logan, Emma, and finally Amelia came in after her and stopped by her side. The great chamber was absolutely empty, with the exception of a person who seemed to be waiting for them at the far end of the room. Behind this person was what looked like an elevator with glass walls.

Ava squinted, studying the stranger thoroughly. It was a young woman of her own age, but her skin was white as snow, her hair jet black, and her eyes a spellbinding green. She was wearing strange clothes of a bright material, which clung to her body like a second skin. Its gold color emphasized all her feminine beauty.

"Come closer, please," she invited them in a sensual voice. They exchanged wary glances, and Logan and Liam activated their Power.

"No confrontation with me will be necessary," she assured them.

"Forgive us if we don't believe you," Ava said roughly.

"My name is Sias, and I bid you welcome to the tower. The end of the way."

"I gather we don't need to tell you who we are," Ava said. "You know perfectly well, or at least your lord does."

"That assumption is correct. Welcome, Ava of the people of the deserts, and welcome, Amelia of the same people. Welcome, Liam. Welcome, Logan. Welcome, Emma."

"We're here for the Cure," Liam said icily. "That's the only thing that matters to us. How do we get it?"

The young woman seemed to think about the answer. Her green eyes flashed twice.

"The first thing is to congratulate you for having gotten this far. It is an accomplishment many have attempted and only a very few have achieved. My lord and master bids you welcome to his palace and extends his recognition for having reached this goal."

"Your lord is presumably Siaais," Ava said. "What's your function?"

"Affirmative. My lord and master is Siaais, as he is yours. My function is to welcome those few who manage to reach his tower."

"And why doesn't he show himself to us instead of sending you?"

"I fear that is not possible. My lord and master does not grant audience to humans."

"Who does he grant audience to?" Amelia put in. "Other Gods?"

The young woman glanced at her for a moment and blinked

hard three times. Ava realized that the question had caught her unprepared, and she had no answer to it.

"Come closer, please, my lord and master wishes to speak to you."

"Then why doesn't he show himself?" Amelia insisted. "Doesn't he want us to see him?"

"Come closer so that my master can speak with you," Sias insisted.

Ava suspected that something strange was going on. She feared a trap, but they were already inside the tower, so if she was right, they were in the trap right now.

Logan nodded at her and so did Emma, who glanced at her right arm as she did so. Ava understood: They had no time left. She had to go on, fast, or else they ran the risk of being transformed.

She nodded to her companions and moved forward. As she took her first steps toward the middle of the room, Logan whispered to her: "I don't trust this beauty, we'll have to be very careful."

Ava nodded, and at her next step she heard a metallic click. The white marble tile she had stepped on sank slightly.

"Trap!" she shouted.

From under their feet a white gas began to rise, as if the floor below was burning. There was a hiss as it surrounded them, forming a thick cloud.

"Don't breathe! It might be poison," Ava called out.

But it was too late. The gas was all around them and had already made its way into their lungs.

"Get back!" Logan snapped.

They tried, but it was useless because the door they had come through was shut. They dropped to the floor unconscious, one after the other. Liam was the last to fall.

Ava woke up to find her companions stretched out on the floor beside her. They were beginning to come to. She noticed something strange: They were all wearing metal collars around their necks. She, too, was wearing one, and in some strange way it was connected to the back of her head, to the nape of her neck. This frightened her.

Amelia looked around nervously at her companions. "Is everyone all right?"

Emma had raised her hand to the back of her head. "I'm fine . . ."

"What's this blasted collar?" Logan asked. He was trying to take it off as he knelt on the floor.

Emma was examining the one around Amelia's neck. "I don't think we can take them off."

"When did they put these on us?" Logan asked.

"It must've been while we were out from the gas."

Emma tried to use her Power on the clasp of the collar, but received a powerful discharge that almost rendered her unconscious.

Liam, who was trying to open his own with his knife, received another powerful jolt and fell to his knees.

"If you persist in trying to remove the collars," Sias warned them, "they'll explode."

"Well, you could've said something before, love," Logan replied as he helped Liam to his feet. "I'm very fond of my head."

Ava was feeling the nape of her neck with her eyes shut and had an odd sensation, as though the collar and the wire were not things that had just been put there. They felt as if they had been there for a long time, as if they had been there forever. Once again she felt the way she did when she had one of her nightmares. Was all this really happening to her, or was it only her imagination? Was she awake, or asleep? Why did she feel that collar had been with her for a long time and she had only now realized it was there?

Amelia's voice brought her out of her thoughts. "Are you all right?"

"Yeah . . . it's just that . . . I don't know . . . I feel as if I was wearing this collar already."

Amelia looked at her, narrowing her eyes as she did so. "I have just the same feeling . . . as if I'd always had it round my neck."

"Exactly. But that's impossible."

"Yes . . . unless something's going wrong with our minds . . ."

"I'm beginning to suspect something is."

Suddenly they heard another metallic sound under their feet.

"Now what?" Logan grumbled.

In the middle of the group, a hole opened in the floor, and the five of them leaped back. A transparent sphere emerged from the floor and closed around them like a glass claw. They were now imprisoned inside it.

"It's some kind of trap," Liam said.

Liam and Logan pummeled the crystal surface with their fists, but it seemed to be solid and tough, some kind of unbreakable glass.

"Let us out of here!" Ava shouted.

"I'm afraid that isn't possible," Sias said in a neutral voice. "If you wish to get to the Cure, you will have to pass this test." She folded her arms.

"She's not going to help us," Amelia said to Ava. "I think she's another of his robots."

Liam and Logan activated their Powers and attacked the surface of the sphere. Liam could not get his Power to damage it, which puzzled them, because it seemed to be glass. Logan, for his part, activated his lighter and sent a steady flame of great intensity onto the surface. Seeing that fire did nothing to it, he changed elements and used water to freeze a large area of it. They waited for a moment to see whether the effect of freezing cracked the surface, but this did not work either.

Liam was still trying, but with equal lack of success. He took the rocks Logan had created and used his Power to hurl them against the top of the sphere. It cracked a little, but he could not manage to break through.

Suddenly, from the hole under their feet, water began to emerge with great force.

"He's trying to drown us!" Emma cried.

The water was coming out with such force that in a few moments it had reached their waists. It was blue and salty, as if it came from the sea.

Ava was hammering the walls, even though she knew it was pointless. "We've got to do something or we'll drown. The water keeps coming up."

Liam dived to try blocking the source of the water, but was repelled by the force of it as it entered the sphere.

"Why can't you let us out of here?" Logan asked Sias.

"I've been strictly ordered not to."

"You cursed robot! Let us out!" Ava yelled, with the water already at her neck.

"The contenders must pass the test by themselves, without any external help."

"Don't let us drown," Amelia begged. "Haven't you got any feelings?"

Sias looked back at her and blinked hard several times. "No."

The water covered Ava's head, and she could say no more. The five were submerged, while the water went on to fill the rest of the sphere until there was nothing left but a bubble of air at the very top.

Liam signaled them to rise to the bubble at the top and

breathe. They swam up and broke the surface, relieved because they were breathing and at the same time desperate because they knew there was no way out of this situation. The bubble was barely larger than their heads together as they kept themselves afloat by kicking and moving their arms.

"How long will this bubble last?" Logan asked, spluttering breathlessly.

"Not long, I'm afraid," Emma said. "A few more moments until we've used up all the oxygen, then there'll be nothing left to breathe and we'll drown."

"And me with my hair in a wet mess," Logan joked.

Ava was feeling a massive sense of frustration. "We can't die here," she gasped, spitting out water.

"I can't hold up anymore, I'm sinking," Amelia said, and let herself fall. Immediately Liam dived after her and held her head out of the water so that she could breathe.

Emma, too, began to sink. Logan dived to help her, but could not manage to push her up and they both sank. Ava gave a cry of rage and despair. She realized that there was no more air left to breathe and let herself sink.

The five companions drowned. One after the other. They were under the surface of the blue water, their bodies inert and lifeless.

CHAPTER 43

Sias waited to be sure they were all dead.

"Simulated reality test over," she called. She walked slowly and carefully over to where the five companions were lying on the floor. The sphere and the water in it had vanished as if they had never been there.

"Failed test," she announced once she was beside the bodies. She stared at them unflinchingly.

Suddenly Logan had a seizure, as if he had received an electrical discharge. His arms and legs began to shake uncontrollably.

"Resuscitation underway," Sias called in her metallic voice.

A moment later it was Liam's turn to be shaking on the floor, and Emma's convulsions were so rapid and massive it looked as if she were having a seizure. Ava and Amelia, too, began to shake, their arms and legs thrashing uncontrollably.

All five were shaking as though they were being tortured with electrical discharges that went down their necks and through their bodies, ending at their hands and feet.

Ava experienced the same nightmare in the midst of the pain that was running through her body. She could now feel it clearly originating at the nape of her neck and spreading from there. She knew it was the nightmare, there was no doubt about it; the problem was how to get out of it. The seizures and the pain were not waking her up.

The great sphere with the flat ring around it appeared, filling her mind completely. It was rotating in an absolutely black space, as if it were floating in the middle of nothing. The spherical surface seemed to be made up of many concentric circles very close to one another, as was the great ring that surrounded the sphere at its equator.

A new discharge shook her body, making her convulse again. An idea began to form in her mind. That sphere was not a sphere at all . . . it was actually . . . something more than that. Something she watched every evening, something she knew was there even though she could not see it. It was a distant planet, a star in the sky. The idea came to her clearly, and she knew it to be true. A new discharge followed by a convulsion etched it in her mind.

The planet vanished, and once again she saw herself floating in a viscous liquid. The back of her neck, as well as her throat and nose, were very painful. Why? What was this horrible nightmare that was tormenting her? Why did she see those things? Why was she feeling this pain?

Suddenly she felt she was being shaken, this time by the shoulders.

"Wake up, Ava, wake up!" she heard. She thought she was back in the nightmare again and that this was one more of its tortures. "Wake up, Ava," the voice said again, and this time she recognized the voice: It was Liam's.

She opened her eyes, looked around her, and saw that they were in the middle of the chamber where they had all drowned. She sat up, not understanding what was going on. The others, too, were also getting up, stunned and baffled.

"Are we alive?" she asked Liam. She could not believe it.

"Looks like it."

"But it's not possible. I can remember us drowning perfectly well. I remember the pain and the anxiety, the lack of air, us dying inside that sphere. Don't you remember the same thing?"

Liam nodded. "Yes, I remember the same thing. I think we all do."

Ava looked around for Amelia and saw her getting up, with Logan's assistance.

"Are you all right, Amelia?"

Her cousin gave the ghost of a smile. "Yeah, for a dead person I'm fine."

"We all are," Logan said, "though I don't really understand how or why, seeing we ought to have drowned."

"Emma?"

"I have no answer to that. We should all have drowned inside that sphere trap. I've no idea why we're alive."

"I can answer that question," Sias said. She was watching them impassively.

They all tensed at once. They had forgotten her presence, as if she were part of the room.

"She's still here," Logan said. He was looking at her sourly.

They reached for their weapons and activated the Powers.

"I assure you it is not necessa—" she began, but she was not allowed to finish. Logan had attacked her with a ball of fire.

"We're the ones who'll decide that," the Elementalist said.

Sias began to burn, yet she didn't seem concerned. She went on talking while her body was consumed.

"You've all been subjected to a test of projected mental reality. What you experienced was not real. It was an experience projected into your minds."

"You have technology that makes us see and experience things?" Emma asked with great interest.

"Yes. We call it Implanted Reality."

"Why? What's it for?" Amelia asked.

"To see whether you were able to pass the test."

"Was that another of Siaais's blasted tests?" Ava protested, although she knew what the answer would be.

"That's right. A test you have to pass in order to progress."

"And did we pass it?"

"Unfortunately you did not, you failed."

Sias was burning from head to foot and beginning to melt. She was made of some material that was neither metallic nor synthetic, and burned more easily. Moments later she was reduced to a viscous puddle that smelled of chemicals.

Logan smiled in satisfaction. "I'm afraid she's not going to do much more talking."

Amelia looked at him, disagreement written all over her face.

Suddenly a hole that had not been visible opened in the floor. Another Sias emerged, identical to the previous one, and rose to the same spot the other had occupied.

"Who are you?" Ava asked.

"I am Sias," was the calm reply.

"We're listening," Amelia said.

"The test was not passed successfully. You failed. Because of this you have two choices. You can give up and leave this place to spend whatever is left of your life in this world . . ."

"No way," Logan snapped instantly.

"In your dreams," Ava cried.

"We've come for the Cure and we're not leaving without it," said Liam.

Sias went on without paying any attention. "Check your Marks of Siaais The other option is to go ahead toward the Cure."

So there really is a Cure after all? "And what's the 'but'?" Ava asked.

"There is a 'but,' true. Because you failed the test, one of you must die here and now in order that the others can go on."

"No way!" Ava cried.

"You're insane!" yelled Logan.

"Those are the rules of the experiment, and are inflexible." Sias gestured, and the floor opened again, this time so a five-sided pedestal could rise, with five buttons on top, one near each edge. Four of them were black. The fifth was red.

"At least one of you will have to press the red button, the others the black one," Sias went on. "If none of you five presses the red button, then you'll forfeit the Cure and leave the building to await your transformations."

"We're not going to condemn one of our own people," said Liam.

"I'll burn you, just like I did your partner," Logan threatened her.

"That will solve nothing. Time is running out. One of you must press the red button and the others the black one, or else all must leave the tower."

Ava looked at her companions, one by one. "We're not doing this."

"If we don't," Amelia pointed out, "we won't get to the Cure . . ."

"Has anybody passed the test?" Logan asked.

"Affirmative. One group has passed it."

"Hellfire, it was Sven," Ava muttered.

"Was it a Nordic with bad manners?"

"Confidential information. I cannot reveal it."

"We're running out of time," Emma pointed out.

Liam turned to Ava. "What are we going to do?"

"I don't know. Let me think."

"Think fast," Logan said. "My markings are flashing too. I'll be transformed any moment now."

"Hellfire!" Ava cried. She put her hands to her head, trying to think of some way out of their situation.

It was Siaais's cruelest test yet, but if one of them did not make the sacrifice, they would never reach the Cure, and in any case they would not last long enough because they were about to be transformed. Ava was sure of that. Siaais was merciless. How could they get out of that impossible situation?

She looked at her companions for help. She was desperate, and to judge by their expressions, so were they. All but one. Amelia's eyes were dull. She showed neither fear nor despair. Suddenly Ava knew what she was about to do.

She reached her hand out to her. "No!"

Amelia looked at her sadly. "I'm sorry. It'll be best for all of us."

And she pressed the red button.

"Nooooooo!" Ava shouted in terror and gripped her arm.

Amelia gazed at her for a single moment with moist eyes and collapsed to the floor.

CHAPTER 44

Ava rushed to Amelia's side with her heart bursting out of her chest. "Why? No! No!" she cried desperately as she knelt down beside her cousin.

"It's for the best, Ava . . . I'm the weakest, the least useful." Her voice began to fail.

"Fight, please don't let yourself give up!"

"I always knew . . . from the moment I was chosen, that I'd never make it. It didn't make sense . . . a weak scholar. I'll never understand why he chose me . . . but it doesn't matter. My purpose was to help as much as I could and get as far as I could . . . I made it, and that's what I wanted to do."

"Amelia . . ." Ava's voice was choked with tears. She lifted her cousin's head onto her lap. "Hold on, my pretty, clever cousin."

Amelia smiled faintly, and her face lost all color. They were all looking on with expressions of sorrow and helplessness.

"How long has she got left?" Ava asked the robot.

"A few moments. The poison is quick and painless. She'll fall asleep and not wake up again."

"Nooo . . ."

Amelia took her hand. "We're not what important, Ava . . . the Cure is. Go get it. Save our people . . . that's all that matters. It's what Amos wanted, it's what I want . . . Do it for us."

"I'm not the one who can do it . . . that's you."

"You're wrong . . . you're the soul of this group . . . you'll make it. I've always known that."

"Don't go, don't leave me."

"We came here . . . to get . . . the Cure . . ."

Her voice began to weaken, and her eyes closed.

"Amelia!"

"Ava . . ." But she never finished, and died.

Ava wailed. She felt her heart breaking into a thousand pieces as she broke into convulsive sobs. In her heart there was a bleeding hole and all she could do was weep. She had lost her cousin forever.

Emma hugged her tightly and wept with her. Logan and Liam looked on with moist eyes, not knowing how to comfort her in this moment of unbearable pain.

"You must press the black button if you wish to go on," Sias informed them.

"Ava," said Liam said gently.

Ava nodded, and gently laid Amelia's head on the marble floor. They each took positions in front of the four black buttons. Liam went first. Nothing happened. Logan went next. Then Emma. Then finally Ava, still sobbing uncontrollably, her heart filled with pain and inexpressible rage, pressed the last black button.

"Test passed. Access to upper levels granted," the robot said.

The spherical chamber slowly vanished before their eyes, to be replaced by a rectangular one that they were now at the center of. Beside them, stretched out dead on the floor, lay Sven's Nordic companion.

"Hell, this whole chamber was a nightmare," said Logan.

"It's a twisted game," Ava said. The tears were still running down her cheeks.

Emma shrugged. "I don't know . . . it has something to do with this place, it's a special chamber . . . and with these collars we're wearing."

"Yeah, with the collars for sure," Logan said. He was feeling the nape of his neck, and gave a grimace of pain.

Liam bent over the Nordic and examined him. "He's dead. And he's wearing a collar, like us."

"Then the same thing happened to them as happened to us," Logan concluded. "They failed the test, and this one paid the price."

"Sven survived," Liam said with an expression of disgust.

"I bet he sacrificed this lad," said Logan. He gave the body a kick to make sure he was really dead.

"That guess is correct," the robot said.

"Well, this beauty's finally giving us some useful information," Logan said. He gave her a flirtatious glance. "Are you going to help us?"

"You've passed the test. I can answer certain questions."

"That's better," Logan said, and blew her a kiss.

"How far ahead are they?" Liam asked.

"Only a little. They've just passed the test."

Liam went over to Ava, who had once again fallen to her knees beside her cousin, weeping. He put a hand on her shoulder.

"We can go on," he said gently. "You stay with her if you want."

Ava heard the words, but did not understand their meaning. Her mind was paralyzed, and it took her a moment to understand what he was telling her. She shook her head.

"No. I'm coming with you."

"Are you sure . . . ?"

"I know what you're trying to do, Liam, and I appreciate

it." She wiped her nose with the sleeve of her tunic. "But I'll go on to the end." She glanced down at Amelia. "It's what she asked me to do."

Liam nodded. "Right. Then let's go." He held out his hand to her.

She looked into the hunter's eyes and accepted it. With a gentle tug he raised her from the floor.

The glass elevator awaited them.

"Permission to access the cupola granted," Sias said.

The four surviving companions went forward. The transparent doors opened, and they went in.

The elevator set off toward the cupola where Siaais was waiting for them. They were on their way to their final test, to their meeting with the God.

The panel showed numbers that changed rapidly: *11*, *12*, *13*, then almost immediately *20*, *21*, *22*. Ava asked Emma what the numbers meant.

"They're the floors of this building, the levels we're going by without stopping. It seems to be taking us directly to the top."

"I wonder what's in all those levels we're passing," said Ava.

"I don't want to know," Liam said.

"Exactly," Logan agreed. "We've seen enough horrors and atrocities to last a lifetime."

"I agree absolutely," Emma said.

"I understand," said Ava. "The sooner we face that God and get hold of the Cure, the sooner we'll get out of here."

Logan had a sour look. "Yeah, if he doesn't kill us all."

"Let's hope not," Emma said, not sounding very convinced.

"And not if we kill him first," whispered Liam.

Ava clenched her fists, buoyed by Liam's determination. "We'll do that and get what we came for."

Logan looked down at his right arm and checked the lower

Mark. "My time's up. The flashes on this are coming faster all the time."

"Mine too," said Emma.

Ava was looking at the panel. *501*, *502*, *503*: the counter was still announcing the floors as they passed them. "We're almost there."

"This tower's endless!" Logan protested. There was fear in his eyes. "Whatever may be waiting for us up there, I want to let you all know it's been a really intense journey, one not to be repeated." He smiled nervously.

Liam gave him a friendly shove. "You can say that again."

"When I was left alone," Emma said, "I thought I wouldn't make it, but finding you all was a real blessing."

Liam, too, was doing his best to cheer them up. "Even meeting Logan?" he joked.

Emma chuckled. "Don't make me laugh, I'm in no state for it. I'm about to collapse. My body and spirit are giving way."

Liam smiled. "We're all in a sorry state, hungry and exhausted, but we're still together and we're going to get to the end. Hang on a bit longer, the reward will be ours."

"There's one thing I can do for you all," Ava said. "I'll use the Blessing, my Power, and leave you all as good as new. Come closer to me."

While the elevator approached the final floors, Ava Felt all three of them and sent feelings of well-being, recovery, and strength into their minds. She left them feeling as though they had been resting for a week and were all strong and full of energy.

"I feel wonderful," Emma said. "Thank you, Ava."

Logan flexed his muscles. "You can say that again. Wow."

Liam nodded with a smile, and Ava felt very proud.

Suddenly the elevator stopped. They had arrived at the cupola. The door opened. The final moment of truth had come.

CHAPTER 45

A long corridor opened out in front of them. Walls, floor, and ceiling seemed to be made of pure white marble. At the end was a double metal door. They went toward it, determination in every step.

Logan began to lag behind. Ava, becoming aware of this, stared at him as she followed Liam and Emma. She was about to ask him if he was all right when he suddenly stopped. She, too, stopped beside him.

"Come on, we're nearly there. Is there something wrong?"

Logan stared back at her, looking as though he could not understand what was happening to him. "I'm . . . coming . . . now . . ." he mumbled.

"But you're better again, aren't you," she asked him in puzzlement.

"Yeah . . . I am . . . I was . . . until a moment ago . . ." He leaned against the marble wall, staring at the floor.

"Are you sure you're okay? You don't look it."

Logan did not answer. He swallowed with difficulty, then

breathed out and wiped away the sweat that was running down his forehead.

"I think your Blessing isn't having any effect on me anymore." He was looking at her with one eye open, the other half-closed. "I feel as if I had a fever or something." He touched his forehead, found that it was sweaty, and wiped it with the sleeve of his coat. "I'm very hot . . . I'm burning . . ."

"Let me see whether it's really fever," she said, and hurried to his side.

He did his best to wave this off. "It's sure to be nothing . . ."

"In your weakened state, it's natural your temperature should rise. My Power only deceives the mind, but the body's still extremely weak." She began to examine him.

"And here I was thinking your wonderful care had healed me forever," he said with a wink and a smile.

"I can't believe that with a fever, sweating like a pig, and barely able to walk, you're still flirting with me."

Logan smiled from ear to ear, and his eyes gleamed suddenly. "Always, my princess. I haven't lost hope."

"You're impossible," she chided him, and crouched down, leaving her satchel and spear on the floor. Logan, meanwhile, was trying to stay on his feet against the wall.

Liam and Emma had reached the end of the corridor. Emma was intent on opening the door, and Liam was looking back at Logan and Ava with a look of concern.

"Everything all right?" he asked.

"Yeah, don't worry, it's a fever."

Logan's eyes suddenly looked up at the ceiling, staring wide. His jaw fell open and he let out an agonizing howl, as if some evil spirit were dragging him to an unfathomable abyss from which he would never return. He put his hands to his throat, apparently choking.

Ava was left petrified. She now knew beyond any doubt this was no fever.

"Oh no," she whispered. "Please, Logan, not now. Don't do this . . ."

Logan could not answer. He seemed to be unable to speak. His mouth was unhinged and his eyes were staring wide as if they wanted to leave his body. He gave another howl, one even more desperate, agonized, and tortured than the first, and fell to his knees.

"Logan, come back to me, don't leave me!" she cried, and gripped his hand.

Logan closed his mouth and looked into her eyes and opened his mouth to speak.

"Run . . . sweetheart . . . go . . ." he said, and suffered a terrible convulsion.

"Logan, don't leave me. You're the most powerful of all of us. Fight! Don't let it defeat you! We need you!"

He shook his head, trying to hold back a convulsion.

"My time's up . . . you can still make it, all of you, go on . . . for me, for all of us." Once again a seizure shook his body.

"Logan!"

"I'd have been so happy to love you . . ." he said with a genuine smile.

"Logan, there's still time. Don't give up!"

A new seizure left him stretched out on the floor. His body began to give off a smell of sulfur, and his skin began to darken. His mouth gaped wide in a terrible, muted howl.

Ava leaped back in terror. She tripped and finally sat down on the floor a few paces away from him, and the substance swallowed him up completely.

"Logan! No! Noooooo!"

The Curse of Siaais was consuming Logan, and he was being transformed. It would be quick. A virus which had been in their bodies all their lives, waiting to escape and transform them, to take over their bodies and minds. Ava watched in horror, with tears in her eyes. Logan's entire skin had turned shining black, as if it were now covered by a shell. His eyes swelled and turned completely white. He lost all his hair in a single moment and his head, too, turned black.

Ava could not stop sobbing. Horror held her there paralyzed, unable to react.

The Transformed One stood up very slowly, as if he were checking the workings of his new body.

"Logan . . . it's me . . ." she said between sobs.

The Transformed One looked at her with those white, lifeless eyes. He opened his unhinged mouth.

"No, Logan. No!"

A black substance, like a mist with a life of its own, issued from his open mouth. It rose, like a black ghost, and began to descend on Ava.

She tried to move, but her muscles had turned stiff. If it touched her she was lost. Unconsciously she reached for her javelin, and at the same time strong arms seized her from behind and pulled her away.

She turned her head and saw that it was Liam. He was carrying her toward the door.

"Emma, open the door!" he shouted.

Ava looked back and saw the Transformed One beginning to move toward them, slowly at first, but then speeding up. She saw her satchel on the floor. She had forgotten it.

Liam set Ava down in front of the closed door. "It's coming for us!"

"I'm almost there," Emma said.

The Transformed One began to run on all fours, like an animal.

"Come on, Emma," Liam urged her, "open the door!"

The Transformed One was now upon them. Ava could not stop thinking that this monster was really Logan.

"I'm sorry, pal," Liam said, and using his Power he pushed the Transformed One down the corridor.

But it got to its feet and came at them again.

"Got it!" Emma cried. And the door opened.

They went in. The Transformed One was coming for them now with great strides.

"Now close it!"

Emma used her Power on the panel on the other side of the door frame, and the door closed.

The Transformed One hissed in rage on the other side.

"Logan . . ." Ava sobbed. She lowered her head, trying unsuccessfully to hold back her tears.

Emma was weeping openly.

Liam's eyes were moist as he said farewell. "I'm sorry, pal, deeply sorry," he said, looking at the door. "A brave heart like yours didn't deserve to end like that. Not when we were so close . . ."

Ava hugged Emma and Liam put his arms round them both. For a moment they stayed locked in an embrace, mourning their loss.

Suddenly they heard a sensuous, feminine voice. "Welcome."

They turned and saw Sias, or one of them. She was in the middle of a round hall, beside an enormous metal box. The whole room was silver, except for two white doors and one golden one. They had come in through one of the white doors.

"Another of them . . ." Liam said with loathing.

"We were waiting for you," the robot said.

The three grasped their weapons, ready for whatever might happen.

"One moment, please," Sias went on.

A door opened at the other end of the hall. From it appeared Sven and the surviving African. To judge by their faces, they had not been enjoying themselves. They were panting and covered in sweat, apparently exhausted, and they could not keep the look of horror from their faces.

"Now all the contenders are present," Sias announced.

Ava, Emma, and Liam stared at their opponents, who glared back at them. They were about to hurl themselves at one another when Sias raised her arms.

"Wait. There's no need to fight among yourselves, not anymore. What you have to do in this final test is to leave this chamber alive."

Ava froze at the sound of this. What was this last test? Why were their rivals here with them? It made no sense.

Sven did not seem convinced. He was brandishing his two axes, and made as if to lunge at them. The African was shielding himself behind Sven's back.

Liam activated his Power, and Emma showed them her katana. Ava aimed her javelin at the African.

CHAPTER 46

"Looks as though we're the only ones left," Sven said with a triumphant grin. He swung both axes in his hands and spread his arms wide to reveal his strong chest. He had lost the bearskin that had hung down his back. Although he still inspired fear, he looked gaunt. His exhaustion and hunger were apparent, particularly around his eyes, where purple circles were visible. His pallor was a clear sign of his weakened physical state.

Behind him, half-hidden, was the African. He did not look much better, and appeared barely able to stand. He said nothing, merely watched them.

Ava realized this was a decisive moment for them, so she stepped in and raised her hand in a sign of peace.

"There's no need for us to fight. Unless I'm misreading the signs, the Cure is behind that golden door. All we have to do is go through it. We're not enemies, it's Siaais who's our enemy. We don't need to give him the satisfaction of killing each other. If we work together instead of fighting, we have a chance."

Sven seemed to consider her words.

"Sorry, but the Cure's only for me. I'm not sharing it with anybody."

Ava nodded toward the African. "Not anybody? Not even with your shadow?"

"Embele's not interested in the Cure, he's only interested in getting out of here alive, and that's the agreement between us. As long as he's with me, he'll stay alive. Once I get the Cure, we'll both get out of here alive."

"And how come you're so eager to get hold of the Cure? You don't strike me as the kind who'd worry too much about his tribe."

"You're right," Sven said, and laughed sourly. "No, I'm not worried about my people. For me, gaining the Cure means the final victory, and that's what I am. I'm a winner, a warrior born and trained for victory. No one can beat me. I'll leave here victorious. My name will be written in the annals of my people. I'll be the first to get it, and they'll venerate me as the Savior. My name will be remembered as the greatest of all warriors, the invincible. I'll go down in history, my name will never be erased like the names of all those who failed before us."

Ava raised one eyebrow. "That's not a very glorious reason . . ."

"I'll be remembered. I'll win. That's all that matters to me. And that's enough chitchat, it's time to die." The Nordic walked toward them, brandishing his axes, and as he advanced he activated his Power. Behind him Embele did the same.

Ava glanced aside at Liam, who was already activating his Power. Emma swung her katana and took up a defensive position.

Liam aimed his hand at the Nordic's neck, intending to strangle him using his telekinetic Power. At the same moment Embele used his own Power. A translucent aura surrounded them all. It was imperceptible before, but somehow in this chamber of Siaais's making, it had become faintly visible.

Liam activated his Power and, as before, was unable to use it against Sven. He pointed to Embele.

"He's canceling my Power."

"Yeah, that really sucks, eh?" Sven said, and delivered a tremendous blow with his axe. Liam threw himself to one side and rolled across the floor. He took out his knife and tomahawk.

Sven went after him. "Don't run away, nothing's going to save you this time."

From the ground, on one knee, Liam tried to use his Power again.

"It's useless," Sven said. "I'm going to tell you a little secret. The reason I allow Embele to come with me is because his Power's a very special one. He can cancel the Power of the ones he chooses, as he's doing with you right now."

Then Liam understood what was happening. He saw Embele pointing his right index finger at him.

"As long as he's protecting my back, none of your Powers'll work on me," Sven said. And he launched a strong axe-blow against Liam, who tried to dodge it by throwing himself to one side. The effort reopened his wounds, and he was left lying on the floor with an expression of pain on his face.

Emma launched herself swiftly at Sven. She made rapid attacks with her katana, which the Nordic did not even bother to block. She slashed at his neck, his groin, even a magnificent stroke to his heart. And yet all she managed to do was to destroy the remains of the armor he was wearing. The steel was unable to penetrate his skin.

The Nordic burst out laughing and launched an axe-blow at Emma, which she sidestepped with a lightning dodge.

"In case you hadn't noticed yet, my skin's impenetrable.

That's the Power my people have. Nothing can wound me. You lot won't be able to defeat me, you can't do a thing to me."

Ava, desperate as she saw Liam stretched out on the floor and Emma unable to kill Sven, lunged at the African with her javelin, yelling like a madwoman. Embele saw her coming and took up a defensive stance. Ava aimed her javelin at the huge African's chest, but with a perfectly measured move turned just enough to let it fly right past him. She hurled herself at him, but he knocked her to one side with his forearm. She was flung backward and was left lying on the floor, barely able to breathe.

Emma went on fighting Sven. With short, agile strokes she lashed at his arms, legs, and neck. The result was always the same: She could not give him even a single miserable scratch.

The Nordic tried to reach her with two massive circular blows from his axes, but Emma dodged them easily. Her small size and her speed were advantages Sven couldn't seem to overcome, but the slightest error on Emma's part would be fatal.

Liam managed to get back to his feet. A moment later Ava did the same, with a terrible pain in her chest and difficulty breathing.

"A magnificent battle," Sias said suddenly. "Nevertheless, before you kill one another, my lord wishes you to observe the last test you will have to pass in order to get to the Cure."

They stopped and turned to listen. Ava had a sense of foreboding.

"In this box there is something very powerful: an enemy greater than any you've previously encountered. Allow me to give you a demonstration."

A side door in the wall opened, and three battle robots came in. They were different from one another, but clearly ready for war.

Ava, Liam, and Emma moved together and backed up

against one wall. Sven and Embele did the same on the opposite side.

"These three robots," Sias said, "are fully capable of putting an end to any threat, including you."

Ava stayed calm and glanced aside at Liam. "What does she want?"

"I've no idea . . ."

"Nothing good," said Emma, who was looking at the robots with narrowed eyes.

"But rest easy, their function is not to kill you but to end the life of the enemy inside this box. Now we'll begin the demonstration." She touched something on her arm, and the box began to rise slowly toward the ceiling. As it rose, the lower part of whatever was imprisoned inside it began to emerge.

The first thing Ava saw was the feet of something more like a great raptor than a human. They were black, with three claws like those of an eagle. As the box went on rising, it revealed more of the creature's body. To her amazement its legs were not those of a bird but looked human, or at least very like it. They, too, were black. In fact its whole skin seemed to be shining black, hairless and without scales, as if it were covered with a black shell, or black armor. The box revealed the creature's thorax, which was indeed humanoid, but its arms ended in hands with claws.

The first robot, which was white, carried a large rifle in its arms connected to a pack on its back by an orange tube. This was presumably either ammunition or some mechanism to give the rifle more power. The red robot was larger, squarer, and more robust. It looked fully armored. Instead of hands it had huge circular machine guns. The third robot was not as large as the other two, but instead was slender, and although parts of its body were of reinforced metal it looked more humanoid, more flexible. In its right hand it held a sword, which it now activated. A red flash indicated that a laser was now active. In its left hand it carried a dagger of the same style, and this, too, it activated, so that another small laser dot appeared on the metal handle.

The box finished its ascent, and they were now able to see the head of that strange being. It was entirely black, without hair, with large yellow eyes like those of a cat and a huge mouth. No ears or nose were visible, though its head was quite human, elongated at the back. A yellow and black crest began at its forehead, continued back across its head and down its back, then forked to continue down the back of both legs as far as the claws.

Ava was unable to restrain herself. "Oh, by the Great Sphinx!" The creature looked utterly insane.

Sias touched her arm, and at the same moment the three robots attacked the creature.

The white robot shot his huge rifle, and a burst of plasma struck the creature with an explosion. Next the red robot activated its two machine guns and fired hundreds of armor-piercing explosive bullets. There was a metallic clatter, and multiple explosions hit the creature in a tremendous cascade.

The creature gave a shriek that was so long and shrill it almost deafened them all, and it took a couple of steps back from the force of the attacks. But something strange was happening: The robots' shots did not seem to be penetrating its skin, or black shell.

It began to move toward the robots, emitting shrill shrieks that made everyone's hair stand on end. The robot with the laser sword and dagger leaped on it and began to attack its legs, arms, and head. But it, too, was unable to pierce its armor.

"As you can see," Sias said, "this creature isn't affected by assault weapons, and not even the most powerful laser can pierce its skin. Its shell is practically indestructible."

The creature reached the robots, lumbering as though its body weighed a ton, in the midst of a ceaseless barrage of shots. It gave a deafening shriek, and its crest stood up stiff so that it now projected a hand-span along its whole body. An instant later it issued a yellow wave that spread from its body and through the whole chamber.

When the wave reached the robots' weapons the machine gun, the rifle, and the laser went out. A moment later the robots themselves stopped working. The lights in their eyes and other illuminated parts went out.

"As you have witnessed," Sias said, "this creature is capable of generating a signal very similar to what is known as an electromagnetic pulse. That's the yellow wave you've just seen. Anything electronic within its range will stop working, just like these robots."

The creature reached the robots and destroyed them with its indestructible metal claws. It only needed four slashes to finish the job.

"There's no need for me to point out that its claws are utterly lethal. They could cut through a wall."

Then Ava realized why Sias was telling them all this: To reach the Cure they would have to defeat this creature, and that was all but impossible.

"But all is not lost," Sias added. "It isn't completely invincible. It's vulnerable to one thing: Powers."

The creature looked at them and suddenly seemed to regard them as possible threats. It gave a shriek.

"Luckily for you this specimen is not an assassin or a hunter, it's an infectious specimen. Its function is to kill all resistance by means of contagion. Hence you have a chance to defeat it."

Ava saw that Liam's eyes showed no fear, but instead were gleaming intensely. His side was bleeding and he was holding his ribs. The color was ebbing from his face and he did not look well at all, which made her wonder how much longer he was going to hold up. As for Emma, she looked terrified.

"What do you think that thing is?" Ava asked her.

"It's organic, like us, a creature . . ."

"But where from? There's no animal like it on Earth. Or is there?"

Liam shook his head. "Not even remotely."

"Which means . . . ?"

Emma sighed. "There are only two options. Either it's a monster created via genetic manipulation, or . . ."

Ava was watching the monster out of the corner of her eye. "Or?"

"Or it's not from this planet."

"What?"

"Siaais has brought it from another planet," Emma explained.

Ava shook her head. "That's not possible."

"Everything is possible in Siaais's realm," said Sias. "The time has come for the final test."

The terrifying black creature, with its lethal claws, began to move toward them.

CHAPTER 47

Ava turned to Sven, and saw the Nordic staring at the creature as it came toward him.

"We'll have to fight together, or it'll be the end of us," she said.

Sven hesitated for a moment. But seeing death approaching he seemed to reconsider, and his expression went from absolute confidence to doubt. He nodded to her.

"We'll get rid of this demon from a lost abyss. We'll draw lots for the Cure afterward."

Ava nodded back in agreement.

The creature advanced toward Sven, who moved forward to meet it. It gave a shrill shriek, and the pain it caused their eardrums almost made them faint. Liam readied his knife and his tomahawk; Emma, her katana. Their chances of victory were minimal, practically nil.

First with one axe and then with the other Sven struck the creature's body with tremendous force, but both weapons bounced off. He had to make an effort to keep the axes from flying out of his hands after the impact.

The creature attacked the Nordic with a similar move, first with a right cross-stroke, then a left one with its other claw. Sven was thrown back by the force of the attack.

Ava thought it had killed him, but she was wrong. While Sven's Power was activated, not even that creature's claws could penetrate his skin.

Liam seized the chance to throw his knife, which went straight to where the creature's heart ought to be if it had one like that of a human, which Ava doubted. The arrow bounced off without even scratching it. Neither blade nor tip could penetrate the armor that covered its body.

The creature's attention was still on Sven, who was trying to get back to his feet after the terrible blow. Emma attacked the monster from behind with lightning speed and launched a series of swift cuts at its legs and arms, but these attacks, too, were ineffective.

Sven tried another attack. His axes battered the creature's head brutally, but every strike bounced off. The creature gave another shrill shriek before attacking. Sven managed to deflect the first blow with one of his axes, but the second caught him squarely in the chest. Once again he was thrown backward.

Emma took a great leap and struck a sharp, precise, and ultimately useless blow to the middle of the creature's forehead with her katana. The creature slashed at her, but she managed to avoid its claws by a hair's breadth.

"Don't just stand there!" Sven called to Embele. "Use your Power on this monster!"

The African activated his Power and pointed at the creature. Sven stood up with a triumphant smile. He lashed out with both axes simultaneously at the creature's shoulders, intending to slice down to its stomach, but he failed.

The monster seized him in its huge claws.

"I said you had an opportunity to defeat it," Sias said. She looked at Embele. "I didn't say it had Powers like you. Hence, if it doesn't have a Power, there's nothing to be nullified."

The monster opened its mouth as if it meant to bite off Sven's head. Liam released again and Emma attacked, but the monster ignored them and focused on Sven.

"You can't kill me," the Nordic boasted. "My skin's as hard as yours."

The monster's eyes gleamed, as if it had understood what he had said. The huge mouth opened even wider, but revealed neither jaws nor tongue. The creature's head seemed to split in two. It gave another shrill shriek, so that they all had to cover their ears. From the monster's mouth there emerged a thick black mist which light was unable to penetrate. It formed a small, ominous cloud that seemed to float in front of the creature with a life of its own. Suddenly it fell on Sven, enveloping him completely.

The Nordic now understood what Sias had meant when she had called it *infectious*. What was enveloping him was sickness. A single moment before the darkness covered him completely, they saw his eyes staring wide.

"No! I don't want to die! Not so close to the final victory!" he yelled, full of rage and fear.

The blackness swallowed him, until he was completely engulfed by it.

The monster dropped him, and he fell to the floor. They could not see his body beneath that black substance. Engulfed by the sickness. By the Curse. By death.

Ava feared they had no chance of defeating the monster. They were not going to leave this place alive. The Curse was going to take them.

It's like a Transformed One. Not exactly, but the resemblance is too close to be a coincidence. What does it mean?

The creature moved toward Embele, who dodged it swiftly, and gave another of its shrill shrieks. Its lethal, infectious mouth opened and the cloud of death fell upon Embele. He tried to reach the door, but the mist pursued him, enveloped him, and left him on the floor while the sickness transformed him.

The creature now turned to Emma, who was the next nearest to it. She hesitated.

"Run to me!" Ava shouted. She, too, had no idea what to do. But they had to get away from it.

Liam activated his Power. He put his hands together, focused on the creature, and caught it. Then with a sudden movement to the left, he hurled the monster against the wall with all the strength of his Power. The monster's body struck the surface and gave a shriek which Ava understood to be pain.

"You're hurting it!" she shouted. "Throw the creature harder!"

Liam concentrated and attacked the monster, slamming it back. Part of the wall was now destroyed, and the monster shrieked again.

Ava could now see a ray of hope. "Keep it up, Liam! Keep it up!"

Liam used his Power again and hurled the monster against the opposite wall. There was another terrible crash, and part of the wall fell on top of the creature as it tried to get up.

"I think it's injured!" Emma cried. She was pointing at its side, where a dark, wet fluid was bleeding.

Liam used his Power again. This time he raised the creature into the air and held it there, trying to strangle it.

It gave another shriek and opened its mouth wide.

"Careful!" Ava shouted in warning. "It's going to release its infection!"

Liam moved his arms quickly and sent the monster against

the right-hand wall. Another crash, and part of that wall fell atop it as well.

The monster got back up very slowly. It looked stunned, but not badly injured.

Liam grimaced in pain. He was very weak, he was bleeding, and he was exhausting himself with the use of his Power. His right arm emitted a series of silver flashes.

"Be careful," Ava said uneasily. "Don't overuse your Power or we'll lose you."

Liam looked her in the eye: a long, deep, determined look.

"I'm sorry, Ava. I have to finish this. If I don't, we'll all die."

"No, Liam! Don't!" She stretched out her hand to him.

The creature began to move toward them with slow but powerful steps. It seemed intent on infecting them.

Liam concentrated, summoning up his Power, barely able to stay on his feet.

"Don't do it, it'll kill you!" she pleaded.

But Liam was determined. He hurled the monster against the stone dome of the ceiling with all that was left of his Power. The creature crashed against it in an explosion of rock and steel. Next he hurled it against the floor with the same brutal intensity. The monster made a hole in the floor with the tremendous impact, filling the hall with rocky debris. It lay still.

Ava, Emma, and Liam watched for a moment, fearful that it would get up again.

It did not.

"You did it!!" Ava cried as Liam fainted. She ran to take him in her arms before he hit the floor, and cradled his head in her lap.

"Why did you do it? I begged you not to." She stroked his hair and his scar. "You're so brave," she added, and kissed him on the lips.

She turned to Emma. "I have to take care of him. If I don't stop the hemorrhage, he'll bleed to death."

"He went beyond the limits of his Power," Emma said.

"And of his body. I'll have to reach into his mind to bring him back, but first I have to deal with his wounds."

"Right. I'm going to try and work on the golden door and get us out of here." She circled the monster and went to the door.

"The test isn't over yet," Sias said when Emma had begun to work on the panel with her Power.

"I don't care," Emma said. "I'm going to open this door, and we're going to get what we came for, and leave this cursed place."

Ava searched in her belt, where she kept extra supplies, for her needle and thread and set to work. She was worried about Liam's loss of blood and weakness from hunger. She applied an ointment against infection when she had finished stitching.

"Don't die on me," she told him, and stroked his cheek.

"I've nearly got it," Emma called.

Ava finished attending to Liam's wound and searched in her belt for another ointment to help it heal.

And then she saw it. The monster had risen and was behind Emma.

"Emma!" Ava yelled with all her might.

The hacker turned . . . an instant too late.

The claws of the creature's right hand plunged into her body.

"Noooooo!" Ava screamed desperately.

Abruptly the monster shook its claws free, and Emma fell to the floor.

Ava ran to the monster without thinking, mad with rage and pain. She leaped onto its back, driven by her fury, feeling its surprisingly soft crests against her stomach. The monster turned and tried to get her off, but its arms could not reach her. And no matter how much it thrashed, she would not let go. She felt so much rage and pain that she was clinging to that horrifying creature's neck and back with strength drawn from her suffering.

The monster let out another shriek, loud enough to hurt Ava's ears. She almost let go, but then she saw Emma lying on the floor, dead in a puddle of her own blood, and felt such despair that she gripped its neck even more tightly.

"You murdering beast!"

The creature raised its claws to its head, trying to reach her face.

Ava closed her eyes, knowing she was about to die. Panic overwhelmed her, and unconsciously she activated her Power in that final moment of utter despair.

Stop!

There was an intense silver flash in her arm that filled the whole room.

To her immense surprise, the creature stopped reaching for her and stood still. She couldn't believe it. She'd managed to make it obey her. But how? It must have been her Power. There was no other explanation.

In that moment she followed her intuition. She concentrated and invaded the monstrous being's mind, armored herself against the savage feelings it might transmit to her. Instead she felt a sense of immense frustration, and she realized why: It was unable to get rid of her. Then she received another feeling which she tried to protect herself against: a sense of utter obligation. The creature had one goal to fulfill, at any cost: It needed to infect every human being.

With Ava still on its back, the creature opened its mouth and gave a searing shriek.

She knew what was coming: It was going to try to infect her with the black mist. She concentrated more deeply, pushing into its mind with an overwhelming need to obey her. *Stop!*

The creature was left with its mouth gaping, but the mist was not released.

Instead, Ava infected *it.*

She remembered all the fear and pain she had experienced during her mother's fatal accident as she relived the event. She remembered her mother's eyes as she fell into the abyss, the fear she herself had felt, the terror of seeing the person she most loved die. She concentrated and sent that feeling, heightened by her gift, to that being.

There was another silver flash on her arm. Suddenly, the monster lowered its arms. It fell to its knees and bowed its head. It was now totally at her mercy.

Ava got off its back and went to stand in front of it. It seemed to be paralyzed by the fear she had transmitted to it. She reached out, without touching its head. Suddenly she knew what she had to do.

She concentrated again, activated her Power, and sent a powerful feeling into the creature's mind.

The feeling was one of death. Of its own death.

The creature raised its right hand, then its left. With a sudden, powerful movement, it plunged its own claws into its eyes until they penetrated its brain.

It fell to one side, dead.

Ava stared at its body in disbelief. She had managed to kill it.

"Test passed," came the Sias's voice suddenly, and the golden door opened.

Ava knelt beside Emma, her heart in her mouth. She examined her in search of any sign of life, but found none. The girl was dead.

She was unable to hold back the tears or the pain she felt. Then she realized that Liam was not yet out of danger, and ran to his side.

"It's time to reach the Cure," Sias said, and motioned her to leave the hall.

She tried to lift Liam up, but he was too heavy for her. She began to drag him to the door with the strength she no longer had.

"Time is running out," Sias said. "You must cross, or you will lose the Cure."

"I'm leaving him!"

Sias began her countdown:

"Ten . . . nine . . . When I finish counting, the door will shut."

"No, you cursed robot!" Ava dragged Liam to the door. She was not going to make it. Her strength had run out.

". . . seven . . . six . . ." Sias went on. "If you don't cross, you'll lose, and you'll die."

Ava had only seconds left. Her heart told her to stay with Liam, to protect him. But her rational mind told her that she had to get it, for the greater good, in the light of her friends' sacrifice. She saw Amelia, Logan, Emma, and Amos, and knew that their deaths must not be in vain. They had given their lives. She could not fail them.

". . . three . . . two . . ."

She let go of Liam, with one final glance.

"I'll come back for you," she said, and hurled herself, head-first, toward the door just as it was beginning to close.

". . . one . . ."

Ava slid along the floor.

The door shut.

She had crossed to the other side.

To the Cure.

CHAPTER 48

Ava spun round, facing the golden door. She stretched out her hand to it, already regretting her decision.

"Liam . . ."

"Welcome," came the voice of Sias.

Ava stood up at once. She had used up all her energy by now, and could barely stand.

She was in a spherical hall. Its upper half was golden, its lower part silver. Thousands of metallic threads ran over both surfaces. Colored lights flashed through them in all directions, at dizzying speed. She nearly fainted, but managed to keep her head.

Sias was watching her with her cold gaze from the center of the room. Beside her was a pedestal of white marble. On top of it lay a glass cylinder containing some blue liquid.

"The Cure!" whispered Ava.

"That is correct. You have passed the last test. As winner, you're entitled to the trophy of victory: the Cure. You may approach and take it." She beckoned with a small bow.

Ava was in a state of shock. *It's the Cure. The Cure! After all the effort, after all the suffering. I made it! My people will be saved!*

"What'll happen if I take it?"

"You will leave here. You will be the winner, the first. No one has ever reached it before. Ever."

"No one? In all this time?"

Sias looked toward the door. "No one has been able to overcome the last test."

Ava examined the room again. There was nothing else in there. She was on the point of fainting and falling. *I have no choice.* With one final impulse she reached the Cure, took it in both hands, and lifted it from the pedestal.

"I did it! Salvation . . ."

And she fainted.

Ava felt a terrible eruption of energy that ran down her back, from the nape of her neck to her feet. She opened her eyes and stared.

Her mind could not understand what was happening. She was lying inside a horizontal metal capsule with a glass cover, floating in some yellowish-green liquid. She was nude, and a multitude of wires came out of her body: arms, legs, torso, and head.

What is this? What have they done to me? Where am I?

She tried to breathe through her mouth, but without success. There was a tube leading into her throat. Fear gave way to terror. She put her hands to her face and found more tubes in her nose, together with a kind of mask covering them. Suddenly she realized that even though she was submerged, she was not drowning. The tubes must be feeding air to her lungs.

I've got to get out of here. I've got to find out what's going on.

She banged the glass with all her strength, but it seemed to be unbreakable. Through the glass surface she caught a glimpse of a ceiling full of cables and conduits and countless wires. She tried to scream, but the tube in her throat prevented this. She turned her head to one side, trying to see what was around her. A blast of energy at her neck forced her to stop. The pain was terrible. Just like what she suffered in her nightmares.

She reached for the back of her neck and found something metallic stuck there. It covered the whole back of her neck and head, and was connected to the metal top of the capsule. Panic took hold of her again. She tried to get the thing off her head, but another spasm of pain forced her to stop.

Suddenly a light shone on her face.

"Subject active," came a machine voice, cold and lifeless.

There was a click, and a hole opened at the bottom of the capsule. The liquid she had been submerged in drained away.

The glass cover of the capsule opened.

When she saw it open, Ava began to pull off all the wires and tubes that were connected to her body. It was excruciating, but it didn't matter, all she wanted was to get out of there as quickly as possible, any way she could. She pulled off the mask that covered her mouth and nose and with it the tubes deep in her throat. She began to cough and retch terribly. Her throat and nose hurt badly, and she almost threw up.

Ava tried to leave the capsule, but she couldn't. The thing connecting her head to the top of the capsule made it impossible. She reached up to touch it, and found that it was cold metal. She gave a little tug to free herself and felt a sharp pain at the base of her skull, coinciding with the same terrible jolt that had so often tormented her in her nightmares.

Fear broke out within her. She had no doubt that taking the thing off would mean risking death. But staying there as she was, trapped, was no better. If she wanted to get out of there, she would have to defeat her fear and pull off that thing from her head.

I have to do it. She gave another tug, and once again the pain forced her to stop. Her fear grew into terror. She realized that her mind would not allow her to do something so dangerous and painful that it might kill her. Unless she managed to trick it somehow.

She looked down at her right arm for the Marks of Siaais. To her great surprise, she saw that they were not quite as she remembered them. There were still two marks, but these looked metallic. One was golden, the other silver, metal covered by some kind of very fine glass.

What's happening to me? Am I going insane? Is this another nightmare?

She touched the upper Mark to activate her Power. A silver light shone in the middle of the Mark and she was able to see numbers in it. They indicated "200 out of 100."

What . . . ?

She set the mystery aside; what mattered now was to get out of there. She put her hands to her head and activated her Power. Everything Ave knew told her that it wouldn't work, that it only possible to use her Power on someone else.

She summoned up all her courage and tried anyway.

Ava felt her fear rising again, growing by the moment and multiplying many times over. She shut her eyes and tried to control them before panic overtook her, but failed. She remembered the fear and pain she had felt when she had lost her mother, and her mother's eyes filled her mind. But this time she took strength from the memory, overcame her mother's desperate eyes, and rose above her terror, quieting her panic, eliminating it from her mind.

She needed a sense of tranquility. She remembered the oasis to the east of the village where she had gathered algae. Her Power produced another silver flash, and the feeling of tranquility from it wrapped around her like a warm cloak.

With her fear vanquished and her mind utterly calm, Ava did the unthinkable: She tugged with all her strength, and amid a terrible pain, broke loose from that strange contraption attached to her head. She opened her eyes wide and held her breath, waited a moment, then took a deep breath. She was still alive. She sat up in the capsule and felt the wounds on her head. She was bleeding from at least twenty places, from the nape of her neck to the front of her skull.

A little calmer now, she turned to inspect the strange half-helmet she had pulled off. She found two dozen needles.

She gave a long, deep sigh. *I'm alive . . . Thank you, Mother. Thank you for giving me the strength I needed. I love you.*

With her beloved mother in her thoughts, Ava looked around to see where she was. The hall was in shadow, so that she could not see very much. With the greatest care, she got out of the capsule. Lights came on in the ceiling, and the room was illuminated. What Ava saw then left her paralyzed.

The room was huge and circular. In it a hundred or so capsules formed a circle around a black tower full of blinking lights of different colors, from red to blue. The capsules were hooked to the wall and to the great black tower by innumerable cables and tubes. A shiver ran down Ava's spine.

She took a single, careful step. She no longer felt weak and hungry but well and strong, which surprised her. She looked into the capsule on her right. It was shut, and inside what might be a young woman floated, just as Ava had done, but in a completely black liquid. She could not see the woman's face, only vaguely guess the silhouette of her body. At the foot of the capsule, she saw a terminal.

It read:

Subject 101002.

State: terminated.

Decontamination stage.

Ava looked at all the capsules around the tower, and her doubts turned into fear as she began to understand what was going on there. She put her face to the capsule's glass and used her hands to try and see better. All she could see was the black liquid and the shadow of someone inside. She tried to open the capsule, but it was sealed.

She noticed three buttons on the capsule, and decided to press them and see if anything would open. It seemed that the first two did nothing, at least nothing that she was aware of, so she decided to try the third.

A light went on inside the capsule, and her heart skipped a beat. The person in the capsule was Amelia.

"Noooooo!"

She tried to open the capsule with all her might, but without success. Full of pain and rage, she began to weep. It was her dear cousin, her pretty, kindhearted cousin.

She reluctantly moved to the next capsule. She read the terminal:

Subject 101003.

State: terminated.

Decontamination stage.

She pressed the button that lit up inside the capsule and saw Amos.

"Nooooooo! Why?"

This can't be real, it can't be happening.

Trying to understand what was happening, seeking some logical explanation, she went back to her own capsule and checked the terminal. It read:

Subject 101001.

State: in progress.

Recovery stage.

This is insane. She went over to the other capsules and began to examine them one by one. All the terminals read the same thing: *state: terminated; decontamination stage.* The only thing that varied was the number for each subject.

Halfway around, she found Sven's capsule next to those of his companions. She went on hoping to find another survivor, someone like her in another capsule. She came to Emma's, and seeing her friend she felt a terrible pang of sadness. She stayed there for a while, wishing she could help her. But she was dead, there was nothing she could do.

She went on still hoping to find someone who had survived, and came to Logan. He was in his capsule in his normal state, not transformed, but he was dead just the same. *I don't understand any of this. What does it all mean?* With her heart in her throat, she went on looking.

At last she found Liam. Full of hope, she looked at the terminal. He must be alive. He was still breathing the last time she saw him. Badly wounded, but alive.

She read the terminal:

Subject 101100.

State: terminated.

Decontamination stage.

Ava's heart shattered into a thousand pieces. She could not bear the pain anymore, the anguish. She stopped looking and collapsed onto the floor, sobbing, with bottomless suffering in her soul. They had all died, but why had they all been put in the capsules? What did all this mean? What was this hall?

She stood up, drew courage from her own pain, and looked for an exit. She found a closed door, and beside it a pedestal with clothes on it. It was then that she noticed her own nakedness, so she put the clothes on. They consisted of a white one-piece suit with boots of the same color. There was a logo on the chest: SIAAIS.

"This is a nightmare," she said between sobs.

On one side of the door was a panel. She did not know what to do, so she put her hand on this as Emma would have done. A light from the panel scanned her hand, and the door opened.

She came out into a long corridor, with another closed door at the end. As she had done when she left the chamber containing the capsules, she put her hand on the panel, and the door opened. Uncertainly, she peeked inside, but it was dark. She went in very carefully. As she did so the lights went on, and what she found left her in a state of shock.

In a vertical capsule she saw herself.

No! This can't be! That's me!

It took her a while to recover and react. She went to the capsule and looked inside. There was no doubt: It was herself.

She read the terminal at the foot of the capsule:

Subject 111002.

State: generation.

Formation stage.

She was baffled. *I must be going crazy. There's no other explanation.*

The chamber was filled with vertical capsules, also placed around a black tower full of blinking lights. These capsules were slightly different from those in the previous chamber where she had woken up in that they were all vertical, not horizontal.

She went closer to see whether her friends, too, were in these capsules, but found none of them. There were another hundred or so capsules, and in each was a person she had never seen before.

She shook her head. She had to find out who all those people were and why one of them was exactly like her.

She left this chamber and found another endless, spotless corridor. At the end she stopped. Above the door, in black letters, was written:

SIAAIS.

Ava felt a shiver so strong that it made her jump.

The door opened, as if whoever was on the other side knew they had a visitor.

She hesitated. What was waiting for her beyond the door? A discovery that would break her even further? She was broken already, and facing that merciless God was the last thing she wanted at that moment, but there was no choice. Siaais was the one who had the answers she wanted.

I'm not going to turn back now. Not after everything I've been through.

She crossed the threshold.

CHAPTER 49

She went in warily and found herself in a huge chamber. Its floors and walls and the crystal dome of the ceiling were black, so that nothing outside was visible. The chamber, lit by a number of very white lights, was empty, with the exception of a huge black tower in the center, larger than those she had found in the previous rooms. It rose from the floor to the domed ceiling, more than twenty-five feet above.

"Welcome," a cold, metallic, inhuman voice greeted her.

Ava turned and saw a blue ring rising and falling around the black tower. It seemed to be made up of thousands of minute rectangles, so that there was a blue-black shade over the entire surface of the tower.

Ava tensed. "Who's speaking to me?"

"It is I," the tower said, and the blue rings vibrated with the metallic voice.

"Who . . . ? What are you?" she asked in confusion as she stared at the tower.

"I am Siaais," said the voice from the tower, and the rings vibrated as they moved up and down along the structure.

"No . . . you can't be Siaais . . . he's a god."

"Affirmative. I am Siaais. That is the designation I was given by those who created me, like you. I am the Survival Investigation, Auto-sustained Artificial Intelligence System."

Ava stared up at the tower. "I don't understand anything you just said . . . what's happening here?" She was almost in tears. "Is this a nightmare? Am I going crazy? Have I died?"

"Negative. Your vital signs are normal. The last encephalogram shows no anomalies. There are no indications of mental illness. You are awake, and your cognitive and motor functions are correct. What you are now experiencing is reality."

"If I'm alive and sane, you can't be Siaais, because he's an evil God!"

"Incorrect. I am Siaais. I have always been Siaais."

"I don't believe you! I don't believe anything you're telling me!"

"Visualizing will help your mind to accept the reality," came the reply, and from the floor in front of the tower there rose a huge screen. On it appeared the face of a woman with fine features, white, lightly freckled skin, brown eyes, and a pointed nose. Her hair was short and chestnut-brown, her expression calm and kind.

"This is my visual representation," the voice said, and as it did so the lips of the woman moved. It was her speaking.

"This isn't helping. It's nothing more than another trick to fool me."

"My creators thought this visual representation would make the connection with humans easier."

Ava considered the face. It was kind but lifeless, like its voice.

"Creators?"

"The scientists who created me."

"What are you? A machine? A system?"

"Affirmative. I am a machine, a system, many in one. I am an AI."

"AI?"

"An artificial intelligence."

Ava blinked, in puzzlement. "I don't understand . . ."

"I am an intelligence embodied in a machine. The one you see in front of you."

"The tower . . ."

"I am a highly evolved artificial mind."

"Mind? Can you think for yourself?"

"Affirmative. I am a very powerful mind, capable of processing large amounts of information with the aim of maximizing the possibilities of success for any task or goal. I can find order in chaos. Every one of the minute nano-cells that form my body is a quantum processor of great power, capable of processing terabytes of data."

Ava breathed out in a gasp as she tried her hardest to understand. "Were you created by the Ancient Ones?"

"Affirmative."

"What for?"

"To solve an extremely complex problem. One which humans have been unable to solve. One of ultimate importance."

"Becoming a God and enslaving us with the Curse?"

"Negative. Saving humanity."

Ava's eyes opened wide. "Is that your mission?"

"It is my final goal. The problem I must solve."

"I'm getting more and more confused." Ava put her head in her hands and let herself fall to the floor. She had reached her limit.

"Expected human reaction. Projecting historical images."

Siaais's face shrank and was left framed in the upper left-hand corner of the screen. A new image now filled this. It showed a huge and advanced city full of shining buildings of glass and steel. The image changed and showed her a bewildering variety of wheeled vehicles, trains like the ones she herself had taken, and people in strange clothes filling the streets. Several flying machines flew past. A great river crossed the city and strange ships moved over it, barely touching the water.

"The city of London. Year: 2225. Year of the arrival," Siaais went on. Suddenly a huge shadow appeared above the great river. "First sighting, over the Thames." The shadow was advancing toward a large palace. "Second sighting, Buckingham Palace."

Ava was trying to understand the meaning of the images, which looked very real. A huge triangular ship, completely black, settled at a hundred and twenty feet or so above the Palace.

"Attack initiated on January first, 13:00 hours," the AI said in its metallic voice.

The image showed a beam of intense red light coming down from the ship to the Palace. There was a shrill whistle, and the building exploded into thousands of fragments of rock. The image showed only an enormous black hole in the ground, with large pieces of rock scattered everywhere.

"First EMP detonation: January first, 13:15 hours," Siaais went on.

A moment later the ship emitted a burst of sound, and a blue wave spread throughout the city as far as the outskirts, followed by several more. The flying combat machines that went to intercept the attacking ship plummeted, crashed into buildings and burst into flames. The boats on the Thames stopped running, as did ground vehicles of every kind. Chaos gripped the population, with everyone running and screaming through the streets. Human war machines appeared on land and several more in the air, but all of them stopped working and crashed with the detonation of additional EMPs.

Suddenly five smaller ships emerged from the alien ship, also black and triangular, like replicas of their mother ship. They spread all over the city, flying at great speed in different directions. As they went, they sent out waves like those emitted by the mother ship, but smaller and less far-reaching.

"Control Positioning of Invader Force: January first, 14:15 hours."

The ships landed, and from them issued a number of creatures, many of them just like the one that killed Emma.

"Sighting of Invader Force: January first, 14:45 hours."

Hundreds of horrible creatures issued from the ships. They attacked the population, bringing death and infection to anyone they met, so that Ava had to look away from the scenes of terror.

"The city fell in three days. Without the weapons disabled by the EMP waves, the soldiers could not stand up to the invaders. They died or were infected with the black epidemic. Those who were infected passed the infection on to others in turn, under the control of the invaders. It is calculated that twelve million people died during the first days of the attack."

"Oh, my God!"

"At the same time they attacked the other great cities of the world: New York, Tokyo, Shanghai, Mexico City, Delhi, São Paulo, Cairo, Dhaka, Karachi, Buenos Aires, Istanbul, Madrid . . ." As Siaais spoke, the same images of horror succeeded one another on the screen. The population fled from the attackers, only to fall dead or infected.

"They're like the monster we fought against in the chamber . . ."

"Affirmative. They have been named Infectors. They are always accompanied by the Assassins, larger and more lethal, which protect them while they infect as many humans as possible."

"That's terrible," Ava said, shaking her head. "Horrible."

"The great cities and their surrounding areas perished in a matter of weeks. A year later, eighty percent of the planet belonged to them. Five years later, ninety percent. Ten years later, ninety-nine percent. And it still goes on."

"Now? What year is this?"

"The present date is April thirty-first of the year 2375."

"It's been a hundred and fifty years since the first attack?"

"Affirmative."

Ava put her hands to her head. "What's happened during all this time?"

"The invaders have infected the whole population. The Earth has been taken over by this alien species."

"Are there any survivors?"

"A few, under the great cities. They took refuge in tunnels, in the subway system, and in similar underground spaces. The aliens do not go underground. The reason for that is unknown."

"Is that how the Ancient Ones perished? Is that what the Curse really is?"

"Affirmative."

"So . . . where are we? Hidden underground so they can't find us? Am I an Ancient One?"

"Negative."

"I don't understand . . ."

"The scientists tried to get rid of the aliens by using chemical weapons, but they, too, failed. At last, seeing that the Earth was lost, scientific teams were sent from Earth to several planets in order to establish bases for research against the invading alien race, as a final hope. The ships were launched before the aliens disabled the launching pads. This is one of those bases."

Suddenly Ava felt an enormous emptiness in her stomach. "What do you mean, this is one of those bases? Where are we?"

"This is Titan Base 010. I will show you."

The walls and the crystal cupola turned rapidly transparent. Ava saw a huge yellow planet in the distance, surrounded at its equator by great rings. She had seen it before, though she did not know where.

"And the sun? And the moon? Where are they? What's that planet I can see?" She came closer to the glass wall and stared at the planet in the distance. Why could she see it so closely? Why was the whole sky black? She could not even see the Eye of Siaais. She moved a little, to make sure it was not some kind of static image or an illusion projected before her eyes.

It was not that. The planet looked real. And suddenly she realized. The explanation came as a discovery that exploded in her mind. That view could only mean one thing.

"This isn't Earth," she murmured.

"Affirmative. The planet you are looking at is Saturn, the sixth planet of the solar system. It is recognizable by its ring system, which can be seen from Earth. This research base you are in is on the largest of its satellites: Titan."

"No, that can't be true! I was on Earth, this can't be happening. It's another test, another trap to finish driving me crazy."

"Negative. You are not being lied to. There are no more tests. You have passed them all."

"No! It can't be! Let me out of here!"

"Request denied. You are in a research center built on a base for space colonization, abandoned two centuries ago, after the period of space exploration. There is nothing out there. There is no one else on this moon. There is only you."

Ava felt that her head was about to explode. None of this was possible. And yet there was the planet, in front of her.

"If it's as you say, if this is Titan and we're in a research base, where are the scientists?"

"Deceased. A hundred and fifty years have passed. An average human being lives for a hundred and twenty-five years."

"So everything you've showed me, what you've told me, is true?"

"Affirmative."

Ava fell to her knees and began to weep.

CHAPTER 50

It took her a moment to regain her calm, and she took a deep breath through her nose. She could not believe any of what Siaais had told her, she just couldn't. It made no sense. What did all this have to do with her? It had to do with the Ancient Ones, and she was not one of them. She thought about her life, her friends, everything they had been through together, and began to feel nervous. Her mind was refusing to accept it all, and rage was beginning to surge up her throat.

"Your pulse is accelerating," Siaais said. "Your biorhythms have altered." She showed her the data on a screen, together with a scanned image of her monitored body.

Ava stood up. "Are you controlling me?" she asked threateningly.

"Negative. I am measuring your vital parameters to ensure your well-being."

"That's what controlling is . . ."

"Negative. It means obtaining data and measuring it in order to make a diagnosis."

Ava made an impatient gesture. "Why are you measuring me? What does it matter to you?"

Siaais's face filled the whole screen once again. "Your well-being is crucial for the objective."

"I don't understand."

"You are crucial for the salvation of humankind."

Ava raised her arms. "All this is madness," she shouted. "How can I be crucial for the salvation of humankind?"

"You are the first specimen to have completed all the tests."

Ava threw her head back in amazement. "Am I the first one to get as far as the Cure?"

"Affirmative."

"So the Cure . . . exists?" she asked, although she had already guessed the answer.

"Negative. No cure has been found for those infected with the alien virus."

Ava swore under her breath and felt rage devouring her inwardly. "You lied to us."

"The learning model made it necessary."

"Why did you call me a specimen? What am I?"

"You are specimen number 101001 created for the heuristic study of quantum artificial intelligence."

"I'm not a specimen!"

"Negative. You were created in the laboratory in order to take part in the Assisted Reality experiment."

Ava's mind exploded with pain and doubt all over again.

"What . . . ? Created? What's that supposed to mean?"

"You were developed in the laboratory you visited immediately before coming in here. You saw the next version of yourself: specimen 111002."

Ava remembered her encounter with her double in the capsule. "No!"

"Affirmative."

"No, that's not possible. I'm of the Kemet people, I remember my childhood perfectly well. I remember playing with Amelia, I remember my mother, my village, the Great Pyramid, the oasis, the choosing, the journey, the tests to get here. All that happened! It must have happened!"

"This is going to be difficult for your mind to accept," Siaais said, and the screen showed the laboratory Ava had just passed through, with the newly-created specimens in their vertical capsules. "You were created in the Genetic Evolution Laboratory exactly ninety-seven days, fifteen hours, thirty minutes, and twenty-nine seconds ago."

"No . . ."

"Once created, and after passing all the genetic and clinical analyses, you were taken to the Laboratory of Assisted Reality."

"No!"

"Everything you remember happened in your mind, it was never real," Siaais said, and the screen showed the laboratory where Ava had woken up. It focused on her open capsule. "You were in that capsule during the whole test cycle. The cycle in an average experiment ends in 10,080 minutes, with a deviation of plus or minus ten percent. No one has ever passed the test. Until now. For the first time this threshold has been passed. You defeated the alien infector. No specimen has ever done this before."

"Don't call me a specimen . . . I'm no specimen, or an experiment, I'm Ava."

"Incorrect. You are specimen 101001, and part of an advanced genetic experiment. I created you and introduced you into the simulation for the assisted development of your physical and mental potential."

Ava felt a strong desire to throw something at the screen and break it, but there was nothing at hand.

"I don't believe a word of what you're saying. I was born from my mother's womb, nothing's going to persuade me otherwise!"

"Humans have difficulties assimilating complex situations. The mind is capable of putting up barriers and even of blocking memories in order to protect the subject."

"And what would you, a machine, know about the human mind?"

"My knowledge of the human mind is the greatest that has ever existed."

"The fact that you have whole heaps of information doesn't mean you know anything."

"Incorrect. My knowledge is extensive and detailed."

"I don't care. I don't believe you."

"I will show you."

The screen showed her the Laboratory of Genetic Evolution. On the top left-hand corner was a date and a meter with the seconds, running fast, and the number of the specimen: 101001. It was herself. Siaais must be showing her a recording of what had happened. She saw a great hall with lines of shelves, and in them thousands of tubes, apparently frozen.

"Storeroom of world genetic material," Siaais explained.

Ava saw a robot with a long mechanical arm taking out one of the tubes. "Is that me? Are you showing me how I was created?"

"Affirmative. You came out of that genetic base."

Ava shook her head. "It can't be . . ."

"The Advanced Genetic Program permits the creation of new specimens without any need for human intervention. I have an extensive genetic bank available, with a world map to choose from. In your case, and for this interaction, I chose a genetic base from the upper delta of the Nile, Egypt."

"No, no, no!" Ava was still shaking her head, refusing to believe.

Then Siaais showed her a machine with a crystal sphere in its center. Inside it she saw a human being taking shape.

"That can't be me . . ." she cried despairingly.

"During the first stages, the specimen is genetically manipulated to obtain a healthy specimen with special characteristics."

"That's an abomination!"

"It is the only hope for humankind."

The image went to a capsule.

"Once the stage of advanced genetic development is finished, we pass to the stage of assisted development in the capsule."

Ava watched the baby continuing to develop at great speed inside the capsule until it had turned into Ava, at sixteen. The marker indicated exactly ninety days.

"You created me in ninety days?"

"Affirmative. All specimens are created in that period of time. We have not succeeded in further reducing the period of development."

"Sixteen years . . . in ninety days . . . how horrible. And what about my mind?"

"During the whole process the subject remains dormant, or in a state of deep sleep. He or she is not aware of anything. Otherwise there would be an irreversible traumatic shock. The subject's mind would be lost."

"It's still horrible."

The screen now showed the Assisted Reality Laboratory.

"You were taken to the laboratory where you woke up. There all your initial experiences were implanted. Until the day of the Ceremony of Choosing."

"My memories, you mean . . . ?"

"Affirmative. Your past history. Your happy moments, your traumas."

"My mother . . ."

"Affirmative. Once selected, the rest of the experiment occurs in real time. The aim of the experiment is to overcome all the stages and reach the end: the Cure. That happens in a simulated reality in your mind and in that of the other contenders."

"It wasn't real? It didn't happen?"

"Incorrect. It was real. It did happen, in your minds. The first experiments were done in real environments. But the cost of recreating surroundings and maintaining them was too high. It was far more efficient to create the environment in the minds of the specimens using virtual reality."

"But Amelia and Amos . . . they were with me . . . from the start."

"In every cycle we create three specimens from the same genetic base. It is more efficient, and covers a greater range of possibilities."

"Possibilities?"

"The genetic factors are determinants in a specimen, but so are environmental factors such as birthplace, era, profession, and experiences."

"You created Amelia, Amos, and me, changing professions and experiences . . ."

"Affirmative. Same genetic base, same era, different professions and experiences. In each experimental cycle thirty combinations are created, with three specimens per combination."

"There are ninety people in every cycle?"

"Affirmative. From thirty different genetic bases."

"Emma, Logan, Liam . . . were from different races and eras."

"Affirmative. In each experimental cycle, the genetic and environmental factors are randomized. Then the personality factors are implanted. In each cycle everything is carried out again randomly, to maximize variability. The greater variety, the more chance of getting the right combination."

She was staring at the two Marks on her arm. "And our Power . . . ? Is that simulated too?"

"The Power is real."

"Do all humans have Powers?"

"Negative. But a specimen is not a standard human. He or she has been augmented genetically."

"I'm not going to like this . . . explain yourself."

"The specimens are genetically altered, mutated, so that they can possess the Powers. Investigations into genetic mutation to date have provided positive tangible results. They have managed to generate a finite number of Powers that can be developed by the specimens: telekinesis, empathy, impenetrable skin, control over the primal elements, control over computer and electrical systems, nullification of Powers, alchemy, physical strength . . . It is a very promising area of investigation. The experimental program is ongoing. The results take time to become concrete, but are critical in the attainment of the goal."

Ava scratched her head. "So . . . what combination am I?"

"Female, not very strong physically, Egyptian, ancient era, healer, mother's death trauma, tough personality, Power: empathy . . ."

"Fine, fine, I get it."

The screen showed Ava's face and all manner of data about her. A seal that blinked green read: *Successful Combination.*

"So in each cycle you combine all the factors to create specimens and see how they'll deal with the tests and whether they'll be able to defeat the Infector. Is that it?"

"Very much simplified, but that is so," Siaais confirmed.

Ava began to walk around the great hall, looking out at Saturn and shaking her head.

"There's something I don't understand . . ."

"I am programmed to answer any question."

"If you already have the laboratories, if you can already create the specimens and test their Powers, why the tests?"

"The tests were created to emulate a hostile environment and extreme conditions. The aim is to drive the specimens to their physical and mental limits, making them experience hunger, exhaustion, stress, and terror, with the intention of seeing how their bodies and minds adapt to these extreme situations. The experiments show that in them the specimens are capable of performing acts which otherwise would be unthinkable, and the same goes for their Powers."

"The Powers increase in strength . . ." Ava said. She was remembering what had happened to them.

"Affirmative. In the laboratory it is not possible to make the specimens improve their Powers."

"That's cruel. Inhuman."

"Affirmative. But necessary. The common good outweighs the individual good."

"You killed my friends."

"Negative. The specimens did not pass the test."

"We're not specimens, and yes, you killed them. I want you to bring them back."

"Negative. A human being, once he or she dies, cannot be brought back to life. That is outside my area of knowledge."

Ava felt an enormous hole beginning to form in her chest. She burst into tears.

"They didn't deserve to die like that. They gave it all they had . . ."

"The experiment was a success. In part this was due to their participation."

"Of course. Without them I'd never have made it."

"I need to study the parameters of the experiment. It will generate new hypotheses for future ones."

"Forget about future experiments. Shouldn't you be investigating a cure for the infection those monsters brought?"

"There is another AI in charge of that objective. It is not my function, or my purpose."

Ava shook her head. "You could look for a weapon to get rid of the invaders."

"There is another AI in charge of that objective," Siaais repeated in the same lifeless voice. "It is not my function or my purpose."

"I see . . . Different AIs study different ways of getting rid of the aliens."

"Affirmative."

"Will you go on experimenting until the end of time?"

"Until we reach our goal. I must save humankind, produce specimens who can defeat the invaders. Either that, or another AI will reach the goal before me."

"And where are those AIs? Here?"

"Negative."

"In other bases on other planets?"

"That information is confidential and must not be revealed without authorization. The risk of interception is too high."

"By the aliens?"

"Affirmative."

"But those other AIs exist . . . and are working on it, wherever that may be . . ."

"Affirmative."

Ava felt a trace of relief. If there were other artificial intelligences trying to find a solution to the terrible situation, then there was hope for humankind, however slight.

"I always believed you were a cruel, ruthless God," she said as she stared at the tower with its blue rings.

"Negative."

"You are not a God, but you're still cruel and ruthless," Ava reasoned with half-closed eyes.

"Negative."

"The end doesn't justify the means."

"Negative. It does justify them. The human race will become extinct in less than twenty-five years according to the latest estimates. Any means is justified in order to stop the extinction."

"Is that what you've been programmed to do?"

"Affirmative. I must achieve that objective. My program cannot be altered."

Ava breathed out heavily. She looked down at her tanned skin, then at the two Marks on her arm, and knew that what the AI was telling her was the truth. She was not in a dream, nor was she being lied to. This was real: a horrible reality, but a reality all the same. She showed Siaais the two implants.

"What are they for?"

"They are meters. The golden one shows the level of infection of the body and of resistance to the invading virus. The second measures the level of development of the Power, its strength. I monitor them. They are critical values for the future survival of the specimen."

"If you create us in the lab, then why are we born infected? Why do we only live a few years?" Ava asked, remembering her life. And as the words were leaving her mouth she realized why. "You're the one who infects us! You're the one who experiments with the level of infection!"

"Affirmative. The resistance to the infection and the time until transformation are variable. I need to study them. The experiment is a complex one, with a multitude of intertwined levels and millions of variables to be analyzed."

"It's ruthless."

The AI did not respond at once, as if it were processing the answer.

"The experiment has been a success. You are the first to defeat an Infector. That is the objective. I have to create specimens who are capable of confronting and defeating the alien invaders. You are the first."

Ava now understood what had happened to them. She took a deep breath and let the air out slowly. She looked up at the dome, at the space outside. She felt alone, lost in that immensity, in a desperate situation. The faces of Amelia, Amos, Logan, Emma, and Liam passed through her mind, and her heart became a block of ice.

"And now what?" she asked the AI.

"Now we save humankind."

ACKNOWLEDGMENTS

I'm lucky enough to have very good friends and a wonderful family, and it's thanks to them that this book is now a reality. I can't express the incredible help they have given me during this epic journey.

To my muse Oihana, thank you with all my heart for your love and support.

Guiller C. for his tireless encouragement and invaluable support and advice.

Mon, master-strategist and exceptional plot-twister. Apart from acting as editor and always having a whip ready for deadlines to be met. A million thanks.

Luis R. for helping me with the rewrites and for all the hours we spent talking and discussing ideas.

Kenneth L. for always being ready to help and for all his support and encouragement.

Fran C. for being an invaluable collaborator and the best CPO.

My parents and my family, who are the best in the world and have helped and supported me so much in this, as in all my projects.

Special thanks to my wonderful collaborators, Christy Cox and Peter Gauld, for caring so much about my books and for always going above and beyond.

To Robert and Mark Gottlieb and the team at Trident Media Group for making this book possible. Thank you for your belief in me.

To Marilyn Kretzer and the team at Blackstone Publishing, thank you for your hard work and the opportunity. I really appreciate it.

And finally: Thank you very much, reader, for supporting this author. I hope you've enjoyed it; if so I'd appreciate it if you recommend it to your family and friends.

Thank you very much, and with warmest regards,

Pedro